THE STEADFAST ONE

HANNAH LEVIN

aethonbooks.com

THE STEADFAST ONE
©2025 HANNAH LEVIN

Aethon Books
www.aethonbooks.com

Print and eBook cover by Steve Beaulieu. Interior formatting by Kevin G. Summers.

Published by Aethon Books LLC.

ALSO BY HANNAH LEVIN

The Treasured One

The Steadfast One

N
W
E
S
AVRILLE
LEIMOR
KERETI
Vhalder
Munarzed
The Rift
Miderrum
WYSALAR

For all the relationships that bring a love for romance books and love for fantasy games under one roof. Maybe this will be the one to bring your two passions together!

PRONUNCIATION GUIDE

In the common fae language, Rs are pronounced with the tongue glancing off the roof of the mouth, creating a sound closer to an L or D. This is indicated with the symbol "r/l." A double n is spoken with a nasal quality as opposed to a singular n and is indicated with "ng."

NAMES

Marcia (MAR-see-uh), goes by Mar. The female main character and a Golden Child with shapeshifting powers. Ran from the White House under care of the U.S. government and snuck through The Rift at sixteen years old, has been living in the fae realm since.

Hohem (HO-hem), an *Alf* and twin brother to Vyrain. A seer told his mother that her child would be a vitally important hero, but no one knows which one of them is the chosen one.

Vyrain (vai-RAIN), an *Alf* and twin brother to Hohem. A seer told his mother that her child would be a vitally important hero, but no one knows which one of them is the chosen one.

Yrralailee (YEER-ah-LAY-lee), goes by **Yrra (YEE-rah)**. An aquatic-based waterfolk fae seeking an unclaimed body of water to inhabit and harem of mates to establish himself.

Daethie (DAY-thee), a member of the militant, pixie-like *Aminkinya* (AH-min-KIN-ee-yah) race and an irritable, self-absorbed kleptomaniac.

Jük (jook), a grumpy *Epitgig*, a faerie race resembling a goblin.

Kereti (keh-R/LEH-tee), one of the 12 fae provinces. Kereti, governed by the Kereti family, makes up the fae realm's geographical equivalent of Canada.

Narille (NAH-ril), the oldest daughter of the main Kereti family.

Luthri (LOO-three), the male main character, a *Peri* with bird-like aspects. An eccentric lone wolf on a quest to copulate with a member of each faerie race.

Cantal (can-TALL), a holy man who tends to a shrine for Hermenia in rural Kereti.

Hermenia (hur-MEN-ee-yah), the Lady of War, patroness of soldiers, justice, and death. A warrior goddess worshiped in the north, the counterpart to Aeil.

Aeil (ale), known as the Mother, patroness of families, love, and life. A deity worshiped in the South, counterpart to Hermenia.

Rugaveld (ROO-gah-veld), Munarzed's acting mayor.

Gerda (GUR-duh), a giantess and ship owner who delivers goods to Munarzed.

Savreen (sah-VREEN), Rugaveld's daughter.

Note: The characters in this book speak languages besides English, but it has been translated to colloquial English for your enjoyment. Fae words that don't translate directly will be italicized. As a human, Marcia occasionally sprinkles in the odd English or Portuguese word. For a complete glossary of fae words and phrases that appear in the story, see appendix.

PROLOGUE

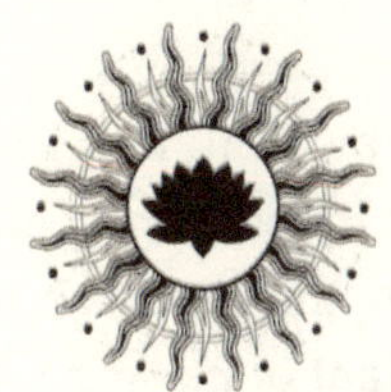

TEN YEARS AGO

DON'T BE SUSPICIOUS. *Don't be suspicious.*

"Hey, Lee," I greeted a passing American soldier, addressing her by the name patch above her right breast. My gaze fell on the M4 carbine resting in her hands. The mantra running through my head faltered, but I kept my features schooled in a mask of nonchalance.

Faint confusion flitted across her face. *Merda. I shouldn't have said anything.*

I'd been watching closely over the last three days to get a feel for their schedule. It was right around shift change, so it shouldn't be strange that I was strolling around unarmed. On the outside, I would appear like a fellow guard heading to my post. Nothing to worry about.

After a beat, Lee returned the greeting, any suspicion forgotten in favor of getting the night over with. "Hey, Cummings."

I nodded and kept walking, releasing a breath that had stagnated in my lungs. *I'll be all right. My training prepared me for this.* It was laughable that my captors never expected I'd use it against them. I smothered a victorious grin at the thought.

The soldiers were here to protect the area against human fanatics and creatures from the other world, keeping each to their respective sides. That's what made my disguise so perfect. It had taken half a thought to turn my body into an adult stranger in an Army uniform. Who would suspect that one of them was a sixteen-year-old girl with shapeshifting powers, much less the "upstart" from Fortaleza who'd vanished some 800 kilometers away two weeks ago?

Salty? Who, me? Besteira.

Recalling that day, the day I left, my heart squeezed in my chest. I shouldn't have ditched my friend, Avery, like that. She was probably worried sick. Knowing her, she ran back to the safety of the White House as soon as she lost sight of me and told them everything. It was the perfect plan, really. The escape would be pinned on me, she'd be accepted back into the fold as the American darling, and I would be across The Rift where they'd never find me.

Still… I regretted leaving things that way.

Agora é tarde, Inês é morta. What's done is done, as they say.

My chin jerked down in acknowledgment as I passed a group of mixed Canadian and American soldiers. Funny how interdimensional portals brought nations together. They nodded back and kept chatting, unconcerned. My breaths came short, and my heart clamored in my rib cage. *Is it really going to be this easy?* That would be a relief after the past two weeks.

The path of paving stones and manufactured landscaping ended up ahead, abruptly giving way to rogue nature. Niagara Falls used to be a hot spot for tourists. Now, a chain-link fence some two and a half meters high topped with barbed wire wrapped around the perimeter of the waterfall. No more idiots throwing themselves over the edge in barrels; instead, this section of The Rift was another Area 51, spoken about in hushed whispers alongside anecdotes about what things were like *before* and assertions that the government was controlled by shapeshifting fae.

Lizard people weren't creative enough, I supposed.

The thunder of the falls and faint glow from below lured me in closer, bolstering my resolve. My steps quickened. *Almost there. Almost free.* When I reached the fence, I paused, taking in rapid lungfuls of moist, fragrant air as I examined the length of it. I gripped a handful of links, testing for weaknesses. It barely wobbled. Secure enough to climb, but the barbed wire would be a bitch. And I'd have to be quick—once I was noticed, I was out of time.

I surreptitiously checked if anyone was looking my way. After the fence sat several meters—twenty feet or so—of overgrown vegetation before the edge of the falls. The Rift was somewhere below, out of sight. I could make a run for it. After that part… I had no boat or plane, no rappelling gear. There was a bridge, but it was the most heavily guarded area.

I'd already thought it through. The best option was to jump from this spot. If I didn't think about it too much, it wasn't too bad. I couldn't afford to hesitate anyway.

Steeling myself for a fight, I gripped the fence with both hands and pulled myself up. My attention was zeroed in on the rushing water before me, my heartbeat in my ears, and the rattle of cold, hard metal under my palms. It was tempting to drop my disguise in favor of my smaller, lighter natural form, but no. If they knew I was one of the Golden Children they expended so much effort to exploit, they might come after me. Better that they think I'm a random deserter.

"Oi!" A shout broke my focus. "Hey! What are you doing?!"

Cover blown, I poured everything I had into scrambling up the chain link. When I reached the section of barbed wire, I gritted my teeth and sent energy from my center to magically harden my skin as best I could before pulling myself over. Metal thorns snagged clothing and flesh without care. I bit back a curse as my hands, abdomen, and thighs took the brunt of it. Tears welled, turning the landscape before me into a blurry canvas of color.

Soldiers shouted orders to each other and into their radios behind me. Boots thumped against the stone path. It was tempting, but I couldn't afford to look back. My landing wasn't pretty—I hit the ground and stumbled, falling onto my hands and knees.

"Stop!" Someone screamed as I surged to my feet. "Stop or we'll shoot!"

Oh, sure, I'll throw away all my hard work and let you take me into custody. Idiots.

Failure was not an option. If I got caught here, they'd never leave me alone. I'd be eating, sleeping, even going to the bathroom under constant guard. No, thank you. I raced to the edge, the roar of water amplifying as I neared, only to stop short at the view that awaited me.

"Merda," I hissed through my teeth.

The waterfall was an impressive sight in and of itself, but The Rift was... something else. When an abundance of magic tore gaps in the fabric of space between our world and the fae realm before I was born, people had been terrified. Seeing this, it was easy to understand why.

Equal parts intimidating and seductive, like the call of the void given physical form, The Rift was a depthless chasm filled with shattered pieces of midnight-purple space in a pattern resembling crystal growth. Mist writhed in undulating tendrils inside and around it, converging with the spray of the waterfall to hide the river underneath.

Anticipation curled in my belly. "Okay," I breathed, nodding to myself. "This is it."

Gunshots rang out in rapid succession, sending clods of dirt spraying into the air and piercing through The Rift's mesmerizing effect. *They're mad. My time's up.* No more doubts—a moment of courage now, and I'd earn the life of freedom that awaited me.

I retreated one step, then two, digging the toe of my boot into the ground in preparation for the leap. Muscles bunched. Launching into motion, I sprinted for the edge. Another, more desperate volley of bullets chased me. Heat seared across my thigh as one hit home, leaving a stinging sensation in its wake, but it didn't matter. I was already airborne and falling toward the open maw of The Rift, any sound I might have made stolen by the wind.

CHAPTER ONE
IN WHICH THE PLAYERS ARE INTRODUCED

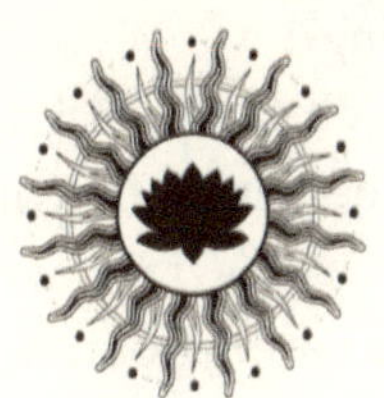

PRESENT

When I first came to this world, it was a night much like this one.

A bright moon. Humid. Lots of screaming.

At that time, the screaming had been mine. Tonight, it was a pair of thieves who'd taken off with a large portion of a local lord's livestock. As I watched them plead for mercy at the hands of my companions, I recalled the evening I stepped into the fae world with a fond smile.

Time was tracked a little differently here—based on lunar cycles rather than months—but if my math was correct, it was around ten years ago. As one of the Golden Children born with magic following the opening of The Rift, a mysterious portal connecting Earth to a dimension where magic and fantastical creatures ran amok, I attracted the attention of the U.S. government. They kidnapped me and smuggled me out of Brazil to have me spy for them.

After a few years of thinly veiled indoctrination, they realized I wasn't as much of a pushover as they thought. That was when they moved me to the White House, hoping the other girl they had, Avery, would rub off on me. She was a sweet girl, timid and malleable in all the ways they liked. I only lasted a couple of years before I couldn't keep pretending that things were okay. However, they wouldn't let me go without a fight.

It took some effort to get to this point, especially with the new language and so many fae species to keep track of. But a couple of years in, I found a group like me—free spirits with nowhere else to go. My merry band of misfits and I did what we pleased, paying our bills through odd jobs like this one. It wasn't exactly the life I pictured for myself, but it was nice.

"Mar! You plan on helping?!"

The sound of my name jolted me back to the present. People came and went over the years. The fair *Alfen* twins—humans might refer to their race as elves—Hohem and Vyrain, were the newest additions to our group. One of them had a thief on the ground in a headlock, the man's struggles growing feeble. It was he who'd interrupted my reminiscing.

"What do you need me for?" I groused. "You look like you've got it covered."

The other criminal was likewise subdued. Another member of our group, Ked, looking mighty pleased with himself, made use of his considerable size by sitting on him. It was hard to say if that thief still breathed—as a half-giant, Ked was around seven feet tall and proportionally wide, with bulbous facial features and hair like damp straw.

"Pay no mind to my brother," the other twin called from nearby. "Despite having the same upbringing, he never learned how to treat a lady. You sit tight, sweetheart, we've got things handled here." He navigated the grassy plain with a green-tinted orb of light in his palm, trying to corral our client's lumbering cattle-like *lya* so that we could herd them back.

Equally tall, blond, and light-skinned, with the same boyish allure to their features and often flaunting the same hairstyle, the twins were a challenge to tell apart by sight. However, it was a breeze once they opened their mouths. While Hohem was an inoffensive fellow, perfectly agreeable in all the ways that mattered, Vyrain was a hopeless romantic who had his sights set on me. It might have been flattering if not for the fact that his attention was likely inspired by a lack of prospects rather than any features I possessed.

Their story, though simpler than my own, was no less entertaining. A seer predicted that their mother would give birth to a hero who would inspire a thousand ballads, or something to that effect. This prophecy became a point of contention as, ironically, the seer hadn't known there would be two of them. I empathized outwardly, but I had to admit it was a decent grift.

Hohem released the now-unconscious thief and let him topple unceremoniously to the ground. Shaking the blood back into his arms, he stepped over the man's prone form.

"There are no 'ladies' when it comes to making a living. We all need to do our fair share," he said, directing a pointed look my way.

"I was the one who found the job, remember?" I pushed off from my spot leaning against our covered wagon and rolled my shoulders back to appear more authoritative. "If you spent as much time hanging around the job boards as you did complaining, maybe you'd also be able to take a break once in a while. It's not all about hard work, you know. Do it right, and you can enjoy the sights while putting food on the table."

"Food?" Ked interjected hopefully, head swiveling at the word. Cunning was prized among giant clans, but Ked was born with a developmental delay. As a result, he'd been abandoned as a child. He would have died if not for Jük and Vee taking him in.

"Soon, big guy," I promised. "Just gotta get these cows back home."

Giving the antlered, horse-like *avida* that pulled our wagon an affectionate scratch on the chin, I examined the herd of livestock animals in the field before me with a critical eye. None of us were animal keepers, but if they were anything like the cattle they resembled, keeping them in check was a matter of having the right equipment. That gave me an idea.

A familiar ache and the welcome heat of magic zigzagged throughout my body, following veins as my body expanded. I shook out my arms and got into a crouch. Like one big, gratifying stretch, joints popped to make room for elongating bones and multiplying muscles. My clothes became a layer of thick, dark fur decorating my sun-bronzed skin. Practiced as I was, the process was complete in seconds, and I stood before my friends on all fours.

"The fuck is that?!" Hohem exclaimed, having never seen a dog before.

I was grateful for my shapeshifting abilities. They'd made sneaking out of the White House a breeze all those years ago. Once I was on the road, I hitchhiked to Niagara Falls. I waited for the cover of night, walked through the area's defenses disguised as a soldier, and jumped to my freedom. That was where the screaming came in.

There weren't many places I could go where the government couldn't find me. What better way to start fresh than in a whole new world across The Rift?

My lips pulled taut against my canine teeth in an approximation of a smirk. Dashing forward with a burst of exhilaration, I made for the stragglers on the edge of the herd. Heads rose from grazing as the beasts sensed a predator in their midst. As I got close to one, it lumbered forward, picking up the pace when I snapped at its heels. A narrow brush with angry hooves had me backing off. My heart pounded in my chest, a combination of nerves and delight.

It took some trial and error, but once I got into the flow of things, the herd made its way slowly but surely down the hill back toward the lord's estate. Whooping with excitement, Vyrain raced for the wagon. Our other friend, Yrra, who had been assisting Vyrain with gathering the herd, followed closely behind. Hohem collected Ked, and they hurried to catch up.

About an hour later, we corralled the stolen *lya* into the fenced field with the rest of them. Vyrain and Hohem helped me get them situated while Ked and Yrra waited with the wagon.

Transforming didn't *hurt,* per se, but it could be uncomfortable, and when I maintained a certain form for a while, it became more difficult to return to myself. Covered with equal parts sweat and dirt, I forced my body back into human shape, wincing as everything settled back into place with a low burn like that of overworked muscles. The satisfaction of a job well done bolstered my strength enough to work through the exhaustion.

Dusting mud off my breeches, I caught my breath while looking around for the lord or any of the stooges we'd spoken to. They should have seen us coming from a distance, but there was no one in sight, only orchards bursting with green fruit and mountains against a starry backdrop beyond that. They'd acted like these animals were a big deal, the way they announced the job in the square and didn't bother negotiating the price.

Something made the hair on the back of my neck prickle with awareness. If my gut was reliable, collecting our payment was going to be a headache. We may have to get mean.

"Hohem. Vyrain."

The boys perked up at the sound of their names. They were the muscle of our unit, their lean builds belying their true strength. I could appreciate how useful it was to have them around. When it had been just me, Vee, Jük, and Ked, I needed to be the strong one, the reliable one. Thanks to their presence, I didn't have to be on my toes all the time.

"Can I get a hand?" I angled my body to indicate the manor. Understanding my intention, the twins came to join me. Next, I directed my attention to Yrra and Ked. Yrra sat in the back of the wagon, helping Ked fix a tear in his sleeve. They'd be fine waiting.

"Hang out here for a moment, will you?" I asked. "We'll be right back."

Yrra gave a measured nod, his big, impassioned eyes never leaving mine, and put a blue-skinned hand protectively over Ked's. "Be careful," he told us, his voice a whisper.

"Of course."

Yrra was a shy, quiet sort whose full name was impossible for even most fae to pronounce. A lanky young waterfolk male, he was seeking an uninhabited river or lake to call home, a process his kind all went through to come of age. Once that was achieved, there was the other part of the process, which involved building a harem and spreading one's seed. Unfortunately, Yrra couldn't look any female in the eye, much less one of his own race. He'd been alone a long time, growing more and more despondent.

I saw him as a sibling, which meant affection but added responsibility.

Squaring my shoulders, I marched the three of us across the sprawling front lawn to the manor. The building was all fieldstone walls organized at right angles for a boxy, old country home in a vineyard effect. At my instruction, Vyrain announced our presence with a booming knock on the dark wood door. My foot had begun to tap the step by the time it opened.

A person resembling a hairless mole rat on two legs peered around the edge of the door. It took a few seconds of squinting in our general direction before recognition dawned. "The master is not available at the moment," he said with about as much enthusiasm as a suburban housewife who'd been told she'd won a lifetime supply of sand.

The offhand response wasn't encouraging.

"Okay, well, if you can get us what we're owed, we'll be on our way," I replied cheerfully.

"You didn't bring back the thieves," the mole-man muttered under his breath.

My eyes narrowed. "What was that?"

Missing the warning in my tone, he raised his voice. "The thieves," he enunciated. "You were to bring back our livestock as well as the thieves for punishment."

Confusion gave way to fury, and I barely kept an insult from slipping past my lips. Abusing a client wouldn't do. "That wasn't discussed," I retorted through clenched teeth. "But they're very sorry, and they'll never do it again. I believe we agreed on a hundred *vodt*."

The mole-man pressed himself into the doorway, perhaps intending to intimidate me into submission. It wasn't the first time someone had tried, and the movement sent me to high alert. Power thundered through my veins, thickening the layer of muscle that wrapped around my torso and giving me extra height. Behind me, Hohem and Vyrain shifted their weight in tandem as a reminder that I was not alone. The steward hesitated before deflating, subdued.

A shame. I'd been looking forward to a fight.

"Wait here," he muttered. He disappeared inside, leaving the door ajar. A moment later, he returned with a purse, which he held out with a look like he'd been sucking a lemon.

Reminding myself that customer service was still a thing in this world, I forced my expression into something resembling a friendly smile. "Pleasure doing business with you. We'll be in the area, so don't hesitate to reach out if you think of anything else we can help with."

Behind me, one of the twins exhaled a sharp puff of air, which I pointedly ignored. The others had no concept of business and thought it was hilarious that I made an effort to do things properly. Honestly, the whole operation would fall apart without me.

Prize in hand, we returned to the wagon. Yrra raised his head at our approach, a question on his face. I raised the purse and gave it a shake, unable to suppress a grin at the resulting rattle of magic-resistant metal that had been worked into usable currency. Sweet relief flooded through me. With this payout, we'd be sitting pretty for the next few days.

"Not bad for a day's work," one of the twins remarked, swinging himself into the wagon and settling on Ked's other side. "For a moment there, I was worried he'd give us trouble."

"Thanks for the backup. You never know if you're going to need to knock some heads around." I strode over to the driver's seat and poured out the contents of the purse. Setting the square coins aside in neat stacks of ten, I counted out thirty, forty, fifty…

My brows drew together. That wasn't right. I counted again, hoping I'd been mistaken, and my stomach dropped. "Puta que pariu! He shorted us twenty!"

Throwing my hands in the air, I whirled about. My fingers itched as nails became claws, ready to raise hell, and my next step fell with murderous intent.

To my surprise, one of the twins held out an arm to stop me. "Let it go, my scowling beauty," Vyrain said, raising a hand to play with a strand of seal-brown hair that had escaped my braid. "It's getting late. And you wanted to make a good impression."

I batted his hand away, opening my mouth to protest.

"Anyway, that's more than we made all of last week," Hohem pointed out from the back of the wagon. "And we should get going. It's late. Some of us are getting hungry." He surreptitiously indicated Ked, who was gripping his stomach with a distraught look on his face. Yrra didn't look up from his work, but his neck was flushing indigo, a sign of emotional distress. He didn't cope well with conflict.

The unfairness of the situation made me grind my teeth, but I was trying to be more easygoing. A reputation for getting physical with customers didn't go over well when one was desperate for work. With some luck, we'd made a repeat client this time. Semiregular work that underpaid was better than struggling to find anything at all, especially with how slow the season had been. As much as it hurt, letting it go was the right move.

"Fine," I grumbled, gathering the coins again to return them to the purse in handfuls. "But just so you know, I'm not going to be the one to tell Daethie."

At my announcement, Yrra shyly met my gaze and touched one finger to his flat nose. The corner of my mouth quirked upward at the familiar human gesture.

"Yrra's not doing it, either. That leaves one of you clowns," I told Hohem and Vyrain as I pulled myself into the driver's seat. They exchanged an uncertain look.

"What is 'klonns?'" Vyrain asked, seating himself beside me.

Not in the mood to come up with a comprehensive explanation of what a clown was, I answered, "People who look funny," which Vyrain appeared to consider quite seriously.

"So it's my appearance that's the problem? I admit I haven't met one of your kind before, but I would have assumed we're perfectly compatible. Unless this isn't your original form."

I didn't miss the thoughtful once-over he gave me. Directing my gaze upward to the sky, I prayed for patience from any holy spirit that might be listening. "It's not a question of 'compatibility.' I'm not interested. That's all."

Vyrain made an unhappy sound somewhere deep in his throat, but to my relief, was silent for the rest of the scenic ride to the encampment we called home.

CHAPTER TWO

IN WHICH THE ADVENTURERS HAVE A MUCH-NEEDED NIGHT OUT

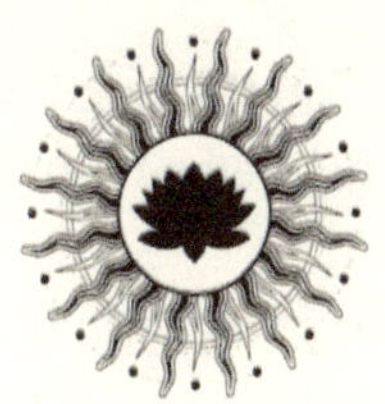

Soap in one hand and fabric in the other, I knelt by the creek to get my washing done.

Modern conveniences were the only things I missed about Earth. There was something satisfying about doing everything by hand, to be sure, but I'd trade that for electricity and tampons in a heartbeat. Also, a proper toilet. And a shower. They did have simple machines and rudimentary plumbing in the cities, but here in the middle of nowhere, options were limited. Boiling your drinking water and burying your shit got old after a while.

The soap was pretty nice. It had a nutty, spicy scent reminiscent of roasted chestnuts and cloves or cinnamon, and it did a good-enough job of getting blood and sweat out of clothing.

We always camped out near towns so that we could find work and get supplies when we needed them, and the soapmaker in this area was one of the better ones. One of the downsides of traveling so much was that you didn't always find the best people, but I'd miss this area and the people here when we inevitably decided to move on. It had begun to feel like home... At least, what I thought a home should feel like.

Leaves and twigs crunched behind me. Shoving my makeshift sanitary pads to the bottom of my laundry basket, I glanced up to see one of the twins approaching. Years of learning to be observant lent me an edge. With an extra moment of care, one might notice Vyrain's slightly slimmer build and how the ends of his hair cupped his ears and cheeks in a way that his brother's pin-straight locks did not. Additionally, there was his body language, an open countenance and near-indiscernible swagger in each step.

That said, there was nothing wrong with waiting for the clearest indicator.

"Lifespring of my heart," Vyrain cooed in greeting.

I got to my feet, squeezing water from the now-clean pants. "They calling for me?"

"Well, the evening meal is prepared. But I figured I'd see how you were feeling about joining me on my mat tonight." He waggled his eyebrows. "There's plenty of room, and it's quite comfortable. We can take it slow—no more than hands and mouths for the time being."

Irritation sent unkind words climbing up my throat, but I forced them down with a harsh exhale. If being the bigger person was easy, everyone would be a saint. I could at least let him down easy. "Look. How about this? You convince Hohem to join us, and it's on. But I'm only interested if it's a package deal, all right? Otherwise, you can stop asking."

Vyrain began to perk up, but in the next moment, he remembered that his brother was not as keen on jumping into bed with me, and his face fell.

"Cursed hot siblings, ruining everything," he muttered under his breath. Gears turned. He cast a sidelong glance my way and tried, "His equipment is out of commission?"

Despite myself, a smile tugged at my mouth. I looked past Vyrain to where his brother descended the hill behind him. "Sorry to hear about your equipment. How unfortunate."

"Could you not bring my dick into this?" Hohem grumbled, making his brother jump. "Come on, you two. Supper's ready, and Jük's real pissed off."

"Don't take that personally," I assured him, bending to rinse my pants one last time in the creek before bundling it into the basket with the rest. "Jük's been in a bad mood since I met him, and that was… oh, about six revolutions ago now. He's a big grump, but he's harmless."

The word the fae used for *years* translated to *dozens,* referring to a dozen lunar months, or a little less than one Earth year. But *revolutions* was close enough.

Hohem wasn't convinced. "I tried to serve myself, and he almost bit me."

Sounded about right. Chuckling to myself, I explained. "Vee likes us all to eat together."

Jük and his mate-slash-wife, Vee, were Ked's adoptive parents, and they kept an eye on our campsite during outings. They were *Epitgig,* resembling creatures humans called goblins. Shorter than my 157 centimeters (or 5'2" for those who refuse to use the metric system), they had large, triangular ears, big hands and feet, and skin the color of ash. Vee was as sweet as Jük was grumpy, and although Jük was far from affectionate, she had him wrapped around her finger.

In many ways, they were the quintessential old, married couple—the relationship that every romantic dreamed of having.

"Well, then, I suppose we'd better get a move on." Vyrain sighed from my left. As he passed, I found myself relieved of my washing basket. Blinking down at empty hands, I realized that he had plucked it from my grip.

"That's not necessary," I protested, hurrying to catch up.

"Oh, but it is, my heart's blood," Vyrain responded sweetly. When I grabbed for my laundry, he shifted the basket to his opposite hip, out of my reach. "Sit back and let me take care of you," he ordered, exasperated. "I'm not doing this for anything in return, I promise."

Unease made my sides prickle. It didn't feel right to leave my work to someone else, and though he'd never tried to use favors against me, I knew his motives weren't entirely honest. Nonetheless, I settled for following him with a glower. I'd begun to learn that it wasn't worth arguing with him; the man was nothing if not persistent, and he seemed to think that my "no" could be nurtured into open arms if he just kept trying. It was pitiable, really.

When we crested the hill to our camp clearing, the others had already congregated around the fire. Yrra, whose turn it was to look after our *avida,* lingered by the tents. The animal was secured to a gnarled tree bough beside one of the canvas constructions. Brush in hand, Yrra worked knots and shed out of the animal's sleek, mint coat as he listened to Daethie, the Tinkerbell-sized Terror, chattering away from her perch on his shoulder.

Daethie was an *Aminkinya,* a race of small, winged warrior women that lived in earthen structures resembling humongous termite hills. She was obsessed with money and, despite her cute, pink-tinted skin and diminutive stature, had a temper worse than mine. She'd only stayed behind because she strained a wing on our last outing; otherwise, she would have been the one shaking that mole-man down for the last twenty *vodt.*

Since she was currently resting her wing, she didn't fly much, but she tended to keep to herself. I couldn't remember the last time she willingly socialized outside of jobs or meals. She and Yrra made an odd pair, what with his quiet, polite demeanor and her… well, lack thereof.

Vyrain ignored my protests and helped me drape my laundry along the clothesline set up for that purpose. It was only a few pieces, so it didn't take long. I did shove him aside when we got to my sanitary cloths; fae might not have the same hangups as humans when it came to bodily fluids, but that part of being raised on Earth stayed with me.

Vee was portioning spoonfuls of cereal grain into clay bowls when we joined the others. They called it *paya* here, but for all intents and purposes, it was rice. A savory gravy with root vegetables and reconstituted meat sat over the fire, waiting to be doled out as a topping. I took a spot on the log next to Yrra and Daethie. Vyrain sat on a dirt lump beside his brother.

"Did Ked help today?" Vee asked, giving her son's knee an affectionate pat. She respected Ked's autonomy, but she couldn't resist worrying about him. It was difficult for her to watch us go out every day, not knowing what we were doing or when we'd return.

"Help," Ked echoed proudly, his eyes fixed on the bubbling pot before him.

"Sure, he did," Hohem confirmed, ever the gracious one where the mom of the group was concerned. "He held one of them down while I dispatched the other."

"We disarmed them first," I interjected, accepting my bowl with a grateful smile.

Jük grunted an indiscernible question through a mouthful of food.

"I'm sure," Vee responded mildly. "After dinner, dear."

"Of course we get a job with some action when I'm out of commission," Daethie grumbled, stabbing a miniature spoon into her bowl. Her hair, the washed-out gray of birch bark, lay against her scalp in a series of crisscrossing braids. Without anything worthwhile to pass the time while recuperating, she'd been putting more effort into her hairstyle as of late.

I should ask her to teach me. All I knew was the typical three-strand braid. Of course, there was no reason to be concerned about appearance here. I wore my hair long because I liked the way it looked. If not for that preference, I'd keep it short for practicality's sake.

Vyrain snickered. "You would have had a blast. The client shorted us twenty—"

My head snapped up. Too far away to pinch him, I had to settle for a sharp look. His words cut off, his expression turning guilty, but the damage was done. Daethie's back went ramrod straight, and her eyes narrowed into scathing pinpricks of emerald.

"They what?!"

Well, that cat was out of the bag. Outrage bubbled up again at the memory of the unobliging mole-man, and I slammed my bowl onto the log with more force than was necessary. "I know. People have no honor anymore. Trust me, I was pissed, too, but it was already getting late, and Ked was hungry. We can always go back for the rest."

Daethie's iridescent wings whipped the air, making Yrra flinch as they grazed his long, pointed ear. "And make a second trip for no reason?" she spat, expression contorted with fury. "You should have taken your payment in fingers! For Valuen's sake. That's it—you're taking me to a mender tomorrow. I'm not sitting around any longer."

Poor Yrra's eyes darted to the ground as his skin darkened to navy around his throat. Even Vee appeared unsettled.

Jük glanced up from his meal to lay down the law. "Shut up and eat," he snarled. "We don't have the money to waste on mending insignificant injuries, and you're being obnoxious. You tweaked a muscle, but you act like you've lost a limb. *Bavga.*"

Vee laid a comforting hand on his forearm and squeezed.

"I can spend my money on whatever I want." Daethie leapt to her feet and went to jump off Yrra's shoulder. She paused to consider the distance to the ground, her wings fluttering uncertainly. Without a word, Yrra raised one hand. She hopped into his palm, and he set her on the trunk beside him. Once settled, Daethie jabbed a finger in Jük's direction.

"And I think I know how my injury impacts me. I'm not a kid; unlike some people in this group, I have the mental capacity to make my own decisions," she growled. Vee's gaze darted to Ked, who was luckily absorbed with his second bowl of food.

"Hey—" Hohem protested at the same time I started to say, "That's not—"

But Yrra surging to his feet had everyone falling silent. He directed a slight frown and something akin to disappointment at Daethie before handing his bowl back to Vee with an abrupt nod of thanks and striding off toward the tents that made up our sleeping area. Daethie watched him go with wide eyes, wings gone as still as the rest of her.

"Great job," Jük started, tone dripping with sarcasm, but Vee's arm flew up to push a mouthful of *paya* into his open mouth before he could piss someone off again.

Someone had to keep the peace.

"Well!" My hands came together with a loud crack, and all eyes turned to me. "The good news is that it's payday. We got eighty *vodt*, and there are eight of us, so it's an even ten each. That should tide us over for another week, two if we're smart about it. And it's almost harvest season, so things should pick up soon."

"Think we should head south," Hohem said through a mouthful of food. Swallowing, he passed his empty bowl to Vee and continued. "Into Wysalar, where Vyrain and I grew up. They're a productive province with mild winters, and the *Ishameti* have always been accommodating of outsiders. None of you would be given any trouble. Plus, they'll need extra hands for harvest season."

My hands balled into fists in my lap at the idea of leaving the Kereti region. That would put us adjacent to the United States side of the continent, closer to D.C. Yes, that was behind me, and yes, it was foolish to let that get in the way of anything, but the feelings remained.

"We could, if need be." I grasped for an adequate reason to shoot down the suggestion. "My gut is saying this will be a good week. I'll spend some more time scoping out potential gigs in town tomorrow. I'll take you, Daethie, if you want to stop by the mender."

"No. It would be a waste," Daethie mumbled, her attention focused on the toes of her slippers. Her wings opened and closed behind her, shedding bits of sparkly dust.

"Let's get a drink," Vyrain suggested, turning to me with a hopeful look. "Take a break. Celebrate a job well done. It's been a while since we had the chance to relax."

At that, Daethie perked up.

"As long as it's not just you and me," I replied with both eyebrows raised, not about to let him set me up for a date. That he thought he could get away with it told me I'd been too soft on him. I'd need to work on finding a balance. Smothering a rising yawn, I added, "Not tonight, though. Maybe tomorrow. See if Yrra wants to come, too. Hohem?"

"Yeah, I'm down."

"Me too," Daethie said quickly.

"Vee? Jük?" I extended the invitation to be polite, even though they rarely left camp unless they needed something. As expected, Vee shook her head.

"Thank you, but no." She sighed. "You all have fun, though. We'll find something to keep us busy here." She turned to gather the dishes. Ked's face was hidden from view as he licked the last remnants of a third serving from his dinnerware.

"Wasn't it Yrra's turn for the dishes?" Vyrain piped up. "Should I get him?"

"No, he was on *avida* care tonight. I'll do them," I volunteered, getting to my feet. He could use some time to himself. One would think he'd be used to our dysfunctional group by now, but he was too gentle for the world. He'd have to grow a thicker skin if he ever wanted to get his home and harem situated. From what I'd heard, territorial skirmishes with other males of his kind weren't uncommon. I couldn't imagine Yrra raising his voice, much less a fist or fang.

The short walk through the trees was pleasant. Clumps of phosphorescent lichen cast areas of the forest in a pale glow, so different from on Earth. As I approached the creek, a small, ferret-like form bounded away with a childlike giggle. This place had so much in common with my world. Even then, it was its own beast, largely untouched by human hands.

I crouched by the shore to run the first bowl under the water. As food particles lifted away, my thoughts strayed back to when I crossed through The Rift. It had been equal parts thrilling and nerve-racking to leave everything I knew behind, but I didn't have many options. I tried to fit in by turning myself into one of the first sentient beings I saw, which happened to be a faun. That didn't work out, because someone tried to talk to me, and neither English nor Portuguese was of any use here.

I'd managed for a little while pretending to be dumb and getting whatever I needed through begging and pilfering. Those early nights, I risked foraged food and slept in doorways, bushes, and stables. It was better than life on Earth in the sense that I was free. Instead of honing my abilities, learning surveillance techniques, and studying foreign languages in a sterile classroom, I could focus on keeping warm and finding my next meal.

When I found Jük and Vee—or, more accurately, when they found me—things changed. While I knew the basics of the common language by that point, they taught me most of what I know now. Being able to communicate made a world of difference. They were also the ones who started calling me Mar, as *Epitgig* traditionally had monosyllabic names. Gratitude made my eyes prick whenever I thought of all they did for me. They'd never met a human before, had no idea what I was or where I came from, and became the closest thing I had to a family since being torn from mine all those years ago.

I could never repay their kindness.

The stack of dirty dishes beside me shrank as I went. Deep in thought, I didn't notice I wasn't alone until I was packing up to return to camp and spotted a blue head bobbing atop the current a few feet from shore. I did a double-take.

There was a brief moment wherein I tried to keep the armful of tableware I was carrying from falling and cover my eyes with the same set of hands. Words tumbled out amidst the chaos. "Good Goddess, I'm sorry. Have you been here the whole time? Wait, are you naked?"

When no response came, I opened one eye, prepared to avert my gaze. Yrra shook his head, and I relaxed. He brooded in the middle of the stream, sitting on the creek bed so that he was submerged to his shoulders. A body of water like this wasn't enough for one of his kind to call home, but it was still in his nature to seek out the comfort the water provided.

Encumbered by an armful of dishes, I approached the stream's edge. "You doing okay?"

I got a nod.

"Want to talk about it?"

A shake.

Yrra ran a wet hand over his hair, slicking it flat against his scalp. Waterfolk had little hair, but what they did have was thin, nonporous, and dried quickly. It was convenient when you lived your life half in the water and half on land.

"Okay." I paused, digging one toe absent-mindedly into the silt at my feet. Silence wasn't new or unusual for him, but it didn't take a genius to tell that his mood had taken a downturn. *Should I push or let it be?* I'd known Yrra for a while now, but with how little he talked, I found him tricky to pin down. He didn't have any trouble getting along with the rest of the crew; even Ked took to him right away. But he still hesitated to open up to us after all this time.

"Well, I'm here if you need a listening ear," I told him, electing to leave it at that. "Also, we were thinking we'd get a drink in town tomorrow if you'd like to join us. Call it a celebration for a job well done today. I have your share of today's payout, too."

Yrra's face tilted toward me. "Is..." At the soft sound, he cleared his throat and tried again, putting a little more strength into the words. "Will Daethie be there?"

A knowing smile graced my lips. "Yes, she's coming," I confirmed.

Yrra stood abruptly. Water sluiced down the hard, flat planes of his chest and abdomen, dripping off the loincloth he wore. My eyes followed before I caught myself. While he wasn't my type, it was fascinating how each part of him was a different hue of blue, from his palms and lips to his nails and lashes. The wonders of the fae realm never ceased.

"Put those away. You're going to poke someone's eyes out," I joked.

Yrra glanced around himself in confusion, overlooking what I was referring to: his nipples, denim blue and pointed like canudinhos from the transition from water to air.

"Never mind." Shaking my head, I adjusted my grip on the stack of bowls and went to head back to camp. "Don't stay out too late, yeah? You'll catch a cold."

I left the gentle fae to splash about and think in peace. As I climbed the little hill leading to our clearing, my train of thought turned to Hohem's earlier suggestion to move south. It wasn't a bad idea. If we kept having trouble finding work as the season changed, we might have to. With a bit of luck, though, tomorrow would come with new opportunities. Having a jingling purse for the first time in a while went a long way in improving my mood.

Hopefully, this optimism could last.

CHAPTER THREE

IN WHICH OUR HERO FLIRTS HIS WAY INTO THE PICTURE

THE TOWN of Vhalder boasted two options for casual drinking. One was Simprekan's, a cozy, family-owned establishment that specialized in food and home-brewed alcohol. The other, with a name translating to The Bitter Brother, was a proper inn where food and drink were decidedly not their specialty but could be had in excess for cheap. By nature, it was the sort of place where people converged to pass the time, spread gossip, and meet new people. I preferred this spot, only because the number of patrons present at any given time meant it was the best place to socialize and advertise our services.

"Let's keep it to a reasonable number of drinks," I reminded everyone, holding the door open as they filed inside. Daethie, riding one of the twin's shoulders today, rolled her eyes at me. I held my tongue; obviously, the statement was not intended for the one person in our group who could get alcohol poisoning from a single flagon.

The interior was warm and well-lit, with large lamps bearing magical light set on windowsills and hanging from ceiling beams. Fermented grains perfumed the air. On the far side of the room was the bar, where two handsome fauns served drinks and entertained guests seated at the counter. Serving girls flitted between tables on the main floor, exchanging empty drinks for new ones. On the left were stairs leading to the second level, with a large man at the bottom to guard the rooms from curious drunks. The whole place buzzed with jovial conversation.

We selected one of the rectangular tables against the wall on the left side of the room. It was a good vantage point to watch the stairs and bar, so I'd be able to keep an eye out for anyone who looked wealthy and in need of a hand. When the waitress came around, we all ordered.

"Something strong," one of the twins requested, the other echoing him.

"Something sweet, if you have it," I told the girl.

When the girl's attention pivoted to Yrra, he struggled to get his words out, hunching in on himself more with every second that passed. Daethie hopped onto the tabletop, beating her wings once to slow her descent, and snapped, "Give me something strong, too, but a half portion. And for him, a full portion, but half drink and half water."

Yrra cast a grateful look at the fierce pixie as the serving girl left to fetch our beverages, and I returned to surveying the dining room and bar area. A few patrons here might be worth speaking to, judging by their dress and the way they carried themselves, but not many. I could also speak to the owner. An establishment like this had a lot of working parts, so chances were good that they could use a hand here or there.

"I hope you'll remember that we're here to relax," the twin sitting beside me remarked.

"Yeah, yeah." I waved away his words. "Don't worry about me."

"He's not worried about you," Daethie interjected with a disdainful sniff. "If you're here to work, you'll rope the rest of us into your schemes, too. Your ass better stay in that chair, Mar."

With Daethie, you had to put your foot down, or she'd walk all over you. In an ideal world, you wouldn't be on her bad side, but you wouldn't be friendly with her either. I'd found a good middle ground in the time we'd known each other.

"And *your* ass better stay out of my business," I retorted, fixing her with a frown. "Someone should keep an eye out so we don't miss any opportunities, and I'm electing to be that person. Why do you care? It's not any bother to you."

"Your business is our business, whether you like it or not, and we're trying to enjoy a day off. Do we need to find you a blindfold so that you can focus, you work animal?"

"Keep it up, and you're going to be on track to another sprained wing—"

"Ladies, ladies." Vyrain put up his hands in a placating gesture. "We have an entire evening to look forward to. Let's keep things cordial, hmm? How about a game of *thracks*?"

He pulled a velvet pouch from a pocket somewhere but was interrupted by the serving girl. She danced around the table, setting cups before their owners with a practiced hand.

"There you are," she said cheerfully as she placed the last one, smaller than the rest, in front of Daethie. "Anything else I can getcha? We've got a lovely *lya* roast on special tonight."

"I don't think we're hungry, thank you." I glanced around the table; everyone seemed to be in agreement. "But, I did want to ask if you've heard of anyone in need of a hand." Ignoring Daethie's groan of protest, I forged onward. "We're staying nearby and looking for work. We do it all: enforcement, deliveries, repairs, menial tasks. Even domestic chores—cooking, childcare, and the like. If you know of anyone who needs anything, send 'em our way."

The girl considered my question, raising one hand to tap at her bottom lip. "Mmm, well, there's always… Oh! Have you heard about the Kereti heiress yet?"

Interest piqued, I leaned forward in my seat. "No, what about her?"

Everyone knew that the Keretis were the leading family in this region, but the municipal seat was far from here, so I'd never seen them. To the best of my knowledge, they had several daughters and at least one son. Extended family governed smaller territories from coast to coast. Beyond that, I knew nothing.

The serving girl smiled, showing deep dimples. "Oh, get ready—it's like something out of a folktale. Their oldest daughter, Narille, was on a diplomatic mission to the island city of Munarzed. There's been a growing civilization there for a long time, but recently there'd been no contact from them, and they didn't pay their taxes. Weird, right? So, she goes to see what's up and, get this, doesn't come back."

There were blank looks around the table. None of us knew what to make of that.

The serving girl continued, vibrating with eagerness at having a captive audience. "Narille sent one message to her family. 'I'm staying here, this is what I want, don't look for me.' Then, nothing. They were distraught, of course, but more than that, confused. She was happy at home, you know, and being brought up to succeed her parents and continue the family line. It's a complete mystery. They sent an envoy to talk with her, and the envoy didn't come back, either. Now, they're trying to find outside help to figure out what's going on there. The pay is ridiculous—it could set a whole family up for life."

My heart was pounding in my chest by the time she finished. Could this be the break we've been looking for, landing in our lap? Hah! What were the chances? *Wait—patience, Mar. Gotta get to the root of this before you get too excited.*

"What's the catch?" I asked, knowing there had to be one.

"Oh, the usual," the serving girl replied, giving a casual shrug. "Nothing in advance, lots of travel…"

She paused for dramatic effect, gripping her tray to her chest as she delivered the kicker: "And nobody who makes it to the island ever returns. Not a single one. The family's been recruiting for several cycles—nearly a full revolution now—so it's got to be, gosh, a hundred people who've attempted? They're so desperate by this point that they're spreading the word far and wide. For the past week, it's all anyone's been talking about!"

Almost a year of this, hundreds of people gone with no explanation, pay that could set a family up for life… No wonder it was all people could talk about. To think, we'd been missing this kind of excitement by keeping to our camp in the woods. We ought to get out more.

I considered the prospect with rising enthusiasm. First, I'd have to confirm this was a legitimate job. Checking the updated job board ought to solve that. Then there was the matter of convincing the others. Daethie would probably be down; she wasn't afraid of anything. Jük, Vee, and Ked would stay behind as usual. Yrra, I couldn't say. The twins—

The waitress heaved a wistful sigh at that moment. "Maybe she's been kidnapped. She could be chained up in a dungeon somewhere, waiting for a handsome hero to rescue her. Wouldn't that be so romantic?"

Vyrain and Hohem exchanged a wide-eyed look as the gears turned in their heads. That would be the perfect recipe for the making of a prophesied chosen one.

"We're in," they said together.

I couldn't believe my luck.

"Hang on! We've got to consider all the angles before we make a decision." I thanked the serving girl for the information, and she took the dismissal for what it was, bobbing on her feet and disappearing to return to work. Pivoting back to the table, I pulled my mug closer and sipped while I got my thoughts in order. An offensive sourness burst across my tongue, making me cringe—the drink was under-fermented, but I wasn't about to waste it.

If I had convincing to do, the first step would be to see where the others' heads were at, but everyone was quiet. Yrra, I expected. Daethie and the others were a surprise.

"What do you guys think?" I asked, raising my head to regard them.

"We're in." Vyrain broke the silence, speaking for himself and his brother. "Saving the Kereti heiress would put us in the history books. We'll be talked about for revolutions to come!"

Daethie, ever the optimist, pointed out, "You know, dying in a horrifically gruesome way while *attempting* a daring rescue might get you in the history books too."

"You can stay here," Hohem muttered against the rim of his mug.

"Not a chance. If there's a fortune to be had, you can bet your buttocks I'm not missing out on that." Daethie fiddled with the assortment of items she wore around her waist, various things she'd collected over the years. Producing a teacup more appropriate for someone of her stature, she dipped it into the cup at her side and guzzled the contents with a sigh of happiness. "Plus, someone will have to bring back the news if you all die horrific deaths."

Yrra smacked his lips thoughtfully, having tasted the concoction in his flagon.

"What do you think?" I asked him. "Is it worth the risk? Would you come with us?"

Upon noticing that all eyes were on him, he blushed dark blue. "Maybe," he whispered, reaching up to tug on one of his pointed ears. "Let me think."

"Of course." I considered our situation for another beat. The kind thing to do was to let them come to their own conclusions; make their own choices. We were halfway there, anyway. "No one's found her after all this time, so there's no rush. At the least, we can sleep on it. The others might not be interested, but we can fill them in too. I'd still ask around about other employment options for the summer, but… a guaranteed payout sure sounds good."

The others murmured their agreement.

I went in for another sip when a door slammed above us, startling me into spilling a mouthful of borderline unpalatable mead down my front. Pushing my cup back, I cursed and searched for something to clean myself up. The din of merriment around us faded as footsteps thundered down the stairs and everyone's attention turned to the two descending.

First came a woman with albino coloring, gray horns peeking out from a cloud of tight white curls on her head. Underneath her skirt, a striped, prehensile tail twitched in a distressed rhythm. A naked man followed close behind, his modesty barely maintained by a sheet around his middle. The shade of his skin, the warm brown of an acorn shell, contrasted beautifully with the woman's pallor. Dark markings decorated his forearms, stretched along his arms, and bled into his chest, caressing each muscle group as though they'd been applied by an artist. On his back were large, black, feathered wings he kept tight against his body.

The man was attempting to console the woman, who appeared distraught. "—came out wrong. I've never pretended to be good with words. What I meant to say is that I'm honored to have you, specifically. You're an exquisite creature, truly! A vision!"

"You must think me a fool," the woman wailed. As she reached the bottom, she whirled, clutching her dangling cloak to her chest. "My mother was right. I can't believe I fell for your… your…" She gestured wildly upon failing to articulate whatever she was trying to say.

"Charm?" the man supplied, striking a pose against the railing.

Is he for real?

At a loss for words, the woman's face scrunched up, her eyes filling with tears. "I should have stayed home!" she cried. With that, she swept across the dining room toward the exit, past numerous patrons who jostled each other and laughed at the lovers' display.

As the man went to follow, I turned away from the debacle and raised my flagon. You didn't have that kind of drama to worry about when living out in the woods. Relationships opened a can of worms. Hell, people in general did. I counted myself lucky that I only had to deal with a select few on a daily basis, and I wasn't tempted to sleep with any of them.

Out of the corner of my eye, I saw Vyrain stiffen, and a strange look came over his face moments before a sultry voice spoke from my right.

"Well, hello there, gorgeous."

The mead went down the wrong pipe.

As I sputtered for air, eyes watering, it registered that the man in a sheet had not gone after his girlfriend. No, he stood two feet away, studying me with his head cocked at a curious angle. Up close, I could see that his eyes were a stunning amber, round and perceptive with big pupils like a predatory bird's and ringed by enviably long, thick lashes. Deep-brown textured hair was tied into a haphazard knot at the nape of his neck, leaving long, pointed ears with tufted tips on display. Several piercings lined the lobe and cartilage.

When I didn't respond, the stranger took my lack of rejection as an invitation. He closed the space between us and leaned against the table, expression nothing short of delighted. I caught a hint of a mouth-watering scent—a warm olfactory hug of fresh-squeezed citrus, spices, and caramelized sugar. To my left, Vyrain inched closer to my side. Hohem appeared amused by the sudden development, while Yrra and Daethie looked on in fascination.

"I have to ask," the man before me began in a low and provocative tone of voice, as though we were the only two people in the entire room. "What are you?"

Record scratch. *What kind of question is that?* I reared back to put space between us and put a hand up, my brows coming together in confusion. "I'm sorry?"

"Forgive me." The man eased up, but his gaze remained intent. "I've never seen someone like you. Your coloring is like a wingless, deformed *Peri,* yet the dull eyes and round ears... With your petite size, you could almost be a land-bound *nykse.* I must know what you are."

Is this guy flirting with me right after having a spat with his girlfriend? And... is he calling me deformed? A familiar heat suffused my chest. I couldn't believe what I was hearing. Caught somewhere between disbelief and anger, my answer came tight. "I'm a human."

The man blinked. "A hyumin," he repeated to himself, tasting the word. "Fascinating. I've never heard of you. Why have I never heard of you before?"

Why did it matter to him? "We're not common around these parts."

"No?" The man considered my answer. A slow smile spread across his face. "Well, then, I *am* a lucky one, aren't I? Tell me, how would you feel about a brief rendezvous in my bed? I have a private room upstairs. It can be as quick as you like, in and out, you'll barely feel a thing."

I was rarely rendered speechless, but audacity of that degree did the trick. Clearly, I'd entertained him too long. My hand twitched with the urge to slap him, and my mouth opened with scathing words at the ready. However, a supportive arm came to rest across my shoulders before I could get violent.

"She's not interested," Vyrain answered for me, his tone as frosty as I'd ever heard it.

When did he get so close?

"I can answer for myself," I snapped, shaking his arm off. Tension had me in a chokehold, the only reason I lashed out at him. I regretted it as soon as it was out of my mouth. Hurt flashed across Vyrain's face, but he returned to the seat without argument.

Pissed now, and more than willing to direct that energy at the cause of my irritation, I turned back to the man in front of me and imbued my voice with a blistering degree of sarcasm. "A tempting proposition, to be sure, but I'm not interested."

"We were leaving anyway," Vyrain added. "Got a quest to get on with."

"I believe Mar was just saying there's no harm in taking our time," Daethie drawled from across the table, fluttering her eyelashes. I shot her a nasty look.

"A quest?" The man perked up. "What a coincidence. I'm on a quest myself, you know, albeit a more personal one. Perhaps they could go hand in hand. Have you got room for another member in your party?"

Though I knew better, curiosity got the best of me. Was he going to be one of our competitors? If so, it might be wise to play nice—he could have valuable information. Mentally pacifying my roiling nerves, I eased my posture into a lean conveying friendly interest.

"Oh, yeah? What kind of quest is that?" I asked, trying to be casual about it.

"To copulate with one of every race," the stranger responded smoothly, with quite a bit more pride than was appropriate for the statement. "Or, at least, those that are compatible. As much as I might want to lie with, say, an *Aminkinya,* it's not exactly feasible. Regrettably."

He cast a saucy wink over his shoulder in Daethie's direction before looking me up and down. A crease appeared between his straight brows. "Hm. I realize now that my lack of familiarity with your race might have me overcommitting. At the risk of coming across as ignorant, I'm assuming you've got some sort of hole or a cock between—"

I stood, the bench underneath me shifting back with a harsh groan. "Respectfully"—my voice rose, attracting the attention of nearby patrons—"what I have or don't have is none of your damn business.

And to be frank, coming across as ignorant should be the least of your worries."

My hand went to the purse at my waist. Realizing I only had the *vodt* from our last job, I gritted my teeth and tossed one on the table, even though it was probably four times the cost of my drink. Had to get out of here.

"Goodbye." I strode toward the door. My friends scrambled to slide out of their chairs.

"Wait, wait, wait." The audacious man followed, almost falling flat on his face when the sheet tangled around his legs. For a moment, the linen dipped, nearly revealing too much—trimmed dark curls and an intriguing shadow—before he hopped upright and yanked it back into place. "Let's try this again. Please?" he implored. "I'm Luthri. You can call me Lu if you like. It's a pleasure to make your acquaintance. And you are?"

God, this guy is worse than Vyrain.

"Not. Interested," I reiterated. When I paused out front to wait for the others, Luthri followed me outside, not taking the hint. Hell, we'd gone way past hints, hadn't we? One had to admire his tenacity by this point. "You're naked," I exclaimed, giving him an incredulous look. "And I'm pretty sure that sheet doesn't belong to you."

"Oh!" His gaze dropped to the fist that held the sheet closed in front of him, as though he were noticing his state of undress for the first time. "So I am."

Telling myself I was doing what I was trained to do and making note of anything that stood out about an individual, I let my eyes follow his movement, taking in the expanse of sculpted abdomen on display. *Hm. On second thought, it might not be such a hardship to sleep with the guy. How long has it been, anyway?*

No, no—there was a principle to be followed. People like this were a plague, and they needed to hear a "no" every once in a while. It didn't do him any favors if I folded.

"Give me a few minutes," Luthri beseeched me, putting his hands together as best he could while holding onto the sheet. "Let me fetch my things and get dressed, and we can talk about it. I promise I can make it worth your while."

I ignored him as the rest of my group filtered outside. Daethie was back on Yrra's shoulder, and Hohem pushed Vyrain along while he stared daggers at our new friend. The night was still young; we could spar or keep going over our options for summer work before bed. Giving Luthri a mock salute, I left him in front of The Bitter Brother with his sheet. I had Vyrain's antics to contend with on a day-to-day basis; that was more than enough for me.

CHAPTER FOUR

IN WHICH THE PARTY GAINS AN ENTHUSIASTIC NEW MEMBER

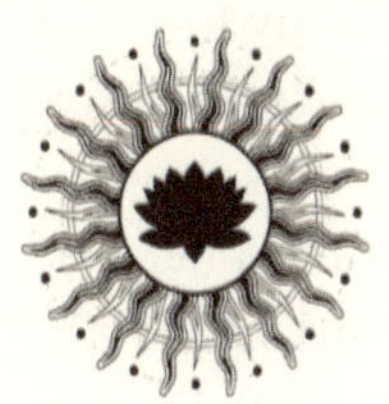

I WOKE TOO EARLY the next morning to an ungodly ruckus outside my tent. Praying it would stop, I spent several moments staring at the canvas ceiling while the shouting, crashing, and occasional jeer carried on outside. When it showed no signs of ceasing, I released a regretful sigh and groped around for my pants. My muscles screamed in protest as I pulled them on.

The night before, I'd ended up going through a few training exercises and running laps around camp with the twins. It was a good way to pass the time and stay fit, but the lingering soreness reminded me that I didn't have a fae body. After taking a deep drink from the canteen of boiled river water I kept by my bedside and grabbing a *zanna* root to clean my teeth, I pushed aside the flap, stepped outside, and drew up short.

What. The fuck.

On the shaded side of the clearing, Vee, Yrra, and Ked worked together to get a section of flaming underbrush under control. In the middle, Hohem and Vyrain circled the man we'd met last night at the inn—now fully clothed, I noted with some degree of disappointment. Luthri, was it? When had he come back? No, that's not the right question. What was he even doing here?

Fighting, by the look of it, perhaps for a while. All three men bore various scratches, burns, and tears in their clothing. Luthri's breathing was labored, and one of Vyrain's eyes had begun to swell shut. What a scene to wake up to.

As I watched, Vyrain rushed the stranger again, throwing a wide punch. Luthri ducked under his arm and responded with an elbow to his back, sending Vyrain sprawling to the ground. Hohem dashed after his brother and managed to sweep Luthri's leg out from underneath him. A cry of warning rose in my throat as he summoned a ball of fire, but it froze on my lips when Luthri effortlessly rolled out of the way and leapt back to his feet.

"Yeah!" Daethie shouted from her vantage point on the log by the fire pit, pumping her little fist in the air. "Hohem's favoring his left side; go for the knee! Punch him in the throat next!"

My eyebrows shot into my hairline. "Whose side are you on?!"

She ignored me, cupping her hands around her mouth. "His hair, pull his hair!"

It was about then that Luthri noticed me. His eyes widened, mouth open in surprise, and the corners of his eyes crinkled in a huge grin. He waved. *Waved*. The nerve.

Vyrain tackled him to the ground with the force of a charging bull.

"Okay, stop!" My feet moved of their own accord. I dropped my *zanna* root and stepped into the fray, clapping my hands to get their attention. Hohem stopped where he was, spitting a mouthful of blood and saliva, but Vyrain and Luthri continued to tussle at my feet.

"That's enough. Break it up," I ordered, clapping again. "Break it up, I said!"

I aimed a kick, not caring who it hit, when they finally released each other. Vyrain crawled a few feet away and rolled onto his back to catch his breath. Hohem went to check on him. Luthri pulled himself to his feet, wincing all the way. His shirt, an odd wraparound style designed to cover his back and sides while leaving openings for his wings to hang free, was torn at the draped neck, and all of him was covered in dirt.

"Hey," I greeted him, unable to help myself. "You look different with clothes on."

He shot me a dazzling smile despite a split lip. "No less attractive, I hope?"

The absurdity of his response caught me off guard. I snorted.

"Let's start over," he suggested, reaching for my hand. His nails were long and black, like an eagle's talons, but he was careful not to hurt me. "I'm Luthri. You can call me Lu."

I expected him to kiss the back of my hand, but as I watched, he rotated it palm-up and brought my wrist to his lips, breathing in. His tongue darted out to taste my pulse point.

There were a lot of things I had to learn after crossing The Rift. Taking things in stride was one of them, especially with the myriad of fae customs someone from Earth might interpret as odd. I kept my expression neutral and, when he released my hand, took the chance to wipe my wrist on my thigh. "Uh… Mar. Nice to meet you. Want to explain what that was about?"

Vyrain was on his feet now, openly scowling in our direction. Using each other for support, he and Hohem limped over to give their side of the story.

"I thought I heard something, so I went to check it out," Vyrain started. "This guy"—he jerked his chin at Luthri—"was creeping around camp. I think he was trying to find your tent."

Lu's eyes went wide. "On my honor," he exclaimed, putting his hands up, "I had no intention of causing harm to anyone or invading the lady's personal space while she was unaware. I was merely hoping to speak with her when she woke."

"How did you find us, anyway?" Hohem demanded. "I thought we left you at the inn."

"I have a good sense of smell," Lu offered. "And through extensive amounts of practice, I can get dressed—or undressed, when the situation calls for it—very quickly."

"That was a blast," Daethie exclaimed. "I'm very impressed." She hopped over from where she'd been watching, beating her wings at intervals to carry her farther.

"Not right now, Daethie." Taking the bridge of my nose between my thumb and forefinger, I centered myself. "Okay, you found us. Congratulations. What can we do for you?"

"Oh! Well, that's..." Lu appeared almost bashful. "I was hoping we could continue our discussion from last night. I realize I may not have gone about it the right way, but—"

I raised a hand to stop him. "Don't tell me..." Tossing an exasperated look over my shoulder at our company, I lowered my voice. "You're still trying to get in my pants?"

"All right, I won't," he replied, matching my volume.

We stared at each other for several beats in silence. When he made no move to clarify or to leave, I threw up my hands and turned to check on Yrra and Vee. They might need backup.

"Just once," Lu pleaded, hurrying to catch up to me.

"I don't like repeating myself," I told him as I lengthened my strides. "And I'm not inclined to jump into bed with a man who can't take 'no' for an answer. For someone who seems to spend quite a bit of time around women, you're surprisingly dense."

He babbled an unconvincing response, but I just shook my head. There was no telling what magical words would get through that thick skull of his. More likely than not, arguing with him was a waste of breath, and if I continued entertaining this, I'd lose it. The best way to deal with an obstinate man in this case was to ignore him.

The bush was, unfortunately, a total loss, but Vee and Yrra both appeared untouched. Vee approached cautiously, dabbing at her temple with her sleeve and eyeing the men as though they might decide to go for each other again. "Well, what an exciting start to the day," she remarked. Her gaze swept over Luthri with unbridled curiosity. "Will we be having one more for supper?"

"Not if I have anything to say about it," Vyrain growled from behind us.

"He was leaving," I added pointedly.

Lu's shoulders dropped.

Around then, Ked returned from another trip to the creek, cresting the hill at a jog with buckets of water dangling from both hands. Upon noticing that things were calm, he slowed his pace. "Everyone good?" he asked, shooting a worried look at Vyrain and Hohem.

"All is well," Vee said, reaching for him as he dumped the last of the water on the charred bush and came to her side. "Ked, honey, this is..."

"Lu," I supplied. "He's not staying. Where's Jük?"

"Out since before dawn," Vee answered, gesturing toward the woods. "He's hunting for some fresh meat for supper today. He'll be disappointed that he missed the excitement."

Lu perked up. "Hunting? I can help. I'd be happy to."

"Don't you have anywhere else to be?" I snapped.

"Yeah, don't you?" Vyrain echoed, crossing his arms and wincing as the movement agitated invisible wounds.

I was debating how to handle this without further bloodshed when Ked stepped forward. His eyes were wide and fixed on Lu's piercings, admiring the way they caught the sunlight. "Shiny," he said in awe, reaching for one of Lu's long, fluffy ears.

I was closer than Vee, so I reached out to stop him.

"His earrings are pretty, huh?" As I redirected his hands, I softened my voice. "Remember what Vee says about touching people without their permission, though? Some people don't like it. You have to ask."

"It's all right," Lu assured me, reading the situation in an instant. He stepped closer, turning his head to make his ear more accessible. I exchanged a look with Vee.

"Pretty." Ked poked one of the gold hoops in Luthri's lobe with one big finger.

"You like them?" he asked. Ked nodded, entranced.

Before I could tell what he was doing, Lu had removed one of the bigger hoops from his ears. He fiddled with it for a split second before holding it out to the half-giant. Ked didn't hesitate to accept. He showed it to Vee, who smiled and nodded.

"I changed it," Lu said, leaning forward to indicate the earring post. "So he can wear it without piercing his ears. It will be a little bit of pressure but shouldn't be painful."

He helped Ked put it on, but I wasn't convinced. I liked to think I was a good judge of character. I'd met the guy not even twenty-four hours ago, and already he'd walked through a crowded tavern wearing nothing but a sheet, publicly propositioned a stranger, and started a fight. That wasn't conducive to a healthy environment. If he thought that being nice to my friends was going to score him brownie points, he was barking up the wrong tree.

Then again, maybe he didn't start that brawl. Vyrain did seem aggressive last night. I'd not known him to pick fights, but I couldn't put it past him either. I shouldn't discount the possibility of Luthri being genuine. Even if he was just here to get his dick wet, everyone deserved a chance, didn't they? Given the timing, he could be a godsend in a way.

"So, apparently, you can fight," I started. When Lu gave me his attention, I dipped my head in the direction of the twins nursing their wounds nearby. "We do odd jobs," I told him. "Right now, we're considering one that might be dangerous. Finding the Kereti heiress?"

Luthri nodded thoughtfully. "I heard about that. Disappeared in Munarzed, didn't she?"

"Yes." *Goddess, please let this be the right decision.* "Would you want to come along?"

That got Vyrain's attention. Fae senses never failed to impress me.

"Excuse me!" Shaking off his brother's grip, he limped forward. "You can't invite a stranger to tag along with us, especially not with something this important," he argued. "And anyway, there are enough of us splitting the payment as it is."

"I don't need any money." Lu held up his hands. "Keep it all; I don't care."

Well, that was the best-case scenario. Extra manpower without a drain on our resources? You'd have to be an idiot to say no to that.

Alas, that was exactly what I dealt with.

"Oh, how magnanimous of you," Vyrain sneered. "So, what, you're going to put your life on hold for weeks or cycles so that you can go on a daring adventure with zero payoff except for the minuscule chance of getting between the legs of a woman you don't even know?"

Shaking her head, Vee went to check on Hohem.

"People have done more for less." Lu sniffed, affronted by the implication. "Ulmar of House Hamra, First of His Name, crossed the barren Fields of Fortitude alone to learn the name of his gods-given soulmate."

"Wha—that's a kid's story!" Vyrain fumed. "There's a reason you won't find that mentioned in any history books. It's complete and utter—"

"Look." I clapped my hands to get their attention. "We can have everyone take a vote if we want. All I'll say is if this job is as dangerous as it sounds, then it won't hurt to have more manpower. Lu's been honest about his motives; you can't fault the guy for that."

"I'm fine with him joining," Daethie chimed in from nearby. "Yrra doesn't mind, either."

Yrra blinked, wondering when he'd said as much, but didn't protest.

"Worried I might grow on you?" Luthri winked at Vyrain, eliciting a disgusted groan from the fair fae. "If the lady was amenable, perhaps you could join us," Lu went on to suggest, waggling his eyebrows. "It wouldn't be the first time I've entertained two lovers at once."

"Absolutely not," Vyrain spat. "I don't share."

The image played out in my head unprompted: lying back on the mat in my tent as pale hands ran along my breasts, teasing the sensitive skin. A dark head settled between my legs, tattooed arms gripping my thighs as he took what he wanted with a hot, flexible tongue—

My silence scandalized poor Vyrain. "Mar?!"

"Oh, yeah, absolutely not," I said quickly, shaking off the daydream. "If you want to join us, Luthri—for this job, I mean—you need to stop antagonizing Vyrain. No ifs, ands, or buts. I need to get a map, but I know that Munarzed is a ways away, and I'm not about to listen to you two squabble nonstop for the next few weeks."

"Oh, please." Daethie waved away my concern. "It's all we ever did before he came along. What's the difference? I, for one, am always glad for more eye candy."

Not for the first time, I considered wringing the pixie's little neck. It was too early in the morning to be letting her get to me. "How about, instead of encouraging that kind of behavior, we strive for a healthy work environment, hmm? Is that all right with you, Daethie?"

She made a noncommittal noise.

"Mar." Vyrain pulled me aside, not missing the chance to cast another glare in Lu's direction. "Consider this from a safety standpoint," he implored in a low voice. "We don't know this guy. He could be a common bandit, for all we know. He might be setting us up so that he and the rest of his ilk can slit our throats in our sleep."

"That's a lot of effort to expend on stealing a handful of *vodt* and a few tents," I responded matter-of-factly. "Plus, we're far from helpless. You know the three of us could give a group of bandits a run for their money. Well, after you and your brother heal up."

"You're being naï—" Vyrain cut himself off when his voice began to climb. Clearing his throat, he started again. "He's traveling alone, staying at establishments of ill repute. We don't know where he came from, or anything about him, for that matter. And Hohem and I weren't pulling our punches that much this morning—that guy can hold his own."

"Then he could have already slit our throats and been done with it, no?" I pointed out.

Vyrain's throat bobbed as he struggled to find a response.

"I appreciate your concern." I patted him on the arm. He flinched away from the contact, rolling his shoulder back with his brows knit together in pain.

"Ah… sorry." Clearing my throat, I continued. "I just wonder how much of it has to do with you being concerned for our safety and how much of it has to do with your ego. I'm not saying that's a problem, but if having another fighter on our team could be the difference between us succeeding or not, the pros outweigh the cons. You know?"

Vyrain sucked his teeth, reluctant to admit as much. I rolled the situation around in my head in hopes of producing another bone to throw him. Better chore distribution? Fresh meat, perhaps, if Luthri had been serious about hunting?

"You don't have to be friends. I'm asking you to tolerate his presence, that's all."

That did the trick. He might not have been excited by any definition of the word, but he at least appeared subdued, even as he grumbled under his breath. Reassured, I let myself relax.

"Promise me you'll be careful?" he muttered as I turned to go.

"When am I not?" I tossed back, though I knew that Vyrain could come up with at least a half-dozen examples in the limited time I'd known him.

Lu was where I'd left him. He and Daethie were deep in conversation by that point. Vee fussed over Hohem, and Yrra stood awkwardly to one side, staring into the distance as though he were no longer sure where he fit in. I approached him first.

"Have you decided?" I asked, tilting my head to regard the shy blue fae.

Yrra shook himself from his daydream. "Hm?"

"If you're coming with us or not. To Munarzed."

I could have imagined it, but his gaze seemed to linger on the pixie speaking with our group's newest addition. "Yes," he answered at last, eyes still distant. "Yes, I think so."

"Great." A smile came naturally to my face as it landed that we were doing this as a group. "It should be a blast, all things considered."

A life like mine could be considered an adventure in its entirety, but as settled as I'd gotten, things had begun to grow stale. Plus, I'd seen precious little of the fae realm despite how long I'd been here. If this job went well, I'd have a lot more opportunities. I could buy a cute little cottage somewhere picturesque and settle down. Was that what I wanted? Well, there was no rush. I had plenty of time to think about future plans.

The excitement was infectious, and soon, we were all smiling and discussing what to do with the money. This payoff could change everything for us—we just had to return in one piece to enjoy it.

CHAPTER FIVE

IN WHICH THE QUEST IS BEGUN

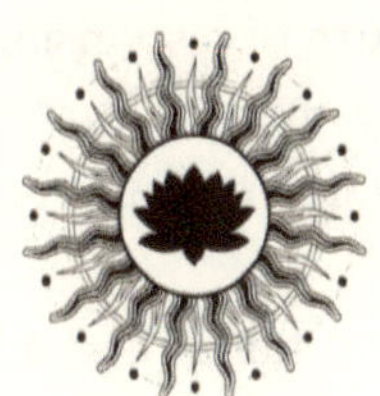

WE DISCUSSED the Kereti heiress as a group that evening. I consulted the town job board again and found the new posting, bringing it back to camp for the group to go over in detail. Likely printed with ink containing the same *mana*-resistant metal that currency was made from, it bore the family crest, and the details were as the waitress had told us.

Excitement reached an all-time high.

Though Vee didn't like the idea, the majority won out, and we agreed to leave the following morning. Vee, Jük, and Ked would stay put, maintaining the section of forest we called home and praying for our safe return. As much as it would have been helpful, the wagon and *avida* also stayed behind, since at least one leg of our journey would be by ship, and it would have been a logistical nightmare. Without further ado, we packed our things and set out with the sun, heading north along the wide path through the forest that served as a main road.

Daethie started the conversation some fifteen minutes in. "How far is it, anyway?"

She told us that morning that she'd nearly regained the use of her wing but wasn't yet ready for a day's worth of flying. Yrra, ever the gentleman, had offered his shoulder on the spot, assuring her that he didn't mind. He also carried her things for her. That was no hardship, given that her diminutive possessions didn't compare to the immense bundles of necessary items the rest of us had strapped to our backs.

"I'm not sure," I responded.

At the same time, Luthri began to say, "We're looking at—"

We both fell silent, indicating for the other to continue with a series of grunts and hand motions. The leadership role in this escapade had fallen to me, something I was equal parts glad and distressed about. I didn't care for the itching burn of responsibility and how it had settled itself in the forefront of my mind like a roosting hen. On the other hand, it meant that I had some deal of control over the rest of these fools, and that felt good.

"Ah. Right." I cleared my throat and adjusted my pack so that it didn't dig into my shoulders. "I don't know yet. Once we find a decent place to stop for the night, I'll see about getting us a map. Then we can figure out the best route."

Lu spoke up. "If I may… If we stay on this road and keep up the pace, we should reach an inn by nightfall. That location is used to getting travelers who are heading this way, so they ought to have some resources we can make use of."

While I didn't trust Luthri enough to take him at his word, it made sense to stay on the main road. We were sure to come across businesses eventually. And if he had been truthful about what he'd been up to, he might very well be familiar with all the inns in the area.

"Great. Perfect. Let's do that."

Vyrain appeared beside me, flanked by his brother. Their bruises from yesterday's scuffle were already faint, though they moved with added care. "May I just say, Mar, that you are looking lovely today," he announced with a pointed look in Luthri's direction.

Hohem made an exaggerated gesture conveying his exasperation. I couldn't agree more.

Not to be outdone, Lu chimed in. "I can't imagine there's been a day when she hasn't."

"You've only known her for a day," Vyrain retorted.

"How about we stick to travel-related topics?" I suggested, barely able to restrain myself from rolling my eyes. I'd have to think of some way to keep them off each other's backs; there was no way I'd be able to make it more than a couple of days listening to the two of them.

"Sounds good to me," said Hohem.

"How about we get to know our newest addition?" Daethie chirped from Yrra's shoulder. "What brought you to this area, Lu?"

He had to give it some thought. "I suppose I've always been a roamer. Haven't yet found a place that felt right. Plus, with a… how to put it… a 'people-centric' quest like mine, you can make enemies quite quickly. It doesn't do me good to stay in one place very long."

"Maybe you could take Yrra under your wing while we're all here," Daethie remarked. "He could use some tips for sealing the deal when it comes to romantic pursuits."

Yrra's ears darkened with a blush.

"Don't your kind have harems?" Lu asked, blinking in surprise.

"Yes," Yrra answered hesitantly. After a moment of expectant silence, his blush deepened, and he added, "They… Our women like strong males. Providers."

"It's a stupid system," Daethie said, folding her arms. "You've got one stud and a load of broodmares. The women sit there looking pretty and popping out babies, and they all play happy family. Sometimes, the men fight each other for their territory or their women, but that's the only redeeming part. Otherwise, it's hopelessly dull."

Yrra's lips pressed together in a thin line.

"Fascinating," Luthri murmured. "Not unlike the lifestyle of *avida*."

"Who are you to judge?" Vyrain butted in on Yrra's behalf. "At least that makes sense. I've never seen or heard of a male *Aminkinya*. Do your young drop from trees when they're ready to go, like *vali* nuts? Do *kainna* fly them to your clan's nest in little baskets?"

"Wouldn't you like to know?" Daethie made a rude gesture that roughly translated to "mind your own business." "It may surprise you to know that genitals aren't everything."

"He's a male." I couldn't hide my smile. "For him, genitals are everything."

"I don't suppose we could come up with a topic that's slightly more mature?" Hohem asked with one eyebrow raised. "As much as I'm sure we'd all love to talk about dicks all day."

"Are you rich?" was Daethie's next question, directed at Luthri.

"Daethie," I hissed.

"It's all right." Lu laughed off her question. "I'm comfortable. It's all luck. My mother is a renowned mender, so my siblings and I had a good start to life. I helped her with business during my teen years. Early experience and learning how to manage money makes certain things easy, which makes other things easy. It's a trickle-down effect."

"How many siblings do you have?" I figured that was a nice, neutral question.

"Eleven. Four sisters, seven brothers."

My jaw dropped.

"We *Peri* have children in broods, you know," he continued conversationally. "Young are born live, of course, usually two to six at a time. Big families are to be expected."

The thought of twelve babies made my vagina ache in solidarity. I couldn't imagine. And having that many young children running around at once? How on Earth did *Peri* moms manage? Were they all wealthy, so they didn't have to work while they focused on family? Did they form communities to help raise each other's children while others worked?

"Speaking of children, I don't know if we ever broached the topic, Mar." Vyrain's attention turned to me. "Do you want children? How many do you hope for?"

I should have been surprised that the line of questioning came to this point… 'Should have' being the operative phrase.

"That would be a decision for future me to make," I responded. "And also none of your business. Even if I was interested, don't you think there are several get-to-know-someone questions you should ask before that? Do you even know what my favorite color is?"

"Green," he replied without missing a beat.

"Nope. Try again."

"Blue?" Luthri suggested.

"Yellow," Daethie guessed.

Even Yrra joined in. "Black?"

Shaking my head, I huffed a laugh. "Whose favorite color is black?"

"Red," Hohem tried.

I pointed. "That's it. You got it."

"The color of blood," Daethie mused. "Fitting."

"Also the most common color of *rinsom,* which happens to be my favorite flower," I countered. "Not that anyone's keeping track."

"*Rinsom,*" Vyrain muttered to himself.

"Won't you tell me about your kind, Mar?" Luthri asked, changing the subject.

"Ah... humans?" I racked my brain for a suitable response. Most fae, in my limited experience, either weren't aware of The Rift or didn't care. But I'd gotten some strange reactions in the past when I tried to explain where I was from, so it was easier to maintain an air of mystery. Vee and Jük knew the truth, but as far as the others were concerned, I was from some super remote area in southern Wysalar. That worked for me. Who knew how they would react if they learned what I was and the fact I'd been keeping the truth from them?

"Well, we're not from around here, obviously. I've been living in Kereti for about ten revolutions now, but I was born in the south. Uh... What do you want to know?"

Where did one start when it came to explaining one's species?

"The average person is like me, for the most part. The same general shape, I mean, but we have males, females, and genders in between. And we come in a few different... colors, so to speak. We have lots of different languages and customs; not everyone's the same."

"Like the *Ishameti,*" Vyrain offered.

"Sure," I agreed. The *Ishameti* weren't a single race, but rather an ethnic group of different races that all lived together in harmony, united under the Wysalar government. They shared a religion, language, and certain other cultural aspects, but remained an amalgamation of peoples from different backgrounds, not unlike the United States.

"We're an advanced people," I continued, thinking of scientific and technological advancements established before I left. "Somewhat, anyway. We've got cars and phones—eh, don't worry about that. But we don't have a lot of magic users. So instead, we use technology. That's, um... advanced tools. And we have medicine instead of menders. Well, we have menders too, but they're not... They can't use magic, so that's where medicine comes in."

Luthri struggled to wrap his head around what I was saying.

"So, not really advanced at all," Daethie commented dryly.

"It's hard to explain." And honestly, I didn't feel like going to the effort. "We do things differently. Society isn't built around magic where I come from."

"It sounds intriguing," Lu proclaimed. "I'd love to hear more about your city sometime."

"Well, it's not a—" I started before realizing the futility of trying to explain that it was a whole different world. Giving up, I settled for a defeated "Yeah. Whatever."

When the sun hit its highest point in the sky, we stopped under the shade of a weeping tree for a quick meal of nuts, fruit, and flatbread from Vee. Huddling together on seats of moss-covered roots, we scarfed down our food in relative silence. Lu turned down offers of food and disappeared toward the end of the meal, telling us to go on ahead. Assuming he was taking a bathroom break, we continued down the road, but minutes became hours with no sign of him.

"Where did he disappear to?" I muttered to myself, surveying the line of trees and thick undergrowth. They offered no answer besides rustling in the breeze. Invisible insects chattered to either side of us, and something large trumpeted in the distance. Had something bad happened to him? An encounter with a wild beast, or an injury? Was he a bandit after all, gathering his buddies for an ambush? We should be prepared for anything.

"Leave it," Hohem said before his brother could comment.

"He probably figured this wasn't worth his time after all." Vyrain shrugged, not one to miss the opportunity. He lowered his voice to sensual tones. "That gives us some time to ourselves, blossom. While we're at it, I thought of a few more questions for you—"

"Oi. You're not alone," Hohem reminded him, reaching out to smack the back of his head. "For Valuen's sake, save the flirting for someone who's receptive. Maybe we'll come across a nice *nykse* for you to practice your skills of seduction on."

"Ow!" Vyrain fixed his brother with a scowl. "See, this is why you'll never be as popular with the ladies as I am. The whole point of flirting is to use your skills to attract someone who's not yet receptive. And you know as well as I do that a *nykse* would sooner drown a man and eat his flesh than sleep with him."

"Maybe they're onto something," I muttered under my breath.

Something rustled to my left. Everyone tensed.

"There you are!" a voice called moments before Luthri appeared from between the trees. The uneasy feeling ebbed. He was out of breath but otherwise no worse for wear, I was glad to see. Only because I felt a degree of responsibility for everyone here.

"Welcome back," Daethie greeted him, eyeing him up and down. "Someone ruffle your feathers? Had to give them a good, hard preening, did you?"

Luthri took the teasing in stride. "You know it," he replied with a saucy wink. "But no, I was finding something more substantial to eat. Alas, nuts and fruit aren't my sustenance of choice. I'm a man in my prime, and being on the road whets the appetite like nothing else."

That ego could use some deflating. But where best to poke? A man like him tended to be caught up in shallow things, like one's pride and appearance. I went for it. "In your prime? I don't know about that. I'm pretty sure I saw a few gray hairs. Not to mention a little pudge around the middle. No shame in that, though—time takes its toll on everyone."

"Gray hairs? Pudge?" Lu put on an affronted air. "Tell me where you see pudge."

With practiced ease, he slid a hand underneath the hem of his shirt and lifted it to reveal the sculpted terrain of his torso. His abdominal muscles flexed under my gaze, transforming his flat stomach into a beautiful landscape of peaks and valleys no doubt best traversed by tongue. The afternoon sun gave his skin a golden glow that called to mind a statue cast in bronze.

My mouth went strangely dry.

Vyrain made a disgusted noise beside me. "Muscle weighs you down," was his input. "Makes you burn more energy. Limits your speed and flexibility. It's a liability."

"Trust me, I'm plenty flexible." Lu drew out the last word with great satisfaction.

"I've got it!" Hohem punched his palm with a resounding *smack*. "You two lechers go ahead and sleep with each other, and the rest of us don't have to listen to this anymore."

I snorted with laughter, not even bothering to disguise it as a cough. Daethie straight up chortled, and even Yrra cracked a smile. Vyrain was not amused.

The curve of Lu's lips bordered on an outright smirk. "I've had more than my share of *Alfen* already, or I would be happy to show you a good time. My offer of a three-way stands, however, should Mar ever change her mind."

Vyrain gritted his teeth, and his hands balled into fists. That was my signal that the fun had gone too far; it was time to intervene before things got ugly.

I stepped between them, putting a hand out to stop Vyrain.

"It's okay; I'll handle it," I told him gently. Turning back to Lu, I hardened my tone. "What did I say about riling each other up? Good Goddess, don't make me gag you."

I realized my mistake as soon as the words left my mouth. For someone like Luthri, a gag probably counted as foreplay. His responding grin was positively devilish, and his eyes twinkled with mischief. But to my surprise and relief, he didn't take it where I expected.

"I'll be good," he promised instead, miming silence by putting a finger to his full lips.

He stayed true to his word. We traveled in peaceful silence for the rest of the afternoon.

Darkness had fallen by the time we came across a suitable place to spend the night: a small but welcoming two-story inn just off the main road with a swinging sign that read "Fill Your Bellies, Rest Your Heads" in the *Ishameti* language. Through the thick cover of trees behind it lay a collection of wood cabins belonging to the establishment. We weren't about to spend our meager funds on private rooms when we had perfectly good tents, but everyone was keen on taking advantage of a hot meal.

A part of me still doubted the authenticity of our quest. Little but widespread rumors to go off of? A tempting reward? People leaving and not coming back? Anyone with a brain would be suspicious. With the group settled at one of the tavern's tables, I strolled up to the bar and took the opportunity to ask the proprietor about it along with my request for a map.

"Ah, right, Miss Kereti." The big man behind the bar—likely part giant, like Ked—scratched his stubbled chin. "Yeah, a few of those groups have come through here. It's legit, as far as I know. Got a cousin farther up north, and he's been complaining about that island for a while now. They're weird folks, the ones that live there. Keep to themselves, mostly, but when they do come to the mainland, there's something off about them."

"Something off? Like what?" With the way everyone socialized with different fae races, it took a lot for someone to consider a certain group "weird." Did they act strangely because they were threatened into hiding something they knew? Were they all in on whatever or whoever was making people who went out that way disappear?

The barkeep shrugged. "How did he describe it," he muttered to himself. "Like, uh… like they're all weirdly pleasant, coming right up to ya, inviting ya to their home. Sometimes unrelated folks be having the same mannerisms and similar speech. It's spooky."

"I can imagine." *Strange. What could that mean? Is it cause for concern?*

"Anyway, let me grab that map for you. It'll be two *jinni*."

"Yes, thank you. Do you have change?" I passed along the money.

Moments later, I joined the others at their table, nudging Hohem aside so that I had room to sit on the bench. Hohem slid closer to his brother, and I unrolled the map and spread it out.

"No trouble?" Yrra asked.

"No, no trouble," I told him. Holding down one side of the paper, I moved my plate to the opposite corner to keep it from folding up.

Vyrain extended a free hand to hold the other corner. "Thanks! Okay, let's see."

I found the line that marked the main road. Following it to the coast, I made a mental note of key points along the way. "All right. The trains won't be useful for us, unfortunately. We can go by foot north-east until the coastal city, Solfarin, and then we'll need to find a ship to get us to the island. If we land over here"—I pointed to a spot on the south side of the island for anyone paying attention—"we can get a feel for the terrain and think about how we'll approach the city.

"I feel like we made pretty good time today, but we can only go so fast on foot. Given the distance we've come so far, and if we're about here..." I gauged the remaining stretch of road, and my heart sank. Looking at it on paper, it seemed so far. "All in all, accounting for setbacks along the way, we're looking at almost a full cycle. Easily one and a half there and back."

"Well, it's a good time for this," Luthri commented from his side of the table. "Even if it takes us a little longer than expected, we'll be back before the snow starts."

"Yeah, that's true—" I looked up and frowned. "What... what is that?"

Everyone at the table had a plate, including Daethie, with hers the size of a bottle cap. Where most of them were loaded with cooked, salted meat with fat drippings and crusty bread to dip, Lu's bore nothing but red meat—neat bite-sized slices of muscle and organs, as raw as it got. As I watched, he picked up a piece between taloned fingers and swallowed it in one gulp.

My stomach churned.

Noticing the way my nose wrinkled, he shifted in his seat. "Oh. I normally... well. Does the meat bother you? Or the fingers? I can eat over there. I thought I'd get my fill before we're back on the road. I can go a couple of days between meals, so in the future—"

"No, no. Sorry." Cheeks warming, I turned my gaze back to the map. I hadn't meant to make him uncomfortable; it took me by surprise, was all. I ought to clarify that so he didn't end up self-conscious. "Eat whatever you like," I added aloud. "We all have our preferences."

Raw meat wasn't unheard of. Steak tartare was a thing, after all. And the others ate with their hands too; that wasn't uncommon. Public eateries didn't tend to offer silverware for their patrons, and when you were hungry, that last thing you wanted was to go digging through your pack for a utensil. After so many years here, even I often slipped into a state of complacency. These reminders were good for me.

You're not in Kansas anymore, Mar.

I put the map away to tackle my dinner, trying to ignore the way that Lu now angled his body to one side to shield his plate from view.

After leaving the inn with full bellies, we found a nice glade not far from the road and set up a temporary camp with our tents clustered together for safety. While I threaded carved poles through loops of fabric, I shifted my weight to relieve the ache in my feet. Not for the first time, I envied the hardiness of the fae. None of the others were bothered by a full day of walking. Even without mending magic, they healed quickly, so they would be fine by morning.

A figure loomed at my back, light from the full moon above casting a shadow on the wall of linen before me. I didn't bother turning to look. "Yes?"

"May I give you a hand?" It was Luthri.

"Thanks for offering, but that's all right. I've got it." In fact, I was done. Stepping back to examine my work, I nodded to myself. With just enough room for one adult and their things, it wasn't anything fancy, but it was serviceable. Summer nights in Kereti were mild.

"Quaint," Lu remarked. Smoke curled from his nose in soft, gray tendrils before dissipating in the wind. He held a petite but ornately carved white pipe in one hand. I didn't take him for a person who smoked, but vices often went hand in hand like that. Whatever he was smoking didn't smell bad—herbal, like thyme, rather than harsh like tobacco or marijuana.

"Do you need help with yours?" I wasn't sure if he even had a tent.

He shook his head, gesturing vaguely to a pile of brush nearby. "I never cared for this kind of shelter. I prefer sleeping out in the open." His tone turned flirtatious. "If you wanted to try it, you'd be more than welcome to join me in my nest. There's plenty of space."

"And waste all my hard work?" I indicated the stakes tying down the structure. "Thanks, but I think I'll stick with my tent. Smaller chance of wild animals getting into my things. Or something falling on my head while I sleep."

"Mm." Luthri took a long, thoughtful pull from his pipe. Upon noticing my curiosity, he offered it to me. "*Mensa* leaf. Have you had it before?" I shook my head, and he continued. "It relaxes the mind and body. I find that it helps me sleep."

"Ah. I prefer to stay sharp." We were in an unfamiliar area and didn't have much but the clothes on our backs. Though I'd dismissed it at the time, Vyrain's warning about bandits hung heavy in some part of my mind. Best to stay alert and on guard.

"How are your feet?" Luthri asked then.

I blinked at the change of subject. "Fine."

His yellow eyes smoldered in the darkness. They captured mine, unblinking, and for a moment, I was a fly caught for an eternity in amber. The inhuman shape and color gave off a hypnotic intensity, as if he could see into my soul and steal secrets from its depths. It should have set me on edge. Strangely enough, it didn't.

"I could massage them for you if you like," Lu murmured, tipping the burnt remains of *mensa* leaf from his pipe and stamping them into the dirt without looking down. "I've been told I'm good with my hands. Among other things."

They *were* nice hands. Shapely, strong, but with a delicate touch. Square joints and understated veins. A hint of dark hair on his knuckles and forearms. The state of his body conveyed an intimate familiarity with physical activity, so I got the feeling that he wasn't a stranger to hard work. Would his hands be calloused and rough? Surely you didn't get a build like that from a life of leisure and sex.

Lu ran his thumb along the edge of the pipe bowl, wiping away a bit of ash. The movement was innocent. His expression was anything but.

Ahh… So *this* was an expert's seduction.

An artificially sweet voice came from my right, breaking the spell before it had the chance to dig too deep. "So kind of you to offer. I'd love a foot massage."

I dragged my attention away from Luthri's mesmerizing gaze to find Vyrain watching us, arms crossed. He and Hohem had finished with their tents. By the look of it, Yrra and Daethie were sharing one, and they'd already disappeared inside for the night.

Merda, that was close. I'd never been so grateful for an interruption.

Lu broke into a grin and disappeared his pipe with a flourish. "Of course. I live to serve." He made to step forward, and Vyrain leapt back, raising his hands as though to ward off evil.

I rolled my eyes at their antics. "Quit it. Get some rest. We've got another long day tomorrow, and another one after that. If you find that you have energy to spare, put it toward something useful, like fetching water or foraging for something fresh to eat."

Hohem clapped his brother on the shoulder. "You heard the lady," he said brightly. "Get some rest. You can get right back to it in the morning."

"Yeah, yeah." Vyrain shook off his brother's hand and met my eyes, his expression earnest. "Good night, Mar. Sleep well. Give me a shout if you need anything."

"Yeah, thanks. Same to you."

Luthri lingered until they'd entered their tents.

"Did you need something?" I asked as I unlatched the door flap of mine.

"Not at all," he replied quietly. "Have a good night, Mar."

His gaze had lost some of its intensity, but I still hesitated to look him in the eyes now that I knew the danger they posed. I would need to tread carefully. "You too."

When he made no move to leave, I gave him an awkward wave and ducked into my tent. Normally, I slept half-naked, but I wasn't about to do that here. Not when I might need to fight off bandits or amorous advances in the middle of the night. Instead, I unrolled my little mat and blanket, fluffed my bag to serve as a pillow, and climbed into bed fully clothed. It wasn't ideal, but we didn't have the luxury of baths and fresh clothes every day while on the road.

Faint rustling sounded outside—Luthri getting into his nest, most likely.

I liked to think I was good at figuring people out. Observing others had been a large part of my training at the White House, in preparation for using my powers to gain intel for the government. The more I could figure out about someone's motives from their speech and mannerisms, the easier it was to pretend to be them. Lu… He had his annoying moments, and he had his amusing ones. Beyond that, I had nothing of substance.

Was he actually here because he wanted to sleep with me, risking his life to gain notches for his bedpost? Or did he have another, more nefarious motive behind his actions? Who was the man behind the winks and quips? It would take patience, but I could crack him given time. People were all the same, after all. At their core, they were all motivated by some self-serving force—money or power, usually. Whatever Lu was after, he wouldn't get it from me. I'd been taken advantage of before, but I'd been weak. Now, I knew better. I knew the signs. And I knew not to let my guard down, no matter how things might seem.

If bedroom eyes were his trump card, he'd have to try a lot harder.

CHAPTER SIX

IN WHICH THE PARTY IS GIVEN THEIR FIRST ENCOUNTER

I WOKE REFRESHED the next morning, although with a residual ache in my feet and calves. After rolling my mat and blanket and returning them to my pack, I braided my hair, dug out a *zanna* root, and exited my tent. Silence met me. The sky was bright and clear, and a fresh-smelling breeze rustled the grass. I took a nibble of the root and chewed, swishing the lather produced by the plant fibers around in my mouth.

Where is everybody?

Hohem and Vyrain had a tendency to get up early. Lu's nest was empty, with no sign of the eccentric flirt in the vicinity. I wasn't going to check if Yrra was in his tent.

Might as well take advantage of the privacy.

Refreshed after attending to my needs, I returned to camp at the same time as Yrra, who had our canteens slung around one shoulder. One of a waterfolk's unique talents was a sixth sense for finding water, which would no doubt be invaluable for the rest of our trip.

"Didn't have to go too far, I hope?" I greeted him in between bites of *zanna*.

He shook his head as he shrugged off the string of canteens. "No rivers nearby," he said, passing me my water, "but the inn had a well."

"Oh, smart. Is that where everyone went?"

"No..."

His hesitation made me frown.

"They went for a run," Daethie announced, emerging from Yrra's tent. She laced her fingers together and stretched her arms above her head with a wanton moan of satisfaction. "Didn't want to bother those of us who were still sleeping. You know how boys get along; if they haven't killed each other, they're probably comparing cocks by now."

How the hell did they have the energy to work out in the morning on top of walking for ten hours straight? "I need a drink," I muttered, one hand coming up to massage my temple. Mentally swatting away the image that accompanied Daethie's comment, I disposed of the *zanna* root and strode back to my tent. Dismantling it for travel took no more than a few minutes. Yrra joined me, wordlessly taking apart his own tent.

We were still packing when the boys returned. Shirtless, out of breath, and shimmering with sweat, they trotted into the clearing. Hohem went straight for his tent, nodding a greeting as he passed by. Noticing that I was up, Luthri and Vyrain exchanged a look of challenge and dropped like stones for a series of push-ups. Up, down, up, down.

"Surprised you manage with all that extra weight," Vyrain taunted through gritted teeth.

"Guess muscle is good for something after all," Lu retorted, showing no signs of fatigue.

"Better save some of that energy for our walk today," I called.

From where I was standing, I had a good vantage point to admire the rippling back muscles, straining biceps, and tightened glutes. I also took the opportunity to appreciate Luthri's large, feathered wings unabashed. They bunched against his back like they'd been tied together to keep them from moving. Was it a pain trying to get them into shirts otherwise? How impressive they must be when unfurled.

Beside me, not nearly as preoccupied with the view, Hohem guzzled water from his canteen. At that rate, he'd need to fill it again before we left.

"How did you get roped into this?" I asked, crossing my arms. He shrugged.

"Vyrain and I usually work out in the mornings. It's nice to have a challenge for once."

"Is it?" Eyeing Lu and his vigorous technique, I clarified, "Is he? A challenge?"

"He can keep up," was all Hohem provided.

A faint humming sounded by my ear. Daethie hovered over my shoulder, her iridescent wings beating so rapidly that they became a lustrous blur. By the look of it, she was similarly enjoying the view, wearing a wide grin that showed off her sharp little teeth.

"Not a bad way to start the day," she remarked.

I could have taken her words at face value, but curiosity got the best of me. "If your race doesn't have males, the implications of that aside, how come you find this attractive?"

Daethie scoffed, "I might be a hand-span tall, but I'm not blind. I can appreciate the male form as much as anyone. Especially when it's so *artfully* presented."

Hmph. Reasonable enough.

With an unfettered groan of exhaustion, Vyrain collapsed to the forest floor and rolled onto his back. Luthri sat back on his heels, the ends of his bundled wings kissing the ground. Together, the two of them looked like models out of a Sports Illustrated magazine.

"Got it out of your system?" I joked, directing the question at both of them. "I hope this means we get to look forward to a nice, quiet stroll today."

"As ruthless as she is beautiful," Vyrain lamented to the open air.

"You always did like the mean ones." Hohem closed his canteen and gave it a lazy, underhanded throw. It landed squarely on his brother's chest, eliciting an indignant yelp. Vyrain sat up with a murderous scowl and grumbled as he helped himself to a drink.

Lu, having proved his point, hopped to his feet and went to collect his things. As he passed, he caught my braid, twisting his fingers around the end before letting it fall. I reacted too slowly, stepping out of reach as he pulled away. My hackles rose. Who was he to casually invade my space? Traveling with us didn't give him permission to touch me.

"I'm afraid I might be out of commission tonight," he said in an apologetic tone. "I'll need a proper night's sleep to recover my strength after today's journey."

"Whatever will I do?" The sarcastic response came easily.

"Tell you what. I'll let you top," he offered. The cocksure attitude annoyed me further. He took too many liberties for my liking. A hand came up, reaching for my braid again. This time, I was ready, and I had no qualms about smacking it away.

"Keep your hands to yourself," I told him in no uncertain terms. "That's going to be your first and last warning. Next time, I bite." A fleeting thought had my teeth sharpening to aggressive points, and I snapped them to punctuate my words.

Lu's eyes widened, and his hand dropped. "I'm sorry," he whispered.

Somewhat mollified, I swiveled to gather my bag and help the others finish getting their things together. Out of the corner of my eye, I saw him discreetly rearrange something between his legs, and to my chagrin, a self-satisfied smile tugged at the corners of my mouth.

The road smoothed out and widened in sections. Daethie flew some of the way, busying herself with braiding Lu's thick, dark locks into neat cornrows as we walked. I focused on putting one foot in front of the other, so most of their conversation faded into background noise. I caught snippets, like Daethie telling him about the time I got physical with a customer who ran us ragged and Lu brushing aside Daethie's invitation to join her for a flight sometime.

Lunchtime arrived, and Luthri ate nothing as the rest of us dined in the dirt. Was it because there was no meat available, or because he was self-conscious due to my blunder at last night's meal? Did he mean it when he said he could comfortably go without eating for days?

I couldn't find a comfortable position, and my own food tasted like cardboard. It was ridiculous to beat myself up about this. Why did I care? He wasn't a street dog that needed someone to look after him. He was a grown-ass man who could make his own decisions.

A hesitant touch on my forearm had me blinking back to awareness. My jaw hurt from the way I'd been gnawing on my flatbread, and I realized I'd been glowering in Lu's general direction. Yrra withdrew his hand, but his somber yet curious expression didn't change.

"It's nothing," I told him, because it was. There was no reason for me to feel guilty for thinking raw meat was gross or for snapping at Lu for touching me that morning—I was within my rights on both counts. And so what if they wanted to run around like a bunch of children in the mornings? As long as they could keep up during the day and weren't quibbling the whole time, it didn't affect me. Since when had I become such a control freak?

Yrra tapped the spot between his eyes. I quickly smoothed the frown from my features. I'd told him once that humans sometimes developed permanent lines on their faces if they held the same expression for too long, and he raised a concern about how often I frowned. That was part of why I wanted to be a nicer person; it wasn't all selfless.

But the important thing was that Yrra and the others shouldn't have to worry about me. "Sorry," I muttered. "Woke up on the wrong side of the tent today."

That was as good an explanation as any.

Yrra nodded and went back to his meal. Not for the first time, I appreciated his quiet, steady presence. Unlike some people, he knew when to offer support and when not to push the issue. I dearly hoped that he would someday find some lovely ladies who would look past his timid personality and be happy to settle down with him. They'd be getting a real gem.

That afternoon, after another couple of hours of walking, we came across a tree branch lying across the road. It had a clear X gouged out of its center, but no other markings in the wood. As if that wasn't foreboding enough, several large stones had been stacked in a pyramid behind it. *What could it mean?*

"Gotta be some kind of warning." Hohem nudged the branch with one foot as though it might come to life and tell us why it was there. To no one's surprise, nothing happened.

"Bandits?" I wondered aloud, glancing up at the overgrown trees to either side of the road. The men all went on high alert. The woods were silent but for the usual: the whispering of wind through leaves, the chirping of birds and small mammals, and the like. No heavy footsteps, muted conversation, or rattle of metal weapons being drawn. No other concerning signs.

"I'll scout ahead," Daethie offered, taking to the air. Wings humming, she flitted forward and disappeared around the bend. The rest of us stood there trying to figure out what this branch was supposed to convey. It had clearly been put there for a reason—the size was such that it couldn't have been casually placed, and there were no trees directly overhead.

"We should go around," I proposed.

"This could be a trap, and someone is hoping we do just that," Vyrain countered. "Straying from the road is rarely a good idea. We're still deep in the woods; it would be too easy to get turned around."

"Well, that's not a problem." Lu shrugged. "I've got a good sense of direction."

Vyrain glared. "Maybe they want to split us up and pick us off one by one."

"So, what do we do?" My question was met with blank stares. I'd need to make the decision, then. Working with so little information, I hesitated to make a call.

A small winged figure reappeared in the distance.

"I don't see anything," Daethie called as she approached. "The road gets rough farther on, but other than that, no problems. I didn't see or hear anything that indicated bandits, either."

Clutching the straps of my pack tighter, I mulled over our options. Neither was playing it safe. Neither was deliberately putting us in the line of danger. If both options were equal as far as we knew… "Let's continue on the road," I decided, "but stay alert, everyone."

We all gingerly stepped over the branch on the road and kept walking.

As Daethie had said, the road was uneven ahead, but nothing

unmanageable. Dark rust-colored stains dotted the ground, which was churned as though a scuffle had occurred or something had been buried there. Was that cause for concern? Why would someone bury something on a main road? Fae didn't have land mines—at least, not that I knew of. However, there was no reason to test that theory.

Uncertainty nagged at me.

"Actually, let's go around." I turned to the trees. No one argued. As we headed for the woods, a bout of dizziness made me pause. What was…? No, not dizziness—the ground was moving, trembling as though it were alive. At the same time, a deep thrumming started all around, growing in volume. An earthquake?

Alarmed, I froze in place.

The churned dirt underneath us shook and shifted. Before my eyes, hundreds—no, thousands—of shiny black insects the size of my fist began to pour out from the earth, responding to our presence. Without delay, they surged toward us in a wave of aggression.

My mouth opened to warn the others, but the fae were a step ahead of me. Hohem summoned flames with both hands. Before I could react, Vyrain scooped me off my feet. Holding me aloft, he darted for the tree line. Even with his speed, however, our pint-sized attackers gained on us. I tried to sit up and see what was going on, but his hold was firm.

"You're overreacting!" I exclaimed, smacking his shoulder. He barely reacted. "Let me down! Good Goddess, they're just bugs. I can help!"

A lot of bugs. Bugs with several spiked legs, thick black shells, and a thundering charge. Bugs that amplified the adrenaline and terror the closer they got, their mandibles clawing the air in excitement. Fae bugs didn't eat meat, did they?

"Catch!" Vyrain shouted.

Fear surged through me. "Don't you d—"

Vyrain tossed me like a sack of potatoes. My body went weightless, and for one heart-stuttering moment, I was scrabbling for purchase in the wind. My fingers hit matter as a new set of arms closed around me. I opened my mouth, but I didn't have to say anything. Luthri released me quickly—almost too quickly—depositing me onto my feet as though the contact singed him.

"Sorry!" he exclaimed, eyes wide.

No time to address it—the bugs were upon us. Yrra cried out. Hohem hastened to his side, scorching the ground at their feet and sending bugs scurrying for cover. The two of them stomped on whatever ones remained within reach. I scrambled backward to put space between me and the bugs, all the while trying to clear my mind enough to use my magic.

Rousing the beast within, I sent massive bursts of energy from my core outward to thicken my skin. I gritted my teeth and pushed faster, harder, shortening my hair and willing my hands and feet to become sharp hooves. It was over in a flash, but the seconds dragged.

The bugs reached me as I fell onto all fours.

My heart pounded in my ears. Even through my transformed hide, I could feel their little legs on me. Their mouths bit and pinched, sending burning darts of pain into my bloodstream. *Are they venomous?* I made it off the path and into the woods, beetles falling from my body in droves. The others followed close behind, throwing fire and blasts of air as they went. Daethie stayed in the air, wringing her hands; she could do nothing.

The few bugs that stubbornly held on reached my stomach. I threw myself to the ground and rolled in hopes of shaking them off before they found softer flesh to ravage. The impact knocked the air from my lungs with a grunt of pain. Twigs snapped under my body, pieces digging into my torso. When I came to a stop, I changed back into myself and dragged my hands down my body, shaking out my clothing to dislodge any stragglers.

No more squirming legs. No more stinging bites.

Gone, all gone. Thank the Goddess. I lay in place, staring at the canopy above me and fighting to catch my breath. My skin still crawled and burned in places. How much of that was a memory, and how much was actual damage? Did we need to go back and find a mender?

Several people started talking at once.

"—all right?" someone asked.

"—there for a reason after all," Luthri wheezed.

"—didn't see anything—" Daethie wailed.

I half listened, closing my eyes to savor the relief.

"Mar? You okay?"

I opened my eyes to Lu leaning over me, concern etched on his features. Behind him, Vyrain stomped toward us. He pushed Luthri, sending the winged fae stumbling back.

"Next time I throw somebody at you, at least *consider* getting them to safety," Vyrain snarled. "For all we knew, those things could have been deadly."

I'd never seen him so irate.

Luthri thrust his chin upward in defiance. "It wasn't your place. She didn't want—"

"For Valuen's sake," Hohem cut in, stepping between the two of them before I could get to my feet. "It's over, yeah? We're fine. Everybody fine?"

Most of us nodded. We were standing, at least. Daethie was untouched, if distraught. Yrra appeared to have gotten the brunt of it. His pants were in tatters from the knees down, the skin underneath raw and red in numerous places. His legs were also beginning to swell.

"Could have been worse." The quip came out thready in the remains of my panic. I took the opportunity to look Luthri over, since he was closest to me. He didn't appear injured. Wiggling a hand at him, I asked, "You? All the important bits still attached?"

Lu's lips curved in an impish smile. "Present and accounted for. Of course, I wouldn't blame you if you wanted to take stock. Shall I take my clothes off so that you can be thorough?"

Vyrain made a sound between frustration and disgust and turned away.

"Hey, hold on." I snagged his sleeve to stop him. "Are you all right? Don't get me wrong, I appreciate the thought, but I can take care of myself. You shouldn't put yourself in danger for me. Just… Be smart about your priorities."

I itched to tell him point-blank that he had overstepped in trying to get me to safety while the others fought, but that would have been like kicking a puppy. Vyrain studied my expression before giving me a brief nod. I let go of his shirt. We could have the discussion about when to be chivalrous and when to let everyone look out for themselves later.

"We're heroes, remember?" Hohem gave me a wry smile. "'Eaten by a thousand bugs on the second day of their journey' doesn't exactly make for an inspiring ballad."

"Speaking of which." I examined a bug bite on my forearm. "Anyone know what those were? I've never heard of carnivorous bugs that nest in the ground. Goddess, they do not pull punches. I don't know if we need to find a mender?"

"Water," Yrra whispered. "Some water would be good."

Multiple people went for their canteens, myself included. Yrra shook his head, raising a hand to point. My eyes followed, but there were only more trees in that direction.

"There's a large river on the way," he said. "Can we… afford a short respite?"

"We'll make it happen. No big deal." Seeing a mender would drain us dry of the little money we had, whereas sitting in a river for a few hours was free. And what was another day out here on top of two months, especially where Yrra's well-being was concerned? Plus, we could get a bath in while we were there. "Lead the way, I guess."

Yrra nodded once. Wincing, he started off in the direction he had indicated. Daethie flitted over to him and landed on his shoulder. The rest of us followed. I elbowed Vyrain as I passed him, and the wounded look he wore gave way to curiosity.

In a teasing tone, I told him, "Maybe Yrra will let you carry him if you ask nicely."

He snorted. "All good. The urge has been satisfied."

We shared a small smile.

CHAPTER SEVEN

IN WHICH THE PARTY NARROWLY AVOIDS A TERRITORIAL SKIRMISH

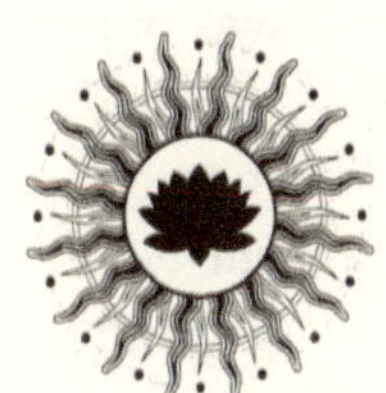

Our run-in with the beetle nest was a minor setback. We didn't make it as far as we did the day before and had to stop before reaching the body of water. That evening, I pored over the map to see if there was a shortcut we could take to reduce the distance. There were several reasons to stick to the main road, but we were going by foot, so it wouldn't be that much harder to go through the woods. Trees only covered another hundred kilometers or so anyway—once we crossed the river, we'd be hitting coastal plains and swampland.

Luthri disappeared into the woods during dinner. He returned with a handful of herbs, combined them with a tin of animal fat he happened to have on him, and cooked it down into a pale green goop over the fire. By the time he finished, the moon was high in the sky. He gave us each a portion of the homemade salve, telling us to apply it to our bites.

"My mother is a mender," he reminded us when faced with suspicious stares. "They do more than throw magic around, you know." He shot me a cocky grin when our eyes met. "Are you impressed? I can think of a way you could show your gratitude."

I wouldn't be 'showing my gratitude' in the way he hoped, and I said as much. However, I wasn't the only one dazzled by his ingenuity.

Even Vyrain was happy to accept his salve. Thanks to the soothing medicinal goop, I was able to get some sleep.

We made it to the river before lunchtime on the following day. The surrounding trees thinned until surrendering to open air and flat, grassy ground, beyond which the expanse of water sparkled in all its glory. The moment that came into view, Yrra stripped down and dove in. Daethie settled by the shore, and I joined her while the rest of the boys undressed.

The moment everyone else was out of earshot, Daethie spoke. "I didn't know about the bugs," she said quietly. "I should have. It's something my people would have come across before, and they would have known how to deal with them, but I never…"

She trailed off, her scowl deepening. *Is this… her version of an apology?*

"It's all right," I replied. "I don't blame you. None of us blame you. In what world is a log with an 'X' on it and a few stones enough to convey that there are man-eating bugs ahead? Whoever did that ought to be ashamed of themselves."

Daethie's mouth twitched in an approximation of a smile. I followed her gaze out to the water. Her eyes were on Yrra, who ducked in and out of sight with the grace of a dolphin. This was his element; he was at home there in a way he never would be on land.

"What's that about?" I asked. When Daethie gave me a blank look, I tipped my head to indicate the young waterfolk male in the distance. "You're close, yeah?"

She shrugged. "Sure. We want the same thing, he and I."

She didn't volunteer anything further, and I didn't press, instead turning my attention back to the others. Judging the distance to the opposite shoreline, I guessed it was a few kilometers. We could save some time by cutting across, but it would be a pain in the ass to swim, especially with our packs. We'd have to find a town and pay for a ferry. That meant more travel, but according to the map, there were a few options along the river to the north and south. It should still save us a day or two.

Yrra pulled himself onto shore as Hohem, Vyrain, and Luthri were preparing to go in. His legs were looking better, not nearly as raw as they were after our unfortunate encounter with the bugs. As our companions went to race down the bank, he held out a hand to stop them.

"This river is claimed by another of my kind," Yrra announced. "We should be brief."

"A quick dip shouldn't be a problem, should it?" Hohem asked, eyeing the water.

Yrra hesitated. "It could be. With me here."

Ah, right. Because another waterfolk male would see him as a challenger, a potential threat to his territory and females. *Men and their cock Olympics.*

They made it quick, sitting in the shallows to wash off the critical bits. Luthri braved the deeper end, submerging himself to rinse away all evidence of our time on the road. He scrubbed at his scalp and straightened up, flipping his head back to toss his wet locks like he was posing for a photo. He never turned my way, but he cupped water in his big hands and let it cascade down his body as if he knew he was being watched. Perceptive, that one.

"Aren't you going to join them?" Daethie asked.

I shook my head. "Not right now. I'll go later. After dark, if need be. I'd rather not strip down to my underthings in front of that lot."

Daethie snorted. "Modesty is the least of your worries. They'll wear you down eventually. If I were you, I'd have jumped all four of them long ago." Her gaze turned critical. "Of course, I also would have given myself a better set of tits."

"My tits are fine, thanks very much." I discreetly glanced downward. They were a perfectly respectable handful, proportional to the rest of me. Who needed breasts weighing them down with this lifestyle? Turning my attention back to the boys, I added, "And don't be gross. They're like family."

"Even Luthri?" Daethie raised an eyebrow.

"Well, no, not him. Not yet, anyway."

"Mm."

A flash of movement out on the water caught my eye. It was subtle, but enough. As I raised a hand to ward away the sun in order to see better, a head the same dark blue-green shade as the water appeared above the surface. It waited there, watching the bathers.

I dropped my hand and bounded to my feet. "Yrra!"

More blue heads popped up behind the first. Yrra and the others retreated, hurrying back to shore as the strangers advanced. A waterfolk male armed with a long, bone-tipped spear led the approach, with six or seven curious females trailing some ways behind him. One of the women carried a toddler, and another was heavily pregnant. The strings of beads and shells they wore as clothing covered little, which was painfully obvious as the male paused in knee-high water, blue balls swinging freely in the breeze.

"We're no threat," Hohem called, holding out his hands. "We're just passing through and wanted to refresh ourselves. We have no intention of causing trouble."

The male's attention didn't leave Yrra. Their gazes met, and a thick layer of tension fell. Yrra stepped forward, his shoulders hunched inward. His neck already turned a deep navy from stress. The male responded by modifying his posture to make full use of his height and frame. He smacked his chest with a fist in an undeniable challenge, a motion that made his beaded arm cuffs and chest piece rattle ominously.

Yrra bowed his head. The male's eyes narrowed. Keeping his gaze downcast, Yrra stepped forward so that he and the male were almost within arm's reach of each other. After another moment of silence, he tilted his head, baring his neck to the other waterfolk male.

Gradually, the stranger relaxed. The females behind him seemed almost… disappointed.

"Today only," the male grunted. Yrra responded in a low voice and kept his head bowed as he retreated to where the others waited. A relieved breath left me in a rush. I hadn't realized how tense I had been, waiting for something to go wrong. Starting a territorial skirmish would have been the cherry on top of the journey so far. And what the hell would we have done with a harem of women and kids after killing their mate and dad?

I hurried to join the others. By the time I reached them, the waterfolk family had disappeared to wherever they'd come from, as if they were never there.

"Well handled," I praised Yrra. Vyrain gave him a friendly slap on the back. Yrra, reeling from the near-altercation and uncomfortable with all the attention, put up a gentle fight.

"I didn't do anything," he protested, ducking his head. "They weren't here to fight, not with the young. And that was a fishing spear."

"Take the credit, seu bobo." I tapped his bicep with a fist.

"Are you coming in?" Luthri asked me, nodding to the water.

Without meaning to, I took in his wet figure once more up close. The unbraided ends of his long, mahogany hair formed artful tendrils where they adhered to his neck and shoulders. Droplets of water gleamed as they trailed down his chest and into the waistband of his boxer-like underwear, which clung to his bulge in the most indecent way. And those *thighs*... Waterfolk were onto something; men who looked like that should wear less clothing.

Goddess, I needed to get laid.

"Later tonight," I answered his question, dragging my gaze back up and ignoring Lu's smirk. *Of course he didn't have the decency to pretend he hadn't noticed.* "I was thinking we could call it an early day. Set up camp close by, try to get some fish or meat for supper, go over the map again, and figure out a way across this river. Then, hope for a good night's rest."

"I think you're better off not stressing over the map," Hohem advised. "It's not going to change on you. We can follow the river north until we hit the closest town. And I disagree with relaxing for the afternoon. We've been on the road for three days; it's going to be a problem if we start taking our time purely for the sake of fresh meat and some rest."

"Oh, yeah, food and sleep? Trivial things." I snorted. "We can take a vote, that's fine. I, for one, would appreciate some hot protein and a bath."

Seizing the opportunity, Luthri put his hands on his hips and waggled his eyebrows. "Well, isn't that convenient? I've got both for you right here."

What a ridiculous man. My hand came up to disguise another snort as a cough, and my lips pressed together to keep from smiling. I was no stranger to suggestive language, lighthearted banter, and the like. So why did his embarrassingly low-effort antics have any effect on me?

Behind Lu, Vyrain made a sound of disgust and pivoted to head toward the water. My smile faded, any residual amusement replaced by an uncomfortable tightness in my chest. This was part of the reason I'd never entertained Vyrain's advances—mixing family, business, and affairs of the heart was never a good idea. Imagine if I did give in and sleep with one of them, and then something went wrong. The next few weeks would be an awkward dance of trying to avoid them while sharing a road and camp. Miserable all around.

Daethie was where I left her, sitting in the dirt to watch the men frolic.

"All good?" she asked as I approached.

"Yeah." I settled into my spot beside her. "We've got today to take advantage of the water. We may have to vote on staying or getting back on the road; some of them are keen on getting back to it and keeping up the momentum."

"Who's in a rush?" Daethie grumbled, echoing my sentiments perfectly. "If something bad happened to the Kereti girl, it happened a long time ago, and if she's safe, she'll stay that way until we get there. Let's enjoy the adventure."

"Yeah… adventure." Recalling the feeling of the bugs and their legs, I shivered.

When the men finished cleaning themselves, Yrra lingered in the water to heal. A body of water for him was like having a mender in his back pocket at all times, which was handy given how fragile he was otherwise. Nature had dealt his kind a strange set of cards.

Once everyone was together, we took a vote. It ended in a tie, but Luthri was able to sway the others with promises of fresh meat. He took off into the woods to hunt while I scouted out a good spot to set up camp. The sky had taken on a subtle golden tint by the time Lu returned, and we rested around a fire with several portions of *paya* cooking in our lone pot.

Raising his empty hands, Lu gave us a sheepish smile.

"Great!" Vyrain, who had been happily chatting moments ago, directed a fierce scowl in his direction. "We've been sitting on our asses all afternoon and have nothing to show for it."

"Don't be mean," I scolded him. "I'm sure Lu tried his best."

But what could salvage this…? Oh! I had a tin of preserved meat in my pack. It was a common way working-class fae prepared protein so that it kept without refrigeration—they broke it up into a fine thread-like texture that, when dried, resembled a nest of brown floss. While it couldn't truly replace the real thing, it wasn't that bad cooked up.

I jumped up to fetch my bag.

Luthri rubbed his neck. "This normally never happens," he admitted with a note of genuine woe. "I'd hoped there was more prey to be had in these woods, but nature can be fickle."

"I can try for fish?" Yrra offered.

"We could see if there are any bugs left on the road," Daethie suggested.

There it is.

"Here!" I held up the items I was looking for and shuffled back to the bubbling pot of *paya* to add the meat along with a handful of spices. "We've still got some things from Vee. It won't hold us over the entire trip, but it'll do for pinches like these."

In another twenty minutes, dinner was ready. We ate with gusto, shoveling *paya* and meat sauce down our throats. After the meal, Yrra took the dishes to wash them in the lake, and Luthri left to hunt down his pipe and private supply of *mensa* leaf. Vyrain scooted closer to me.

"How are your legs?" he asked, glancing down. "The bites?"

"Good, thanks." I uncrossed my legs and wiggled my toes in my boots to prove it. "Almost back to normal. Those pants were pretty much a total loss, though."

"Yeah, mine too." He cracked a smile. "Might need to pick up another pair somewhere along the way. Make a quick stop at the next town, perhaps."

Luthri returned with his *mensa* and claimed the spot next to Hohem, directly across from me. "The salve helped," I remarked as he settled in to fill his pipe.

Lu beamed. "Happy to be of assistance. And if anyone needs, I've made clothing in the past from animal skin or tree bark. It's a tricky process, but the end result is passable. Handy for those situations when you're rushed outside without any clothes."

"Happens to you a lot, does it?" Vyrain's tone was sarcastic but lacked bite.

"Not a lot." Lu shrugged. "But more than once, strangely enough."

He offered the pipe, now lit, to Hohem. After a moment's hesitation, Hohem accepted it. He held it awkwardly in front of his face, as though it would give up its secrets with enough eye contact. Lu leaned forward to help, pointing out the mouthpiece.

"Put your lips here and suck in. Start with a small breath."

Hohem obeyed, drawing in a steady, intentional lungful of the herb. Almost immediately, he began to cough, smoke pouring out from between his lips. He passed the pipe back to Luthri, who offered it to Vyrain without hesitation. They eyed each other for a beat. Vyrain's mouth set in a stubborn line, but he reached out to take it.

My heart warmed at the sight. Given some time, maybe they could get along. We'd adjusted to strangers joining our group in the past, so why should this be any different?

"Oh, that's nice." Hohem sighed, setting his hands on the ground and leaning back. His head tipped, making the cords in his neck stand out. "Subtle. Takes the edge off."

"What edge?" I asked, curious.

"You know." Hohem waved a hand. "The edge of life."

A sudden outburst of coughing from beside me told me that Vyrain had helped himself. Wheezing, he handed the pipe back to Luthri, who held it out to me next. It would have been easy to accept, but I shook my head.

"Nah. At least one of us should stay sober."

"What could happen?" Hohem argued.

Lu accepted my answer without complaint, taking the next hit himself.

"Oh, you know. Man-eating bugs, ornery lake kings. Nothing crazy," I answered breezily. Hohem grunted in acknowledgment as he borrowed the pipe from Luthri for another puff.

"So, how did you all meet?" Lu asked, shifting so that he lay on his side. He propped his head up with one hand and watched us with bright eyes.

Now that was a question. Where had my canteen gone? Rooting around for the hard cloth texture, I dipped out of the conversation. "You guys want to take that one?"

"My brother and I," Vyrain began, studying the sky, "are destined for greatness. Before we were born, our mother went to a seer to have our fortune told. Upon reading the stars, the seer predicted that her son would be a hero who inspires a thousand ballads."

"A thousand ballads, huh?" Luthri sounded suitably impressed.

"Well…" Some of the superiority drained from Vyrain's voice. "You know seers like to be poetic about it. Anyway, my brother and I were always competing with each other growing up, trying to prove who was the chosen one and who was the spare."

"It got intense at times," Hohem remarked, staring into the distance.

"No more than the usual sibling rivalry," Vyrain protested.

"Really? Pretty sure you tried to kill me on more than one occasion."

"We were kids. Everyone does stupid things when they're kids."

Canteen in hand, I settled back down and gestured for them to get on with it.

Vyrain cleared his throat. "Yeah. Anyway, we grew up in a small town, but we studied hard. Trained in archery and hand-to-hand combat, learned how to use *mana,* speak multiple languages. We started small, helping out around town. Once we felt we were ready, we set out to advertise our services. We wandered for a bit before finding Mar and her group."

"It's not the best idea to travel without a direction," Hohem mused. "But, well, we got lucky. Someone told us about a group that traveled around doing odd jobs, and we thought, 'What better way to make a living while keeping an ear out for the right heroic opportunity?'"

"Of course," Luthri agreed amicably.

"So we went north, into Kereti, to find this group," Vyrain continued. "They traveled around, so they were tricky to hunt down, but eventually our paths crossed. And then…"

Vyrain's gaze shifted to me, and his expression softened. I knew exactly where the story was going before he said it. "I saw the lovely Mar, and it was love at first sight."

I loosed a long-suffering sigh. "There you have it. I'm sorry the story is so anticlimactic."

"Not at all." Luthri couldn't hide his smile. "In my opinion, the world could use more people who love with abandon. And it's a pleasure to learn more about you."

Oddly enough, he appeared to be telling the truth. I wasn't sure how to take that. If his goal was to sleep with me and then move on in pursuit of the ultimate bragging rights, why would he care about learning more about me or getting along with us? Was it possible that he was hoping for a family of sorts, same as me when I first joined?

I met Lu's eyes from across the fire. They usually glowed in the darkness, but with the added light from the flames, they were radiant, like gilded suns underneath his dark lashes.

Being direct about these things was always best. If not knowing his true plan bothered me, we could have a conversation about it. A good, old-fashioned "What are your intentions with my daughter?" Except… I was both the father and the daughter in that scenario.

What?

Anyway. I told myself that it wasn't cowardice that kept me from doing so, we just weren't at that point yet. When we were, I wouldn't hesitate to pull him aside.

I told myself that… But it might have been a lie.

CHAPTER EIGHT

IN WHICH THE HEROINE'S ICY HEART SHOWS SIGNS OF THAWING

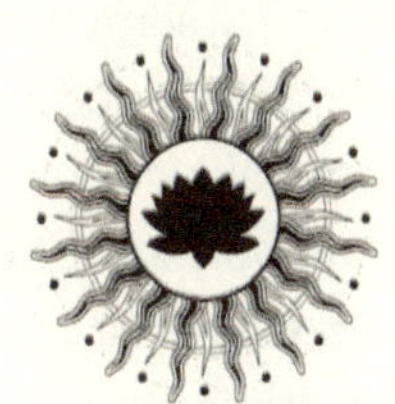

WHEN THE SUN dipped out of sight, bathing the terrain in shadows, I made my move.

A change of clothes bundled in my arms, I stepped out of my tent. Quiet voices chattered away in the tents beside me, only just audible above the deep croaking calls of the fae equivalent of frogs. I was paying too much attention to where my feet landed and not enough to my surroundings. As a result, the sound of a throat clearing made me jump.

"Sorry! I didn't mean to startle you."

I whirled about, ready to give the offender a firm scolding, but the words died in my throat when I saw it was Luthri. His still-damp hair framed his square face in waves. He sat by the fire pit, which was a nest of sand and ashes by now. The location put him only a few steps from my tent. My eyes narrowed as he sprang to his feet.

"Were you waiting for me?" I inquired. Maybe we'd be having that 'talk' sooner than I'd expected. Starting with "I don't like to be surprised at night while heading out to bathe."

Lu brightened. "Oh, yes!"

At the way my brows drew down in warning, the smile dropped from his face. "Er… no? Not exactly. Well, I hoped to catch you, but it didn't have to be now. If you'd rather... It's just that Daethie said the other day that you liked the scent of *vali* soap, and I..."

He fumbled for a moment before thrusting out a handful of fabric.

"Daethie has a big mouth. What is this?"

"It's an oil for the skin and hair," he explained with some degree of pride, quickly unwrapping the fabric to reveal a small, stoppered jar of golden liquid. "It cleanses and softens. Moisturizes. I wanted to offer it to you, in case you didn't have... Well, no, I'm sure you have something, but in case you wanted to try something new. It's a gift."

The jar stared me down. Was it innocent or a bribe? Could I trust that if I accepted this, there would be no expectations put upon me later? *He's being nice, you pessimist, just being nice.* Like with the salve, only this time it was more personal. That was the part I didn't care for.

"Ah. So this is the secret behind your good looks." The quip broke the silence but did little to mitigate the uncomfortable lump that had developed in my chest.

"Well, no, that would be my father. A bath oil can only do so much, I'm afraid."

I blinked, so deep in thought that it took a moment for his response to register. Once it did, the tension drained from my body. At least he didn't seem bothered by my hesitation... Then again, he had no idea what thoughts circulated behind my skull.

"Thank you." I reached for the oil.

Lu pressed it into my palm. "You're welcome."

He held it there for perhaps half a second longer than was necessary, a full second after my fingers had closed around it. I wasn't sure why that was something worth noticing, but it was. He kept speaking, his tone light. "If you need a hand applying it, you know where to find me."

That was the Luthri I expected. Letting the hand that held the bottle fall to my side, I allowed the smile I'd been pushing down to rise to the surface.

"Oh, we're not nearly close enough for me to inconvenience you like that," I crooned, each word dripping with saccharine sweetness. "But I appreciate the offer."

"It would be my pleasure, truly," he countered, similarly sweet.

Shaking my head, I turned to go.

"When was the last time you let someone else take care of you, Mar?"

His soft-spoken question hit me in the back like an arrow tip, making my shoulders tense and my steps falter. I recentered my thoughts to keep my temper in check.

"I don't need someone to take care of me," I said without turning around.

"I know," Lu assured me. "But most of us are social creatures. We're meant to have not just company, but family, comrades. People who look after us when we're unwell or lacking energy. People we rely on to have our interests at heart. Is that not also true for hyumin?"

Branches snapped underfoot as he made his way over. He left a degree of space between us, but somehow I could still feel his breath against my nape. A shiver ran down my spine.

"Humans." My free hand balled into a fist at my side. I wasn't antisocial; I was selective about whom I trusted. Who would blame me? Since I was a child, everyone I came across wanted to use me for their own gain. Right now, Vee, Jük, and Ked were the only people I considered real family. The others I enjoyed having around, but as far as trust went…

"And what about you?" I swiveled back around to face him. Lu was closer than I had expected, only an arm's length between us. I refused to fidget under his piercing gaze. Releasing a shuddering breath, I continued. "You travel by yourself. Flirt with anyone who'll lend you an ear. No doubt you had a different person in your bed every night, yet now you sleep alone. Does that superficial half-life give you the right to judge? The way I see it, you and I aren't all that different."

"The difference between you and me is that I would let another person close." Luthri's hand came up, reaching for my face. Without intending to, I recoiled. Something flashed across his face, gone as quickly as it had appeared, but he withdrew his hand and let it fall. Clearing his throat, he continued. "Being vulnerable is not always a weakness. Most people hope for a connection with someone they can be vulnerable around, whether they realize it or not.

"If I had a person like that in my life, I would cherish them. My priority would be to learn them so completely that I could anticipate their every need without a word. I would consider it a blessing to have them invade my waking thoughts and be the last thing I think of before sleep takes me. I would give everything I have and everything I am, even if fate itself stood against us, because there is peace to be found in that kind of surrender. Would you?"

Luthri knew how to hit where it hurt. Rather than dissect the thread of sadness his words elicited, I kept my attention trained on a pretty five-pointed leaf to my left. "I haven't met anyone who deserved that."

Out of the corner of my eye, I saw Lu's expression soften. He swayed ever so slightly, almost as though he wanted to haul me into an embrace but stopped himself through sheer force of will. "I hope you'll let me know when you do," he said softly, the words hanging between us as frail as a strand of spider silk standing against the breeze.

I didn't respond. If this was a dance, it was done far too close to danger and with no regard for consequences. There was no inviting whatever this was. No giving in to temptation, no thinking about what this could be, no chance of making an irreversible mistake.

He was an attractive man, and a charming one. But couldn't be more than that.

Without giving him an answer, I whirled around and made for the water. Each step fell heavy with the weight of my emotions. Luckily, Luthri knew what was good for him and didn't follow. I wouldn't have appreciated having to put him in his place.

My bath was only somewhat satisfying, but the oil did smell wonderful.

With Yrra's help and some attractive trinkets provided by Lu, we convinced the waterfolk to take us across the river on floating rafts they used as beds. Their assistance saved us a couple of days of travel and a host of headaches. No sooner had we landed on the other side than the male passed the trinkets to his most favored wives. They began to purr—an odd, sultry clicking not unlike the sound of a spinning bicycle wheel—and rub themselves against his body.

We got the hell out of dodge before the orgy started.

The days after that passed uneventfully, thank the Goddess. We rose with the sun each morning and walked until dusk, stopping for bathroom breaks and meals. Before I knew it, it had been another week, and our limited supplies were nearly depleted.

With a sizable distance before the next town, we were forced to dedicate a large portion of time to foraging for food. Most of the edible plants near the road were picked clean, but Luthri redeemed himself for his past hunting failure by catching a young forest pig. It was none too soon, judging by the dark clouds on the horizon, as beautiful as they were ominous. We were prepared to call it an early night, but the pig was not the only surprise Lu came back with.

"I saw a building out that way," he said, raising an arm to point. "I'm not sure if it's inhabited. It didn't look that promising from a distance, but it might be worth checking out. It's another span's walk, but not too far out of the way."

"Think there's food there?" Daethie's wings fluttered with excitement.

"I have no idea," Lu answered. "It wasn't on the map, so it could be an old hunter's shack, a rural cabin, an abandoned woodshed, anything. At the least, we could have a solid roof over our heads." He studied our grim expressions. "You find anything?"

"Not much. A few handfuls of bitterweed and some bark that will be edible once we boil it to death." I nodded at Vyrain, who carried our disappointing haul. "I hoped for something more nutritious, but this area is picked clean. I guess it makes sense, being so close to the road."

"I'm not complaining." Hohem eyed the carcass dangling from Lu's hand with undisguised hunger. "Let's get a move on so we can get that thing cooked. Lead the way."

Daethie made a rough landing on Yrra's pack and tucked her legs under the handle like a seatbelt. Looking forward to a break, we trudged after Luthri into the darkening woods.

I couldn't wait to be out of this forest. It wasn't so much the walking all day that got to me as it was seeing the same scenery all day, every day—nothing but trees and more trees for miles. If we were lucky, the occasional boulder or funny-shaped bush. Foliage could be colorful year-round in the fae realm, which was magical, but not enough to shake up the monotony.

The terrain changed somewhat as we headed uphill, the earth under our feet becoming rocky and unsteady. I stepped carefully among the pebbles to avoid a twisted ankle.

"You sure you know where you're going?" Vyrain grumbled beside me.

"Of course," came Luthri's confident response.

Eventually, the greenery began to thin, and our destination came into view. How Luthri spotted it while hunting and remembered the location was a complete mystery, but it was as he'd said: a random shack standing by itself in the woods. Shallow stone steps led the way to the structure. The tall, thick trees in the immediate area had been cleared away in a neat circle, which hinted at it being inhabited. As we drew closer and details came into view, my confusion grew.

The building was square and no larger than the small huts one might see in the poorer city districts. While it had walls and a well-maintained roof, there was no clear door, though the front jutted out in an approximation of a porch. Before the structure sat an imposing metal statue of a waifish fae woman about my height. She was dressed in aesthetically arranged layers of fabric and rope, with a severe face and a long weapon with a curved blade resting against her shoulder. A generous pile of small, shiny, dark stones was stacked precariously at her feet, covering the statue to her knees.

The area was quiet, but I didn't dare let my guard down. Something was off about all this. If the structure didn't have a door, what was its purpose? A hunter's shelter? A traveler's temple? There was nothing else around. Was it meant to be a home to someone… or something?

The others were likewise wary. Luthri raised his head to sniff the air as though that might reveal a clue. All I could detect was damp mulch, but then again, I had a human nose.

In the distance, a twig snapped, the warning carrying on a breeze. Multiple heads turned. The next moment, a *thing* emerged from the woods.

"Diabéisso?!" The Portuguese expression dropped from my lips.

There was no way to describe it other than a beast. It was a disconcerting amalgamation of various creatures, from the stature of a massive bear and the majestic antlers of a male *avida* to the spines of a porcupine and the large, triangular ears of an *Epitgig*. The thing was gigantic, horrifying, grotesque, and… held a basket in one paw.

Its intelligent eyes narrowed as it regarded us. Nothing moved but for Daethie's wings, which began to buzz and jerk in an odd pattern—a threat, although it didn't quite have the intended effect without the rest of the hive around. I tensed, prepared to fight. To my left, flames surged to life in Vyrain's hand. Hohem and Lu stood equally ready.

The beast grunted, a low, inhuman sound, but made no aggressive moves. Instead, a low hissing filled the air as its skin gave off a white, almost glowing smoke. Before our eyes, it began to shrink, deflating as though the fur was a costume or special effects.

Not a muscle twitched among our group.

When the smoke cleared, it revealed an old man in a simple draped robe. At least, I assumed he was old, given the sparseness of his hair and the texture of his hands, neck, and face. It was hard to tell with fae. Black script covered nearly every centimeter of visible skin, distracting me from the rest of his appearance until he spoke, shaking me from my stupor.

"Have you come to pray?" was the first thing out of his mouth. The stranger's eyes sparkled as something long-dead deep in their depths was resurrected.

Lu was the first to compose himself. "Ah… no," he managed.

The man's shoulders dropped. "But of course not," he muttered to himself, rebalancing the basket that hung from his arm. His gaze grew sharper as it flitted from person to person, taking us in. "You're all so young. I can't imagine you do much worship."

A moment of silence passed before he realized that we were all still poised for defense.

"My apologies," he said finally, softening his voice to break the tension. "I didn't mean to startle you. I tend to the shrine here, and visitors do not always mean well. As a result, I've learned to lead with a show of strength and ask questions later."

The fire Vyrain held winked out in an instant.

"*Opashi.*" Hohem choked on the word, a form of address used for clergymen. He and Vyrain wore identical looks of horror, having almost attacked a man of the cloth. Distantly, I remembered that they'd been raised religious, even if they didn't practice these days.

"We're just passing through," Lu offered.

I shoved down numerous questions to put up a friendly front. "Yeah. That. Sorry if we gave you a fright." I had a feeling *we* hadn't worried *him* in the slightest, but it still seemed like the right thing to say. *What was that thing? And... how?* "We're on our way to Munarzed and saw your shrine from a distance. We thought we might be able to use the shelter."

A theatrical gesture to the advancing storm got my point across.

"Ah." The cleric stared into the sky as though measuring the distance. The air had begun to thicken with the promise of rain. "You... would be welcome to stay. However, the building was not designed for guests. I don't have much space to offer you, and there's only—"

"—one bed?" Lu interjected. He sidled closer to me, as though preparing to throw me over one shoulder like a caveman and make a run for the single bed. Sending a prayer for patience into the ether, I stepped to one side to put space between us.

"Erm... no." The *opashi*'s silver brows drew together. "One outhouse. There are no beds beyond mine. You can use the vestibule, but it will be tight for all of you."

"They'll be fine," Daethie piped up from her perch on Yrra's shoulder. She leaned forward with an eager gleam in her eye. "More importantly, have you got any food?"

The old man hesitated. "Hermenia provides."

"Who?"

The priest inclined his head toward the statue. "The Lady of War. Of course, you wouldn't know... So many haven't spoken the Goddess's name since the Battle of Caersinde, which decided how this continent would be broken into provinces, as you know. Ironic, isn't it, that we are closest to the divine when our grievances with the world are many?"

Uncertain glances were exchanged among our group.

"Sure, ironic," I ventured as a fat drop of water hit the ground. "Perhaps we could move inside while we work out the details? We don't have a lot of money, but we could exchange work for the food and shelter…"

"We've got this, too." Lu held up the pig.

The *opashi* grimaced. "I don't partake of flesh, thank you. If you must, please butcher it outside. Do save the pieces you won't use; they can be utilized for the garden."

Vyrain hurried forward, shooting a withering glance in Lu's direction. "Of course, *Opashi*. Our apologies. This one isn't familiar with the finer aspects of life, such as the faith. Please, allow me to assist you with your things." He stooped to tap two fingers against the top of the cleric's bare, tattooed feet before reaching for the basket.

"Indeed?" Eyebrows raised, the cleric handed over his burden. Hohem came to hover behind his brother—to provide moral support? —as the old man stepped onto the scant porch. He raised one thin hand and ran it along the wall. Where it passed, a seam sprang from the wood grain. The newly made door swept open with a light push to reveal the inside of the shrine. With a wave of the cleric's hand, golden balls of magic found strategically placed glass lamps throughout the interior, bathing the horseshoe-shaped hall in low, warm light.

"You're a *shahim*," Vyrain announced in a voice filled with wonder.

There weren't many words I didn't know. "A what?"

"A mage proficient in the four common types of magic," Lu explained under his breath.

"I never thought I'd meet one in my lifetime." Vyrain's eyes remained fixed on the man. "What in the name of the Goddess are you doing out here, in the middle of nowhere?"

"I told you," the old man responded patiently, "I care for this shrine."

"That doesn't—"

Hohem put a hand on his brother's shoulder, silencing him.

"We're honored to be in your presence," he said sincerely. I couldn't hide my bewilderment at the current sequence of events, but everyone else went along with it, so I followed the rest of them inside. Hohem and Yrra divested themselves of their packs in the tight hallway, and I did the same. The holy man went around the bend to the right, where a small kitchen was set up. He waved Vyrain over and took the basket from him.

"Perhaps one of you could fetch some root vegetables from the garden," he suggested without looking back. "It's just around the corner, behind the shrine. There is a pump for drinking water as well—feel free to make use of it."

"We can do that," Daethie volunteered. She tugged at Yrra's ear as though steering an *avida*. Yrra heeded her direction and made for the door, beyond which the melodic cascade of rain had begun. In the distance, the sky grumbled a warning to be quick.

"I'll get this... er... squared away." Lu indicated the carcass, turning to go.

Vyrain remained enraptured by the cleric. "What can I do?"

I resisted the urge to tell him he could divorce his lips from the man's ass, instead opting for, "How about you drop off your pack and get settled first? You're taking up the entire hall." I slapped the bundle on his back to punctuate my words. With an apologetic smile, he scooted past me and Hohem to leave his pack with the rest by the entrance.

"Grab the stuff we found while you're at it," I called after him.

I swiveled back to watch the old man pull handfuls of moss and fungi from his basket. Despite his apparent age, his fingers flew across the countertop to set up a cutting board. The words tattooed across his hands were impossible to make out from where I was, but there was something about "day of judgment" on the forearm closest to me and "believers will be blessed" along the skin that peeked out from his loose collar. A prayer? Lines of scripture?

"How long have you been in the area?" I inquired.

"Oh, it's hard to keep track of the revolutions." He rinsed the mushrooms by hand in a small pail that was already set up on the counter. "Decades. I took over from the previous caretaker about eighty revolutions ago. Back then, there was more to do. These days…"

The old man trailed off, his gaze becoming distant, as Yrra and Daethie returned with freshly picked vegetables. Vyrain followed on their heels with our meager provisions in hand.

"Is this enough?" Daethie asked as Yrra held up their offerings.

Looking over the items with a critical eye, the cleric put the mushrooms aside to tie his sleeves back. "It will do. Let's get to work, shall we?"

CHAPTER NINE

IN WHICH THE HERO ROLLS HIGH FOR CHARISMA

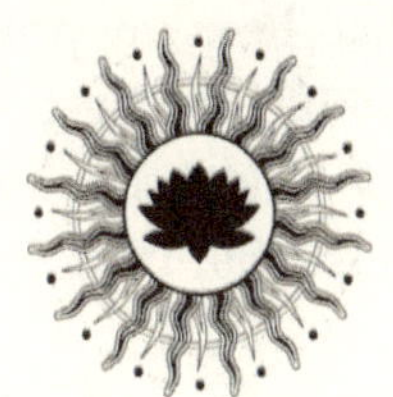

NOT BY CHOICE, we all huddled together on the floor that night. I picked a spot against the front wall of the shrine while Vyrain and Luthri argued over who would get to sleep next to me. When the dust settled, Lu was content at my back, Hohem and Vyrain snored in each other's arms by my feet, and Yrra was established on the far side of the hall. Daethie tucked herself out of accidental crushing distance on one of the shelves that had borne a *mana* lamp.

I lay on my side, head resting in the crook of my arm, and faced the wall. My eyes traced the wood grain as Mother Nature unleashed her rage against the roof overhead. The abusive pounding above and muted trickling all around echoed in the small space, making it difficult to find sleep. Even when I closed my eyes, the audible barrage continued, made worse by awareness of the male body behind me.

To his credit, Luthri had squeezed himself against the opposite wall to give me as much space as possible. I wasn't sure which way he was facing, and I didn't care. Spooning or butt-to-butt came with the same degree of intimacy as far as I was concerned. And regardless, it was unavoidable given the circumstances, so there was no point in feeling a way about it.

He put forward a certain persona, but I was beginning to think the shallow image I had of him wasn't entirely accurate. He was considerate in his own way. Pulled his weight. Had a sense of humor, even if it could be annoying at times. It wasn't all bad. That was probably how he'd been so successful at his "quest" thus far, come to think of it. One didn't repeatedly score with a wide range of people without having at least some redeemable features.

It was fair to assume he was decent in bed too.

That didn't negate the dangers of sleeping with someone you had to live with, though. That had been my primary excuse when it came to rejecting Vyrain, so it would hardly be fair to overlook that for Luthri. But... why think that way? I shouldn't need an excuse. People could judge me all they wanted, but I made my own choices, and "no" was a complete sentence.

A body by my feet turned over, the friction of linen against a sleeping mat temporarily harmonizing with the rainfall. My breath caught at the sudden rise of guilt.

What is this all about? No one knew my thoughts. I didn't owe Vyrain anything, either. He was an acquaintance, nothing more. He didn't have a chance to begin with.

Something else rustled in the dark.

"Mar? Are you asleep?" Lu's low voice had my heart stuttering in my chest.

"What?" I grumbled, hoping that one word wouldn't betray where my mind had been.

"I think I get the attraction of sleeping under a roof now."

What sort of nonsense...? Taking care to keep quiet, I shimmied around to face the man-shaped lump that was Luthri and leveled him with a scathing look that I hoped he could see. "Is this your first time experiencing weather?"

"No." Teeth flashed in the dim light. "I thought the opportunity to tease me for saying something stupid would be tempting enough to make you turn around."

My mouth opened and shut. He had me there. I met his apparent delight with a scowl but didn't go back to facing the wall. Not yet. "So? Why did you need me to turn around?"

Lu shuffled closer. When I didn't react, he stole another inch. While his elbow nudged the edge of my mat, his arms remained folded against his chest so as not to invade my space further. "Is this all right?" he asked in a whisper.

The warmth of his breath hovered in the air between us. I was tempted to say no. He would back up if I did, for the same reason he put me on my feet when we faced a horde of man-eating bugs. The knowledge settled any trepidation I may have had. Plus, he smelled amazing—like caramelized oranges with the bitter edge of cloves.

"It's fine," I said, discreetly trying to get another whiff. "What's up?"

"What do you think?" Lu jerked his head toward the rear of the building to indicate the old man sleeping on the other side of the wall. "The monk. You get a read on him at all?"

Why did he ask? Had I missed a warning sign? "I think there's no reason to assume he isn't who he says he is, but there's always the possibility that he's hiding something. Why?"

"No reason. Just wanted your opinion."

I blinked. When was the last time someone had genuinely wanted my opinion? Something somersaulted into my throat and stayed there, making it difficult to get the next few words out. "That's, uh… well, yeah. That's my opinion."

"Okay. Good."

I got another smile. It shouldn't make me feel anything—he gave them out like candy—but he did have a nice smile. And when it was directed my way, I almost forgot that I wasn't supposed to like him. Right now, I was even tempted to smile back.

I brought the conversation back around to the cleric before things got weird. "The beast he turned into. I want to know more about that, like how he made himself so much bigger than his normal size. I've changed myself into a lot of things, but that shouldn't be possible."

"Maybe it's a *shahim* thing?" Lu suggested.

"Maybe so." Tomorrow, I'd ask him about it. If it was, no harm done. But if it was something I could learn… Most of what I knew about my powers had been discovered through trial and error. Before I came through The Rift, I didn't even know about *mana*. I felt the difference with my first change on this side. Using my magic had been unpleasant back on Earth, but here, it was more like shifting into a second skin. Literally and figuratively.

Luthri broke the silence, derailing my train of thought. "I have something for you."

He propped himself on one elbow to reach his pack. As the rain pounded away above our heads, he struggled one-handed with the ties, trying not to make noise. Daethie muttered something about a challenge to the death as she rolled over in her sleep.

"While I was out foraging earlier," Lu began in hushed tones, sliding his hand into the main pocket, "I came across a *rinsom* bush, and—oh. That's unfortunate."

He'd withdrawn his hand to show me a large red blossom, its brilliance pitifully mangled by travel. The petals were crumpled and hanging on by a thread. As we stared at it, he loosed a defeated sigh. "Well, it *was* the nicest one of the bunch."

Pressing my lips together to hold back a smile, I said, "I'll take your word for it."

I couldn't tear my eyes away, not because it was a tragedy—though it was—but because I couldn't believe what I was seeing. Luthri, the man on a mission to notch a member of every fae race in his bedpost, had thought of me while out hunting for necessities? He'd remembered a throwaway comment I made about a flower and thought to pick one for me along the way?

I'd have to revise my earlier assessments of him. Maybe there was a universe in which he would make someone a reliable partner. Not me, of course. But… would it be such a problem if we used each other to let off some steam? No expectations, no strings attached. That was what he wanted too, wasn't it? And we were both adults; we could be mature about it.

He kept talking. "It's early in the season for them, you know, so most of them hadn't bloomed yet, but I remembered you had said that *rinsom* was your favorite flower, and I thought, 'Well, isn't that a wonderful coincidence?' But obviously, flowers don't travel well. I should have pressed it. I wasn't sure when I would be able to give it to you, and I didn't want—"

"It's lovely," I interrupted him. "Thank you."

Lu hesitated, eyeing my outstretched hand with the same look one might bestow upon a beggar child holding its hand out for coin. "I'll get you a different one," he said.

"No, I want that one." I snatched for his arm before he turned away. My blanket slipped down, pooling in my lap. "You got it for me, didn't you? So hand it over."

He lingered a moment before giving in to my touch. The arm underneath my hand eased out of my grip. His fingers trailed along the bottom of my forearm to my hand, wordlessly directing me to offer my palm. When I obeyed, the flower at last exchanged hands. I closed my fingers around the cool stem and brought it to my nose to appreciate the subdued almond scent. Across from me, the twin orbs of warm light that were Lu's eyes remained steady.

"Thanks," I repeated quietly, meeting his stare. We locked eyes for several seconds.

"You're welcome," Lu said, finally looking away. I could have sworn I caught a hint of a blush in his coloring, but it could have been the shadows in the hall.

My pack was too far to reach, and there was no windowsill, so I settled for placing the flower on the floor between the wall and my makeshift pillow. By the time I'd plonked back into place on my mat and pulled my blanket to my chin, Luthri hadn't moved from his spot. If it had been anyone else, I would have ignored it in favor of trying to get some sleep, but there was something vulnerable in the curve of his spine and the heaviness of his head.

"Can't sleep either?" I found myself asking.

He shrugged, leaning back against the wall. "You'll laugh. I thought it might be inappropriate to smoke around a holy man, but I hadn't realized how much I'd miss it."

Well, that's what happens when you grow reliant on mood-altering drugs. I tamped down the words that sprang to mind. Not the time or place. "Do you need it? Every night?"

"Do I need it?" Lu turned his face to the ceiling and sighed. "No, I suppose not. In the same way that no one requires a nest to sleep. Or a pillow, I suppose, for those pampered individuals who use such a thing."

The rain picked up outside. Good Goddess, would the deluge never end? Casting a glance at the sleeping forms a few feet away, I raised my voice past a whisper in order to be heard. "I'd hardly call it pampered to want a soft place to rest one's head."

"Exactly what a pampered person would say," Lu teased.

I rolled my eyes. "Oh, yes, I'm a princess."

The English word made him blink. "A what? Prinses?"

"A powerful daughter. Like Lady Narille." My explanation was met with nothing but confusion. "You know, the Kereti heiress? The one we're on a search and rescue mission for?"

"Oh, right." He didn't appear bothered by the fact that he'd forgotten the entire reason we were out here. Must be nice to be that carefree. "Well, in any case, we all have our vices."

"Sure," I agreed, shaking my head. "I will say, though, you might have better success getting to sleep if you lie down and shut up. That's how most of us do it."

"Will you hold me?"

"No."

"Sing me a lullaby, at least?"

"Absolutely not."

"Why don't you let other people close?" Lu's disarmingly playful tone turned serious out of nowhere. My breath left me as if I'd been punched.

"Can we not?" I managed.

"Not what?"

"Not do whatever this—" I grappled for the words, clenching and unclenching my hands. "Just—not talk? It's late, and I'm tired. Thank you for the flower. Good night."

"A secret for a secret," Lu cajoled, even as I turned over again to block him out. "Come on. Isn't there anything you've been dying to know about me? I could tell you the harrowing tale of my first experience warming the sheets with company. Want to know which of my siblings is my least favorite? Or, what about how I earned the scar on my left cheek?"

"You don't have a scar on your cheek," I countered without thinking.

"I wasn't talking about my face."

No retort worth a damn came to mind, leaving me to simmer in silence. The rain, at least, was beginning to let up, judging by the way the prior torrent had petered out to a dull trickle. It didn't escape me that the lack of background noise would make it harder to maintain a conversation without waking the others. Despite that…

"Mar?"

I closed my eyes. "What?"

"I don't mean to push. It's just that… I'd really like to know you better."

The statement, whispered in that plaintive tone, wormed its way into the pit of my stomach, where it settled into an uncomfortable lump. My eyes closed. Why was I still scared? He meant well. If anything, this was a good opportunity for practice. When I opened my eyes, my gaze fell on the flower by my pillow, and the bitter taste of regret coated my throat.

"You're fine," I murmured. "It's not your fault. I've gotten better with time, but I'm… I wasn't always good with people. Or I'm still not, I guess. It's not on purpose. In the past, there were people in my life who were supposed to look after me and didn't. I think that makes it hard for me to trust that people I meet now don't have an ulterior motive."

Silence followed my admission. Even the steady rhythm of water dripping outside seemed to pause, like the air had put a stop to it in order to listen in.

Luthri made a decisive sound in his throat. "I feel the need to clarify. You know I'd like to do extremely naughty things to you, right? That won't be a surprise when the time comes?"

A bark of laughter escaped me before I could smother the sound. I snatched the blanket gathered around my chest and pressed my face into it to hide the groan that followed.

The fae didn't have the same hangups as most people back on Earth. With menders, there was no need to be worried about sexually transmitted diseases, and most men had magical vasectomies done early on to prevent accidental pregnancies. Thus, sex was simply a way to explore your body or pass the time. Hell, I'd taken advantage of that mindset a time or two. That said, I hadn't expected him to put it so plainly.

As I struggled to pull myself together, Lu gave a light chuckle.

"Except for that, I don't have any motives beyond getting to know you," the *Peri* man continued in a low voice. "So you can rest easy. For now, let's be friends, yeah?"

"Friends," I muttered into the bundle of fabric. The word was innocent enough. We were all friends, weren't we? I was comfortable with Yrra and Daethie and the others. Well, I assumed they didn't want to sleep with me. Lu's forwardness was admirable, but there was the issue of having to look him in the eyes afterward if we did go through with it. That was the main problem, wasn't it? A one-night stand with someone I'd never see again was one thing, but this felt too much like a commitment to be comfortable.

A friendship with the possibility of something more… That came with a new level of intimacy. It had been too long since I had a true friend, much less something more. I'd have to be strong. I couldn't let myself be seduced by the promise of closeness, no matter how much I craved it. Being friends was manageable, so long as I didn't fall into that trap.

I pulled the blanket down and gulped in fresh air before formulating a verbal response. "Friends," I confirmed once I'd caught my breath, keeping my eyes pinned to the ceiling so that I didn't have to look Lu in the face. "Yeah. Let's be friends."

When there was no reply, I risked a glance in his direction. He lay on his side facing me, head propped up by one hand. The dazzling smile he wore made the corners of his eyes crinkle becomingly. For once, I met his eerie yellow stare head-on.

"Good night, Mar," he said.

That wasn't affection in his tone, just the weird intimacy of the situation, with him being two feet away and having to whisper. That was all. It probably would have had a similar effect on me with someone other than Luthri.

I told myself that, but my heart had trouble getting the message, and it was some time until it had calmed enough that I could fall asleep.

CHAPTER TEN

IN WHICH THE HEROINE IS AWARDED A SIDE QUEST

Vyrain chattered away as we ate a satisfying breakfast of flaky, seeded flatbread and soft-boiled eggs courtesy of the cleric's free-range poultry. The rest of us were content to keep to ourselves, which I was grateful for. The lack of sleep put me in a grumpy mood. And for some unrelated reason, I was starting to feel self-conscious around Lu too.

"You snore," had been the first thing he said to me that morning, nose scrunched as though he was personally affronted by that fact. I don't know what I'd expected after last night—odes to my beauty? An endless string of creative pet names à la Vyrain?

"We never did catch your name," Hohem interjected at some point during the conversation. "Yesterday went by so quickly with everything that happened."

"Cantal," the old man supplied. We did a round of introductions for his sake.

In the second of silence afterward, I seized my chance before Vyrain started again. "That thing you turned into yesterday. How did you do it?"

Cantal wiped up a bit of yolk with a piece of bread, unbothered by my question. "Changing magic," he replied absently. "Using *mana* from the air and ground to fuel the shift."

"Yes, but how?" I set my empty plate aside. "I use changing magic. I can make bones into a different shape and change skin and hair into fur, claws, and spines, but I can't make myself that much bigger or smaller. You were as tall as a house."

"Oh, that. I use a bit of making too."

I sucked in a breath. *Do I dare hope?* "So I could learn how? Can you teach me?"

"I can try." Cantal studied me with a critical eye. "How long do you have?"

"How long do I…?" My spirits plummeted. We were on an important mission; we couldn't afford the delay. But learning magic from a *shahim* might be a once-in-a-lifetime opportunity. For someone like me, someone who grew up in a land with no magic and no teachers, it was a dream come true. One I hadn't even thought to dream.

"We could visit again on our way back," Vyrain suggested, noticing my hesitation. He reached out as though to take my hand before letting his arm fall. "Once we've gotten the reward money, we'll be set for life. We can do whatever we want—travel the world, see all the sights, find a place that makes us happy to call home."

We hadn't ever discussed what would happen after this. But he knew we'd go our separate ways, right? None of us had the same calling. I could stick with Vee, Jük, and Ked for a while, but I'd also have to figure out what I wanted to do long-term—I didn't plan to mooch off of them for the rest of my life. Now wasn't the time to argue, however.

"I don't know," I answered the holy man. "How long do I need?"

Cantal shrugged. "Everyone is different. I did not become *shahim* overnight. I am no teacher, mind, so I can only tell you what I've done. The rest is up to you."

He got to his feet. I scrambled to collect my plate and follow suit, not wanting to miss a minute of time that could be spent learning.

"When can we start?" I asked as I trailed him to the kitchen area.

"I have some chores to attend to, but you can accompany me, and we can talk while I work." Stopping by his sink, Cantal held out a hand to take my plate.

I clutched the dinnerware closer. "Please, let me. You've been such a good host that it's the least I can do. And the others can help with your chores too. We'll be done in no time."

"No need." Cantal's tone left no room for argument. "Assisting in the preparation of your meals is one thing, but it is my duty and my pleasure to care for this shrine and the surrounding land as I have for decades. Besides, I have no desire to delegate."

Odd to turn down help when it was offered, but I didn't pretend to understand how religion worked. He'd gotten too comfortable being on his own, perhaps. "All right, then… I'll meet you outside?"

He inclined his head. Passing over the plate, I turned on my heel to fetch my boots from where they sat in the hall. As I bent to collect them, I also took a moment to move the *rinsom* flower off the floor, which was when Vyrain appeared behind me.

"What's that?" He nodded toward the splash of red atop my bundle.

"Hm?" I followed his gaze. "Oh, Lu gave me a flower last night."

"He what?"

"Gift-giving is an essential part of a proper wooing," Luthri remarked from his spot by the door. Daethie, perched nearby, crossed her arms and gave me a wide, shit-eating grin.

"Is that what's going on here?" Vyrain's expression remained unreadable but for the way his jawline bounced as a muscle ticked under the surface.

"It's a flower," I reiterated as I pulled my boots on. "It doesn't mean anything."

"Well, in some cultures," Lu began, rubbing absently at a kink in his neck, "presenting a female with attractive foliage is a way to signal one's intention to mate—"

"Read the room, seu bobo." Shaking my head, I yanked the laces tight and straightened. Daethie caught my eye on the way to the door and shook her head, still grinning that ridiculous grin. Yrra gave me a small smile. Heat crept up the sides of my neck. So help me, if they teased me for entertaining the vaguest idea of a fling with Luthri…

A thought stopped me dead in my tracks. They hadn't overheard our chat the night before, had they? It was raining, sure, but the hall was tiny, and sound could travel in what was essentially a big wooden box. What if we'd woken them up, and they kept quiet out of kindness? Or, more likely, for the sake of being nosy. They could have overheard the whole conversation.

I was trying to recall exactly what we'd spoken about when Cantal returned.

"Shall we?" he asked, looking from face to face. Vyrain perked up.

"Sorry, he's talking to me," I told him. "I was planning on asking him some things about changing magic while I have the opportunity. You could, uh..."

I racked my brain for something to give the rest of them to do.

"We'll manage," Yrra said softly.

"No way we're sitting around doing nothing," Daethie announced, clapping her hands. "I wouldn't mind another physical competition. We can pick up some nice fat worms for my lunch while we're at it. Let's go, boys. How about a run to start? Shirtless, of course. For your sakes—you'll soak through them in this humidity."

"Sounds like a plan. Perhaps we ought to go pantsless too. For our sakes." Luthri shot me a dazzling smile as he went for the ties of his shirt, deliberately tugging each one out of place.

I dragged my eyes away before I got invested. "You have fun with that."

Cantal pushed between us to head outside. I followed, stepping onto the wet grass with an unattractive squelch. Shadowy branches crisscrossed over pale gray skies above. Birds sang in the distance, thanking the rain for puddles to bathe in and worms to eat.

Apathetic to nature by this point, Cantal paid no mind, going straight for the statue. A touch of his hand, and it refreshed itself—moisture evaporated in a snap, and dirt sloughed off to leave the paint vivid once more. The old man stooped to rearrange the stones around the base.

"What did you say her name was again?" I asked, figuring that was a good way to break the ice. Given how he and Vyrain got along, he seemed to like talking about his goddess. It made sense, given that he'd devoted his entire life to her.

"Hermenia." Cantal spoke the word with reverence. He ran a thumb along the hard fold of her skirt, his gaze becoming distant. "The

Lady of War, patroness of soldiers, justice, and death. Counterpart to Aeil the Mother, patroness of families, love, and life. If you also grew up in Wysalar, you may be more familiar with her." He paused before adding, "Some say that Hermenia and Aeil were lovers before the Goddess took her consort, Valuen."

"I'm not really familiar with either," I confessed, shifting from one foot to the other. "I'm from… farther south. We have different gods there. How do you serve a goddess?"

"Hermenia asks seven things of her followers." Cantal straightened, pulling one side of his robe open to reveal the writing underneath. With one wiry finger, he indicated the lines of text that decorated his ribs from breast to stomach. "'Love all creatures. Be fair always. Speak the truth. Be generous with what you have been given. Work without complaint. Protect those who cannot protect themselves. If you must take another's life, be quick, not cruel.'"

He arranged his robe so that it covered him once more. Noticing the way my gaze lingered on his tattoos, he continued. "The Lady of War's followers serve through action, not words. This is another way I choose to serve: by wearing my commitment for all to see."

"More power to you." The phrase didn't translate well to the common fae tongue, and I got a blank look for my trouble. "Good for you," I clarified. "Be yourself. That's good."

"Yes." The lines on Cantal's forehead deepened. He waved me along, and we headed toward the back of the shrine as the others were emerging, shirtless and glorious, from the front. Yrra joined them this time, with Daethie loosing a victory cackle from atop his head.

"Onward!" she crowed, pointing with great enthusiasm.

"See ya, Mar!" Vyrain called.

"Later!" I waved goodbye as they took off jogging toward the woods.

"You seem like good people," Cantal remarked when I turned my attention back to him.

My eyebrow twitched upward. "I'd like to think we are."

He watched them go too, as if a part of him did regret going the path of a hermit in the woods. Anyone would miss human interaction, but perhaps serving the Lady of War was not quite as rewarding as he let on. I wouldn't be able to stand decades of quiet and a meatless diet.

Around the back of the shrine was the priest's vegetable garden. A short picket fence with tight slats encircled the space, likely to keep out potential pests. Inside, deep planters were stacked neatly to head height, bearing a variety of root vegetables, herbs, and fungi, most of which I didn't recognize at a glance. A swell of admiration for the obvious amount of effort that had gone into the design and upkeep washed through me.

"You'll be able to bathe later if you wish." Cantal gestured to a spout and rope dangling off the edge of the roof. "The water reservoir will be full after last night's rain. You'll have to be quick if you'd all like a turn, though."

It took me a moment to determine what he meant, but once I did, I pumped my fists in excitement. "A shower!" I exclaimed. "Thank you."

"Of course." He fetched a bucket sitting by the fence and dumped out the water inside. "Why don't you start by telling me how much you know about *mana*?"

This was general knowledge for most people in the fae realm, whether they could use it or not. Jük and Vee had told me a little about my changing magic once I'd gotten a handle on the language; that had been the first time I heard the term *mana*. I summarized for Cantal's sake. "It's an extra element—an energy all around us, in the air, the water, the ground. Mages can draw from it at will to fuel their abilities. Its presence also makes us stronger, faster, and live longer."

"Right." Cantal entered the garden and began the tedious process of examining each plant for vermin. When he found a colorful little slug/caterpillar scaling a stem or clinging to the underside of a leaf, it went in the bucket. "The types of magic?" he asked as he worked.

"Making, changing, mending, and breaking. And the gifts, which vary."

A distracted grunt of approval told me I got it right. "And what have you learned to do with *mana* so far? Tell me about your abilities."

That one was harder to answer. I had the basics down. Was there anything that made my abilities unique? "At first, I studied anatomy and mannerisms to make the changes convincing. I practiced speed and variety until I could be fast and get different materials right—fur and fleece, scales, feathers, that sort of thing. I can keep the change small, like if I need to cut something. But I can also change my whole body if the situation calls for it."

Cantal shot me a strange look. "Is that all? Do you change things external to yourself?"

"I learned to change my clothes with me," I offered, shifting on my feet under his beady stare. "What do you mean, 'is that all'? Is that a problem?"

"Problem," Cantal repeated as he plucked another slug. "No. Not exactly. Most learn it the other way around—using objects before they practice on themselves. But… perhaps there's something different about your ability. When did you first start using magic?"

"Let me think." Those memories were faint, living in a dusty corner somewhere in the darker recesses of my mind. My first transformation scared the shit out of my mamãe and papai. A stray dog came at me, and I sprouted feathers in my desperation to get away. My primo took a video that ended up on the Internet. The rest, as they say, is history. "I guess I was six or seven?"

"You transformed yourself?"

"Yes. Not well, but I had the feathers."

Cantal felt around in the planter, tilling the wet, compacted dirt with his fingers as he digested my words. Watching an old man do manual labor on his own was all kinds of wrong.

"Are you sure I can't help?"

"I'm sure." He shook off the dirt and moved to the next planter. "Given what you've told me, I have a feeling that you'll find this particular technique easy. The first part, at least. It involves drawing in *mana* the same way you usually do, but instead of channeling it into the change, you'll keep it inside. It may be uncomfortable at first. Like heartburn."

"Great. No pain, no gain." That uniquely human phrase didn't get me any more recognition than the last. I forged ahead. "And after that?"

"After that comes learning to make. Making and changing aren't all that different. Instead of changing something that already exists into another thing using *mana* as the catalyst, you'll start with *mana*. Once you've summoned enough, tell it what form to take, the same way you get your body to respond to you during a change. It will take practice to attune your attention."

"I'm not afraid of a little hard work," I assured him. It had taken me years to fine-tune my changing abilities, but I hadn't had so much as an inkling of what to do. This would be a walk in the park compared to feeling my way through with instinct alone.

"Oh, that's not the hard part." Cantal gave a low chuckle. "The hard part is changing it back to energy and letting it go. It's counter-intuitive. Once you get the hang of it, though…" The planter beside him began to warp under his hand, twisting in on itself and reaching upward in the same movement. In a matter of seconds, the vegetation within was cradled in the boughs of a large tree. Stray clumps of dirt skittered down the trunk, narrowly missing another planter.

"Wow," I breathed.

The demonstration continued. Much like when Cantal transformed back to himself in the woods, the tree hissed and smoked, then deflated and shrank. Now I knew what I was seeing: matter melting away into nothing as *mana* returned to the air it came from. It should have been impossible, and yet… the laws of science didn't have a place in the world of magic.

"That's incredible." I cracked my knuckles. "Okay, I'll try it. Should I start with something in particular? Are there any levels to it?"

Cantal didn't reply until the planter was back to the right size and shape. "You could say that. I recommend you start by taking in *mana* and holding it. Get used to the feeling of having more than usual inside you for an extended duration. Once you've gotten to that point, you can give making a try. Normally, I would recommend you first do something outside of yourself… summoning an element or similar. But it could be that you pick it up quickly."

"I have been told that I'm an excellent student." In any case, Jük and Vee had been impressed when I'd gotten to a conversational level of the *Ishameti* language within my first year living across The Rift.

The cleric didn't miss a beat. "While humility is not technically a commandment, I believe it's still considered something to strive for among the general population."

A puff of air left my nose. Reaching my hands out in front of me, palms up, I tried to clear my mind and focus on the task at hand. *Mana, mana, mana...*

My magic inhabited a particular place inside me. I often pictured it as a cave in my chest where an assortment of creatures lived, and I only had to reach out and take what I needed. The thought of being able to transform into something beyond any of those had me giddy. I could be a bear or dragon. I could take pieces from multiple sources, as Cantal had when he took his beast form. I could make myself wings!

"We'll work on this later," the cleric announced, breaking my concentration. He came toward me with his bucket of slugs. "I have to finish some things before I can watch you. The autumn equinox isn't far off, and it's one of the only times we get any visitors. Can you find enough to do until this evening?"

"Can I—" Miffed, I followed him to the edge of the woods, where he dumped the contents of the bucket into the underbrush. "Yes, I'll be able to entertain myself. I'm not a child."

"Good. Go. Do so." Cantal turned back to me and made a shooing motion.

I huffed as he strode past me. He was doing me a favor; I should be grateful for whatever time I got. I hovered by the garden another moment in case he changed his mind, but he appeared invested in his work. The others would probably be out a while longer, but I could get my own workout in and steal the first shower while they were gone.

Solid plan. Mentally patting myself on the back, I headed back toward the building.

CHAPTER ELEVEN

IN WHICH THE HEROINE IS PUT IN HER PLACE

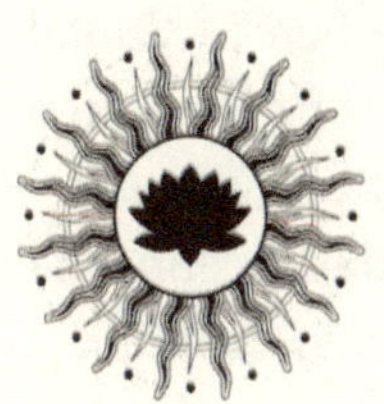

CANTAL AND I sat together in the hall while the others worked to prepare dinner. Legs crossed, hands resting on our thighs, we faced each other. The position, he'd told me, was optimal for honing one's focus to learn *mana* control. For the last few minutes, I'd been turning my attention inward to carry out the delicate process that was asked of me. Raised voices tumbled around in the background before Daethie's shrill voice scolded them into silence.

For Valuen's sake, couldn't they keep quiet for ten minutes?

"You can draw the *mana* now."

I cracked open one eye to level a frown in Cantal's direction. "I am."

"You're not." The cleric mirrored my frown. "The amount around you hasn't changed."

I checked again in case I had it wrong, but the power was a purring cat curled in my chest, ready to pounce as soon as I gave the word. "I don't know what to tell you." I raised one shoulder and let it fall. "I could change right now."

Disbelief was scrawled across my teacher's face.

"I swear to the Goddess." To prove my point, I lifted a hand.

Warmth rushed to my fingertips as my fingers sprouted massive talons.

"Ah." Understanding dawned. "No, no, no, child. You're not doing it right. The consort have mercy."

My hand landed hard against my thigh and gripped a handful of fabric. "All right, well, how about you tell me how I should be doing it, then? Directions never hurt anyone."

"I thought you'd… Well, that's not important, I suppose. Let's start over. You have a receptacle here"—Cantal tapped his sternum—"that houses your personal store of *mana*. An amount you're born with. It naturally replenishes itself from whatever is around you, whether you use magic or not, until one day it cannot, and you die."

"And?" I wished he'd get to the point.

"You don't use that to fuel a change. You've got to use external *mana*, like I showed you in the garden. Try again. Close your eyes if it helps. Whatever you just used, whatever you've been using in the past, ignore that. You have to feel for the *mana* around you. You may only be able to draw small amounts at first, but this will improve with practice."

Trying to ignore the flustered heat rising in my chest, I settled back into place. *Feel for the* mana, *huh? Easier said than done. Not doing it right? Would have been nice to know that about fifteen years ago. How long have I been behind the curve?*

I had to focus my thoughts. The air smelled of wood, the same wood that was hard against my backside and ankle bones. Underneath that was cold, wet earth, humming with power if only I knew how to take advantage of it. The inner seam of my sleeve itched; I ignored it. Breathed in, breathed out. If I looked for it, maybe it would come to me. *Mana* might feel like a big ball of spiritual yarn, and getting the amount I need like pulling on a loose thread—

"Dinner's ready," one of the twins announced.

My eyes popped open.

"Thank you, Hohem." Cantal unfolded his legs and got to his feet. "We can resume this later. But that will be the first step—until you learn to draw *mana* properly, I cannot help you."

A swell of disappointment washed over me. I ground my teeth

together, unwilling to admit defeat. "You go on ahead," I told them. "I'm going to keep practicing."

Cantal inclined his head and went to join the others.

"Want me to bring you a plate?" Hohem asked, hovering in the hallway.

"Ah… yeah, I guess. Thanks."

It wasn't even a full minute before footsteps approached, interrupting me for a second time. I held a hand out for the plate without opening my eyes. "Thanks, Hohem."

"It's Vyrain, actually."

The handoff complete, Vyrain took a seat beside me with his own plate. Down the hall, cheerful voices chattered away, Daethie's enthusiastic voice carrying above the din.

"How was your workout today?" I asked when he didn't try to initiate conversation.

Instead of answering, Vyrain used his fingers to scoop up a mouthful of his dinner and chewed with a determined set to his jaw. I followed suit, too lazy to fetch cutlery from my bag. We ate a few bites in silence, each swallow getting progressively heavier.

"What's up with the others?" I wondered aloud when they remained out of sight.

Vyrain's throat bobbed as he swallowed. "I… asked them for a moment. Alone."

My fingers paused on the way to my mouth. "Oh. I see."

His attention narrowed on the bite hovering in front of my lips. Without any fanfare, I dropped it back on the plate, licked my fingers clean, and set my half-finished meal aside.

"Out with it, then," I ordered.

Vyrain pushed a piece of indiscernible vegetable from one side of his dish to the other while he considered his words. "It's nothing crazy. While we were out today, we got to chatting, and it made me think. I know we were never… I was never clear, I suppose. About my intentions. I was being frivolous about it, but… I like you, Mar."

I opened my mouth, and his hand shot out to stop me.

"You don't feel the same," he continued, studying my expression. Whatever he might have been looking for—a rebuttal, perhaps—he didn't find it. He dropped his gaze. "I knew that—know it. My mother used to say that women don't always know what they want, and it's a man's role to take charge. That we needed to be relentless. That's obviously not the case, and I never meant to make things difficult for you."

Able to guess where this was going, I gave him silence to keep going.

"I just wanted to say that I'm sorry. And I get it." His volume dropped to slightly above a whisper. Nodding in the direction of the kitchen area, his expression grew longing. "He's a personality, that one. I would never have thought that was your type, but I guess I can see it."

Did I imagine it, or was there a touch of admiration in his tone?

"What is that supposed to mean?"

"His energy complements yours." Vyrain punctuated his words with a vague gesture. "You seem to enjoy his company. And as strange as it sounds, I think he's genuine, deep down." At my look of utter confusion, he at last got to the point. "I'm saying that I give up. On you. Us. Live your life. Be happy, Mar."

I almost laughed. The whole situation was ridiculous. *Vyrain thinks he's genuine? I'd trade both pinky fingers to know what they talked about while running today.* As silly as it was, him coming to terms with the fact that I was never going to entertain his advances made things easier for me. This was a good thing. So, not without difficulty, I kept a straight face.

"Where is this coming from?" I inquired. Having the context would go a long way in determining the best way to deal with this. *Did Luthri say something?*

Vyrain gave me a subdued smile. "It's nothing, really. I was just thinking I ought to tie up any loose ends before we rescue that lady. You know, in case her family wants to thank me with her hand. You would be welcome to attend the coupling ceremony, of course."

I didn't know whether it was okay to laugh. I ought to assume that for him, this was serious, not a simple crush. The melancholic mood killed any desire to poke fun. I retrieved my plate and stuffed my mouth while I thought of an adequate response. Regardless of where I considered us, his perspective deserved respect.

"Of course," I agreed. "Well, I appreciate your honesty, and I hope we can still be friends. For what it's worth, you're making the right decision." Feeling as though I should say something more, I added, "And I hope it works out between you and Miss Kereti."

Vyrain nodded, the motion causing his blond hair to flop into his eyes. He ran his fingers through it with a drawn-out exhale before responding. "Yeah. Thank you."

We sat together without speaking for another moment before he sprang to his feet, nearly upsetting the plate resting on my knees. "Oi," I protested, snatching it out of harm's way.

"Sorry! Sorry." Vyrain backed up. "I'll go join the others. Enjoy your dinner. There's, uh, more where that came from if you're still hungry."

"Yeah, yeah." I shooed him away. "Tell them they can come out now."

"Will do. Thanks, Mar. For hearing me out." With one last smile, which I mirrored for his sake, he about-faced and disappeared around the corner. Once he was out of sight, I loosed a deep sigh and slumped against the wall. The ceiling hadn't changed since last night. I hadn't expected it to, but took the time to assure myself of that.

Then, plate in hand, I went to find Luthri.

He wasn't in the kitchen. Daethie directed me outside, where I found him leaning against the garden fence with his back to me. I led with a friendly inquiry.

"Did you threaten Vyrain into leaving me alone?"

He whirled around, and his expression shifted from surprise to pain as whatever he was eating went down the wrong pipe. I waited for the coughing to taper off.

"One more time," he wheezed, thumping his fist against his chest. "Did I—what?"

"Vyrain," I enunciated, looking around for a place I could set my plate while we talked. "He said you talked during your run today.

What about? Did you threaten him into leaving me alone to give yourself a better chance?"

Lu's dark brows drew together. "I might be a touch competitive—it's not my finest quality, I'll admit—but I'm not a bully. Is that what he told you?"

"I inferred." Settling for holding my dinner, I slouched against the fence and fixed Luthri with a wordless stare. It didn't work quite the way I'd hoped, as he stared back with an infuriating amount of composure.

"How was your day?" he asked, cocking his head.

"Don't change the subject," I warned him. My gaze fell on his hand. He held a small wrapped package instead of a plate. Raw meat again? Guilt gnawed at my insides. "You don't have to eat outside, you know. I'm sorry if I made you uncomfortable about the meat the other day… I shouldn't have commented. It surprised me is all; it's not that weird."

Lu shrugged and set the package aside. "It's all right. Even with magic, there are things we can't change about the way we are. If I could digest grains, I'd happily be eating bread and *paya* with the rest of you. However, it gives me the runs like you would not believe."

My nose wrinkled. "That's way too much information, but okay. No worries."

Chuckling to himself, Luthri relaxed against the fence, regarding me with something akin to fondness. There was no wonder he had women—and others—falling over themselves to get into bed with him. He'd perfected the sort of look that could convince a person to forget themselves and spread their legs.

"Anyway." I studied the ground at my feet, ignoring the little voice that called me a coward as I did so. "Just because Vyrain has decided to seek out greener pastures doesn't mean I'm about to make things easy for you."

"I wouldn't have it any other way."

"Nothing's changed from last night. Relationships can be messy—not that I'm entertaining a relationship, mind you." What was wrong with me? I'd never been flustered around a guy before. "I'd rather focus on this. The job we're doing. That being said, if something happens..." I lifted one shoulder. "We're both adults. I expect we can come to an agreement."

When I glanced back to determine how Lu felt about that, there was pure, unadulterated pleasure written across his face.

"Mar," he began. "You would make me the happiest man in the realm—"

"Ah-bup-bup!" I silenced him with an outstretched finger. "I don't want flowery language. I don't need it. I don't need gifts, either. We're not dating, and I'd prefer not to flaunt anything in front of the others. Oh, and the whole 'wanting to fuck a human, any human' thing... Frankly, it's a turn-off, but don't mention it again, and we'll be good."

Luthri waited to be sure I was done before replying.

"All right," he conceded. "I agree to your terms, with a few addendums so that you know where I stand. First and foremost, being a hyumin aside, I find you incredibly attractive. Not just that"—his voice dropped to a purr—"but I think we would be *very* compatible in certain areas."

I could only blink.

Returning to a normal tone, he continued. "But I don't intend to push or rush you into anything, physical or otherwise. Like I said, friends. I'm having a blast either way. And if the door is open to more at some point, well... That's good to know."

"Okay. Great." A weight lifted from my shoulders. I nodded once, content with the course of the conversation, and pushed away from the fence. "Glad we're on the same page. Now, will you join us inside? Your dinner will—well, my dinner's going cold, anyway."

Lu snatched his bundle of meat and trailed behind me. "A pet name doesn't count as flowery language, does it? What do you like to be called? Beautiful? Precious? Darling?"

"Are you trying to make me regret this already?"

He responded with a sheepish smile. "Oh, all right. Just once in a while. How did your day go? Did you have the chance to speak with Cantal about changing?"

"Yeah." Cycling through what he'd told me, I breathed a sigh. "Apparently, I've been using magic wrong all my life, so that's fun. I'm going to have to acquaint myself with *mana* properly and learn making in addition to changing. I'm not sure when I'll find the time, but there you have it. It might need to wait until after all this."

"I'll help you!" Lu's gaze was earnest, but behind that was a familiar sparkle of mischief. I could almost have anticipated the next words out of his mouth. "The teacher/student scenario is every man's fantasy. To enact it with you would be an honor."

"Well, aren't you generous?" I reached to slide open the door, and another hand shot out to plant itself beside mine. Luthri stepped in closer. He was careful not to touch me, but I was all too aware of the heat of his body, the presence he exuded. It was enough for my imagination to run wild. Rogue images sprang to mind: naked bodies twisting together atop the sheets, teeth and tongues and fingernails battling for dominion over one another. The plate I held bobbed, and my tongue darted out to moisten lips that suddenly felt parched.

"You smell lovely," he murmured into my hair. A shiver threaded down my spine, sending a swarm of goosebumps to my arms. "How is the oil treating you?"

It took me a moment to find my voice. "My skin has never been softer," I admitted. It wasn't a lie—the oil was heavenly, from the warm, spicy scent to the way it melted on contact. *It's been hours since I used it during my shower. Can he really still smell it on me?*

"Good." Luthri pulled back, and my lungs drew in the fresh air left behind. It took a beat for my train of thought to resume, which made me realize that I'd been frozen in place with my hand on the door frame for the better part of a minute.

"Stop doing that," I snapped, unnerved by how easily he threw me off.

"What?" Lu flashed a disarming smile as I wrenched the door aside. The shouting was the first clue that I was stepping into a den of chaos. Something large came flying out of nowhere, nearly clipping me in the nose before it hit the wall with a resounding clatter. If not for Luthri behind me, I would have staggered backward and landed on my ass.

"The consort have mercy." Cantal's booming voice carried into the hall. "Out, out! Everybody *out*!"

I sought out the source of the trouble as the twins stumbled around the corner. The one in front spotted me, and his features crumpled in an unmistakable wince.

"We were only trying to help, I swear," he proclaimed before I could comment.

Daethie whizzed into view, chortling with glee, a flushed Yrra hot on her heels. "How stupid do you have to be to set fire to a completely wooden structure without even trying?" she exclaimed between fits of laughter. "It's a miracle you haven't killed yourself by now!"

"We were going to heat water for the dishes!"

I had stopped listening after the operative word—fire—and my hand tightened on the door frame as I prepared to cast down my plate and leap into action. Priorities, what were the priorities? *Someone should grab the packs. Do we need water? Maybe the shower had some left. I could use the buckets from the garden to haul it?*

"No, no. Cantal has things well in hand." Hohem herded everyone outside with outstretched arms, forcing me out of the doorway. "Honestly, everyone is overreacting. It was a tiny fire. A few sparks, really."

"A tiny—!" My throat closed around the words. "Porra-louca! Do you have any idea how dangerous that is? You could have *killed* somebody."

"Technically, it was Vyrain." Hohem jerked a thumb in his brother's direction.

"I got a little distracted," Vyrain grumbled, depositing himself on the stoop in a huff. "Normally, magic like that would be a cinch. But anyway, nobody got hurt, so I don't see what the big deal is."

"Don't see—!"

Luthri's hand fell on my shoulder before I could tear into Vyrain for his flippant attitude. My head swiveled around to pin him with a glare, but he just smiled.

"It seems there was no lasting harm done," Lu remarked, removing his hand. "We'll call it a learning opportunity and move on, yes?"

Vyrain rolled his eyes. "You got it, dad."

Luthri grimaced. "Ooh, not my favorite. Might I suggest 'sir' or 'my lord'?"

"How about assface?" Vyrain countered, not one to let someone else have the final word.

"Keep talking. I'm not opposed to taming the occasional brat."

It was Vyrain's turn to pull a face.

No longer hungry, I dumped the rest of my ice-cold dinner and set the empty plate on the platform beside Vyrain. An outraged buzzing sound drew my attention to Daethie, sitting cross-legged on Yrra's shoulder.

"What a waste," she scolded, gesturing to the food on the ground. "Someone else could've eaten that."

A guilty lump formed in the pit of my stomach. "It was stone-cold," I argued. "I've been hauling it around the past span. Besides, it was just a few mouthfuls."

Before anyone else could chip in, the front door slammed open, making us all jump.

"You may come in now," Cantal intoned, his expression carefully blank.

Vyrain hopped to his feet and bowed his head. "Sorry about all that," he said as he straightened. "If you need help cleaning up, I'm happy to lend a—"

"No," Cantal cut him off. He didn't appear angry; rather, he had the air of a disappointed father about him. *I know the feeling.* "Everything has been taken care of, thank you. Find something else to occupy your time. Mar, let's resume your practice."

I sprang to attention. "Yes, *Opashi.*"

As I followed him inside, I ran through the timeline once more in my head. How much longer could we spend here before we had to move on? We might have made good ground thus far, but we had weeks of travel left to go. It wasn't reasonable to take more than a couple of days on detours like these, no matter how rewarding they might be.

The thought hardened my resolve. *I'll throw myself into this and figure out how to draw* mana *properly, even if it takes me all night.*

CHAPTER TWELVE

IN WHICH A NEW SKILL IS ACQUIRED

IT DID, in fact, take me all night, but I discovered the missing link shortly before dawn. Rather than coercing the magic to suit my needs, I had to meet it as it was. *Mana* was not meant for me alone—it was this world's essence, its lifeblood, the snake digesting its latest meal in the shadow of the shrine and the raptor watching it from the trees all at once. I had to seek it out on its level, join the cycle, and ask rather than demand its attention. Give and take.

I spent the last hour before the sun rose kicking myself for overlooking such a simple thing. When Cantal emerged from his space in the back of the shrine, I showed off my newfound skills by transforming into him, even turning my breeches and blouse into his robe. Having discovered the ocean of power that lay ripe for the taking, changing was effortless. Gone was the uncomfortable ache as muscle and bone shifted into new places, replaced by giddiness at the thought of having near-endless potential at my fingertips.

It was well worth a lack of sleep.

"Good," was all Cantal had to say. "We can move on to the next part today."

"Are we staying another day?" one of the twins asked from the hallway, covering a massive yawn with one hand. There was an *Epitgig* saying along the lines of the stupider you were, the better you slept. Or maybe that was just something Jük said.

Either way, the twins were pretty convincing evidence.

"One more day," I proposed, though I hated to hold the others back. This was important enough to make time for. "It'll be useful to have this down in case things go awry at any point. We can head out first thing tomorrow morning."

Daethie let loose an exaggerated groan from somewhere out of sight. "All right, boys, you heard the boss. Up and at 'em. Shirts off. Let's get that blood pumping."

As the grumbles of protest started, a familiar dark head popped out from behind the wall. "Mar?" Lu scanned my figure from head to toe. I returned the perusal, my gaze catching on his bare shoulders. "Did you stay up all night?" he asked, aghast.

"I figured out how to draw *mana* properly is what I did," I answered, dragging my eyes back to his face. "Still can't believe I was doing it wrong for twenty revolutions, but I guess that's what happens when you don't have any other mages around to teach you."

"No magic users at all?" Cantal interjected.

I realized the implication as soon as the words left my mouth. In the fae realm, it was exceedingly rare not to be able to use *mana,* and those few unlucky souls were treated like they were made of glass. An entire area lacking magic users would be well known. Revealing that I was from Earth right now would raise numerous questions, and it wasn't a fact to carelessly throw around a stranger whose motivations were unknown. So I backtracked.

"Well, there were plenty of magic users, of course. But alas, no one who wanted to spare the time or energy to teach a bratty kid how to get a hold of her abilities."

The cleric's lips pursed. "Your parents didn't ensure your education?"

"They were… a little absent. Kept busy with work and such." Too many eyes focused on me. The only one who showed any doubt was Cantal, but the confusion and pity in the expressions of my companions wasn't much better.

I clapped my hands together. "In any case, we should get a move on. Running on limited time and all. Shall we move outside or set up in the hall?"

Cantal spoke over his shoulder as he headed for the kitchen. "We'll go over the essentials in a minute, and then I'll leave you to practice. I won't have the time to walk you through the process in its entirety, but you'll be fine. It's not a difficult concept to grasp."

I wasn't sure how to take that. The thought must have shown on my face, because Luthri motioned to catch my attention. "I've got you," he mouthed. My lips pressed together in a thin line. I wasn't *that* worried—I'd managed to figure things out on my own just fine over the last couple of decades. Not that I was opposed to having help, but I didn't *need* it.

Grumbling to myself, I followed Cantal to the kitchen to help prepare breakfast.

Hours passed sitting cross-legged in the hall in silence, focusing every ounce of energy I had into holding *mana* and attempting to force it into matter. Counter-intuitive was an understatement—creating something out of nothing went against everything I knew. I'd already expanded myself to my limit, a six-foot-plus-tall version of me. The extra *mana* thrummed in my veins. My skin began to crawl—literally and figuratively—with the need for release, but I gritted my teeth and told myself that I would get used to it.

Cantal came in and out over the course of the day as he made preparations for the equinox. Other than that, I was alone. I had no complaints—the peace made it easier to focus. Trying to force *mana* into another form felt like shoving a square peg into a circular hole. The edges caught every time, and my frustration grew the longer I attempted it. I couldn't imagine trying to do this with the others around. As time passed, the air filtering through the open doorway cooled, and the sky darkened to the dull shade of twilight.

Burnout hovered within reach when voices carried on the breeze, signaling the return of my friends. Releasing an unhurried breath, I shifted my attention from inside to out. The adjustment was a slap to the face. Sweat coated my body in a fine layer, pooling around my hairline and plastering hair to the back of my neck. My hands shook where they rested on my knees. My teeth were clenched so tightly that my jaw ached. Whatever *mana* I had gathered slipped from my grip, and I slumped forward as dizziness overtook me.

"Hey."

My face tilted up. Colors swam into each other before my eyes, painting an abstract picture of two identical figures crouched in front of me. Over the next second, the images merged to become one before sharpening into a person.

Cantal patted my cheek with one hand as his other closed around my limp wrist. Mending magic swept through my body in a surge of pleasant warmth, seeking out misfiring nerves and sore muscles with precision. I bit back a groan of relief.

"I realize you're in a rush, but maybe take it a little easier," he suggested, no cruelty in his tone. "Work yourself too hard, and you'll cause permanent damage to your personal magic source. Being unable to draw *mana* is a death sentence to a mage."

Thoroughly abashed, I muttered a "thank you" and slipped my hand from his grip. Cantal remained at my side until the dizziness subsided enough to stand. My cheeks warmed, but I wasn't cocky enough to turn down his help. I'd overdone it—that much was evident. The depletion remained etched in my bones even with a *shahim*'s mending.

Splashing sounds and snippets of conversation coming from outside told me that the boys were taking advantage of Cantal's shower system one more time before we left.

"I'm good," I assured the *opashi* hovering next to me. "Thanks."

He didn't believe me, but stepped back anyway. "Rather than forcing it, let it come to you. You can't accomplish everything with sheer stubbornness alone."

I wanted to say, "Watch me." Instead, I settled for a meek nod and went to join the others.

Yrra stood in his loincloth under the shower spout, pulling the rope at regular intervals to get a short spurt of rainwater to rinse with. The rest of the men and Daethie lounged on the ground nearby, deep in conversation. Lu spoke while the others listened, engrossed. I did a double take. One of the twins—Vyrain, I realized—had cropped his hair close to his scalp.

Had our conversation been that difficult for him? Or… Hah. It was probably so that Narille would be able to tell him apart from his brother. He was thinking ahead, after all.

As I approached, the lilting mix of consonants and vowels became comprehensible.

"—are most fascinating. See, externally, the males and females look similar, but the females have one hole that does it all. And all of their pleasure points are internal. That was an adventure trying to figure out, let me tell you. The male genitalia, on the other hand, is internal until he's aroused, at which point the penis extrudes from a slit in the gr—"

Vyrain was the first to spot me. "Mar!" he exclaimed, shoving Luthri aside in his scramble to simultaneously get to his feet and silence the *Peri* male. Lu fell backward against the fence, his mouth making a perfect *O*, while Hohem and Daethie looked on with amusement.

"Oh, please, don't let me interrupt." My lips twitched with the effort to hold back a smile. "You were just getting to the good part. After the penis extrudes, then what?"

"That's it!" Vyrain hurried to speak before Luthri could condemn them. "We were—it was an anatomy lesson. Luthri has, ah, had experience with several races, as you know, and we were curious to know if they differed. I mean, of course they differ physically, but it's not like we've seen all there is to see—in regards to the various races, not in terms of their uh, attributes or accessories thereof—"

Hohem smacked him upside the head.

"Very smooth." Daethie folded her little arms. "But I, for one, am not ashamed. We're all adults here, and I wanted to know about Lu's experiences with interracial sex."

I turned my attention to Luthri, who squatted by the gate, rubbing his backside. "You know you don't have to tell her anything you don't want to, right?"

"She scares me," Luthri muttered. "Besides, it's not like my past is a secret."

"She might be annoying, but when it comes down to it, you could step on her."

"I'm right here," Daethie reminded us with a sneer. "Try it. Hope you aren't too fond of your balls."

Luthri pushed himself to his feet, casting a wary glance at the pixie as he dusted dirt from the seat of his pants. "How did your training go?" he asked, directing the question at me.

I went to sit on the fence, but thought better of it after examining the width and bend of the slats. Instead, I settled for leaning against one of the posts. "I can hold *mana* for a while, but I don't think I'm any closer to making something out of it. I was trying all day and only tired myself out with nothing to show for it."

"Well, you can't force it. You've got to be persuasive."

"You don't think I'm persuasive?" I challenged.

"I didn't say that," Lu hedged. "This might just need a… more delicate touch."

"Oh, so I'm not delicate?"

Vyrain turned away, but he couldn't hide the way his shoulders shook with the effort to keep quiet. Hohem chortled outright, having no such compunctions.

"Delicate like an *Aminkinya,* perhaps," he remarked.

We all shared a giggle. Daethie's kind might be small, but they were nearly indestructible. That, combined with their sharp teeth, claws, and wings, made them a force to be reckoned with. Some might consider the comparison to be an insult, but you could be likened to worse.

"Um…"

The hesitant interjection was Yrra, who had finished his shower and was stuffing his shirt into the waistband of his pants. He nodded toward the building, where Cantal stood poised outside. "He's calling us. Time to get started on dinner."

The twins jumped to attention, and Daethie whizzed ahead.

I pushed away from the fence and was hit with a bout of dizziness. My arms extended, automatically seeking support as I teetered in place. Yrra noticed, stepping forward to help, but a solid forearm met my palm before Yrra could make it to me. I gripped Luthri's sleeve like a lifeline until the dancing gray spots faded from my vision.

"You all right?" he asked, studying my expression with a frown.

"Yeah. Thanks. Sorry." I released the handful of fabric and gave his arm an awkward pat. "Practice today took a lot out of me, that's all. I'll be fine with food and a good night's sleep."

Lu's arm remained outstretched. Yrra glanced between the two of us, his thoughtful eyes taking in the way the *Peri* hovered at the edge of my personal bubble, before moving on.

"I'm good," I reiterated as my face warmed. "I don't need an escort to the dinner table."

"I understand. But would you like one?"

He waited there patiently, respecting my space. My stomach flipped.

"No. Let's go."

In my hurry to move on, my answer was more of a grunt than words. I strode after the others without looking back. *Goddess, what's wrong with me?* I'd become a teenager again, worrying about useless things. How were we supposed to get along if I couldn't look him in the face? There was no pressure; we agreed to be friends. And who cared if the others noticed? It was none of their business if we decided to have a physical relationship.

Keeping myself busy seemed the smart thing to do. It had served me well before.

We prepared a dinner of *massiya,* a tasty crescent-shaped pastry similar to a pastel. The egg-and-mashed-root-vegetable dough was filled with a savory mix of other vegetables and baked on the fire for a delicious and convenient meal. When they were ready, we convened on the floor and ate with our hands. Cantal broke out a bottle of fae wine and elegant little serving cups. Everyone got a glass but Luthri, who declined on account of his delicate constitution, and Daethie, who split one with Yrra.

I was relishing a pleasant buzz and daydreaming about what a *massiya* would be like with a cheese and chicken filling when a lull in the conversation made me look up.

"We're heading out tomorrow, yeah?" Hohem inquired, putting down his empty plate.

I answered him. "Yeah. I looked at the map the other day. We've got about another week until we reach the edge of the mainland, so long as we can keep up a good pace all the way through the wetlands. Then we have to catch a boat the rest of the way to Munarzed."

"Can we afford a boat?" Daethie licked her fingers from her spot on Yrra's knee.

"Hopefully." That, I wasn't sure about. I'd never had to take a boat before.

"I believe shippers make the trip every six days," Cantal informed us. "I can't say how much it would cost, but they surely have enough room to transport a handful of people alongside the usual supplies. It's a four-day round trip—I'm not sure how that would impact your plans."

"I'm not sure either." I hadn't thought past making it to the island. If we couldn't learn anything by asking around in the city, we'd be going in blind. How long would it take to find Narille? Where would we even start? Chewing on the inside of my cheek, I mulled over what little we knew. Hopefully, the shippers could tell us more about the people on the island. They might even know what happened to Narille.

"Well, let's make the most of our last night off," Luthri suggested, leaning back against the wall. He'd sucked down four raw eggs while we prepared dinner; I had no doubt that Cantal was looking forward to us no longer draining his limited resources.

"How about a story?" Vyrain looked to the cleric. "Do you have any about Hermenia?"

"Mm." Cantal scratched at his jawline. "I do, of course. But most of the sacred stories are not pleasant. Back then, the world was dark. Hopeless. Any tales that survived from that period are much the same. Take the Sacking of Sinsanad, for example."

At our blank looks, Cantal loosed a weary sigh. "It's a particularly depressing one," he warned. "Sinsanad was the capital of North Hamra during the Settling Age, a thousand-odd revolutions ago. The city prospered for generations under its leading family, who were followers of Hermenia. Naturally, other powers grew envious of their bounty. Fueled by greed, a powerful *amafarin* put together an army to take the city and everything in it."

The unfamiliar word caught my attention. "*Amafarin*? What's that?"

"Someone who uses their magic for evil," Vyrain supplied. I nodded, filing away that word in the same place of my brain inhabited by "witch."

"Sinsanad was not prepared for an attack of that scale, but the men went to fight nonetheless. The king was killed in the initial battle. The queen, distraught, prayed to Hermenia for guidance. Now, the Lady of War is strong, but not all-powerful. The army was too much for them. So, she summoned the women and told them that they had a choice to make."

The *opashi*'s throat bobbed. He laced his fingers together in front of him and blinked to clear the moisture that had gathered in his eyes.

"They could sit back and let themselves be taken as spoils of war," he murmured, "or they could make a stand. However, none of them knew how to fight—their abilities were put toward home, health, and crafts, not taking lives. All armor and weapons had gone with the men, and they were left with nothing but stones and fire. With few options, they threw boulders and burning coals from the walls to delay the advancing army while they built a fire that could be seen from a great distance."

His voice cracked as he spoke. He took a moment to compose himself before finishing.

"When the enemy at last breached the city, there was nothing left but fire and bone. The women had cast themselves into the flames rather than be subjected to their evil intentions. The *amafarin* and his army couldn't get the blaze under control, so the city burned to ash. Just like that, the long, happy reign of Sinsanad was ended. The city was renamed and rebuilt some decades later. I believe it's called Riyacal or something like that now."

A pregnant silence fell. None of us quite knew how to respond until Luthri spoke up.

"You weren't wrong. That *was* depressing," he said matter-of-factly.

Cantal shrugged. "It was the way of things back then. They

recorded these stories—if the history is accurate—as warnings more than anything else. They're meant to teach important values. Things like patience, kindness, generosity. The importance of education for all, regardless of their gender or background. And to help people connect with their goddess."

"A story like that doesn't reflect all that well on Hermenia," I said without thinking. Vyrain's sharp intake of breath made me realize how that might come across. "Then again, I don't know what I'm talking about. Gods and goddesses aren't my realm of expertise."

I flashed Cantal what I hoped was a charming smile.

"You're not the only one who feels that way," he admitted, unruffled. "But in my opinion, it is not our place to measure a divine being against the standards of mortals."

Right... Ours is not to reason why. Why was the sentiment so familiar?

"How about another story?" Hohem swirled his wine. "Something lighter, perhaps?"

"I've got one." A devious glint appeared in Luthri's eyes. "Have you ever been to northern Leimor? There's a tribe of indigenous people, the *Santouri*, where they look like us from the waist up but have the bottom half of an *avida*. It's a struggle getting out there—"

"Let's keep it PG," I interrupted, having more than an inkling of where his story was headed. "That is, appropriate for the current audience."

Cantal shook his head. "I appreciate your discretion, but it's not necessary. I assure you I've seen and heard it all. Besides, there's nothing inappropriate about a little romance."

"I highly doubt there was any *romance* involved."

Lu's countenance was the picture of innocence.

Chuckling to himself, Cantal took up the storytelling mantle once more. "Speaking of romance, there is an old... legend, let's say, that claims *mana* does more than we give it credit for. It's a somewhat popular belief in the east. They say each individual has a unique magic signature, and that when two signatures on the same wavelength meet, the individuals will feel an almost irresistible pull toward each other. A fated connection, some call it."

An emphatic hiccup drew my attention to Daethie. Her peach-toned cheeks bore a rosy flush. "*Gian du tiannar,*" she stated, baring her teeth in a sleepy grin. "Fate knows best. We respect those feelings, especially if it's telling us to kill someone. And back in the clan, we formed households based on positive connections with other members."

"That's… sweet," I ventured as Yrra moved the cup of wine out of her reach. *Forming households based on connections… Isn't that normal friend groups?* Anyone would choose to surround themselves with people they vibe with. It's how people worked.

"Here, I have another one." Cantal cleared his throat.

I shifted my position to settle in for the long haul. Across the way, Luthri did the same, stretching an arm out over a raised knee and tucking his hand under his chin. Our eyes met, and he winked. This time, I powered through the urge to look away, even as heat crept up the sides of my neck. I couldn't afford to lose a battle of wills—what precedent would that create?

Brown eyes bored into gold, the competitive intent a living, tangible thing felt by no one but us. It became a game wherein Luthri and I were similarly committed. Who would break first? But the game was over before it truly began, as Lu's expression gentled, the intensity of his stare going from an electrifying stroke of lightning to the kiss of dawn after a long night.

How had I thought his eyes were eerie? They were beautiful.

Cantal's smooth, pleasant voice carried on in the background. "The *vali* nut tree, as you know, is a valuable resource for the people of Kereti and Wysalar, used for its fruit, nuts, and bark. The origin of the tree, however, is highly contested. It's said that long ago…"

CHAPTER THIRTEEN

IN WHICH THE PARTY RESUMES THEIR CROSS-COUNTRY JOURNEY

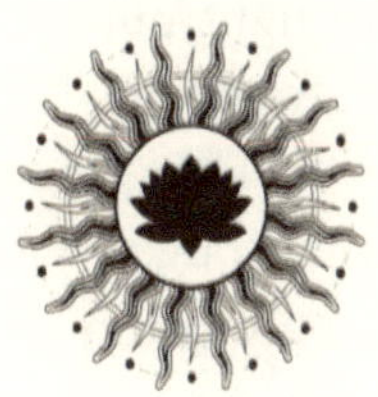

KNOWING we had a lot of time to make up, we were packed and ready to go by dawn.

Cantal surprised us on the way out with homemade sweets—bite-sized pieces of a sticky, chewy substance that reminded me of brigadeiro with a harder bite. The nostalgic flavor coated my tongue and gave me flashbacks to my last birthday in Brazil.

"A northern specialty," he said with pride, "to give you strength for the journey ahead."

If I thought they would keep, I would have demanded another dozen. I had to settle for stuffing my mouth and giving Hohem a dirty look when he took the last one.

We said our goodbyes at the door. Stumbling across Cantal when we did was a blessing, and it was a crying shame that we didn't have any way to thank him. I expressed as much, but Cantal assured us that he had things covered, wanted for nothing, and was happy to see us on our way. The last, at least, I believed wholeheartedly.

So we hit the road once more. Resting over the last couple of days made it difficult for me to get back in the groove, and I flagged by the time we stopped for lunch. Part of it may have been due to the fact that I was trying to draw and hold *mana* while walking, but I wasn't sure how I'd find any time for my magic practice otherwise. Walking all day left few options. I could squeeze in an hour or so of meditation before bed, but I'd be dead on my feet.

That evening, I picked at my food. *Is this worth it?* We could turn around. The others would be disappointed, but they trusted my judgment. Things were only going to get more convoluted from here on out. Adventuring was for adventurous people, people who had experience with the pitfalls and were well-armed. Not a random group of homeless young adults with light purses, lofty goals, and a lack of common sense. That was fair, wasn't it?

Something poked me in the side, causing me to jump. Images of being smothered in man-eating bugs flashed through my mind, but when I turned to look, it was only Luthri.

"What sorts of thoughts are ruminating in that delightful brain of yours?" he asked, eyes twinkling.

"Honestly?" I sighed. "I'm wondering if it's too late to give up and go home."

Lu made an expression of mock outrage. "The Mar I know would never!"

"You don't know me," I pointed out, not in the mood to entertain his eccentricity at that moment. "We're barely acquaintances."

"But we've slept together." His shameless statement had even Yrra's head swinging around. Daethie gasped and clapped her hands together in delight.

Thank heavens I hadn't put anything in my mouth, or I would have choked. I was quick to correct him. "We've slept *next to* each other. Very different."

"We've all slept next to Mar," Vyrain grumbled. His brother gave him a friendly shove.

"What do you miss most about home?" Lu's question was directed at me, but judging by the thoughtful looks that resulted, it got us all thinking.

"Jük, Vee, and Ked," I admitted. "They were fine before I came around, so I'm sure they're still doing fine, but they're family, and I can't help but worry." When no one else responded, I poked them with a, "What about you guys?"

"I was trying to think what home is for us," Hohem said slowly, looking to his brother. Vyrain appeared equally lost. "It's been revolutions now since we left Wysalar in search of work, and we haven't made as much headway as we hoped. We appreciate being able to tag along, but... camping on the outskirts of Vhalder was never a long-term plan."

"What do your plans look like now?" I asked.

Vyrain shrugged. "Haven't thought that far. Maybe we'll go see what our parents have been up to. Or maybe we'll keep traveling the world, going wherever we're needed. A hero's job is never done, right? If the money is enough, we could retire. The world is ours."

"Isn't that the dream?" Luthri mused. "Kick back on a beach somewhere for the rest of our lives. Build a fancy treehouse. Keep a shrine out in the middle of nowhere."

Vyrain's eyes narrowed. "You're not getting a share, remember?"

"I remember." Lu put up his hands. "Just giving you some ideas."

Yrra made a small, dejected sound in his throat. All eyes went to him. "I haven't found home yet," he whispered. He didn't say it outright, but the way his shoulders slumped hinted that he didn't believe it would ever happen. My heart squeezed in my chest.

"It'll happen," I stated, reaching out to set a hand on his knee. "Until you find it, you can stay with us. We're happy to have you."

"If all else fails, you could go back to your family, couldn't you?" Vyrain asked. "Or your clan, or whatever you'd call them. Wherever your parents are now."

Yrra winced. "That's not possible. I'm an adult now, a threat to my own father. He would sooner..." His lips pressed together, keeping himself from saying something more. After a beat of silence, he finished on a quiet, "It's not possible."

"Who needs a home?" Daethie hopped onto Yrra's knee with a short pump of her wings. "I don't look back anymore, only forward. That's the best way to do it."

The non-answer from Daethie was no surprise. She didn't like to talk about her past—to this day, I had no clue what happened between her and her clan. Something to do with mismatched personalities, if I had to guess. She wasn't the type to take direction well.

"And you?"

Luthri blinked, realizing his initial inquiry had turned on him. "Oh! Home, huh?" He studied the ground. A crease appeared between his brows as he formulated an acceptable answer. "It's complicated. My family came to this continent a long time ago from across the sea. I grew up in Wysalar, and my mother's still there. My siblings are all over the place, living their lives. I suppose after this… I'll be back to my usual shenanigans."

Going from place to place, spending his money and sleeping around, he meant. Not sure why disappointment was my first reaction to the statement—it had nothing to do with me.

I took pity on him. "That's fine. If there's anything I've learned from life, it's that home isn't always a place. It can be with the people you love, wherever they are."

"Well said." Lu gave a soft smile. Was it my imagination that it seemed… sad?

"Need a pick-me-up?" Daethie chirped, vigorously rubbing her hands together. "I lifted some curious things off the old man. They're in Yrra's pack."

My eyes widened in horror as Yrra's hand shot to his bag.

"Daethie, you didn't!" I exclaimed.

"Heaven help us," Hohem muttered. Vyrain's mouth opened, but he had no words.

"Bunch of fusspots." Daethie exaggerated sticking her tongue out. "I'll have you know I did him a favor. As it turns out, strong wine wasn't his only vice—not everything in that garden was innocent, and I'm pretty sure his precious Goddess would not approve."

I'd opened my mouth to tell her off when Luthri laughed, an unfettered, head-thrown-back, slapping-his-knee cackle. Wiping tears from his eyes, he announced, "Well, it's too late to return them. Who knows, maybe those souvenirs will come in handy."

Vyrain's face had taken on a decidedly green tint, but he found his voice. "You can't seriously think it's okay to steal from a holy man."

"Of course not. But what's done is done." Luthri shrugged.

He had a point. I wasn't about to turn around and waste a day because of Daethie and her sticky fingers, no matter how much I appreciated Cantal and what he'd done for us. Anything she'd taken from his garden would grow back.

I shoved the rest of my paltry lunch into my mouth. "Let's get a move on, then," I said through the mouthful of bread. "Adventure waits for no one, and we're behind schedule."

"Hear, hear!" Daethie crowed, taking to the sky as we packed up.

The terrain changed gradually as we walked. Where it was once firm and rocky, the ground became spongy underfoot, and the trees fewer and farther between. The road became harder to follow, so I kept an eye out for markers that could reassure me we were on the right path. The next day, we passed the train tracks going from north to south on the map. When night fell, we were still out in the open. We slept on our tents, using them as a layer between us and the moist earth, and took turns keeping watch in case of hungry predators or worse.

Humidity struck like a damp blanket thrown over our heads before the swamps came into view. The sea of rich pinks, greens, and browns all around gave way to stretches of tan mud and wild grass dotted by spindly trees and sorry excuses for shrubs. From the height of the plateau, we could make out the wetlands below us and the city beyond that, a jagged shadow against the pale blue sky.

"We're almost there," I stated, relieved, as we paused to appreciate the view and catch our breaths before descending into the penultimate stretch of our journey.

"That's Munarzed?" Vyrain eyed the horizon dubiously.

"Well, no. That's Solfarin, the coastal city." Its name literally meant "oceanside."

"Haven't you been paying attention?" Daethie rolled her eyes. "Munarzed is an island, *skair*. If we could walk there, we wouldn't need to take a boat, now would we?"

"It's big." Luthri sounded delighted. Likely imagining being in proper civilization again.

"Yeah," I agreed, no less enthusiastic. "We should be able to stock up on some necessities while we're there. Start thinking about what you might need. I know I ran out of *zanna* root. Be sensible, though—anything that's not urgent, we can pick up on the way back."

Everyone made their way down the hill. Already I dreaded the thought of picking our way through waterlogged trenches and drowned vegetation. My boots weren't even waterproof in normal rain conditions. But realistically speaking, wet socks were the least of my worries. What sorts of things lurked in the water, with no telling how deep it went in places? The fine coating of vivid blue-green algae could be innocuous or poisonous to the touch.

"Stay sharp," I warned the others as we approached. Yrra nodded, big blue eyes solemn. Scanning the terrain ahead of us for signs of danger, I adjusted my pack and forged forward. Almost immediately after crossing the tree line into the wetlands, the soft earth became thick mud that gripped the soles of my boots and tried to swallow my feet whole.

"Isn't that pleasant," I muttered to myself, yanking my legs into motion one after the other. I raised my voice to be heard over the chorus of sloshing and squelching footsteps around me. "If the carrying mood strikes anyone, you know where to find me."

"Goddess, Mar, do you want a faceful of mud?" Vyrain exclaimed. Beads of perspiration already dotted his hairline. "Because that's how you get a faceful of mud."

"Hostile much?" I grinned even as I considered my next step.

"I didn't mean *I* would—oh, never mind."

The mud was a short stretch followed by stagnant pools of algae-infested water. We had no choice but to continue onward. I broke the surface with my first step, and my nose wrinkled at the pungent bouquet of rotten eggs and decomposing plant matter that wafted up. The ground dropped off under my foot. My leg sank in to the knee, and I stumbled forward, almost face-planting in the dark water. I caught myself just in time, flailing for purchase.

"You all right?" Lu called. He lowered himself into the water with a grimace and waded toward me, arm extended, but I waved off his approach. Jokes aside, I didn't need babying. Still, I was oddly grateful that Luthri chose to trudge along beside us instead of flying, though it would have been difficult to navigate the trees as a full-grown man. Daethie had an easier time of it, cruising along on the breeze, making lazy loops when it suited her.

Those of us who walked made our way steadily through the water, mud, and underbrush. As we went, the water became clearer, and the smell faded until it was nothing more than earth with an eggy undertone. Some areas were deeper than others. We weren't even halfway through, and I was soaked to my waist. The others removed their packs to carry them above the surface. I followed suit, grumbling all the way.

Shiny winged insects skimmed along the water, diving under in places. They didn't bother us, thankfully. I didn't have hands to swat them away.

I was fit enough, but I wasn't built for *this*.

Half-swimming, half-walking with my bag above my head, I'd begun to tremble from the weight when Yrra paused where he was. His nostrils flared, and his tongue darted out to taste the air. A deep line appeared between the twin curves of his brow ridge.

"Wait," he murmured. I paused. The twins were ahead of us and didn't hear him.

"Wait," I repeated louder for their sake. When they stopped and turned back, I looked to Yrra. He said nothing, only scanned our surroundings with a sharp-eyed intent.

That's when the singing started. It began low and sweet, a melodic hum that reverberated over our watery surroundings and caressed my ears with the care of a lover. The sound skimmed over my flesh, sending goosebumps scattering in its wake. I couldn't make out the source. I should have found that odd, but instead, I found it remarkable. My eyes closed, and my arms sagged. I didn't even care that my bag slipped into the water—simple pleasures ought to be enjoyed without distractions, and this brand of pleasure was something special.

A malignant hiss burst from Yrra, causing my eyes to snap back open. "*Nykse,*" he spat with a vehemence I'd never imagined he was capable of. "Quick, cover their ears!"

He dropped his pack and sprinted toward the twins, cutting

through the water with a level of efficiency that only a water-dwelling species could achieve. Daethie shouted his name and dove after him.

It took me a moment to snap out of it, but when the meaning of his words registered, I leapt into action. Letting my burden fall, I surged toward Luthri. He stood rooted in place, eyes wide and empty, his wings trailing forgotten into the water behind him. He didn't so much as twitch, even when I sloshed to his side and clapped my hands forcefully over his ears.

The tune shifted. Layers of sound braided together, rising and falling in volume, invading my senses. I could *feel* it, as though it had a physical presence, or as though it were a chemical and not a song. Lu repositioned under my hands and stepped forward, almost dragging me with him. Was he back to himself?

"Luthri?" I looked up hopefully, but his face remained blank.

"Their ears!" Yrra cried. The twins pulled away from him, even as he tried to stuff their ears with whatever plant debris he could gather. It made no difference. They didn't so much as lift a hand to deflect him, steadily making their way forward as if they were zombies. They turned right. My head whipped around to scrutinize the terrain in that direction. More trees. Deeper water. And there, in the water, were creatures I'd never seen before.

Only their heads were visible above the surface. Three… no, four of them, their faces narrow strips of luminescent white blighted by huge, bottomless black eyes. Long, dark hair floated behind them like a shroud. Somehow, they sang with their mouths barely open, but the strength of it sent the water before them fleeing in tight ripples. They advanced, each step revealing more of their forms. Slim shoulders emerged, followed by nipple-less chests and flat abdomens. They carried their willowy frames in graceful beats to the music—stepping forward, swaying to one side, stepping forward, swaying to the other side.

"Yrra?!" I had to shout to be heard over their noise.

He couldn't help me; he was too busy trying to block the twins. And Daethie flitted from person to person, desperately trying to keep their ear stuffing in place. Ugly scenes flashed before my eyes, visions of the men willingly walking into the *nykse* pod and being torn apart.

The twins screaming with pain as *nykse* tore into their backs with sharp teeth. Luthri's body—what was left of it—floating away to decay alongside the algae.

Heartbeat shrieking in my ears, I pushed through the water to snatch a hold of Luthri's arm. My feet dug into the mud as I grappled with it, putting everything I had into holding him back. His progress was slowed, but not halted. My own strength wasn't enough.

Which left me with one option. I gritted my teeth and drew *mana* like a woman possessed, expanding muscle and bone so quickly it hurt. Magic burned through my veins. My skin stretched to make room for the new bulk, and I expanded in all directions. But in the end, even with what I'd learned from Cantal, I couldn't spread my reach any farther than usual. The excess *mana* pooled in my chest, heavy and useless. Acid climbed my throat like fire.

Goddess, it didn't matter. It wasn't enough; I couldn't do it. I released the breath I'd been holding and gulped fresh air in short pants. When my grip on Lu's arm slackened, he shook me off. The *nykse* beckoned, almost licking their lips at the prospect of fresh meat. I watched his back retreat from me, his waterlogged wings dragging through the swamp water behind him.

What do I do now? What can I do? Angry tears blurred my vision. *It's not fair.*

Yrra threw himself in front of the twins, between them and the *nykse* pod. His long ears drew back against his head, his lips peeled back from his teeth, and he loosed a vicious rattling hiss that had the *nykse* rearing back in surprise. Their song stuttered.

And for a fleeting moment, Luthri hesitated.

"That worked." I lunged forward to grasp Lu's hand once more. "That worked! Do it again! That's right—we mean business!"

The *mana* I'd already gathered leapt at my command, bulking my body to its limit once more. I turned my clothes into blue skin and sharpened my teeth. Pushing aside any embarrassment, I flattened my own ears against my head and hissed in the best approximation of Yrra's. The *nykse* in front closed its mouth abruptly and shook its head, taken aback.

But the others kept singing. And despite Yrra's best efforts, the twins reached the edge of their big pool. Any farther and they'd be climbing in for a casual swim with the sharks.

We were running out of time.

Yrra realized it too. He glanced back, and his eyes ran over the twins and Luthri as he sized them up. "Could you carry him? Or Vyrain?"

If it was our only option? I would somehow, so help me. "Yes," I breathed. "Yes, I can."

Yrra wasted no time in snatching the arm of the man nearest him and, faster than I could blink, sank his teeth into Hohem's wrist. He did the same to Vyrain. Without a word, I did what I could to pull Luthri closer, and Yrra dashed to us to repeat the process on him.

"Be prepared to catch him," he ordered, eyes wide, before returning to the twins. I watched as he tugged them backward. They fought his grip, struggling to make it to the *nykse* that called them, and then they… stopped. Vyrain went down first, slumping into the water. Yrra quickly slipped an arm around him to keep his head above the surface. Hohem went next, falling back with a splash and eliciting a grunt from the waterfolk male as he caught him.

Lu crumpled in place, collapsing into my waiting arms. *Good Goddess, he's heavy!* I fought against gobs of mud and nearly went under, having underestimated his bulk. Spitting mouthfuls of swamp water, I shook my head to get my bangs out of my face and hauled him toward me, sending a shot of *mana* to shorten my hair at the same time.

Daethie released a ululating war cry and engaged the *nykse* pod without prompting, becoming a projectile of light and color. She zipped around and between the monsters, causing them to screech and recoil in pain as her sharp claws, teeth, and wings cut into their delicate skin. Black blood oozed from the shallow slices she made. They swiped at her but couldn't maintain focus, and their songs stuttered as a result. It didn't make a difference at this point—Lu was unconscious, his eyes closed. Whatever Yrra did was effective.

Together, he and I hauled our companions through muddy swamp and wet, tangled weeds toward Solfarin. When the *nykse* noticed that we were moving away from them, their songs petered out one by one. The one in front straightened up, its hair falling in a dark curtain around it, and watched us go with an almost comical frown on its face.

Daethie shot a crude gesture their way and went to join us. As she turned her back on the creatures, the one nearest her lurched forward, arm outstretched. Daethie's progress was abruptly halted as bone-white fingers closed around her torso, trapping her wings against her body.

My heart might have stopped. "Daethie!"

Yrra's head whipped up at the terror in my voice. His grip on the twins faltered, nearly upending Hohem into the water. A dozen expressions crossed his face at once—surprise, fear, horror, resignation—contorting his features. His gaze catapulted between the unconscious Luthri in my arms and Daethie struggling in the *nykse*'s grip.

The monster held her aloft, a victorious grin splitting its narrow mouth. Yrra and I could only watch as the monster brought its other hand around to snatch one of Daethie's little windmilling arms. Gritting its teeth in a nightmarish sneer, it began to pull.

My eyes squeezed shut.

Water splashed beside me as Yrra launched himself forward, coming to her rescue even laden as he was. But as it turned out, we underestimated the pint-sized fairy. Almost faster than the eye could follow, she wrenched her arm back and twisted around to sink her teeth into the hand that held her. Mouthfuls of flesh fell to her onslaught. The *nykse* shrieked in pain and dropped her like a hot potato, plunging back into the water to ensure it was free of her. The others retreated uncertainly, their eyes wide.

Daethie crossed the space between us in an instant. "Woo, that was a rush!" she exclaimed, shaking any residual tension from her small frame. "You guys okay?"

Were *we* okay? The Goddess have mercy. This was doing no favors for my blood pressure. "We will be," I grunted out, focused on dragging Luthri over a section of land. I jerked my chin in the direction we'd come from. "Are they following us?"

The pixie spun around to check. "Nope. They're off to find easier prey."

"Oh, thank the Goddess." I let Luthri fall back against the ground and collapsed next to him. Raising a hand to wipe away some of the mess from my face, I returned to my usual appearance. My heart knocked against my rib cage as if it was eager to join the fray.

Yrra fared slightly better, even with Hohem and Vyrain both to handle. A shadow remained over his features, but other than that, he appeared unshaken. He paused in the next watery section for me to catch my breath. How did he do it? I'd faced down some things in my life, but drunkards and bullies, nothing like that. Those were straight out of hell.

"How is something like that even here?" I wondered aloud. We were so close to the city. How many travelers and residents had fallen prey to this pod in the past? Were there even more of them somewhere out there? The wetlands continued for several kilometers.

"It's not a bad spot." Yrra corrected his grip on the twins. "The water is not all salt; many things can live in it. And there's nothing higher on the food chain that might bother them."

He stared into the marsh, deep in thought.

Taking stock of the situation, I looked Daethie over next. Remnants of black blood coated her arms and wings, but she was otherwise no worse for wear. I didn't look much better, as covered in sludge as I was. But we were alive, and that's what counted.

We would live to fight another day.

CHAPTER FOURTEEN
IN WHICH THE PARTY RECOVERS WITH A SHORT REST

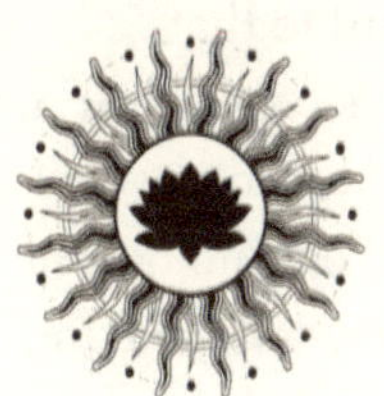

"ARE THEY GOING TO BE OKAY?"

Yrra, Daethie, and I sat together on the outskirts of the wetlands, admiring the city skyline and watching the sun make its way down to the horizon. The rest of our gang lined the ground in front of us, sleeping peacefully. Getting them through the swamp had been a massive pain in the ass, but we hadn't encountered any other dangers.

This line of work was anything but glamorous. Most people didn't realize that a life without rules meant hard work and sometimes going days without a bath or clean clothes. Not knowing where your next meal would come from, or facing things out of a nightmare.

Yrra considered my question before responding. "They'll wake soon, but given the combination of *nykse* song and my venom, they'll probably be dazed for a while."

I nodded, making myself comfortable. "You did well out there," I told Yrra. That didn't even come close to being the praise he deserved, so I kept going. "I couldn't have done it without you. I mean, you legitimately saved all of our butts."

"He wasn't the only one putting in work, if you'll recall," Daethie interjected, even as a little satisfied smile pulled at Yrra's lips.

"Good point. I take it back—that was a team effort."

"Hm." Yrra tapped a finger to his cheek. "You have mud on your face."

I quickly wiped at my face with the cleanest part of my sleeve, which wasn't saying much. Remembering that all of my clothes were at the bottom of the swamp along with our packs, I heaved a sigh. "Do you think it would be worth going back to get our stuff?"

Yrra cast a sidelong glance in the direction of the swamp. "We should."

"Tsk. Not looking forward to that."

"I can babysit the boys until you get back," Daethie offered, hopping over to Yrra and plopping herself beside him. Yrra offered his hand as a seat, and she climbed into his palm.

"How kind of you," I drawled. Shaking my head, I lay back against the cool moss and squinted at the summer sky. It was going to be a cloudless night, by the look of it. Stars were already beginning to emerge, eager to start their shift. Could be worse. It could be storming like nobody's business on top of being a miserable day of travel.

"So you're familiar with *nykse*." I didn't want to push Yrra to talk more than he was comfortable, but it was difficult to wrap my head around how he'd risen to the occasion.

"Nope. Never seen one before," Daethie responded.

I shot her a scathing look. "Then maybe I wasn't talking to you."

"It's not my first experience with them," Yrra admitted. "It's not uncommon to come across other water dwellers. They might resemble people, but they're mindless animals. Nuisances at best… and to males who haven't evolved to be immune, a fate worse than death."

Something lit up in a shadowed corner of my memory. Hohem had said something about them in the past, hadn't he? *Nykse* weren't that different from the human concept of sirens, with a twist. They couldn't reproduce alone, so they lured in men of other races for breeding purposes. Once they were… *finished,* they would drown and eat them. A cold shiver ran through my body at the thought of what would have been our friends' fate if we hadn't been able to do anything.

Or maybe the shiver was due to the fact I was still soaked through. What I wouldn't give for a warm, fluffy towel right about now.

"Well, we were lucky you were there," I said quietly. "All of us."

Yrra ducked his head, uncomfortable with the praise. It was crazy to think that he'd taken charge of the situation and gotten us to safety a matter of hours ago. The thought brought a smile to my face. Perhaps fueled by residual adrenaline, a giddy mirth overtook me.

Yrra and Daethie looked at me like I was crazy.

I squeezed words out in between bouts of laughter. "It just occurred to me that you've spoken more today than you have in the last revolution. To think, all it took to get you out of your shell was the threat of a near-death experience."

Yrra blinked, not sure how to respond.

"You're not wrong!" Daethie nodded thoughtfully. She leaned against Yrra's thumb, not unlike a cat cuddling up to someone's leg. "But it's all right that you're quiet. Makes it easier for someone else to get a word in compared to some people around here."

Yrra didn't respond, but the tips of his ears took on a darker shade, and his thumb moved against her cheek as if giving her an affectionate stroke in return.

We sat together in companionable silence. Figuring we had some time to spare, I practiced drawing and holding *mana* as best I could while running on limited rest. It was difficult to sit in place and focus past the discomfort of being tired, hungry, thirsty, and wearing wet clothes. My neck could barely support the weight of my head.

Night arrived. A curious volleyball-sized moth covered in downy fluff visited our meadow, observing us from a respectful distance as it tried to determine if there was any carrion for the taking. Yrra shooed it off. At last, the boys began to stir. Lu roused first, an intelligible groan emanating from his chest like an off-tune instrument.

"Why am I on the ground?" he mumbled. He tried to sit up, his wings jerking underneath him in an attempt to give him a boost, before settling back against the ground. His next exhale was an indignant huff. Slowly, he tilted his head one way, then the other. Debris skittered down his shoulder in clumps. He looked down at it, eyes crossing with the effort.

"And... why are my ears full of moss?"

I got up to help him. "It's a special gift. From the Goddess of stupid questions."

"Huh." Lu blinked. "Haven't heard of her. Must be a southern one?"

My lips pressed together to hold back laughter. "Yeah, a southern one." I offered a hand, but he made no move to take it, maintaining a distant stare instead.

"Maybe… I ought to stay here awhile," he reasoned, his tone apologetic. "But I'd like answers, if it's all the same. What happened?"

I crouched beside him, brushing swamp debris out of his hair. "Apparently, the swamp wasn't uninhabited. We ran across a pod of hungry *nykse*. Yrra saved us—if not for him, we'd be dead. Well, you guys would be." I nodded at the twins lying nearby.

Yrra looked away, embarrassed.

Lu raised the hand the waterfolk had bitten, scrutinizing it with narrowed eyes. It dangled from his wrist, limp. "Waterfolk venom. Smart. With a paralytic in our systems, we couldn't have moved for anything, not even a *nykse*'s song. Can't say I'm fond of the sensation, though."

Yrra ducked his head. "I'm sorry."

Lu let his hand fall and heaved a sigh. "Don't be. So, what are we doing now?"

"Well…" I exchanged a glance with Yrra. "We were waiting for you guys to wake up. We sort of had to leave our packs behind. I have our money still"—I patted my belt, from which the pouch of *vodt* dangled—"but our clothes, food, tents—all that is gone."

Lu's hand went to the waterlogged satchels at his waist. His eyes closed.

"It was necessary," Yrra said quietly.

"It was. Unfortunately." We didn't even have fresh water, and it had been too long since I last had something to drink. Clearing my parched throat, I continued. "We have to decide if it's worth going back for them. Otherwise, we should move on to Solfarin. We're so close, and we can get supplies there."

I tried to keep the longing out of my tone, but I couldn't quite help it. We were almost there; we could be in Munarzed in less than a week. If all went well, and we found the Kereti girl quickly, we could be back home within another month. Or a month and a half after the pit stop to drop her off home and get our reward—couldn't forget that.

Spending the night digging through muck to recover our things wasn't particularly appealing by comparison. Plus, I wasn't looking forward to another run-in with *nykse*.

A faint rustling in the grass drew my attention to where Hohem pulled himself onto his elbows, wincing all the way. His gaze fell on the body an arm's length away. "Vyrain?" he whispered. When there was no response, he dragged himself across the distance. I hurried to his side as he none-too-gently shook his brother's arm.

"Careful," I warned him, reaching out to stop him. "He'll be fine. Just sleeping it off. You should rest too; you've been through a lot."

Hohem paused his efforts to fix me with a bewildered stare. "Sleeping what off?"

"*Nykse*," came the grim response from Luthri behind me. "I don't remember any of it either, but apparently they were hiding in the pools. Yrra and Mar got us to safety."

Hohem's eyes fluttered shut.

"You're welcome," I added, eyeing the scuffs and scratches along his limbs. "You and Vyrain got the worst of it. You were closer when they started singing, and Yrra had to carry you both. Pretty sure your heads knocked together more than a few times."

"With any luck, it'll have knocked some of my sense into him," Vyrain muttered from the ground. Relief flooded through me. I'd known we were all in one piece, but seeing everyone awake and alert was reassurance I hadn't realized I needed. The band was whole once more.

Hohem's head snapped around, and his shoulders dropped when he saw Vyrain was all right. He slouched against his brother with an exaggerated sigh.

"Goddess, I hope not. I could do without your idea of 'sense.'"

Vyrain gave Hohem's arm an affectionate pat before letting his hand fall back to the ground. "Respectfully, you don't know what you're talking about."

"Disrespectfully, I know exactly what I'm talking about."

"Well, then." I clapped my hands together. "Now that everybody's awake, we have a decision to make. Obviously, it's late. You may have noticed that we don't have the tents set up."

Blinking, Vyrain surveyed our surroundings. "What happened to the tents?"

"They're gone," Daethie piped up as she came to join us. "Lost to the swamp."

Hohem sat bolt upright. "You can't be serious," he exclaimed.

"Excuse me?" I crossed my arms. "How exactly do you see the two of us hauling our packs out alongside your unconscious asses? It was all I could do to keep Lu's head above water."

"So I have your tender love and care to thank," came an abrupt purr by one ear. Startled by Luthri's silent approach, I nearly smacked him silly.

"Don't do that," I hissed, putting space between us.

"What about our water?" Vyrain asked, wincing as he sat up. "I could use a drink."

"Gone too," I admitted. "Everything except what we have on us. And I don't even know if I could find our bags again if I looked. We don't all have Luthri's directional prowess."

"So moving on seems like the best course, no?" Hohem studied our faces one by one. "We'll pick up the necessities in town and get this job done. Do we have enough money?"

"It'll depend on what prices are like around here, but we should have enough for the basics." Untying the pouch from my belt, I knelt on the ground to count. We'd barely spent anything thus far, with Cantal's help and living off the land, but we also hadn't started with much. As I stacked coins, my lips moving without sound, a hand bearing another pouch was thrust into my view.

"This too." Luthri gestured for me to take it.

"Been holding out on us, bird boy?" Vyrain remarked, eyeing the pouch.

"Ooh." Daethie half-flew, half-skipped to kneel by my side. "We finally get to see what the son of a great mender travels with. A fortune awaits!" She rubbed her hands together eagerly as I opened the pouch to pool our money together.

Lu reached up to scratch at the back of his head. "Well, it's not like that's my life savings. But we're friends now, so might as well share. It should be enough to replenish what we lost."

I stared at the money in my hands. Combined, it was more than I'd ever seen in one place—easily enough to cover a few canteens, food, and even proper lodging if we wanted to splurge. I could only hope that it would be enough for passage to Munarzed. Shippers were going that way multiple times a week anyway, right? It shouldn't be—

"Put it back, Daethie."

Grumbling, the pixie returned the coin she'd pilfered. Where had she thought to hide it? I gathered the money again, filling the two pouches equally, and handed Lu's back to him.

"Hang onto it for now," I told him, straightening up. "It wouldn't be good to have all our money in one place. I don't know what crime is like in these parts, so keep your eyes open." Considering the shade of the sky, I added, "Let's focus on finding a safe place to stay the rest of the night. We can ask around to figure out our next move in the morning."

Second to the excitement of being one step closer to calling this job done was that of sleeping in a real bed. How long had it been? Several years, to be sure.

"You good?" I offered Hohem a hand. He waved it off and helped his brother to his feet, maintaining his grip on Vyrain's forearm until he stopped swaying.

"All right, then." Luthri faced the group with a dazzling smile. "Shall we?"

CHAPTER FIFTEEN

IN WHICH THE PARTY ARRIVES AT THE COASTAL CITY

PERHAPS WE WERE STILL RECOVERING, or perhaps the distance to cover was farther than it appeared by eye, but making it to Solfarin took longer than expected. By the time we reached the outskirts of the city, it was nearly dawn. Feet dragged as dreams of curling up on a wool-stuffed mattress dissipated with the darkness.

We passed several houses that were little more than shacks on our way to rejoin the main road, which carried us underneath arching pillars carved into twin statues of a familiar lady with a spear. The statues guarded the official entrance, where constables and a representative of the city administration waited to screen visitors. Towns like Vhalder didn't bother with such formalities. Traveling in the fae world was informal in general—a side effect of changing magic, since common forms of identification were rendered useless.

"Welcome to Solfarin," a young lady with cute, rounded features in a square hat called as we approached. She sat behind a tall podium, her feet dangling off the stool. I might have mistaken her for a child if not for the crafted leather armor adorning her torso and legs and the authority in her appearance. While her overall air was that of a professional, with a straight back and a quill gripped in one hand, the fatigue in her voice and dull glint in her eyes suggested that they were coming off the night shift.

"Hello," I started, putting a hand on the podium.

The constable nearest us, who resembled a crocodile person stuffed into a uniform, adjusted its weight. They all took us in, hard gazes lingering as we were committed to memory. To them, we might have appeared to be bandits scoping out the security.

"Full names, please, any associations, and the reason for your visit." The girl—woman?—poised her quill to take down our information.

"Marcia de Souza," I told her. The others introduced themselves one by one as the pen scratched against paper, immortalizing our visit.

"Luthri Mendersson. No title."

"Hohem Sinthaid of Wysalar, and this is my brother Vyrain, of the same."

"Daethie the Unconquerable."

"Yrralailee."

"We're looking for the Kereti heiress?" I offered.

The woman nodded. "Anything to declare?" At my look of confusion, she clarified, "Any weapons, herbal compounds, or other potentially hazardous materials on you at this time?"

"Why would we decl—"

Hohem shut his brother up with a kick to the shin.

Pasting an easy smile onto my face, I answered, "Nothing. Actually, we lost all of our gear in the wetlands. We're hoping to pick up a few things in the city."

The pen slipped in the clerk's hand, and her eyes went big. "You came through the wetlands? Lady watch over you. You're lucky you made it out! There are *nykse*!"

"No," Lu gasped sarcastically under his breath.

"Well, yes. Therein lies the problem," I admitted. "Without knowing the landscape, it seemed the most direct route. We made it through intact but had to sacrifice our things. Food, clothes, all of it. If you could point us to the best place to replenish what we need, it would be appreciated. And then… I suppose we ought to see about catching a ship out to Munarzed?"

The last bit came out as a question, half because I wasn't sure if she'd be able to help us, and half because I wasn't sure what the plan was. As much as I would have liked to get some sleep, the chance for that was behind us. Did we ask around town and find out what we could? Would people talk to us? Was it best to head straight to Munarzed, knowing that was Lady Narille's last known location?

But the clerk was stuck on the fact we'd come through the wetlands. "Why didn't you take the bridge?" She set her pen down and leaned back on her stool. "Goodness. Is this your first time this far north?"

Well, that was one way to make someone feel stupid. "It is, actually. What bridge?"

"You come up by da tracks?" grunted a hairy constable with squinty eyes and tusks muffling his speech. "You shouldn'ta missed it. Dere's a toll, but not too 'spensive."

"We passed the tracks but didn't see a bridge or toll." An odd queasiness took root in my gut. I must have looked at the map a dozen times—there was no way I'd miss that. A problem with the map, then? We must have been sold an outdated one. Pity I couldn't check now, but if we ever crossed paths with that bartender again, he'd be getting a stern talking-to.

"Well. No matter. You'll know for your return trip." Back to business, the petite clerk took up her pen and made a few more notes before beaming at us with a mouthful of short, square teeth. "Thank you, you're all set. If you should take advantage of lodging, we ask that you report the estimated duration of your stay. Otherwise, enjoy your visit."

Easy enough. "Thanks!" I lingered a moment, unsure if we were supposed to get paperwork or proceed, until the hulking crocodile constable waved us forward. I led the way. Luthri fell into step behind me, a comforting presence at my back. Yrra and Daethie held up the rear as we entered Solfarin and got our first good look at the coastal city.

It appeared to be one of those places where people from all walks of life gathered, not unlike Fortaleza or D.C. And, as luck would have it, we arrived just as it was waking up. It was inspirational to see the spread of fashions, from the gauzy shirts and dresses of the Southern regions to the full-body ornamental armor worn by officials, and the myriad of different races. You couldn't turn your head without seeing someone with a tail, fur, horns, wings, pointy ears, or some combination of nonhuman attributes.

The average Earth resident would be overwhelmed to know such things existed across The Rift.

People we passed were living their lives—striding confidently to work, pulling petulant children along, selling homemade goods out of baskets to anyone who would stop and entertain their pitch. Storefronts and merchant carts stocked with incredible wares took up both sides of the main street. There were fabrics, books, medicines, spices, wood and metal crafts… anything the heart desired. Some awnings and shutters remained shut, their owners late to open.

The mouthwatering scent of fresh bread drew my gaze to a nearby pastelaria cart laden with baked goods, where a faun in an apron stacked *massiya* and other delicacies in neat rows. An uncomfortable cramp in my stomach reminded me that it had been a long time since my last meal. We had other priorities, but I made a mental note to come back this way.

Taking it all in, I kept walking. Houses became more tightly packed as we went. Buildings in the fae world were constructed from wood, stone, or brick using a combination of skill and magic. Windows were glass, and most of the roads were paved with attractive stone. While they didn't have electricity, *mana* lamps lined the streets to provide light at night. All in all, it felt cozy, like a historic village in the countryside untouched by time.

A sliver of sunlight reflecting off water caught my attention through a break in the skyline. When I paused to get a better look, my breath left me in a whoosh.

"It's the ocean!" I blurted, raising a hand to point. The view, combined with the smell of salt and scales that carried to us on the wind, brought back memories long hidden away that made my heart hurt to recall. I vaguely remembered visiting the beach in Brazil before being taken from my family—eating sorvete as it dripped down my hand onto the ruffles of my swimsuit, digging holes in the sand, and watching the cool surf caress my toes.

Daethie took off from Yrra's shoulder and darted higher to get a better view. Loud whoops came from behind, making me jump as the twins pushed past me. They raced each other down the street to the harbor, dodging bewildered locals along the way.

"Let's go!" Luthri seized my hand. My initial reaction was to shake him off, and my arm tensed to do so. But the excitement was infectious, and as I stared at where our limbs connected, I relaxed and let it guide me instead, giving him a little squeeze in return.

Lu's face split in a wide smile. That was all the warning I got before he tugged me forward. I'd seen him run—for someone who, according to Vyrain, was "weighed down by muscle," the man was fast. Yet, I didn't have to struggle to keep up with him. My face mirrored his smile as we flew after the others, all exhaustion forgotten.

The harbor at dawn was an impressive sight, from the wooden pier that ran along the shoreline as far as the eye could see to the assortment of boats and ships decorating the golden water. Smaller fishing vessels prepared to take off for the day. Some already had, growing smaller in the distance. What caught my eye next was the behemoth with off-white sails and elegant black rigging moored some thirty meters away. The massive wooden paddle affixed to the side and the smokestack protruding from the deck told me there was more to it than met the eye. Perhaps this was one of the shipping vessels we could contract to take us to the island?

Luthri and I caught up with Hohem and Vyrain where the cobblestone road ended and the wood pier began. As we slowed to a walk, I pulled my hand from Lu's to catch my breath.

"What's the plan?" Hohem asked.

"Ooh." Hands on hips, I surveyed our surroundings. "Let's split up," I suggested. "Ask around, see if anyone knows something about Narille or what's going on in Munarzed. I'll try to find out when the next ship heads that way and how much passage will be."

"Might be worth starting there," Luthri observed, inclining his head in the direction of the large ship. It wasn't clear if the individuals milling about the immediate area were members of the ship's crew or not, but it wouldn't take me long to find out.

"I've got this side." Pointing the opposite way, I suggested, "Someone should head that way, and someone else down the street we came from. Meet up in a span or two?"

Luthri opened his mouth, but Daethie beat him to it. "Yrra and I will take the other side of the pier," she proposed. "The boys can take main street—they'll need the numbers."

"Someone should go with Mar," Lu countered immediately. "Two, two, and two. I'll do it. Hohem, Vyrain, you can take main street. It'll be more fun anyway."

"No, you should go with someone else." I tapped the pouch at my belt and lowered my voice. "Splitting up the money is less of a risk. You should take main street."

Lu clicked his tongue. "Then take Yrra. For your safety."

The groups ended up being Luthri and Vyrain, Hohem and Daethie, and me and Yrra. We said our goodbyes with the understanding we'd reconvene soon to determine the next course of action, and Yrra and I made a beeline for the big ship. A bearded dwarf ate breakfast alone by where the boat was tied off. It was as good a place to start as any.

"Hello!" I raised a hand in greeting. "Is that your ship?"

The dwarf, either distracted or disinterested, didn't bother looking up. He said something I didn't catch.

"I'm sorry?"

He repeated himself more slowly in a guttural language I wasn't familiar with. At my look of confusion, he jerked his chin toward a large group surrounded by wooden cases. Half of the group appeared to be standing off against the other half, and their conversation was loud enough to be heard from where we stood. Inserting ourselves into a tense situation wasn't ideal, but I wasn't about to stand around and wait for them to finish.

Yrra could only follow as I marched up to them. "Excuse me!"

"—because you can't *count*," a woman's voice snarled in the sudden silence that followed. Several sets of eyes turned our way, along with one eyeless face. The group was diverse, with a bald, green-tinted waterfolk male; a seething she-giant; an ancient, grizzled woman with smooth pits where her eyes should have been; and an androgynous being that was relatively humanoid but for the long, scaled snake tail trailing behind them.

It was the giantess who had spoken. She was dressed in the light, form-fitting layers often worn by the Northern houses, designed to keep one warm in the cooler months and be adaptable to other weather conditions. Upon noticing us, she pulled herself to her full height—nearly three meters—and jabbed a sun-tanned, sausage-sized finger at me.

"Are you their boss?" she demanded, nose wrinkling. "This delay is unacceptable. We have a standing order every week, and we don't make our money until the delivery is complete. There is NO reason we should have to wait for your team to get it together. Every time, at that!"

I held up my hands. "Sorry, no, I'm not involved in this. I might have a job for you, though. The little guy with the beard said you were the person to talk to about that ship?"

The giantess's eyes narrowed. "It's not for sale." Behind her, the people she'd been arguing with took the opportunity to slink off and continue pulling crates together.

"I don't want to buy it," I said quickly. What in the world would I do with a ship like that? A pirate's life was *not* for me. "I'm trying to get to Munarzed."

Her expression went slack, then broke out in an obliging smile as she made the connection. "Oho, an adventurer! Yeah, we could work something out. How many in your party?"

"Six. Well, five and a half."

"I charge based on mouths and assholes, not height."

"Six, then."

The giantess faced me, revealing another, more compact figure disguised in swathes of dark fabric who'd been sheltered in the shadow of her frame. I blinked, unnerved by its sudden appearance, before remembering what I was supposed to be doing.

"Uh… yes, so, six," I repeated, angling my head to meet the she-giant's eyes and wincing as the motion put me directly in the glare of the morning sun.

"You know there's something weird going on out there?" she advised before confirming.

Her offhand comment made my heart skip a beat. Leaping at the opportunity to drive the conversation in that direction, I replied, "I'd heard. But if you have any more information, I'd love to have it. Honestly, we know very little."

"Not unlike most of the people that go out there, then." The giantess sucked her teeth before gesturing to her companions. "Start loading up. I don't want to waste any more time," she directed them. Turning back to me, she continued. "Munarzed was a big, ugly rock in the middle of nowhere until a couple of revolutions ago. New management came in, a foreigner named Rugaveld, and all of a sudden, everybody was goody-goody. The city expanded at record pace. Problems with crime were a thing of the past, and business was booming.

"That was around the time they stopped paying taxes. Didn't respond to census requests either, and that was a big deal, because a lot of people who went out there were choosing to stay. Obviously, the lack of communication was an issue for the leading family. Munarzed might be a municipality, but they're still a Kereti territory." She glanced down to be sure I was listening. I held my breath and gave an enthusiastic nod of encouragement.

"So Narille goes out there to see what's up. Now, she's the heir, so she's in line to take over when her parents step back. That's a lot of responsibility, to be fair, but it's something she's been prepared for her whole life. She goes to see Rugaveld and figure out what's going on, and bam, she's dropping everything to stay there. Sends a bird home and that's that. Anyone who tries to convince her otherwise also ends up staying. Strange, isn't it?"

"That's… helpful, thank you. It seems like I found the right person to ask." I exchanged a look with Yrra. Strange didn't begin to cover it —what was going on over there? Was their island the ultimate paradise, or was there something darker afoot?

"Gossip is one of the few pleasures of land." The giantess grinned, revealing a mouthful of even white teeth she'd probably paid a fortune to a cosmetic change-mage for. "But that's not all I have to tell you. You work with people at all? It sucks. You've always got people like these" —she jerked a thumb toward the suppliers she tore into moments before—"making your job harder.

"Delivering to Munarzed? Smooth sailing the whole way. They've got a team waiting and ready to help you unload. As soon as you set foot on shore, they're asking you to stop by and offering you food. Every damn one of them's as friendly and welcoming as the next. Rugaveld lives in this grand old house, and his door is always open, no matter what you come to him for. It's nice, sure, but it rubs me the wrong way. People don't get along like that. It's like they're all part of some happy cult."

A cult wasn't that far-fetched, given the evidence. If that was the case, it made sense to try avoiding the residents so that we could investigate the situation on the island without interference. It was large enough, so long as we could find an uninhabited area to land. "I don't suppose you could take us around to a quieter part of the island and drop us off where there aren't any people?"

"Smart." Nodding, the giantess folded her arms. "I could manage that. Go the long way 'round and drop you on the barren side of the island. It'll cost you extra."

The corners of my mouth twisted downward. "If that's the only way," I agreed. Better not to take any unnecessary risks. With some luck, Luthri's contribution would cover the cost. "I'm Mar, by the way." I indicated myself, then nodded toward my companion. "And this is Yrra; he's one of our party. The rest are around here somewhere."

"Gerda." The giantess extended one huge hand.

Muscle memory had me reaching out to grasp it before I remembered where I was and paused, arm extended. Gerda didn't hesitate. She took hold of my hand, being mindful of her size and strength, and gave it a single firm shake, then released it to slam a fist against her breast with a ferocity that made me flinch. Stepping back, she indicated the people with her, who were hauling the crates one by one to where the ship waited.

"This is my crew," she said proudly. "I'll introduce you later. But you're in good hands."

"I'm sure, thank you." My gaze lingered on the knee-high creature hovering behind her. It gave off the image of a shy child clutching its mother's leg. "Are, uh… they with you too?"

"Huh?" Gerda glanced down. "Oh, there you are, Firag. Yes, my errand-runner. He's been a more recent addition. Quick as a snap, even if he does wear more clothes than my north-born elders. The sunlight disagrees with him, or so he tells me."

We regarded the mysterious, awkwardly shaped figure together. He appeared to stare back, though it was impossible to tell, and didn't seem inclined to introduce himself.

"Tongue doesn't wag much on that one," Gerda said by way of apology.

"No worries." I dragged my eyes back up. "Okay, so… how much are we talking? For transporting all of us to the island?"

"How much you got on you?"

My hand itched to fondle my money pouch, but that would be a dead giveaway. "That's not how this works."

"Fine." Gerda shrugged. "Thirty *vodt* per person. Does that seem fair?"

I bit back a curse. That would wipe out our entire purse, and we needed money for supplies too. We'd have to be frugal as it was. "Ten," I countered through gritted teeth.

Gerda scoffed, "I'm running a business, little one, not a charity. Twenty-five."

"You're going that way anyway," I argued. "But I can do fifteen."

"Twenty. No less."

It would be tight. Did we wait for another shipper to come along? We weren't in any rush. Or were we? We'd lost our tents after all, and the idea of sleeping on the streets wasn't appealing. There was no guarantee the next ship that came through would be any cheaper.

As if reading my mind, Gerda tutted. "It's a two-day trip. The price covers your fare, bed, and food. Trust me when I say you won't find a more generous offer."

"Fine," I snapped, already seeing the few coins we had slipping out of my hands. "You have a deal. Half when we board, half when we arrive at the island. When do we leave?"

"As soon as we get the merchandise loaded," Gerda responded immediately. "Should be ready to cast off around midday. Have your group ready to go, or we leave without you."

A final nod, and the deal was made. Gerda left to hash out details with the suppliers and oversee the loading, leaving me and Yrra to figure out our next move.

"All right. We have some time before we meet up again. Let's keep asking around, see if anyone else knows anything." I was already surveying the pier for a likely suspect. "With any luck, we'll have a little more to go on by the time we have to head out."

Nodding, Yrra slipped his hands into his pockets. "I'll follow your lead."

"Great." My attention snagged on one of the little fishing boats coming back to shore to drop off a haul. They ought to be a good source of information. As my feet moved, I called, "This way!" over one shoulder, and we headed over to interrogate the new victim.

CHAPTER SIXTEEN

IN WHICH THE PARTY INVESTIGATES THE SITUATION

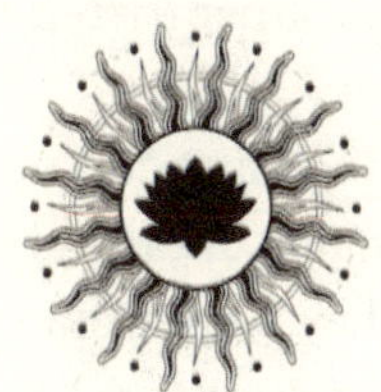

YRRA and I were first to the meeting point and feeling rather good about ourselves. We had transportation to Munarzed lined up, a plan for how to approach the island, and a vague idea of what we would be getting ourselves into. It was a pretty good start.

Daethie and Hohem arrived next, their raised voices preceding them. Somewhat out of respect but mostly due to my own curiosity, I didn't interrupt.

"There's a wrong and a right way to ask someone for a favor," Hohem was saying, throwing up his hands. "You lead with that kind of attitude every time, and we might as well be talking to the cobblestones. That guy was about ready to twist your wings off."

"As I told you," Daethie retorted from her spot on his shoulder, "there's no guarantee someone's telling the truth. Put a little fear in them and they're more likely to give you what you want without a fuss."

"They weren't afraid of you; they wanted to shut you up. There's a difference." Shaking his head, Hohem let the matter drop and turned his attention to Yrra and me. "Next time, one of you gets Daethie. If I have to do this again, I'll wring her neck myself."

Yrra extended his hand—was it my imagination, or was that a little smile on his face?—for Daethie to clamber up to his shoulder.

"Am I to assume that you two didn't get anything helpful?" I asked.

"Not much." Hohem scratched the back of his head. "We found some fishermen who go out that way. There's a rare type of mollusk that breeds in coves around the island. Anyway, they deal with the islanders sometimes and had mostly nice things to say."

"Let me guess—they're all super friendly and cooperative."

"Yeah. You heard the same?"

"Basically. Let's see what Vyrain and Luthri have to say."

It took several more minutes until they returned. Their arms were full of assorted goods, and they were making every effort not to look at each other. When they saw us, Lu's face lit up, and Vyrain's darkened. I was tempted to lead with a comment about how they'd gotten on well, but it didn't seem like the time.

"Any luck?" I eyed the bundles they carried. *Did they buy out a whole store?*

Vyrain snorted. "None of it was luck. He's so charming it's disgusting." Throwing himself on the ground, he set down his burden and dug into it to pull out five *massiya*. My mouth watered at the sight... but all that cost money.

"We really don't have—" I began, only to lose my train of thought when I found myself with a still-warm pastry in my hands. There were hums of delight as the others bit into theirs. Breathing a helpless sigh, I followed suit, swallowing a moan along with the first bite of rich, spiced seafood that danced across my palate.

Luthri joined Vyrain on the ground and passed out full water skins. The rest of us sank to our knees to relax and enjoy a much-deserved lunch while he filled us in.

"All right, let's see. We stopped by a few of the shops and found several folks who had done business with the islanders, directly or indirectly. Jasya—nice girl, she sells beautiful handmade jewelry—knows a mason who did work for the mayor over there, Rugaveld. The guy's a delight, apparently. Real stand-up guy."

"Big surprise," I muttered through a mouthful of fish and bread.

"I'm not sure what you mean by that."

"Nothing. Sorry. Keep going."

"Mm. Well, he spends his days basking in the sun, indulging in luxuries. Who knew administrative positions had it so good? I ought to have gone into local government."

At my pointed look, he cleared his throat. "That's not relevant, I suppose. But it took about two weeks for the upgrades to his home to be completed, and in that time, the mason didn't see him do any actual work. No paperwork, no sorting grievances, nothing. It was more of an envious observation than anything else, but I thought it could be worth mentioning.

"Then there's the baker's son, who dated a girl who worked on one of the shipping crews. On one trip, she ended up declining a return trip without so much as sending a note back to her family. So the Kereti girl wasn't the first time someone's gone to Munarzed and decided to stay out of nowhere. In fact, there's a superstition circulating among some of the townspeople that the island has some sort of aura capable of hypnotizing the feeble-minded. Sounds like idle gossip to me, but then again, I've seen stranger things."

Finishing the last bite of *massiya,* I swept the remaining crumbs from my pants. "Okay. Hypnotizing auras aside, I think it's safe to say there's something weird going on here. I spoke to one of the shippers —we have transportation lined up, by the way—and she mentioned how everyone on the island seems to share the same positive attitude. Could be a cult scenario."

Through his last mouthful, Vyrain asked, "Would that be a problem? I mean, hear me out." He choked down the bite before continuing. "If everyone's happy, why is that bad?"

"It's not. They can do what they like; it's no business of ours." So long as they weren't throwing virgins in volcanos or molesting kids, it didn't matter to me what they were involved in. "Our job is to find Narille and get her out. Or at least find out what happened to her."

"What if we find her, and she doesn't want to come with us?" Daethie posited.

What *would* we do in that case? "Then we ask her again, very nicely."

Rolling her eyes, she tried again. "And after that doesn't work?"

Ah. Eyes narrowing, I told her in no uncertain terms, "We will not be threatening the leading family's heir. If she won't come with us, then... then we'll tell her family we tried. They should at least give us part of the reward, since we found her."

"Wouldn't it be lovely if that was how it worked?" Hohem mused.

"I'm with Daethie." Vyrain slapped his knees and leaned forward. "We've come all this way; we shouldn't leave without her. If you don't want to hurt her, you can keep her distracted, and one of us will give her a good whack to the back of the head."

My mouth dropped open. "Do you hear yourself?"

"Maybe we should take a vote?" Daethie suggested.

"How about we leave the decision to an older and wiser version of ourselves?" Luthri offered me a waterskin, which I took gratefully. As he opened his own to take a long drink, he added, "You said you found transportation, didn't you, Mar?"

Nodding, I pointed to the majestic beast on the water. "That one there. I spoke with the owner. It's not the first time they've had guests who were looking for Narille, and she seems to know what she's doing. She wants twenty *vodt* each, and we set out midday."

Lu's hand went to his money pouch. My eyes followed the movement.

"How much did you spend?" I dreaded the answer.

"Not as much as it looks," Vyrain piped up. "We stuck to the necessities—dried foods, water, *zanna,* clothes, and two packs to carry it all in. We didn't bother with tents, only a tarp, but so long as we can find a standing surface to work with on the island, we'll be set. Most of them liked Luthri so much that they threw something in for free or gave us a discount."

"Happy to be of service." Lu grinned. "Anyway, that left me with seventeen *vodt*. But you should be able to make up the rest, right?"

The others watched with bated breath as I counted what I had, the *clink* of coin against coin filling the empty air. Ten, twenty, thirty... My heart sank. Eighty. Combined with Luthri's seventeen, it made ninety-seven. Where could we scrounge up another twenty-three *vodt* in the space of—I cast a quick glance upward to judge the sun's position—two spans?

"It's not that far. Luthri could fly."

Silence met Daethie's hopeful comment. Lu's throat bobbed.

"I… would," he hedged. "It's only… with the aftereffects of Yrra's venom, my stamina might not be what it's supposed to be, and there aren't many places to land—"

"It's all right."

My head swung around at Yrra's gentle statement. He stared down at his hands, folded in his lap. His lips were curved in a smile that didn't reach his eyes. "I've been giving it some thought," he said, looking up to meet our questioning stares. "The wetlands we came through… the water is a little salty, but not unlivable. Deep enough in places. Food would be easy to find, and the *nykse*… they wouldn't be a problem for me."

The *massiya* I'd eaten stirred in the depths of my stomach. "What are you saying?" The question came out more accusatory than I had intended. Softening my tone to something more appropriate for a friend, I tried again. "Are you…?"

Yrra hesitated before nodding. "I know it doesn't look like much, but I think… I found my place. With a little work, it could be home. A good one."

None of us seemed to know what to say to that. Hohem and Vyrain were exchanging wide-eyed looks. Daethie's mouth opened and closed, but nothing came out.

"I can look out for other travelers who come that way," Yrra continued, a measure of excitement slipping into his voice. "I can search for our things too. You could swing by on the way back to pick them up. And see me, if you wanted. One last time before…"

"Ah-bup-bup." I stopped him there. Took a moment to let the sea air soothe my burning sinuses. This was inevitable; people always came and went. We each had our own goals in our ragtag group. If Yrra had accomplished his, that was something to celebrate, not bemoan. My mouth formed words of congratulations when—

"I'll stay too," Daethie announced. Yrra's gaze snapped to hers. She crossed her little arms and stared back, lips pressed together in a stubborn line. "I've already decided, so there's no use trying to change my mind. You could use the company."

Yrra made a distraught sound in his throat, but he didn't deny it.

"Well." Luthri's cordial tone cut through the mounting melancholy. "Though it hasn't been long, it was a pleasure traveling in your company, Yeeralilly."

He didn't appear to notice Yrra's wince at the butchering of his name.

"And knowing you, Daethie, has been a true honor," Lu continued. "I will never forget your delightful company and sparkling conversation these past weeks."

Daethie's chest puffed at that.

"Are you sure about this?" I inquired, leaning over to place a hand on Yrra's. He was a grown man, more than capable of making his own decisions, but I'd watched him acclimate to his lanky adult frame, navigate unfamiliar feelings and new roads, and now face life-threatening trials. Through all of that, he had become like a brother to me. And I knew this world wasn't made for people like him, people who were gentle and pure and *good*.

Beneath my palm, his hand rotated so that his long fingers could lock with mine. He gave my hand a reassuring squeeze. "Daethie and I have been looking for a place to belong for too long," he said, soft and firm all at once. "I'll miss you all, but I've dallied enough."

His face fell. "I only wish I could have said a proper goodbye to the others. Ked expects me to return with you, and…"

"We'll pass the message along," I assured him, swallowing past the lump in my throat. My hand slipped out of his to pick a loose hair from his shoulder and smooth the collar of his shirt, though it wasn't truly out of place. "This isn't goodbye, anyway. A couple of days there, a couple of days back… With some luck, we'll see you again within the week. Can't wait to fill you in—you and Daethie will regret missing all the action, I bet."

"One of us, at least." Yrra's mouth twisted in a wry smile. He looked down at Daethie, who hopped onto his knee and beckoned me to come closer.

As I leaned in, Daethie put one of her braids between her lips.

Before I could tell what she was up to, she'd split off a chunk of her hair with a vicious twist of her head. A fist was thrust at me in all sincerity. I offered my palm and found myself the proud owner of a miniature tuft of loose gray hair not even two centimeters in length.

"Er… Thank you?"

Daethie sniffed, reaching up to push at my fingers until I closed my hand around her gift. "An *Aminkinya*'s hair is worth an immeasurable favor among our people," she explained, her voice gruffer than usual. "Consider that my thanks. For being a good friend."

"You don't owe me anything," I protested, hand still outstretched. As she sniffed again and rubbed at her nose, my heart squeezed with emotion. "Are you crying?"

"I'm not," Daethie denied with a jerk of her head. Her shoulders shook.

Seeing Daethie get emotional had me following suit, my vision blurring. My arm undulated in the air. I had no idea what I'd be able to do with a bit of loose fairy hair, but the depth of meaning behind her gift didn't escape me. She wasn't a sentimentalist.

"Allow me," Luthri interjected, gently taking my hand. He plucked the hairs from their place and rubbed them between his thumb and forefinger with tender care. When he released my hand, I reared back to admire the thin woven ring encircling my pinky finger.

My eyes flicked up to meet his.

"I thought I saw a sign for a birdkeeper," Vyrain murmured. "Should we get a letter sent to Jük and Vee before we set off? We'd have to be quick—it's almost midday."

"Yes! Let's do that." I scrambled to my feet.

Yrra paused long enough for Daethie to take to the air before he also stood. "Good luck," he said, all business. Letting his expression soften, he added, "Don't do anything I wouldn't do."

My cheeks ached with the effort to maintain a straight face. "Well, considering that facing off against a pod of *nykse*, dragging two grown men through a swamp, and biting are all on that list now, I'm not sure that's the best guide on what is and isn't appropriate."

"Biting can be a lot of fun depending on who else is involved," Luthri remarked.

"Shush, you," I told him as I stooped to collect our things from the ground. Vyrain and Hohem leapt into motion. As a group, we gathered the new supplies and bundled them onto the twins' backs. Silver lining —I'd appreciate not having to lug a pack around all day.

Yrra and Daethie accompanied us to send a letter back to Vhalder. We each wrote a paragraph for Vee, with Yrra adding in his happy news of finding a place to stay. I filled in the rest and paid the bird-keeper, wincing as our purse lightened by another two *tarn*. It being a necessary expense didn't make the loss any less cutting.

Before we parted ways, Daethie made me promise I'd make sure she and Yrra got their cut of the reward money, because of course she wouldn't let that go. We negotiated a reduced percentage based on the distance they'd traveled. She proclaimed, "It'll do," and reluctantly sealed the deal with a normal handshake after I stood my ground on a blood bond (the *Aminkinya* way) being out of the question. We said our final goodbyes.

As we made our way back to the dock to the boat that would take us to Munarzed, it felt as though a weight had been lifted. The path forward was clear for once. And a relaxing cruise across the wide blue channel sounded like just the thing to lift our spirits.

CHAPTER SEVENTEEN

IN WHICH THE PARTY BECOMES SEAFARERS

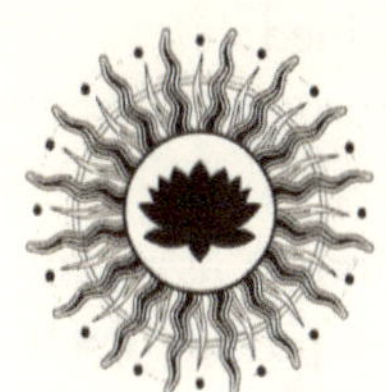

I COULDN'T REMEMBER if I'd ever been on a ship before. Cars, sure. An airplane, certainly. But a ship? Such was a feature of books and movies, not my life—which had been relatively humdrum since crossing The Rift. I liked it that way and had no complaints, especially not after the events of the last two weeks showing me what life in the fae realm could be.

Then again, a little excitement once in a while never hurt anybody.

Busying myself with these thoughts was how I'd decided to cope with the raw absence of Yrra and Daethie. I had to pull myself away from the railing so as not to be tempted by the urge to watch them leave. Hands balled into fists at my sides, I took my time examining the crafted wooden deck, the great wooden masts holding swollen sails, and the base of the smokestack where it disappeared into the hold beneath.

It wasn't long before the giant wheels on either side lurched into motion, and we pulled away from shore. I fiddled with the pinky ring made from Daethie's hair as the visible expanse of water between us and the dock lengthened.

"That'll be eighty *vodt*."

I knew I wasn't alone on the ship, but the voice still made me jump.

It was Gerda, who wasted no time in motioning me to hand over my coin.

"Half now, half on arrival, wasn't it?" I checked. Gerda nodded her assent. As I counted out the amount, I made polite conversation. "About how long did you say the trip was again?"

"Two days in fair weather. We've got a *galyak* with us, so that's all but guaranteed."

My hand paused on the way to Gerda's. "A *galyak*?"

"A weather hag," she clarified.

I was passing over the money when a timely voice shrieked, "Did you bring me an eye?!"

Startled for the second time in as many minutes, I stepped back to make room for the body that pushed itself between me and Gerda. A wrinkled face framed by wild gray hair stared up at me—or, stared as best it could with shadowy pits where eyes should have been.

It was a good thing she couldn't see my expression.

"It's got to be fresh! I won't have an old one!" she exclaimed, waggling a gnarled finger.

"She's having you on," Gerda said dismissively, stepping out from behind her. "They have a strange sense of humor, hags."

The *galyak* dropped her finger and grinned. "You're younger than most of the folks who come looking for the Kereti heiress. What's a fledgling like you doing so far from home?"

So she could see, somehow. I gave her a cursory once-over. While she didn't appear to be a threat, there was clearly more to her than met the eye… No pun intended.

"I'm making my way in life, same as anyone," I answered stiffly. "Is the interrogation included as part of the transportation fee, or is that extra?"

A short bark of laughter escaped Gerda. "Keep your secrets, little one. It's curiosity, that's all. You're not the first group that's come through here, and I'm sure you won't be the last. We're happy where we are, but I can see the attraction. Even if I don't trust the islanders."

"You'll do business with them, though."

"Sure," Gerda agreed. "Their money's as good as the next guy's."

The statement hit home. I'd been there—doing strange jobs for questionable people to afford food and a roof over my head. After a certain point, the money was all that mattered.

"Oi!" Gerda snapped her fingers at someone loosening the sails. "Excuse me," she said to me briskly, already moving to intervene. "I'll show your group around once we're off!"

The hag regarded me a moment longer, head tilted to one side, before wandering off to prepare the ship. I watched her go, thoroughly confounded. Her kind was new to me. How did that even work? And what came after vampire gremlins and weather-controlling crones?

"Nothing quite like the sea air," Luthri remarked from behind me. Being on high alert, I'd whirled about and slapped him straight across the face before realizing who it was.

"Sorry!" I exclaimed, holding the offending appendage in front of me.

Rather than hurt, Lu appeared faintly amused. One hand came up to probe his reddening cheek. "No harm done; I've had worse. If that's how you greet a friend, though, I think I would do drastic things in order to see how you receive an enemy."

"It was an accident," I informed him, sweeping my braid over my shoulder. "You startled me. Maybe you should consider being more deliberate with your approaches."

"That's odd. I should think I've been quite deliberate in my approach." His eyes had gone molten gold. How did he manage to turn something innocent into flirting so effortlessly?

"Oh, you have," Vyrain grumbled, coming up on his right. His shortened locks stood to attention in the sea air, bringing to mind the image of an accident involving several volts of electricity. "Do they have rooms on this thing? It'd be nice to put these down somewhere."

"Oh, Gerda was going to show us." Hand jerking in an aimless gesture, I scanned the deck until my eyes snagged on the giantess. She was chewing out the green waterfolk male for whatever he had done to the sails. "Hm. She looks busy. Can you hang out for a while?"

With an exaggerated groan, Vyrain stomped over to his brother. They ended up removing the packs and collapsing on the floor against the railing. A smart move. I looked forward to being able to take a load off for the next couple of days. It was too optimistic to hope for a shower and real beds, but the skin under my collar itched something awful thanks to long-dried swamp water and who knew what else. I'd settle for tipping a canteen over my head at this point.

I turned my attention back to Luthri, who surveyed the horizon with a distant expression. He fit into my idea of a sailor: a well-traveled vagabond going with the flow of life along with the flow of the sea. What sorts of things had he seen? Beyond a myriad of bedrooms.

"It's been a long time since I was on a ship like this," he commented without prompting. "Brings back memories." Clearing his throat, he tipped his head back and, much to my surprise, began to sing a jovial shanty. It took a moment for my brain to catch onto the lyrics.

"I once knew a girl from a port down south, with golden hair and a mighty skilled—"

Grimacing, I walked away before I was subjected to the rest.

When Solfarin was a strip of color and motion in the distance, an apologetic Gerda found us to proceed with the tour. The ship was large, but most of the available space was reserved for cargo. We were shown the kitchen and dining space, bathrooms, and finally, our quarters. Showers and beds had indeed been too much to hope for, but they'd made the most out of what they had. The toilets were a proper system that flushed waste out to sea. Barrels of fresh water were available to wash with as well as drink, and our quarters, though little larger than a closet, were private and included clean, comfortable hammocks. I couldn't complain.

Well, I could, but was that the brightest idea? I could imagine what a refund looked like on a shipping vessel in the middle of the sea, and even for a strong swimmer, the distance from here to shore was dizzying.

On second thought, maybe it was the steady back-and-forth motion of the ship that was dizzying. My stomach raised periodic protests that would become full-blown nausea if I didn't find a way to take my mind off of it. With that thought, I made sure our bags were secure in our sleeping quarters and sought out the others.

My companions were in the dining hall, playing a card game with several members of the crew. Vyrain mumbled a greeting as I approached. He and his brother appeared to be finished with the round—that, or they'd already lost. Lu was holding his own against the *galyak*, who played with her cards face down and seemed to be doing everything in her power to unnerve Luthri with an eyeless glare that would have sent a lesser man cowering.

All seating in the vicinity of their table was taken. As I considered dragging over one of the benches from another, Luthri glanced up from his hand. With the same ease as nominating a particular dish for lunch, he suggested, "You can sit on my face."

A smattering of laughter rippled through our audience. Vyrain rolled his eyes, unimpressed by Lu's forwardness, as my teeth ground together.

Couldn't he be a bit more subtle? Smarmy commentary was more suited to a randy teenager than an adult male. Still, I couldn't let a statement like that go without a retort. I landed on, "Hardly the time or place for me to break you in, don't you think?"

Lu slapped his cards on the table and angled his body toward me with a scrutinizing tilt of the head. Yellow eyes pinned me in place. His gaze swept down the span of my body, as though considering what he could get away with at this time, in this place. Despite myself, my heartbeat quickened, a swell of heat accompanying my body's response.

For a moment, it was like we were the only two people in the room.

The waterfolk male, also at their table, stood abruptly, eyes wide. "Was that Gerda calling?" he exclaimed, sidling toward the exit. "I'd better go see what she needs."

The dwarf slipped off his stool and followed, grumbling something unintelligible.

"Nice job," I told Luthri. "You're making our hosts uncomfortable."

The corners of his lips curved up. "As long as you're not uncomfortable, that's all that matters."

"Oh, I've heard worse," the hag interjected breezily, tossing a card onto the table between them. "And done quite a bit worse than that. There's a seat available now, dear; come join us. I'm about to show you what your boyfriend looks like when he cries."

Luthri appeared to remember what he was doing before I entered the room and turned back to the table. He stared at the card the *galyak* had played, mouth open in an *O*. A stack of coins next to the card caught my eye. They weren't… He wasn't…?

"You can't do that," he hissed.

"Oh, but I can." The old woman sat back, looking mighty pleased with herself. "A north star takes the place of a matching pair when two players remain." She smirked. "Unless you draw a card that will somehow give you three more matches on your next turn, I win."

"Ha!" Vyrain crowed, jumping to his feet and pointing. Hohem loosed a low groan and dropped his head into his hands. Luthri continued to stare, having no words.

Coming to his side, I examined the table. I didn't recognize whatever game they were playing, but the contextual clues were enough, though I was afraid to believe what my eyes were seeing. Luthri was impulsive, but he wasn't stupid. Certainly not *that* stupid.

"Did you gamble away our last few coins?" I injected the question with warning.

"I goofed," Lu admitted, his left knee bouncing under the table.

"Mar—" Hohem began.

My head snapped in his direction, and he decided against whatever it was he was about to say, holding up his hands and shrinking down in his seat.

Angry words bubbled up my throat, ready to be wielded. My nostrils flared. No, no—I could be better than this. My lips pressed together, and I closed my eyes to focus on my breathing. Sucked in air through my nose, parted my lips to release it. In and out. When I opened my eyes again, the hag was standing. If she had eyes, she would have winked.

"Keep your money," she said, nodding at the coins. "Thanks for the game."

As she made for the door, the last breath I inhaled left me in a whoosh. Cresting anger was replaced by the soothing balm of relief. Luthri didn't need to die tonight after all.

"That's not—" he began.

I interrupted him with a firm, sincere "Thank you," a smile frozen on my face. My hand dropped to his forearm and squeezed as she left, hopefully hard enough to convey the message of *close your big, fat mouth, or I will shut it for you.*

"Let's play something with lower stakes," a handsome faun I hadn't seen before suggested, trying to break the tension. "A simple game of questions to get to know each other."

He and the half-man, half-snake were the only two members of the crew that remained. Their attempt to be hospitable even after that whole debacle deserved to be rewarded. I rounded the table and sank into one of the empty chairs across from Luthri with a glower, intent on putting together a proper scolding as soon as we were in private. That wouldn't be too harsh, would it? It wasn't as though I didn't know how to have fun, but there were limits to reckless behavior. He crossed a line—that needed to be called out.

"Shall I start?" The faun asked, turning to Hohem. "How old are you?"

"Thirty revolutions," the fair fae muttered. When silence fell, the faun inclined his head encouragingly. Hohem's eyes darted around the table before landing on Luthri.

"Uhh, where were you born?"

"The Eastern continent," Lu replied immediately. "An island off the coast of Pfilai." His gaze shifted in my direction, the motion calling to mind a predator seeking out its prey from behind tall grass. "Mar. Tell me about the first time you had sex."

Where does he get off—

Finding my voice, I snapped, "Vá encher o saco do cão com reza," before remembering where I was and switching to *Ishameti*. "That's none of your business. And anyway, that goes against the spirit of the game, don't you think?"

"How so? It's a question, and I'd like an answer."

"It was more like a demand. Anyway, this is a game about getting to know each other, not spilling embarrassing secrets. Unless you'd like to tell us..."—I grasped for something on the same level—"I don't know, if you've ever crapped your pants."

"Two revolutions ago," Lu answered without missing a beat, his gaze unwavering. "A fling didn't believe the extent of my carbohydrate intolerance and tampered with my food."

Outrage cut through the haze of resentment. "What the fuck? That's messed up."

Lu blinked. "It's—well. I suppose it was."

The poor faun's smile had faded into an awkward grimace since our heated exchange began. No doubt he wished he hadn't started the whole thing. Being disconnected from polite society for so long, it became easy to forget yourself, to forget about manners and playing nice with others. But we weren't barbarians.

"I apologize for the detour. Let's try that again." My eyes found the snake-man, the only person at the table who hadn't yet had the chance to speak. I tried for a pleasant smile. "Hi. How about, uh... what's your role on the ship? Your job here?"

A few cordial rounds later, it was Luthri's turn again.

"Tell me something you're afraid of," he asked me. So now we were getting vulnerable?

My arms crossed. "*Nykse.* What do you think is your greatest flaw?"

Luthri exhaled a puff of air, but took my challenge in stride. "As you know," he began, keeping his gaze downcast, "I've had many... sexual partners. The fact is—and this is truly difficult to say—I'm so good in bed that the people I've slept with in the past keep coming back, begging for more. And I have to disappoint them time and again."

Hohem snorted. "What a hardship."

I couldn't help but notice the lack of an answer. Luthri had been truthful in the past, so why did he skirt around the question now? Was it that he didn't understand what I was asking, or that he wasn't capable of letting himself be vulnerable, even for a moment? For all of his speeches about trusting people, he wasn't exactly Mr. Open Book himself.

"Got it." I kept my tone light. "Too many shortcomings to narrow them down. A monumental braggart, insatiable flirt, bulky build…"

"Don't forget 'strikingly handsome' and 'outrageously clever,'" Lu chipped in.

"Outrageously simple, more like. Do you know what the word 'flaw' means?"

The snake man threw back his head and laughed, interrupting our back and forth. "You're a witty one, aren't you? Bet that temper keeps people on their toes."

Luthri face split with a feline grin. "It's what I love most about her," he replied.

I scoffed, but his choice of words slithered its way into the recesses of my mind, clunking into place with an attitude that let me know it was there to stay. Oh, boy.

The faun provided a welcome distraction. "In the mood for supper?" he asked brightly, his hooves clicking against the floor as he hopped off his stool.

"I could eat," Hohem agreed, the sentiment echoed by his brother.

The crew members had us follow them to the kitchen, where drums of flour, lard, salt, and other staples were stacked together—more than enough for a week at sea. It turned out that the faun was the cook. He put together a quick meal of cured meats, crisp biscuits that he claimed were homemade, and a fruit like a softball-sized lychee.

Luthri and I sat beside each other in silence as we ate. Me, the full spread; him, nothing but a plate of the salted meat. Some frustration over the earlier situation remained, but thanks to the *galyak*'s kindness, no lasting damage had been done. I wanted to discuss the issue with him at some point, but it was a trivial matter in the grand scheme of things.

Besides, we could set aside some time to talk once this job was over.

CHAPTER EIGHTEEN

IN WHICH THE HERO MAKES A PLAY

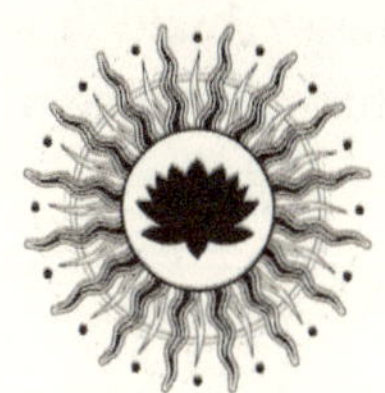

THE SWAYING of the ship became harder to ignore with a full belly.

In hopes of some relief, I made my way to the top deck. Leaning against the polished wood railing, I basked in the moonlight and listened to the faint *whumps* of wind buffeting the open sails, which kept us moving now that we were in open water.

Meat and biscuits sat heavy in my throat no matter how many times I swallowed. Staring into the distance didn't make a difference either. My body knew where it was, and no amount of watching the clouds calmed the nauseating swells.

"Have mercy," I mumbled, resting my head against my forearm as another wave hit.

Wood creaked under a heavy boot.

"Looks like you found a nice spot," Luthri remarked, coming to rest against the barrier beside me. I didn't bother raising my head. I didn't have the strength to ask him to leave, either.

"I wanted to apologize for my behavior before," he continued in a low voice. "Both… for the cards and for the question I asked. It wasn't right. This isn't an excuse, by any means, but I think I was affected more than I thought by the situation in the swamps. The fact that I wasn't—"

Saliva pooled in my mouth.

"Hold that thought," I managed seconds before my stomach clenched with a vengeance and my supper was lost to the black water below.

"May I?"

I couldn't do much else but nod my permission as I heaved. Immediately, kind hands pulled stray hair back from my face. I closed my eyes and tried to focus on the cool breeze hitting my neck, the gentle tugs at my scalp as the messy braid from two mornings ago was undone and reworked. A stubborn piece of swamp debris caught my cheek as it was flicked into the ocean.

"Dibs on the bathing sponge," I mumbled in English, only half-aware.

"Would talking help?" Luthri asked, letting the new braid fall against my back. One of his hands, big and warm, made contact with the spot between my shoulder blades and moved in unhurried circles, sending pleasant ripples through my body. My eyes closed again.

"You could try," I agreed in a whisper.

Lu didn't hesitate. "I was born in the eighth cycle under the First Quarter moon, second of my brood. Talithri, my sister, was last and smallest. They weren't sure she would survive. My mother told me that I hugged her constantly to share body heat, even though we were both babes. She seemed to think it was out of a desire to help. I never told her this, but… I think I must have simply been a hungry thing and mistaken my sister for my mother's breast."

A chuckle tore from my sore throat, leading to another bout of retching. As Lu continued to speak, his hand never faltered in its soothing pattern. "We competed for our parents' attention those first few years. Most would say it was innocent sibling rivalry, but it could be cutthroat at times. We were often kicked out of the house so that our mother could work without being interrupted. By our early teens, we'd gotten through the worst of it, thank the Goddess. Turned our attention to schooling, helping with the family business on the side."

My head raised. "Your father?" I croaked.

"Oh, he was a land surveyor. Always traveling, away for long stretches of time."

I took a few deep, cleansing breaths of sea air to soothe my sore throat before offering a story from my own past. "My mamãe—mother, I mean—was a teacher, from what I remember. Father was a sanitation worker, cleaning trash. I'd stay with my grandparents or cousins during the day. One time, my cousins and I were playing hide and seek —it's a game, you know, where someone hides and tries not to be found. I climbed onto the roof. Suppertime came, the others went to eat, and I realized I couldn't get down."

Luthri's hand on my back paused. "Did you call for help?"

"And lose the game? Of course not. I stayed up there until my parents started calling neighbors together to help look for me. Someone spotted me eventually. I went without dinner that night." I fell quiet, watching the water ebb and flow as the ship cut through. *Should I keep going? Friends shared these kinds of things, didn't they?*

It took a few seconds to build up the courage, but I continued. "I think I always hesitated to rely on others. Even before I left… home. Back then, it was out of a desire to not be a burden on anyone. To not… take more of their attention than was my share. After that, I didn't have great experiences with the people I came across. Don't want to get attached to someone who isn't going to stick around, you know?"

That wasn't entirely true. I'd been friendly with everyone who'd tagged along with our group over the years, even the ones who didn't stay long. My problem had more to do with the people I'd known during my last few years on Earth, but that wasn't easy to explain without additional context. Where could I begin? Clarifying would take more effort than it was worth.

Luthri hadn't said anything in a while, which meant that I could change the subject. It might have been the coward's way out, but I took the opportunity.

"I always wanted to make myself wings," I said, raising my gaze enough that I could study the shadowy clouds on the horizon, their edges lined in moonlight. "I could never get it right—the combination of feather shapes, the right muscles, and the wingspan needed to get me off the ground. Maybe when I get the making magic down, you'd let me study yours?"

Luthri's hand vanished from my back. I mourned its comforting weight. He came to lean on the railing next to me, on my right this time, and trained his gaze on the same view. The ocean breeze carried with it his signature scent of caramelized oranges and spice. Breathing in, I closed my eyes to savor it. Was it weird? Maybe. But it settled my stomach.

My eyes opened again when the quality of silence changed. I couldn't put it into words. Maybe it had something to do with the low set of Lu's brow, the way his eyes narrowed at the horizon as though it personally offended him. The shadows in the sky were reflected in his deep gold irises, and his ears didn't stand to attention the way they usually did. I knew that look, though I hadn't seen it on him before. Had I inadvertently touched on a sore topic?

When he opened his mouth, the words were low but clear.

"My people mate for life," he began, absently tilting his head from side to side to release the tension in his neck. He didn't look at me as he spoke. "There's an elaborate process to it. First, the male courts the female—sweet words, gifts, acts of grooming. This can take many weeks or months. Sometimes even revolutions. If the female decides to return our affections, we perform a showing. It's a rather silly thing, that. The male flaunts his physical prowess and shows off his wings with a series of exercises or dances. Finally, they perform a mating flight together, which culminates, of course, in sex."

I was tempted to ask him to get to the point, but something told me not to interrupt. Instead, I watched his profile, watched his chest deflate as an exhale left him. Gave him time, like he'd given me. His next words were spoken so quietly, I almost missed them.

"I can't fly."

That got my attention. I stared, mouth ajar, caught somewhere between wanting to ask questions and expressing my condolences. His expression softened into something serene, even as a sad smile graced his lips. He kept going without prompting. "My wings are useless. Deformed. They have been since birth. So I'm afraid I couldn't help you."

Since birth? That didn't…

"Isn't your mom a mender?" What kind of mother would leave her son like that?

"The best," Lu assured me, a note of pride entering his tone. "But alas, she couldn't do much. Conditions you're born with... They're usually impossible to heal. They're working on addressing such defects in the womb, before the body is fully formed, but the technique hasn't been developed yet. In fact, it's one of my mother's passions because of me."

At my look of devastation, he hurried to reassure me. "It's all right. I came to terms with the fact that I'd never find a lifemate of my kind a long time ago. And as for my silly, self-serving quest, I had the thought—or the hope, perhaps—that maybe, if I was thorough enough, I could find another race... more specifically, a person, who was both compatible with me and able to look past my abnormality."

He shifted to the side, opening his body to face me. His hands locked together in front of him, so tightly that the color washed from his knuckles—at odds with the relaxed slant of his hips and the softness of his words. Those discerning owl eyes must have picked up the indecision written across my features, as he offered me a small, endlessly patient smile.

I turned my attention back to the ocean's dark valleys and peaks dotted by silver foam. I wanted to comfort him, to tell him it was all right and that he'd find someone, but it was never that easy, was it? Especially when you'd lived your whole life a certain way, had the same thoughts about yourself all the while, and gotten comfortable with that. Deep-set beliefs didn't adjust in a blink because someone said something on the contrary.

And... I couldn't promise that I was that person. Not even for the sake of his feelings.

I let myself drift two steps to the right along with the motion of the ship, which landed me squarely against a firm chest. Luthri's arm came around my shoulders.

"I've got you," he murmured above me.

It was tempting to argue that *I* had *him*, but rather than disturb the comfortable silence with semantics, I let him have the last word. Leaning into the heat of his body, I nuzzled at his chest until I found the steady *thump-thump* of his heart and pressed into it. My arm, tucked between us, encircled his waist and squeezed. He squeezed back.

Goddess, what a firm man.

When had I last held someone? Been held like this? I'd almost forgotten what it was like. I was irrationally pleased when my nose caught a hint of musky swamp water underneath the sweet orange. That proved a barrel of water and a washcloth only went so far, even for him. It would have been entirely unfair if he went around smelling glorious all the time.

Lips brushed my forehead, painting a path from my temple to the ridge above my right eye. I was too aware of their suppleness, their warmth. The way my skin sang at the contact. When Luthri sighed, his breath ruffled the hair atop my head, making my scalp prickle.

"I would kiss you right now," he whispered, "but you absolutely *reek.*"

I huffed a laugh against his pectoral. "Some other time," I told him. And, since it didn't feel right to sit in silence after sharing such a poignant moment, I added, "You could sing that shanty from before now, if you wanted to. The one about the blonde girl."

A grin split Luthri's face from ear to ear. All too happy to accommodate me, he cleared his throat and began to sing. His voice was deep and smooth—untrained, but not unpleasant.

"I once knew a girl from a port down south
With golden hair and a mighty skilled mouth.
She was tan and lean and as tall as a tree
With a bosom that just begged to be free.

And when the days at sea led to nights at sea,
I was glad to have a girl in my bed for free.
She could take any man to the promised land,
Now I have to settle for my hand..."

CHAPTER NINETEEN

IN WHICH THE PARTY PASSES THE TIME WITH A GOOD-NATURED SPARRING SESSION

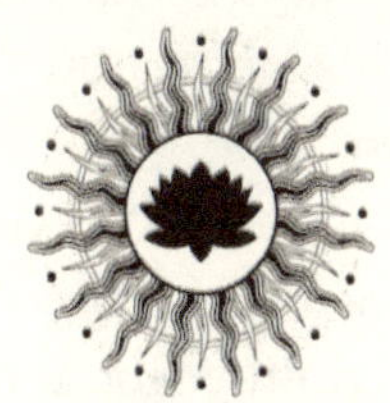

THE HAMMOCKS WERE MORE comfortable than they looked. When I emerged from the bowels of the ship the next morning, it was nearly midday, and the main deck bustled with activity. I found Luthri and the twins idling toward the bow, shirtless. The twins were doused in sweat, apparently taking a breather after intense activity, while Lu lay on his back, soaking in the sunlight with a serene expression on his face.

Did his wings bother him like that? Or did they not have any sensation? Could he still move them, or would they drag behind him if not tied up?

"Sleep well, darling?" Luthri asked, shooting me a grin as I approached. He laced his fingers together behind his head, which made the muscles in his upper arms stand out. Last time I saw his half-naked body, it hadn't felt appropriate to stare. Now, I savored the view unabashed.

"Very well," I answered, crouching by his side. "It's a miracle what a solid night's sleep plus a sponge bath, fresh clothes, and a *zanna* root can do. I feel like a new person."

"I believe it. You certainly smell like one."

Tsking, I reached out to flick Lu's forehead. He was too quick for me, thwarting my attack with the confidence of one who knew he had the upper hand. His fingers closed around my wrist as he scanned my face for signs of discontent. Was he checking to see if I'd changed my mind since last night? I wasn't about to dismiss that moment as a mistake—he had earned that much. A woman who wants to be taken seriously never goes back on her word.

"Did you eat?" he murmured, releasing my hand.

I made a face. "What was breakfast, more meat and crackers?"

"Hari caught us fish." Lu nodded toward the waterfolk male, who treated a length of rope in his lap nearby. "There might be some left. You should check the kitchen."

I went to straighten up and nearly tripped over an odd combination of soft and hard textures. Regaining my footing, I glared down to see the knee-high, sun-shy creature whose name I couldn't remember. He adjusted his bulky head wrap to hide a section of bright green scales from view.

"Merda!" I exclaimed. "Are you okay? For Valuen's sake, say something if you're going to stand right behind someone!"

Even Luthri stared, similarly puzzled by the little thing's sudden appearance. It waddled away, unbothered, to go do whatever it did on the ship. Stand behind other people, maybe.

Vyrain hopped to his feet and came to join Luthri and me. "We were thinking we'd do a run around the deck," he announced, jogging in place. "Want to join us?"

He inclined his head as I pointed to myself in question. My head shook quickly. "No, thanks. I've been on my feet enough the past couple of weeks to last me a lifetime. How you all still have energy for cardio is beyond me."

"Needed something to do." Vyrain shrugged.

Of all the activities that could be used to fill time, running was lowest on my list. That reminded me, though—I had meditating to do. I couldn't figure out the key to making magic back at the shrine, and after the swamp, I'd been too tired to focus past the basic *mana* exercises. But I was so close. Once whatever I was missing clicked, the rest would fall into place. Honestly, it should be easier without Cantal and his cryptic explanations.

"We could do another round of sparring now that Mar is here," Luthri suggested, sitting up. A slow-moving smirk made its way across his face. "Unless, of course, that would be too much for the lady's feeble stomach."

"Oh, you want to play that game?" It had been a while since I put my formal training to use, but from where I stood, it would be all too easy to tackle him to the deck. I remembered a few things—a couple of basic takedowns, chokes, arm bars. It was never the focus of my training—if a spy ended up in a fight, they'd made a serious error along the way—but I knew enough for basic self-defense. For all the good it did me in a land of magic.

"You up for it?" Vyrain appeared eager. Between him, his brother, and Luthri, he was closest to my size. Still had a good eighteen kilograms/forty pounds or so on me, but I used to roll with men his size and larger all the time back at the facility where I spent my first few years in America. Most of the time I was my usual self, too, though I practiced in other forms.

That made the initial takedown quite natural.

The fae were stronger and faster than humans thanks to their connection to and regular use of *mana*. Vyrain was a good sport about it, only reacting after we hit the deck. I let him roll underneath me so that I could take his back, locking my arms like a seatbelt over his chest. He gave a half-hearted yank, testing my hold, before tucking to try throwing me over his head. When that didn't work, he came back down on all fours, preparing to roll again.

The moment he paused, I transitioned into a rear naked choke, slinging my right arm around his neck and tucking my hand into the crook of my opposite arm's elbow. I squeezed to make my point, restricting the flow of blood to his brain for a second before releasing him. He threw himself forward to put space between us, performed a tight roll, and sprang upright.

We circled each other. Hohem had made his way over to watch, and Luthri stood now, observing us with an eager glint in his eye. My attention snapped back to my opponent as Vyrain barreled into my midsection, tackling me to the ground. My legs wrapped around his waist even as the breath was knocked from me. As he reached back to unlock my legs, I snatched his wrist, grasped his ankle, and bridged off my shoulders to send him toppling. In a blink, he was flat on his back, and I had the advantage, straddling his waist.

An exhilarated grin split my face. He barely resisted, letting me go through the motions without much of a challenge, but still. It was a thrill to put my limited talents to work again. Brought back memories of before everything went to shit.

"I'm next," Luthri interjected, eyes pinned on our compromising position.

"That's pretty cool," Vyrain admitted from under me, thoroughly at ease. A bout of that length wasn't even enough to steal his breath; the sheen to his skin was all from earlier.

"Yeah, well. Not very useful when everybody's got magic to throw around." I hopped off my companion and offered a hand to help him to his feet. It took most of my strength to counter his weight enough for him to stand. I could have laughed. Magic was the great equalizer here—all the more reason for me to figure out how to make the most of mine.

A shout rang out across the deck. Everyone looked up as one. There was no instant panic, no one rushing to defense positions or scrambling to look. Hohem, who was nearest the side of the ship, spotted the issue first, pointing out toward the water. A long, scaled neck protruded from the ocean's surface, glittering in the bright afternoon light. The rest of the beast's body was a rainbow of color underneath the water. It paddled alongside the ship as though it weren't large enough to crush the ship in half and swallow any of us whole.

The image had my body tensing in preparation for a brutal fight, a flurry of fear and adrenaline driving my heartbeat to quicken, but that intention petered out a moment later. It would be hopeless, I realized, even with all of us. We'd be crushed, or drown, or worse.

The waterfolk male, Hari, stripped down to bare skin before I could get myself together. He dashed for the side of the ship, family jewels swinging in the breeze, as hands came over my eyes. I batted them away, more to make a point than for the sake of enjoying the view.

"That's just unnecessary," Luthri muttered from behind me.

Caught in the throes of my fight-or-flight instinct, I asked the ship at large, "Shouldn't we… do something?"

No one else appeared to mind the monster's presence. In fact, Hari was swimming with it, weaving around and underneath the beast as it released a proud trumpeting call.

"No cause for concern," Gerda announced from behind us. For someone so large, she had a light step. "Sea beasts. We see those every so often in our line of work. They're curious but won't bother us unless we give them reason to. Think of them like the *lya* of the ocean."

The creature I was looking at more resembled a dragon/Loch Ness Monster hybrid than the docile cattle beasts that provided food and milk for much of the Kereti and Wysalar regions, but it wasn't a point worth arguing. Especially since the fae had no concept of dragons or the Loch Ness Monster.

As the instinct to fight faded, the cadence of my heart gradually steadied. Resting against the railing, I leaned forward to admire the beast's narrow snout and wide head framed by fierce frills, sleek neck studded with spines, and what I could make out of a lithe body distorted by waves. Its long front arms doubled as fins. Smaller back legs hugged its body as it swam, giving the illusion that they melted into the massive tail.

"Beautiful," I breathed, suitably awed.

"Indeed." Luthri's soft agreement came from somewhere behind me.

"Have you ever seen anything like this?" I swiveled around to face him. His gaze flicked to the view beyond us and softened as some distant memory played under the surface.

"Once before. When my family came to this continent many revolutions ago."

Nodding, I turned back to the water. One of these days I would have to ask him about his adventures before he tagged along with us. What parts of the fae realm had he seen? What kinds of stories did he have to tell? Surely they didn't all have to do with his "quest."

Well, we had plenty of time to have those conversations. I pulled myself away from the railing, intent on taking advantage of the free time and sparring partners while I had them.

"All right," I announced, hands rubbing together. "Where were we?"

Approximately an hour later, Luthri and I circled each other. I tried to look past his smile—which bordered on unhinged—to watch for signs of weakness. Fresh from a round with Hohem, he favored his left wrist, and his chest rose and fell rapidly. If I could get underneath him, I could use his weight against him. The best opportunity for that would be when he charged.

"Are we dancing, love?" Lu teased, the endearment making something flutter in my gut.

"I'm ready when you are," I told him. My hands were in front of me, ready to redirect his advance. I shifted my weight from side to side as I studied his shoulders, hips, and feet for a balance adjustment that would key me into his next move. The anticipation was intoxicating.

His shoulders pitched forward without warning. It was a reckless dive for my knees, easily thwarted by catching his torso and extending my legs in a sprawl. He twisted underneath me, more flexible than I had expected, wrapped his arms around my waist, and yanked. We fell together, his quick thinking earning him a faceful of armpit.

I smothered a laugh against his side before releasing him and sitting back on my heels.

"Not the most effective of takedowns," I remarked, "but points for effort."

Lu grinned at me, a familiar spark of mischief lighting up his features. "Maybe I just wanted to see you on your knees."

I met his taunt with one of my own. "If that's the case, all you had to do was ask."

Vyrain grumbled something about "flirting when lives were on the line being plain inconsiderate," but my focus remained on Luthri as the grin faded from his face. His jaw went slack, his chin bobbed. Mischief was replaced by thinly veiled hunger. Before the mood could shift too much in the wrong direction, I was on my feet and helping Lu to his.

"Shall we go again?" I asked brightly.

"Sure, but I won't go easy on you this time," he warned, shaking out both arms. His gaze smoldered with heat, but he got the message: not now.

I ducked my head to hide my smile and leaned into a hamstring stretch for good measure. "Wouldn't have it any other way," I told him. "Try to end up on top this time?"

Pulling a face, Luthri waited until I was upright before lunging. This time he skirted around my reach, much faster than before, and clamped his arms around me from behind. I thrashed for a moment and went limp. Luthri corrected his footing to accommodate my dead weight but was otherwise unaffected. Built like a brick wall, he revealed no weaknesses.

Luthri tittered. "Are you fighting me, or are we cuddling? I can't tell."

My blood heated. I reached back to slip my hand in between my back and his front in search of the bulge of tender flesh all males had between their legs. My fingers closed like a vise, eliciting a choked squeak from my victim. His hold loosened as he prepared to push away—I didn't hesitate. Shifting my body underneath his, I captured his waistband and yanked, rolling him over the curve of my pelvis. He hit the deck with a dull thud and muted hiss.

"Are we fighting, or are you taking a nap? I can't tell," I mocked. Luthri made a motion like blowing a kiss, and the next thing I knew, a powerful gust of wind put me on my ass.

"If underhanded tricks are on the table," he retorted with a wink.

We kept at it most of the afternoon, rotating partners and switching between hand-to-hand combat and magic practice. Luthri was a little rougher than the twins, but I appreciated that he didn't pull his punches to the point that they were love taps.

That wasn't all there was to appreciate about Lu. When the topic of my training with Cantal came up, he was eager to help me figure out the combination of making and changing magics. Regrettably, he wasn't the most articulate teacher.

"You're trying too hard," he exclaimed when I threw my hands up after the latest attempt.

"It's harder than it looks," I growled, collapsing in a heap on the deck. I grabbed for the nearest canteen and helped myself to a drink. Staying in motion was a good distraction from the swaying of the ship, but it wasn't a permanent solution. Good thing I'd skipped breakfast.

Lu settled beside me, stretching his arms over his head with a satisfied grunt. I followed the ripple of muscle out of the corner of my eye as he spoke. "If changing comes naturally to you, this shouldn't be that difficult. That means you're doing it wrong."

Looking to the sky for patience, I responded, "As helpful as that is to know, perhaps instead of telling me I'm doing it wrong, you'd like to tell me how to do it right?"

"It's like..." One clawed hand opened and closed as if trying to pluck the words from the ether. "When you hold your breath, you crave air. The sensation builds until you either breathe or fall unconscious. It's like that. When you take in *mana,* you can either use it or let it go. If you don't use it, you risk burnout—your body's way of resetting."

"And?"

"It should be like breathing. But instead of using your lungs, you're using your magic ability. Instead of air, you're taking in *mana* and putting out whatever you're trying to make." Luthri showed me his palm as he nurtured a small purple flame into existence. "The initial change is the hardest part. Well, that and returning it to a neutral state. Once you've changed *mana* into another form, it doesn't take much energy to control it."

My free hand flexed. *Would I also be able to make fire if I tried?* Well, best to focus on one thing at a time. The breathing analogy made sense... Maybe switching up my approach was all I needed to get a handle on this.

Hohem and Vyrain took a break from their drilling to join us. Luthri dropped his hand, and the little flame he'd kindled winked out.

"Don't stress if you can't get it," Vyrain said, crouching by my side as his brother slumped against the wall to catch his breath. "Certain kinds of magic come more naturally to certain people than others. If it were as easy as he's making it sound, we'd all be *shahim*."

"I'll get it." My hand curled into a fist. "I'm close. I can feel it."

"Keep at it," Lu encouraged. "It might help to raise the stakes. Drive yourself to physical exhaustion and then try it, or, I don't know, have someone choke you." The corner of his mouth twitched. "If you opt for the latter option, I happen to have some experience."

"We could tie you to the front of the ship," Hohem proposed.

"Or drag you behind it," Vyrain chimed in, raising his canteen to his mouth.

"Oh, gosh. Tempting, but I'll go at my own pace." I did take a moment to savor the image that popped into mind at Luthri's words: the two of us pressed together so close that our breaths mingled, his fingers locked loosely around my throat while his other hand got acquainted with lower parts of my body. It wasn't a terrible option. Especially next to getting keelhauled.

"Think we could bother someone for some food?" Vyrain wondered aloud.

His brother perked up at the suggestion. "I could eat," he agreed, looking around for signs of life from the crew. "It's almost suppertime anyway. Crazy how the time flew."

My stomach growled in accord, reminding me that it had been a while since I last ate. *Could I handle something light? A few crackers or a piece of fruit?*

"You didn't have breakfast." Lu phrased the statement like an accusation.

"Or lunch," I admitted. "But it's all right. I can afford to skip a few meals. Better that than be bent over the side of the ship for the rest of the evening."

His lips clamped together, holding back the suggestive comment that surely sprang to his mind as soon as the words were out of my mouth. I had to admit the same came to mine.

"Let's find something to eat," he said instead, getting to his feet and offering me a hand. When I accepted it, he drew me upright so quickly that my head spun. I steadied myself using his forearm, helping myself to a subtle grope since the opportunity presented itself.

The twins also stood, expressions eager and flushed with the evidence of an afternoon spent toiling away, and we made for the galley as a group in search of sustenance.

CHAPTER TWENTY

IN WHICH THE PARTY ENCOUNTERS LIFE ON THE ISLAND

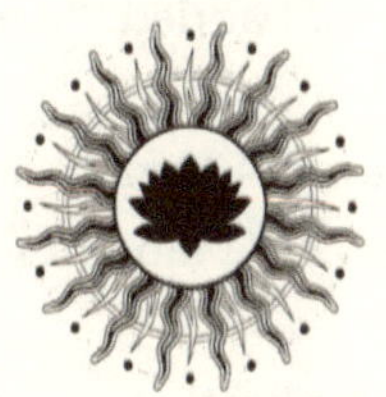

THE SHIP DOCKED on the far side of the island before the sun rose on the third day. After assembling our things, we paid Gerda the rest of our fee, shuffled down the rickety old gangway, and watched our transportation pull away from shore through bleary eyes. Despite the calm night, something itched under my skin, making it difficult to sit still. Whether it was residual *mana* from practicing the evening before or nerves, I couldn't tell.

"No going back now," Vyrain remarked, straightening the strap over his shoulder.

"No shit," his brother mumbled.

In the ensuing silence, I racked my brain for a suitable plan of attack. We couldn't avoid the islanders completely since we'd need to ask around to figure out what happened to Narille, but we could take the time to get a feel for the lay of the land. What I wouldn't give for a map of the island. It was small enough that we didn't have to worry about getting lost, but knowing where the city was and knowing how best to approach it were two different things.

The area we stood on now was only just above sea level, with a short drop to the ocean behind us as a steep hill ahead. A bird's-eye view would be helpful. Could Luthri fly at all, even for a short time? I opened my mouth to ask but thought better of it.

"Let's head that way." I pointed to a section of elevated, grassy terrain up ahead. On the edge of my vision, a shadow darted out of a bush to disappear behind a ridge of dirt. An animal? "Uh… It'll be a hike, but it should be a good vantage point. We can figure out a plan from there."

"Works for me." Lu eyed the hill, sizing it up.

Noting the twins' burdens, I added, "And we'll take turns with the bags. It's only fair."

"That's all right. I'm good." Vyrain looked to his brother, who inclined his head in agreement. "Yeah, these are nothing. You focus on the walk."

I might have taken the implication as an insult, but at this point in the journey, I didn't have the energy to care. We made our way uphill from the shore, fighting every step as a mix of mud and sand clung to our boots. The next thirty meters or so were covered in tall, stiff grass that sliced at exposed skin, leaving shallow wounds equivalent to a dozen paper cuts.

"No wonder this side of the island is less traveled," I groused as I drew in *mana* to harden the skin on my limbs and reinforce my clothing. My fae companions fared better, their rapid healing allowing them to better meet the plant's assault.

"Shall I carry you?" Luthri offered, coming to my side.

I waved him away, getting warm at the thought of being princess-carried up the hill while the others trudged behind us with our things. *That* was going a step too far. "I'm complaining for the sake of it, is all. There's nothing wrong with my feet."

We continued to climb, one foot in front of the other. Upon reaching the top of the hill, I paused to admire the view, shielding my eyes from the glare of first light. This was a corner of paradise, with sheer cliffs to one side and deep blue water stretching in all directions. All was calm but for the occasional wave crashing against rocks below. The ship chugged along in the distance, steam-powered wheels engaged once more now that they were no longer journeying through the open sea. It was a remarkable sight.

Something else caught my eye—a flutter of movement.

The hill beside ours was smaller, bare of vegetation, and riddled with lumps and holes that would have made hiking it a chore. Now that I examined it more closely, there was something off about it. For one thing, it was a shade too light—a dull tan compared to the gray-brown of the beach, like mud gone pallid in the sun. It was also... sparkling?

No, that wasn't it. The *holes* were sparkling—and not the holes themselves, but rather the familiar little figures emerging from within them. The shimmering was hundreds of iridescent wings reflecting the morning light as the *Aminkinya* horde took to the air in droves.

I said a reprehensible word.

It wasn't a hill at all, but an *Aminkinya* nest larger than I'd thought possible. The twins threw down our packs to face the ambush, and Luthri raised his fists, but we had no chance. There had to be hundreds of them, and we knew from personal experience how dangerous even a single *Aminkinya* could be. Our only hope was to talk our way out of this.

Praying the boys kept their mouths shut, I forced a nonthreatening smile to my face and held up my hands to show I was unarmed as the pixies swarmed us. They flew close, the threat of their sharp wings forcing us back-to-back into a tight circle.

"*Ailou vas tan'ga*?" one in front demanded, her wings making a threatening chirp.

There goes that idea. Cold sweat moistened my palms. What alternative was there to talking—an awkward game of charades? A monetary bribe to let us pass in one piece? Would we need to fight our way out after all? It would be a bloodbath on both sides.

"I'm sorry, I don't understand. Do you speak the *Ishameti* language?"

"*Kap Danagil,*" someone barked, inspiring a flurry of motion.

The one who had spoken first regarded our group anew, her pale green eyes sweeping over us. She held out an authoritative hand and ordered, "Stay. Do not move."

I released the breath I'd been holding and let my hands fall. From his spot beside me, Luthri edged closer and slipped his hand into mine, giving it a reassuring squeeze. His jaw was set, his gaze dark—no doubt seeing the situation the same as I did. I glanced back to catch Hohem's questioning look and shook my head once, hoping that was enough to convey that they should leave this to me.

Behind the defensive line of angry pixies, a new figure emerged from one of the nest's many tunnels. This one was larger than the rest, though still no taller than my knee, and several pieces of polished bronze armor protected her torso while accentuating her curves. She walked rather than flew, long, bright green braids swaying behind her.

This must be their clan head. I didn't dare speak for fear of saying the wrong thing.

The clan parted to make room for their leader, and Luthri released my hand. Probably for the best, all things considered. If we did end up having to fight our way out of this, it would help to have both hands free.

"You're not of the island," the pixie leader observed, looking us over one by one. Her gaze lingered on me and narrowed. "And you're… not of this world at all."

My blood chilled in my veins. *How did she know?*

Sensing my shock, Luthri took the lead. "Please pardon our intrusion on your lands," he implored, stepping forward. "We were passing through and didn't recognize these hills were inhabited. We don't want any trouble."

"That's a shame." The pixie leader grinned. "Been a long time since we saw any action."

Wings thrummed around her like screaming applause. One of the twins shifted against my back, and I fumbled for his sleeve to hold him back.

"Please," I said through gritted teeth, my grip tightening.

The pixie leader's wings beat once, twice, taking her to the air in an elegant hop. She landed in front of me, making Luthri's spine snap straight. I held my position as she reached out to graze the fingers of my free hand—the hand that bore Daethie's hair ring.

"A friend doesn't beg," she remarked before turning back to her clan. A snap of her fingers sent the crowd scattering back into their holes, with a handful remaining to keep an eye on their queen. She swiveled back around and continued speaking.

"They call me Danagil the Quick-Witted. I'm afraid our halls are not built for guests of your generous size, so I can't offer you much in terms of hospitality."

It took a few seconds for the meaning of her words to sink in. The flood of adrenaline seeping into my bloodstream hesitantly tapered off. Relaxing my hold on the person behind me, I let my guard drop enough to appear amiable.

"Oh, that's—" I cleared my throat. "That's quite all right. We don't want to intrude. We're headed to the city. Looking for the Kereti heiress, if you know about that."

"I do. Guessed as much." Danagil eyed our group. "Should have had them drop you on the other side of the island, though. There's a reason no one bothers us here."

That's because a bunch of killer pixies scared them off. But rather than say as much, I kept the conversation cordial. "We were hoping to avoid the islanders—er, the city residents, specifically. Get acquainted with the area before running into anyone."

"I would have done the same," the pixie agreed. "Have you a map?"

"Not of the island itself."

Danagil tilted her head. "Well. If you'd like to continue avoiding unwanted company, you can go through the Blights. It's a cave system on the northern side of the island. Largely left alone, although the occasional group ventures in. Your other option is through fishing territories and farmland, where you're sure to encounter people. My scouts tell me some never make it to the city, but I have nothing else to offer. The risk is up to you."

"What happens to them, to keep them from the city? Do you know?" Perhaps the *Aminkinya* saw something the shippers didn't, being neighbors in a sense.

"They give up," Danagil supplied, tone dripping with distaste. "Only they know why. Could be they are threatened or bested in combat. They live here, serving Rugaveld now."

Threatened? That could explain it. But what could someone hold over a stranger's head that would make them abandon everything they knew to be subservient? It sounded more and more like we wouldn't be able to get away with not meeting this Rugaveld.

Vyrain stepped forward. "Have you seen the lady Narille?" he inquired.

Danagil tapped her lips. "When she first arrived. No sign of her since. I suspect she's being held in Rugaveld's manor, if she's still alive. Equally possible that she was fed to the birds and what was left of her given to the ocean."

Our group collectively grimaced. I'd considered that she might be dead, to be sure, but the possibility at this stage in our search and rescue attempt was a miserable thought.

"That would be the final flourish on an otherwise sensational journey," Hohem grumbled, voicing what we were all thinking.

Before I could level an exasperated look his way, a hand tugged at mine.

"We appreciate the information." Luthri none-too-subtly drew me toward him. He stood at an angle, and his gaze darted back toward the *Aminkinya* nest as though they might reemerge to tear us apart after all. Nonetheless, I planted my feet.

"You can go on ahead," I told him. "I'll catch up."

The boys all stalled, looking to each other for cues. Lu wet his lips.

"We should figure out what we're doing as a group," he reasoned. Still, I hesitated. There was more Danagil could tell me. What did she know of the city? Navigating the cave system? Most importantly, how did she know what I was?

"Males," Danagil scoffed. Pinning Luthri with a glare, she made a shooing motion. "Let the women talk, boy. I swear on my grandmother's spirit that she'll return to you in one piece."

Once they were out of earshot, I turned back to the little chieftain.

"How did you know about me?" I asked in a low voice. "That I'm… not from here?"

My question didn't surprise her. "We have a sister clan in Miderrum, the capital of Wysalar. Some revolutions ago, they met a human mender there—one of the only humans seen this side of The Rift. The rest I could piece together. Such creatures, their original forms raw and untouched by *mana*, are not common here, you know."

I could wonder at how news traveled among the *Aminkinya* later. My immediate concern was that I might not be living far enough from the U.S. government's reach after all. "The humans, they haven't given them trouble? Wysalar, I mean?"

I hadn't heard of a war or other transfer of power, but I wouldn't put it past them. It wouldn't be the first time they'd taken something that didn't belong to them.

Danagil shook her head. "They are allies, last I heard. The human was staying with the *Ishameti* leading family. She seemed quite friendly with the younger prince."

"This human… Did she look like me?"

The fairy's eyes roved over my body, considering my question. "The same general shape, but different coloring. Pink skin, orange hair. Gold eyes. Someone you know?"

Avery. It had to be. A lump developed in my throat. It was a pleasant surprise to hear news of my old friend, but I couldn't think of a reason for her to cross The Rift except as collateral or a diplomat. Hopefully, she wasn't being used as a political tool these days.

"Maybe," I admitted. Flashing a quick smile, I glanced back to where my companions waited for me with narrowed eyes and tense bodies. I couldn't dally here. "Thank you for your help. We'd best be on our way now."

Danagil inclined her head. "May Fate smile on your journey. Should you meet a violent end, we shall hope they tell your tale in songs."

"Er… I hope there's no need, but thank you." Nodding my farewell, I pivoted to go.

"Oh, and a word of advice," the pixie chief called after me. "The islanders—don't take anything they give you."

"Huh?" I turned back to see a flash of lime green disappear into the ground. Left to ponder the meaning of her words, I joined the others, and we continued onward.

CHAPTER TWENTY-ONE

IN WHICH THE PARTY IS GIVEN THEIR GREATEST CHALLENGE YET

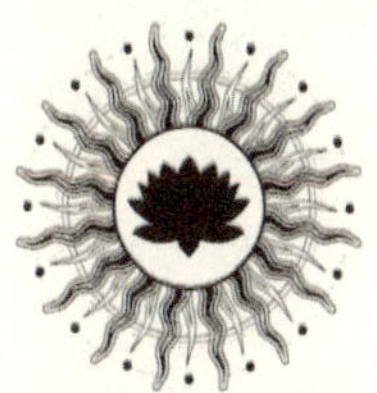

After much deliberation, we elected to go with the caves. Traversing some uneven ground didn't scare us, and Luthri was confident that he would be able to guide us through with his uncanny sense of direction.

The Blights were carved out of smooth, dark rock along the north side of the island where Danagil said they'd be. Remains of a volcanic eruption long past, perhaps, dipping toward the water in peaks and pits that went deeper than expected. Picking each step carefully, we made our way down the ridge to the largest of the holes, an entrance to the main cave system.

Vyrain led the group, pulling himself over the initial lip of the tunnel before pausing to face the darkness in front of us. "This is it, yeah? The 'Blights'?"

"It's not like there are any signs, but I would assume so," I answered, testing a handhold with my weight. Luthri reached down to help me the rest of the way.

The cavern was, well, cavernous—a pitch-black cave, as light didn't reach beyond the first few feet, filled with damp, stale air. I wandered ahead with a hand extended to feel for the walls. They were cool to the touch and almost sharp in places where the surface had chipped. Pale green light ignited behind me as one of the boys cultivated a handful of flames.

"Can't go that far," I reasoned, swiveling around to face them. "The island's only so big. With any luck, it's a straight shot to the city."

"I guess that leaves us with one question." Hohem grinned. "Are we feeling lucky?" The flames in his hand cast stripes of light and shadow over his features, lending a menacing air.

A perfectly timed breeze threaded through the cave, wrapping around our bodies and sending a warning shiver down my spine. The ominous shift sent me back a step. Rather than more stone, my heel met something soft. I didn't think, turning my nails to claws and whirling on a startled Vyrain, who stumbled back, arms flailing, to dodge my clumsy swipe.

Luthri was there, catching his arm to right him before he fell. "Let's not lose our minds," he remarked, giving Vyrain's shoulder a friendly pat. "A little darkness never hurt anyone."

"He surprised me, is all." Grateful that at least the low light would hide the evidence of my embarrassment, I paused to let Hohem move up and light the path ahead.

"You could've killed me!" Vyrain sputtered, pointing an accusatory finger.

"If that was enough to take you out, you would have deserved it." His brother gestured with the flame in his hand. "Let's get a move on, shall we? The sooner we get to the city, the sooner we'll be done with this whole thing."

Luthri lit a violet flame to further illuminate the space around us, and we made our way deeper into the chamber. Nothing stood out from the gloomy surroundings beyond our own echoing footsteps and the occasional whistle of wind or sound of dripping water that one might expect to encounter in a cave. An indistinct hiss and rustle had us all tensing at one point, but the light revealed a harmless sea snake slithering into a murky pool and out of sight.

"We could pass the time with a game?" Lu suggested.

I exhaled a puff of air. "I spy with my little eye something black."

"Hm?"

"It's nothing. What kind of game?"

"*Kapitiya*?" Vyrain spoke up.

The word was familiar, but I couldn't place it. "What's that?"

"A word association game," Hohem explained, speaking up to be heard over the escalating roar of waves hitting the shore that carried through the tunnel. "The first person provides a word, then the next person has to come up with a word that begins with the last syllable of the first word. The round ends when someone can't find a word within a few seconds, and they're disqualified. Keeps going until you have a winner."

At least one of us should stay alert. I shook my head, bowing out of the game, but the boys played a few rounds. The air took on a salty tang as we walked, and the roaring grew deafening as we passed an alcove with a large split overlooking the ocean. If one could look past the doom and gloom of the surroundings, the rock provided a pretty frame for the water. Already, I missed the sight of open space more than I cared to admit.

Wind howled through the cavern, making us all jump and causing the flames to flicker. If they hadn't been magically fueled, we would have been out of luck. The hair on my arms stood on end.

"Let's pick up the pace, please," I urged, my voice coming out thready. There was no reason to panic—not that I was panicking—but if we could get out of here soon, that would be great. Vyrain's wide eyes told me he agreed with the sentiment.

Luthri fell into step beside me, his arm grazing mine. His pretty flames did something to chase away the chill, but it was no comfort to know that my apprehension was so plain to see. Settling down in a cute cottage when this was all over sounded more appealing by the second. Maybe somewhere with a view of the ocean… That would be nice.

The path we were on opened into an even larger cavern, at which point the boys all poured a little more *mana* into their flames. The light revealed several passages through the rock. It would have been too easy to get turned around in here—you take the wrong path, twist your ankle in the dark, and *poof,* never heard from again. I pushed down the unwelcome thought.

"This way." Lu nodded toward one of the paths to our right. Even he was twitchy, eyes darting about, but it made sense for a fae species normally capable of flight to be uncomfortable underground. Hohem and Vyrain went on ahead, dodging stalagmites and chunks of rock along the way. I busied myself with studying the cracked walls when the ceiling groaned above us—a deep, echoing moan that carried like the cry of a grieving mother.

It was all the warning we had before it came crashing down.

Instinct had me diving for shelter in the space beside one of many large stones littering the ground. Someone yelled over the ruckus, but the words were unintelligible. I pressed myself into a gap, forced my head between my knees to protect soft parts from the barrage of stone, and drew in *mana* as quickly as I could to harden the rest. The collapse robbed me of all my senses in an instant. Blackness swallowed the light, dust stole my breath, and weight pounded against my limbs in rapid succession. *That'll leave a mark.*

My ears rang even after things stopped moving. I gave it another moment before trying to raise my head. Unyielding stone blocked me in on all sides, trapping me in place. The next inhale caused me to hack and wheeze, lungs convulsing to force out unclean air.

I have to get out.

Heart fluttering in my throat, I scrabbled for gaps in the rock. The ones near the top should be less weighed down, shouldn't they? I should focus my efforts upward.

As I got oriented and gathered the energy to dig myself out, another cough came from beyond the wall of stone, making me pause. Something shifted, a muffled clatter betraying movement. There was a beat of silence and a single croaked word: "Mar?"

Luthri. Relief made my next breath come a little easier.

"Mar?!" The clattering grew louder, insistent. Stone cracked against stone as it was hauled aside without care. A momentary pause had purple light flaring to life, illuminating the boundaries of my prison in hazy definition.

"Here," I tried to say, but only managed another cough. I cleared my throat and gave it another attempt, reaching out for the source of light. "Here! I'm here." My fingers found an edge. I braced myself and pushed, grunting with effort. No sooner had I created a noticeable gap then a hand invaded the space to seize my arm. The light winked out.

"I'm here," Luthri's voice gasped as hands tugged at me. "I have you."

Grinding and clacking followed as debris was pushed aside to better access my alcove. I went limp and let him drag me from the wreckage. Two dull orange pinpricks stared down at me, Lu's glowing eyes the only thing I could make out in the darkness. Before I could say anything, I was hauled into a warm lap. Hands roved my body as he muttered under his breath.

"I'm okay," I assured him, fumbling to catch his hands. "I'm not hurt. Where's the light?"

Those owl eyes went wide. "Light—yes, light."

A pale mauve glow started by my hip. It brightened gradually, casting dancing shadows against the walls as the hand that held it shook. His chest heaved, breaths coming short and fast. My fingers closed around his wrist to hold it steady. As I raised it higher, my gaze landed on his ravaged hands. The skin was torn, and at least two of his nails were broken, with another hanging by a thread.

"What—" I started to ask, but Luthri cut me off.

"I'm all right," he said quietly. "I just—I didn't—I'm sorry. I'm so sorry."

Bewildered, I shook my head. "You have nothing to be sorry for."

Luthri exhaled sharply, his shoulder jerking to indicate the mess around us. Squinting in the low light, I took in our situation. The nearest tunnel—the route we'd planned on taking—was blocked. It was unfortunate, to be sure, but we were alive.

"That's not your fault," I said, putting a hand on his. "We had no way of knowing this section of the cave was unstable. What about Vyrain and Hohem? Are they okay?"

Lu's throat bobbed as he swallowed. "Yes. On the other side, I think. I heard them shouting. We'll have to go around another way. I'll get us through."

"Okay." I ran my hand down his forearm, dusting off the grit from his skin. Movement caught my eye. His wings, though bound in place as usual, shuddered and jerked like they had a life of their own. My hand slowed. "Um…"

"Ahh, sorry." Lu's face turned as though trying to hide. "They do that sometimes. Could I—" He reached for me. I watched his hand hover in the space between us, trembling, before I brought mine to meet it, offering my permission.

He didn't hesitate, pulling me close and burying his face in my hair.

"I'm filthy," I protested, but didn't push him away. His free hand came around to cradle the back of my head. Soft breaths warmed the crook of my neck. At one point, I could have sworn I felt his lips. A slight shiver shook my frame, but I wrapped my arms around him, encouraging the contact. We sat like that for several minutes.

When gentle tugs at my scalp signaled that he'd begun to play with my hair, I pulled away. Was the cave warmer than it had been a minute ago? And so quiet. Instead of dwelling on that thought, I set myself to untangling our limbs while avoiding eye contact.

"We have to get moving," I said as I got to my feet. "They'll be concerned about us."

Luthri leapt into action, the light in his hand bobbing emphatically. He nodded toward the way we'd come. "Let's circle back and check out that other opening we passed. If there's solid ground underneath, we can use it as an exit and walk along the outside."

"Sounds like a plan," I agreed. As he turned to go, I slipped my hand into his. His eyebrows rose, but he tightened his hold and gave me a decisive nod. Without further ado, we marched down the cavern back in the direction of the entrance.

The lack of Hohem and Vyrain's commentary made every sound in the tunnel that much more significant. Along with our footsteps and the faint rush of the sea was a dull scraping I couldn't place. Other animals living out their lives in the shelter of this labyrinth? The fae realm had an eclectic mix of creatures not dissimilar to those found on Earth. One could reasonably expect there to be all kinds of insects, rodents, and other vermin lurking in the shadows. Perhaps even things like sand scorpions and spiders the size of dinner plates.

Why is my brain choosing now of all times to focus on the worst-case scenario?

One of Luthri's long, tufted ears twitched. He glanced back and did a double take. With no warning, his spine went rigid, and his grip tightened to the point of borderline pain.

"What's got you—" I began, starting to turn.

"Don't look!" Lu dropped my hand. Clawed fingers took a hold of my chin and directed my head forward. In the corner of my eye, Lu also centered his gaze on the terrain before us. Sweat beaded along his hairline and rolled downward, tracking faint lines in his dusty skin.

What in the world could have him so nervous? Could it be that I'd been on the right track with my unsettling line of thinking? Lowering my voice, I hissed, "What? What is it now?"

"Nightmares. Look forward or at me. Don't look back, and don't stop moving."

His uncharacteristically serious tone made my blood run cold, but the pieces hadn't yet fallen into place. I must have misheard him. "Nightmares? As in, bad dreams?"

"Not dreams—monsters that feed on fear. They have a paralyzing stare and produce chemical signals that multiply the terror in their prey. If you acknowledge them, they'll put you under and help themselves until you're nothing but an empty husk." Under his breath, he added, "Aeil's laudable tits. Could we be any more unlucky?"

The back of my neck prickled as a low *click-click-click* echoed along the walls. To make matters worse, another series of clicks responded to the first. We picked up the pace. The scraping and shuffling were impossible to ignore now. It was heavy. I couldn't hope for something as innocent as a cute little mouse, then. My imagination conjured an image of two massive praying mantises, their mandibles clacking excitedly at the prospect of lunch.

By some miracle, I kept my voice steady. "How many of them are there?"

"I don't know. Trust me, it doesn't matter."

"What if it does?"

"What?"

"Maybe it matters to me."

"What are you going to do, sass them to death?"

"Gosh, I didn't think of that. Do you think I could?"

Luthri rewarded my cheek with a spectacular grimace, somehow managed with only one side of his face. "If it were anyone else, I'd say no. But you might have a chance."

A gradual smile tugged at my lips. "I'm not sure if that's a compliment or an insult."

"Why can't it be both?"

The alcove wasn't far now. What would we do if that wasn't a serviceable way out? We could risk the ocean, so long as the drop wouldn't kill us. That assumed Luthri could swim—I'd learned my limits as far as carrying a full-grown man. The alternatives were running or fighting. As disadvantaged as I was not knowing anything about nightmares or the threat they posed, I had claws and teeth. At the least, I'd go down kicking.

We reached the gap in the rock. The way it jutted from the rest of the cave to overlook the sea was almost like a natural balcony. In any other situation, I would have marveled.

Luthri slipped into the space and crouched by the opening. Steadying himself with one raised arm, he poked his head out. "We're good," he announced, having to raise his voice to be heard over the crashing of the waves below. "It's not a short way down, but there's sand. Here, you go first." Sitting back on his haunches to make room, he reached for me.

I shuffled to the opening beside him, putting a hand on either side of the rock window for support. The distance to the ground—several meters of air—mocked me. I couldn't hear the creatures anymore, but I didn't dare glance behind. Time was of the essence, yet… I hesitated. It had been a long time since I was in a position like this. Ten years, in fact.

"All right." Lu interrupted my trip down memory lane. He'd noticed my uncertainty. "I'll go first, then I'll catch you."

He waited for my nod before throwing himself off the ledge, taking my breath with him. I craned my neck to see. Faster than I could track, he slid down the cliff face to the beach below, sending fragments of slate scattering. When he reached the bottom, he leapt off the wall with fluid proficiency to land on his feet.

He makes it look so effortless. I teetered in the gap, trying to shake off the fear that threatened to lock my limbs in place. Since when did heights make me nervous? This was nothing. Not at all like the drop into The Rift, and that, I managed fine. This should be easy.

A whisper of a breath behind me had my muscles tensing. *Did I imagine it?* Sheer willpower kept me from looking back, the effort making my neck hurt.

"Mar, come on!" Luthri encouraged, arms outstretched and ready.

Fuck. My heart thrashed inside my rib cage as I forced my feet forward. The clicks started up again, much closer than they were before. Maybe even within arm's reach.

Lu's voice carried on the wind. "Mar, it's them!" he called, cupping his hands over his mouth. "What you're feeling is their miasma—what they use to trap prey. They're amplifying your fear and turning it against you. Please, trust me. I swear to you, I will catch you."

What other option did I have?

Heartbeat screaming in my ears, I closed my eyes and jumped.

CHAPTER TWENTY-TWO

IN WHICH THE PARTY CONTEMPLATES A LIFE OF DOMESTICITY

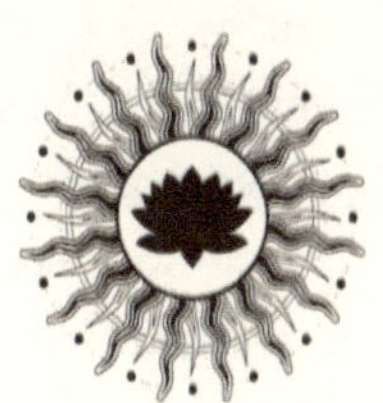

Despite my awkward trajectory, Luthri caught me. Of course, he did—what did I expect, that he'd pull his arms out from under me at the last minute, and I'd face-plant in the sand?

As it happened, we still ended up in the sand, as my weight sent Luthri to the ground. We landed in a tangle of limbs, both of us loosing a harsh puff of breath at the impact. I opened my eyes to his face inches from mine, lips curved in a sunny smile that did not seem appropriate given the situation. Seabirds called to each other in the background, a symphony of sound—laughing at us, or egging us on? Surely an outside observer would find this funny.

We don't have time for this.

His arms, locked around my waist, thwarted my initial attempt to stand. I was tempted to "accidentally" knee him in the groin. Luckily, a pointed glare got the message across without having to resort to more barbaric methods. He'd softened my landing, after all.

As I dusted sand and gravel from my knees, I took stock of our surroundings. The strip of beach went a few meters up the coast before giving way to rock formations half buried by the water. It would be a challenging walk, but better than being trapped in tight quarters with literal nightmares. Since venting my frustrations with a good, old-fashioned beat-down wasn't an option, I settled for making a face at the opening in the rock.

Luthri cast an amused look my way.

"That was an experience," I remarked as we started down the beach, avoiding the stretch that had been moistened by the surf. I kicked a clump of seaweed out of my path. My heart fluttered, but the crippling fear had faded. The memory of that feeling was too raw, eliciting a shiver. I could comfortably go the rest of my life without encountering a nightmare again.

"I should have figured something was strange earlier." Luthri's brows drew down. "The signs were there—we all felt it. I thought it was odd how our reactions were so visceral, but I thought… Well. There being nightmares living in the caves makes sense."

"Come across them often?" A gust of wind, trapped by the wall of rock, whipped at my hair. I yanked my hair tie from its place and shortened it with a fleeting burst of *mana*.

Lu's head tilted to one side, scrutinizing the new hairstyle as he answered me. "No, thank the Goddess. Only once before, a long time ago. I saw firsthand what they're capable of, and that was more than enough for me. It's not a pretty sight."

The shadow that crossed his face kept me from asking more questions, so I turned my attention to our progress. Lu helped me over a boulder slicked by algae and seawater. As he went to follow, his boot slipped into a tide pool, sending him careening forward.

"Steady," I chided, seizing his arm. "Do I have to tell you to be careful?"

Luthri flashed me a dazzling smile. "If I hurt myself, would you kiss it better?"

I would *not* reward such a cheap come-on by smiling back. "Glad to know that two near-death experiences in a row aren't enough to put a damper on your charming personality."

"Spoken like someone who hasn't nearly died before."

"I didn't say I haven't." I paused, hand on the rock I was climbing, to process. "But… wouldn't it be a good thing if I hadn't? Or does everyone live on the edge where you're from?"

"There's nothing like a near-death experience to remind you of the important things in life," Lu insisted.

"Mm-hm. And what would those be?"

Luthri's chest puffed as though he was prepared to give a sermon. "Well, the sensual pleasures, of course, food and comfort," he listed, counting on his fingers. "A good night's sleep. Quality company. Taking a moment to appreciate the beauty in the world around us and the endless possibilities each new day brings."

"Huh. That's… nice." I'd half expected him to pull out something like "gambling the night away and a tight pussy." Pulling myself over the next obstacle, I considered what the important things were to me. It wasn't like my life had flashed before my eyes or anything, but this journey had me thinking. If I didn't have to work anymore, what came next?

"Do you ever think of settling down?" I asked without thinking.

"Why?" Eyes widening, Luthri put a hand on his heart. "Mar… are you proposing?"

"I'm making conversation," I corrected him, shaking my head. For the sake of his ego, I could never admit it, but his presence helped chase away the lingering chill of the caves. Lately, I'd come to expect the teasing remarks and outrageous statements, and they almost put me at ease instead of riling me up. It was a good thing he and I had gotten separated together in the collapse… He made a nice distraction.

Luthri's expression grew serious as he contemplated my initial query. "To answer your question, it depends on your definition of 'settling down.' Do I want a life of domesticity, kissing my wife and broodlings goodbye every sunrise to go do the same thing I do every day? No. But there is something to be said for security. A stable nest, a steady income, and consistent companions."

He glanced my way on that last point. I met his gaze to show I was listening, and he averted his, busying himself with scaling the next arrangement of rocks.

"You're still young," I commented, parroting a phrase I must have heard a dozen times myself. "You have time to figure all that out. Priorities change too, you know."

"Oh, I'm not worried. And I'm well aware that priorities change."

A subtle smile graced his lips as some unknown thought came to mind.

Why did he put it that way? Have his priorities shifted recently? I almost asked about it, but movement in the distance took precedence over our conversation.

"Ho!" someone shouted. Luthri's head swiveled around. Two bulky figures stood on an outcropping, arms waving emphatically. There was no mistaking the twins.

A relieved grin split my face, and I waved back with a murmured, "Thank the Goddess."

We found our way to the far side of the cave system where Hohem and Vyrain waited for us and, after some cooperation from all parties to ascend the final incline, had a touching reunion. The boys clapped each other on the back as I doled out heartfelt hugs.

"We were going to circle back for you," Vyrain said as we pulled apart. "Luckily, Hohem remembered that hole in the wall we passed. I thought we'd have to dig through all that rock."

"Fate was smiling on us," Luthri agreed, patting Vyrain's shoulder.

"It's a blessing no one was hurt. That could have been bad." I hated to think of what might have happened if we'd been caught under the brunt of the collapse. None of us had a useful amount of mending magic, and the chances Luthri had a recipe for a salve that treated head trauma were slim.

Hohem wore a solemn expression. "Well, we were mostly untouched. As for Vyrain's face…" Gesturing to the visage in question, he continued, "I don't know if he'll ever recover. It's a good thing I've always been the handsome one, or the loss would be truly devastating."

"Stuff it," Vyrain responded with a scowl. "I wasn't even hit in the face."

"No?" His brother feigned innocence. Vyrain tackled him, resulting in a brief tussle.

"The nightmares didn't give you any trouble?" I asked as Hohem broke free from his brother's hold. The questioning look he gave me was enough of an answer. "Never mind."

No need to worry them if they hadn't.

"Shall we find a place to set up camp before going on to the city?" Luthri suggested, examining the horizon. "It's been an eventful day. Perhaps we could use time to recharge."

As much as the drive to finish this job nagged at me, I had some bruises to nurse. And a dull burn in the pit of my stomach reminded me that we hadn't yet had the chance to eat the late morning meal. "That's a good idea," I admitted. "We can take the evening. But we should figure out our angle of attack first thing in the morning."

After another hour, we found a quaint area nestled beside a rocky plateau that would shield us from the wind and keep us out of sight from anyone approaching from the city. Given that we now traveled parallel to the fields that Danagil had mentioned, I prepared for the inevitability of coming across a resident. Asking probing questions while keeping responses short would be best. That way, we could get a handle on the situation while giving away as little about us as possible. I didn't look forward to walking that line.

The twins set down their packs and began pulling out supplies—an extra water canteen, a waxed canvas tarp, pots and utensils, and prepared goods for a quick meal. While Luthri and Hohem put together a temporary shelter, Vyrain and I cleared the space and dug out a fire pit.

As the boys finished up, I announced, "I'll find us some kindling."

"I'll come with you," Luthri volunteered, nearly tripping over the half-empty pack on the ground in his haste to join me. An unexpected image sprang to mind—a young, overly eager puppy bounding after a treat. I disguised a laugh by coughing into the crook of my elbow.

"We might as well all look." Hohem surveyed the bare ground with doubt.

"We'll look over here," Vyrain offered, nodding in the direction of the field. Grass the height of a man's waist would make it difficult to find anything useful, but maybe the seeded crests on top of each frond were edible. Or perhaps the grass itself would burn well.

"By all means." Indicating that Luthri should follow, I turned toward the shoreline. The swish and crackle of boots in the grass signaled his compliance.

As he drew beside me, Lu had a knowing glint in his eye. He led with, "You didn't have the chance to express your thoughts on settling down."

I should have known he was eager for the chance to turn our conversation around on me. "It's not something I've given much thought to," I responded. "To be honest, I always figured I'd work until the day I die. For now, I'm content with the way things are."

"Well, that's no way to live." Luthri's lips pursed. "No grand aspirations? Never so much as entertained the daydream of an ideal world? With the payout from this job, you wouldn't need to work anymore, right? That puts a lot of opportunities in your lap."

When he put it that way, it did sound like a dream, but an idle lifestyle didn't suit me. *What would I do with disposable income?* I listed things aloud as they came to mind. "I might pick up a new hobby or two. Treat myself to some luxury goods, like nice soaps. Travel. Take the load off and drink myself silly once in a while."

Luthri cocked his head, studying me. His expression, blank as it was, revealed nothing, and I wasn't about to concern myself with groundless speculation.

"What, too boring for you?" I quipped. "What can I say, I'm a simple woman."

"I don't think you're simple at all," Lu denied with a shake of his head.

"Oh, yeah? Go ahead, then, tell me what I am." My tone took on a sharper edge. People like Luthri weren't the worst of the bunch—he came from a place of privilege and misplaced confidence rather than a desire to manipulate—but few things irked me more than people who asserted their influence over others when it wasn't their place to do so. Besides, he and I were so different. What opinion did someone like him hold about someone like me?

"I believed you when you said you hadn't given much thought to it. That doesn't make you simple. It's a matter of"—he searched for the right choice of words, mouth opening and closing before he settled on —"...figuring things out. Everyone goes through that phase."

"Well, when I 'figure things out,' you'll be the first to know."

"For me," he continued, ignoring my sarcastic remark, "Most things I needed were provided for me. A privilege, I know. But with those needs met, I had the chance to explore myself—dwell on my desires, my shortcomings, my goals. Even if some things weren't possible for me, I could travel the world, meet new people, and find companionship in other ways."

Aquele é criado a pão-de-ló—how nice to be born with a silver spoon in one's mouth. "Enlightening. I'll have to give the privilege thing a try sometime." I stooped to retrieve a piece of driftwood, but Luthri touched my shoulder, stopping me.

"Not that," he said, indicating the wood with a jerk of his chin. "It will be saturated with salt. We'll have better luck combing the grasses for withered fronds and dry undergrowth."

Releasing the stick, I straightened. "Won't that make a lot of smoke?"

"The smoke is manageable. It will burn cleaner, without irritating our lungs."

I nodded my assent and gestured for him to lead the way.

"Anyway," he spoke over one shoulder as he shifted onto the path lined with tall grass, "Everyone goes at their own pace. When you're young, it's all about making mistakes. You try a few things so that you know what works and what doesn't. You figure out where your talents lie and which of your dreams are achievable versus which are doomed to remain dreams."

Before Luthri established himself as a father figure in my book, I interrupted his monologue. "If I wanted a lecture, I would have asked for one. Can we get to the point, please?"

"Yes, the point. The point is…"

The next word faltered, and he paused, every muscle freezing in place. A blur of color later, a firm hand clasped over my mouth, and I was pulled to the ground alongside him. My first reaction was to fight, but logic argued that he had a good reason to tackle me—he'd proved trustworthy before. Nevertheless, relaxing into his hold didn't come naturally. I had to force my hands to unclench and moderate my breathing by counting the beats.

For several tense seconds, we huddled together on the path, barely hidden by greenery, the pounding of our heartbeats harmonizing. I held my breath, straining to hear whatever it was that had scared him.

Was it islanders approaching? Were the nightmares from the cave stalking us? Some other island terror hellbent on hunting down a living lunch?

After another beat, Luthri's hand softened against my lips and drew away. "Sorry about that." The whispered apology tickled the top of my head. "Thought I saw someone coming."

No retort came to me, so I dedicated my energy to recovery instead, resting a cheek against his chest as I caught my breath. It wasn't long before fingers tentatively raked through my shortened hair, making my scalp tingle in their wake.

"Did I mention how much I like your hair like this?" Luthri murmured. "I mean, I'm partial to long in general, but you pull it off. Could be the boyish figure."

I lifted my head enough to manage a glare. More to make a point than for practicality's sake, I sent a bolt of *mana* to return my hair to its original length. I'd go digging for another hair tie later. Underneath me, Luthri grunted his approval, and the fondling intensified.

"You had a point," I said into his chest. "Before we were interrupted."

"Hm? Oh, I don't remember… But I'm sure I'll recall soon. You'd be surprised at the level of introspection that can be achieved between another person's thighs."

I *was* straddling him, come to think of it. "Is that so? I'll have to take your word for it."

"You could give it a try sometime," he suggested. Tender strokes transitioned into a light massaging motion that melted away any residual exasperation. My eyelids grew heavy.

I shifted, threading my fingers together over his chest and resting my chin on the bridge they created so that I could look him in the eyes. "I've always found that there were more interesting things to do between another person's thighs than thinking. So maybe it's not for me."

Lu's head dropped back against the ground, and the rhythm of the massage slowed as he considered my response. From my position, I could admire the fluffy tufts adorning his ears, the artfully crafted gold piercings, the strong ridge of his brow, and the curve of his lips.

They looked so soft, his lips. Full and inviting. A shade darker than the rest of his skin, and touched by a hint of pink that bordered on berry when combined with his coloring.

If I was going to act on my attraction to him at any point, the timing wouldn't get much better than now. We had a moment to ourselves for once, with no one else around to see. Emboldened, I reached for him. His gaze sharpened with the movement, and his breath caught as my fingers threaded into the knot of hair at his nape. I used my hold to draw him to me, propping myself up at the same moment to capture his lips.

CHAPTER TWENTY-THREE

IN WHICH THE FLAMES OF PASSION BEGIN TO SMOLDER

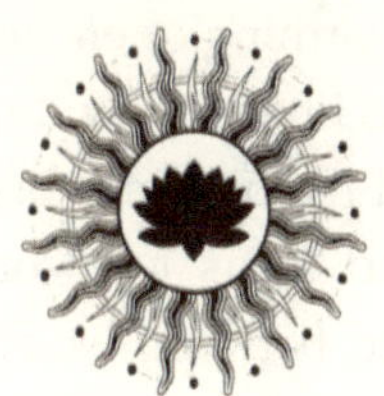

LUTHRI FROZE UNDERNEATH ME—UNABLE to believe how lucky he was, perhaps—but recovered quickly. The muscles of his abdomen flexed between my thighs as he bolted upright, his hand coming around my back to keep me from retreating. My hands shot to his shoulders, gripping the firm flesh around his neck for support.

Settled into the new position, he sought my lips again. Our restraint was admirable given the circumstances. Rather than open my mouth for him immediately, I tested the give of his bottom lip with light nibbles. His breath quickened, but he allowed the exploration, not unlike how a wildlife specialist would deal with a skittish animal. After a few moments, his tongue grazed the seam of my mouth—a gentle request. I let my lips part for him.

Like a flip was switched, the tempo between us picked up, and his tongue ravaged me. It was firmer than a human's and slightly pointed. I shouldn't have been surprised at the way it moved, the skill with which he coaxed little gasps from my throat. How many people had he practiced this on to perfect his technique? A brief pang of insecurity hit, smothered quickly by desire and a commitment to not let the past get in the way of the present.

My hands moved to either side of his face, and I lost myself in him—meeting every swirl and prod of his tongue with one of my own, interspersing explorative licks with playful nips and a suckling of that full bottom lip I was quickly becoming obsessed with. A low moan tore from his throat, a heady, purely masculine sound. His hands roamed my upper body, leaving a scorching path under my clothes.

I wrapped my arm around his neck as he helped himself to two handfuls of my backside, nearly lifting me off him in a heated frenzy. My teeth caught his lip—a warning or encouragement, I wasn't sure. It did nothing to deter him; his fingers only dug in further.

"You're incorrigible," I breathed into his mouth, too distracted by the way he gripped me to focus on words. He answered with a subdued growl that vibrated between us, zipping through my core to settle between my legs in an addictive tingle that had me squirming to seek more. I had to disconnect from him before I dissolved into a creature of depravity.

Lowering my head to the crook of his neck, I sucked in air, basking in the sweet and spicy scent of his heated skin. He pressed kisses to the side of my face, my temple, the crown of my head.

"Goddess, Mar," he groaned into my hair. "You have no idea how hard it is to hold back. You're so beautiful, so vibrant, and the things I want to do to you... They're *ugly*."

My breath caught. Butterflies took flight in the pit of my stomach, a sensation a man hadn't made me feel in a long, long time. "Yeah? Like what?" I whispered.

Luthri huffed a laugh against my head. After a beat of hesitation, his hands sought out the grooves of my hips and came to rest there. Then, he gave me what I was looking for.

"I want to spend the afternoon tracing those little round ears of yours with my tongue," he said hoarsely, his breath fanning the side of my face. "I want to worship every bit of you with my hands and mouth. Map every inch of your skin with my touch, taste each finger and toe."

His hips bucked to accentuate his next words. "I want to bend you over and bury myself in deep, savor the feeling of your cunt clenching around my cock, and stay inside you until the dawn... Then do it again the next day. I want to fuck you so hard that I leave marks inside and out, marks that make it so you'll never forget me."

His fingers dug into my love handles. I almost missed what he said next, as his voice lowered until it could barely be heard over the breeze that investigated the grass around us.

"I've never wanted someone this much. It hurts, Mar."

The emotion in his confession wrapped around my heart and squeezed. In the end, we were all beasts at the whim of our instincts, but I understood Luthri a little better every day. Even the best of us needed reassurance sometimes.

"I want you too," I murmured, running my fingers through the ends of his hair as I met his hopeful gaze. "And you don't scare me."

His lips parted, but I stopped him with a finger. We had all the time in the world for talking. "Tell me later," I urged him, dragging one hand down the stretch of chest that peeked out from his low neckline. "Now's not the time."

The starstruck expression on his face didn't suit the situation. Friends with a little something more, that's all we agreed on. If I hadn't already been committed to this, the unrestrained adoration there might have intimidated me, but I couldn't think about that.

Luthri's hold shifted, and we rolled so that I was comfortably nestled in the divot of the path with him a comforting weight atop me. His hands roamed my body reverently before he picked up where we left off, ducking down to kiss me again. I met his fervor, fisting a handful of his shirt for better leverage, and we engaged in a sensual back-and-forth dance.

With his heat at my front and the cool ground at my back, I was at peace. Lu, to his credit, knew how to read a partner well. He didn't rush or fumble, and there was no battling for dominance or awkward clashing of teeth—we were two people in perfect sync, enjoying each other without pressure. And God, was that doing it for me. Even the undercurrent of dirt and male sweat perfuming the air was intoxicating. Why hadn't we done this earlier?

When one of his hands nudged my breast, it sparked a deeper need. I expressed my approval with a breathy "mm-hmm" against his lips. Grasping for my shirt, I yanked the fabric from where it was tucked into my belt to provide access. It wasn't that I intended to go all the way right here and now… But if it happened, I wouldn't be mad.

Luthri ended the kiss and reared back, giving us both a moment to catch our breath. We gulped fresh air in tandem. As his eyes raked down my relaxed body, he took the opportunity to slide one hand under the hem of my shirt. His fingers skimmed one nipple, the touch accompanied by the lightest scratch of his pointed nails, and it was as though something within me went molten, rushing to heat my core. My back arched on instinct.

"No undergarments?" Luthri murmured in a tone between awed and playful. His head ducked to greet my collarbone with a trail of kisses ending in a light dusting of his lips.

"Inconvenient and uncomfortable," I retorted, squirming underneath him. I'd never been so upset to be wearing clothing before. "Are you complaining?"

"Not at all. In fact, I approve."

The pad of his finger teased my nipple. It took an immense amount of self-control to not press myself into his touch, demanding more. Keen on exploring his body in return, I shifted to put my hands between us. His dark and downy wings beckoned, and I longed to find out if they were as soft as they looked, but I didn't dare reach for those first. Instead, my hand journeyed downward to seek the junction of his thighs.

The combination of our position and height difference put his bulge beyond reach, and I had to settle for pawing at the abdominal muscles I'd admired so often during our travels. As my hand made its way into his shirt, appreciating the subtle curves of his torso, Luthri lowered his head once more to my neck. His lips grazed my skin.

Any coherent thoughts scattered when he suckled the flesh there and plucked my nipple in the same movement. A hot flush spread through my chest, turning into a smothered whimper somewhere along the way. I closed my eyes and tilted my head back, surrendering myself to his attention. Though his mouth remained occupied with my neck, his hand abandoned my breast to seek out the waistband of my pants. I rolled my hips in invitation.

His fingers separated fabric and skin without delay. He took his time traversing what lay beneath, hand gliding over my pubic mound with lazy, assured strokes of his thumb. So close, but not where I needed him. The suspense had me trembling in his grip. He brushed against my clit and paused at my sharp inhale.

"Aha!" A self-satisfied smirk was audible in that one word. Having discovered what he was looking for, he continued his tactile exploration, hand dipping between my legs. Fingers tested my wetness, slipping inside before retreating to paint my own moisture across my clit. The tight, deliberate circles he drew around that small but mighty cluster of nerves had my body tightening like a bowstring on the edge of snapping.

What do you know—most fae women must have the same parts. He certainly knew his way around them. But I couldn't be satisfied letting him do all the work.

I squeezed my legs, trapping his hand where it was. His head lifted, but before he could ask what was wrong, I'd trapped his arm, hooked a leg, and bridged against the ground to flip us. He pulled me with him, and our roles reversed so that his back was against the ground. Straddling him, I paused to let him work his hand from my pants. He and I were similarly disheveled, hair a tangled mess and lips bruised by passion. I took some pride in that, my cheeks aching from the resulting grin.

Once he'd retrieved the wayward appendage, I wasted no time. My lips burned a determined path down the side of his neck. He went pliant underneath me, his breathing becoming stifled. Oh, but he was perfect—skilled and obedient, passionate and responsive. Excitement made me giddy as possibilities came to mind, each more tantalizing than the last.

"We're going to have so much fun, you and I," I whispered against the column of his throat, reveling in the little shiver my words evoked. My hips made a slow, intimate circle.

"I can—hah…"

His response faded into indiscernible sounds as I placed open-mouthed kisses along the expanse of golden-brown skin dusted by dark hair that was bared to me. His shirt was loose enough that I could shift it to one side, uncovering a dark-brown nipple. I met it eagerly with tongue and teeth. It wasn't long before my ministrations tore needy sounds from the depth of his chest, the sort of sounds that would haunt my nights in all the best ways.

I played with his waistband at the same time, but with the way things were, I couldn't go any farther. Impatient, I released his nipple from my mouth and shuffled down to his thighs to give myself better access. Nimble fingers made quick work of the ties on his pants, and I was reaching in—but though his cock jerked in excitement through the fabric, his hands came up to stop me. Cool air filled the space between us, refreshing and dampening all at once.

"Not here. Not now." His words came out strangled.

Confusion shot through me. "What? Why not?"

Had I moved too fast? No, he had been just as eager. Our position? I backed off his legs in case his bones were delicate. Was it the location? Perhaps he was used to seducing women in a place with four walls and a comfortable bed. Perhaps that had become his preference. He could be a romantic when he wanted to, after all, from what little I'd seen of him in action.

"There's no one else around," Luthri groaned, running a hand over his face and peeking from between his fingers. "I need a witness; otherwise, no one will believe me."

It took a moment for his meaning to sink in. Torn between laughing and wringing his neck, I settled for a long sigh even as the corner of my mouth twitched. "You won't be able to keep that ass scar from me forever," I warned him before pulling away.

He gave me a suspicious look. "How did you know about that?"

"You told me, seu bobo."

The amount of patience I could summon for this man was truly inspirational. Really, I ought to be canonized.

Adjusting my clothing, I scanned the immediate area. The field spread out around us as far as the eye could see. Now that I was standing, I could also make out the two figures not fifty meters from our position. One of the twins raised a hand to wave, a quizzical look on his face. Probably because we were fooling around instead of gathering kindling like we were supposed to be doing. Shame brought an uncomfortable warmth to my cheeks.

"Was it one of the twins you saw earlier?" I asked as Luthri came to stand next to me, tucking in his shirt. His sheepish expression was answer enough.

"Well, I hate to make assumptions where safety is concerned," he replied.

I flicked my fingers at him in a rude gesture I'd picked up from Daethie before making an attempt to smooth my hair. With any luck, it would be believable that I'd lost my hair tie to the wind. "Let's get going. They'll be wondering what we were doing all this time if we go back with a handful of twigs."

We made quick work of combing through the grass for usable tinder, but by the time we returned to the campsite, Hohem and Vyrain were waiting for us inside the shelter. It wasn't pretty—a borderline serviceable lean-to more than a traveler's haven—but it would do. The tarp would shield us from the afternoon sun and help us blend in with the rock face.

Luthri set up the fire, and we were dining on a hot meal in no time.

"We'll have to talk to the natives at some point, won't we?" Hohem asked between bites.

Putting down my empty bowl, I directed my energy back to business. "I was considering that. We can't avoid them forever. If anyone knows what happened to Narille, it would be Rugaveld, so... I suppose we ought to make for the city tomorrow."

"We'll keep our guard up," Luthri murmured. We all nodded our agreement.

"Stay cordial, but don't volunteer information you don't need to." I watched the flames dance in the fire pit as I racked my brain for anything relevant to add. "Stay close to each other. Oh, and don't take anything they offer us. Danagil said something about that."

Vyrain's brow furrowed. "Who?"

"The pixie chieftain?"

"Ah."

I accidentally caught Lu's gaze from across the fire. We looked away at the same time. If I was the type to blush, I'd be burning up, but that would be asking for probing questions. Even though we didn't do anything wrong, I preferred to keep our little tryst between us. Hopefully Luthri felt the same. For all that he joked about needing an audience, I was confident that he would follow my lead.

"Well." Hohem set his dish aside with a resounding clatter. "This Rugaveld may be used to having his way, but I think he'll find we're a force to be reckoned with."

"That he will," I agreed, my face splitting in a wide grin. "We won't back down without a fight. This job is going to be what puts us in songs. When it's all over, we'll retire some place beautiful, where we can live out the rest of our lives fat and happy."

"Maybe he's paying people off?" Vyrain mused, stroking his chin. "If that's the case… Most people would be doing this for the money, right? If he were to say, 'I'll give you a million *vodt* to drop the mission and go home'… Why would we say no?"

"Where would the mayor of a small island nation get a million *vodt* to throw at every group that comes looking for the missing lady?" Hohem shook his head. "No. I'm inclined to believe there's something much darker going on here."

Vyrain looked to me for support, but I could only shrug.

"It's all conjecture at this point. We'll have to wait and see."

Grudging nods all around ended that dialogue. After taking care of the fire, we passed the afternoon with conversation and games, including *thracks* with pebbles that were too flat to effectively roll. As the sky darkened, we set up our bedrolls—regrettably, not nearly as nice as the ones we lost to the swamp—side by side under the tarp.

Before all daylight was lost, I dug up a hair tie and set to combing out and braiding my tangled mane. Luthri sidled up to where I sat cross-legged on my mat and observed the process, his eyes markedly bright in the light of the waning sun.

It wouldn't be overreacting to set a few boundaries now, would it? Starting with ensuring that I wasn't panting after him like a groupie. I tied off the braid with a flourish before giving him my attention. "Did you need something?"

"No, no." He absently drew patterns in the dirt between our mats. His nails, while still hard and black, had short, rounded tips now—when had he changed them?

"All right." I waited another moment in case he wanted to say something. Vyrain and Hohem were in earshot, but we were all adults. If he wanted to address what happened in the field, I was more than willing to have that discussion. If he was satisfied leaving things the way they were, that was fine too. It wasn't something worth dwelling on.

His lips parted, and I had an inkling some great confession was to follow. But in the end, all he said was, "Good night," before burrowing into his covers.

I could pin him down and force the words out whenever I wanted; that knowledge made it easy to let the matter be. I returned the well-wishes, fluffed the clothing bundle I was using for a pillow, and lay down to join him.

CHAPTER TWENTY-FOUR

IN WHICH THE PARTY AT LAST ARRIVES AT THE ISLAND CITY

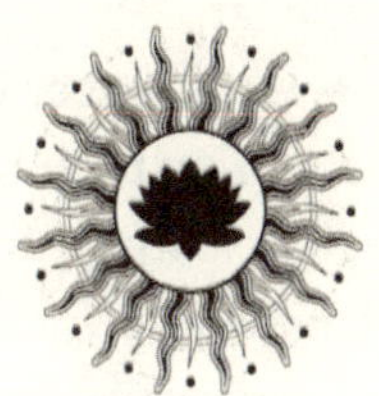

"YOU TWO LOOK COMFORTABLE."

Roused by the random remark, I opened my eyes to see Hohem standing over me, grinning around a *zanna* root. Weight across my chest prevented me from sitting up. I turned my head and was met by Luthri nestled against my side. Face slack, hair mussed, and a hint of drool at the corner of his mouth, he clung to me in sleep as though I was his personal body pillow.

"Lovely," I muttered under my breath as I shifted his arm back into his bubble. Once freed, I retrieved a *zanna* root from our luggage and chewed as I re-braided my hair.

Hohem spat his root onto the ground and moved to begin disassembling our shelter, not appearing too bothered by the fact that Luthri was passed out inside.

"Get a move on. We haven't got all day," he remarked.

"Sun's barely up!" I protested, glancing at the pale orange sky. "Where's Vyrain?"

"Taking a shit."

No sooner had he gotten the answer out than the man returned, plodding up the path from the direction of the beach. He mumbled a greeting to me before helping Hohem pack our things. They took apart the lean-to together, leaving Lu exposed in his cozy nest of blankets. I joined them to retrieve the bedding. When I got to Luthri's mat, I nudged him with one foot.

He startled awake with a disgruntled "Hmph?!"

"We're packing up. Sai do mêi—out of the way."

"Couldn't you have been a little gentler?" Lu grumbled as he bundled his sleeping mat.

"I could have," I tossed over my shoulder, stuffing the items I'd amassed into our pack after the tarp. While I was at it, I rooted around for the food supplies. As we were all eager to get back on the road, we had a quick breakfast of dehydrated fruit, nuts, and the last of the bread from the ship's cook before loading up and setting out.

The fields of high grass gave way to neat sections of manufactured wetlands, for lack of a better term, as we drew closer to the island capital. Borders were carefully laid out in parallel squares like a draughts board. The water in these sections appeared perhaps knee height and clean, with lush, green plant matter peeking above the surface.

It was there that we encountered our first residents of Munarzed: a small group of farmers in wide-brimmed hats combing through the waterlogged rows in near-perfect sync to clear weeds and pests. My lips pressed into a thin line. They hadn't noticed us yet, but they would—the widest path through the water-grown crops, which could be called a road if one were feeling generous, passed by the sections where they worked.

Sure enough, a head raised, then another. The first worker straightened up, leaning against their tool as we approached. The second mirrored the movement a beat later. Both their faces broke out in welcoming smiles at the same time, giving them identical expressions. Maybe they were related? The smiles seemed genuine, but something about it made me itch.

The first worker, a short, stout man with scruffy facial hair and earlobes that reached his shoulders, raised a hand in greeting. "Ho!" he exclaimed. "Welcome to Munarzed!"

I met his eyes, gave a friendly nod and little wave in return, and kept walking. The boys followed my lead. In the distance, the other workers had paused to observe our exchange. Similarly, their faces bore wide, disarming smiles, though they didn't approach. When we made no effort to speak to them, they returned to their work one by one.

"That wasn't bad at all," Vyrain remarked once we were out of earshot. "I expected… I'm not sure what I expected, actually. But something really weird."

"Mm." I looked to Luthri. He appeared thoughtful, still pondering the interaction. I had yet to relax, but I hoped this was a sign that they wouldn't give us any trouble.

"I can't say I found anything concerning about their attitude." Hohem scratched the back of his head. "All the *Ishameti* people I've encountered are just as friendly. Most of Kereti too. I guess we'll see what they mean about acting strange."

"Don't let your guard down," I reminded him, glancing behind to make sure we weren't followed. "Things will change when we're in the city. For better or worse."

When we reached the city boundary, I was inclined to think things had changed for the better. The capital appeared a paradise by every definition of the word.

To begin, there was no checkpoint, not even so much as an *Epitgig* with an abacus. The boundary was defined by no fence or wall, only a transition from nature's glory to man-made. Streets went from trampled dirt to neat cobblestones lined with *mana* lamps and decorative trees whose green- and peach-toned leaves were taking on the rich orange tint of early autumn. Along the main road were brand-new buildings of vibrant red brick and tan stone with glass windows and slate roofs, planters providing splashes of flowers and climbing plants to enrich the exteriors.

Cute wood cottages with dainty, carefully cultivated gardens sat beyond the main road, spaced from one another so that each resident had their own property. One side of the city had been built beside farmland—what little of it there was to be had on the island—while the other side spread onto cliffs overlooking the ocean. Chalk it up to timing, but sunlight caught the buildings at an angle that made the entire space glow.

The area bustled with activity, much like Solfarin, the coastal city. But where Solfarin was life and heart, all the passion, the unexpected, and the rough edges that came with it, things here were… different. Those heading in the same direction kept to one side of the street, avoiding the awkward dance to keep from bumping into someone else. Everyone moved with intention. Motions appeared well-practiced. Muted conversation drifted in between the shuffling of feet, goods exchanging hands, and the occasional bray or bark of a working animal.

I couldn't place what was wrong, but whatever it was made my skin prickle.

As we ventured farther inside, residents began to take note of our presence. The mood shifted. People paused in waves to look up, smile, and raise a hand in greeting. We didn't make it ten meters past the entrance before one of the passersby, a short, older woman slathered in freckles, split off to approach us—smiling widely, of course.

"Hi!" she began, waving with both hands as she scrutinized our party. "Welcome to Munarzed. What brings you to our little island?"

"Thank you. We're, ah…" I paused. Could I ask after Narille without giving it away that we were looking for her? If that was all anyone came for these days, they already knew why we were here. Subterfuge wouldn't get us the answers we needed. With that in mind, I told her, "We're looking for Narille, the Kereti heiress."

"That's great!"

I jumped at the voice coming from behind us. Luthri slid closer, coming to stand half in between me and the pale young man with a head of curly, off-white hair who had spoken.

"We've had so many visitors since the Lady Narille chose to move here," the man continued, nodding to himself. "It's a dream come true! Have you decided where you'll stay?"

One of the twins made a nervous sound in his throat. I whipped around to see the lady tugging at Vyrain's hand, beaming. "You must come by my home for a drink and some sweets," she cajoled. "I'd be honored to give you a taste of Munarzed hospitality!"

Hohem grasped his brother's shoulder. "Thank you, but we've got a schedule to stick to." He shot me a meaningful look.

"Ah, that's right." I put on a rueful expression. "We're already behind schedule. Maybe if there's time before we leave. If you could tell us where we can find Miss Kereti, though, that would speed things up—we'd be much obliged!"

A hand plucked at my belt. I stiffened, looking down to see… a toddler, its cherubic face a veritable sunbeam of joy. Well, it wasn't the strangest thing I'd seen in the fae realm.

"You've got to visit Rugaveld," it said before transitioning the hand it had used to get my attention to its mouth, resulting in a heavy speech impediment. "He'w be abuw to hewp."

"You're sure you haven't a moment to spare?" The woman pouted. "I haven't gotten to entertain guests in far too long. I have a recipe for suncakes that will change your lives!"

Luthri swooped in, clasping the lady's hand in his. "Your kindness is a blessing," he murmured, brushing his lips against the back of her hand, "and we'll never forget it. But alas, we must be leaving. If you are inclined to show the next group of travelers this hospitality in our stead, your deity will surely reward your efforts."

"Oh, it's no bother!" She waved off his words, putting her free hand to her ruddy cheek. "It would be entirely my pleasure to have you. Should Rugaveld not have what you need, do return. We will be happy to help in any way we can."

Lu gave her a sad smile. "So kind." He patted her hand and released it, returning to my side. "Would you do us one more kindness and point us toward this Rugaveld?"

"Fowwow da woad." The toddler popped its hand from its mouth to give us clearer directions. "The big house all the way at the end. You can't miss it."

"Safe travels," the young man chimed in. "Hope to see you again soon!"

Behind him, a picture-perfect *Alfen* couple had also split from the traffic to make for us, arms spread wide in welcome. If we didn't get moving soon, we'd be surrounded.

"Thank you, thank you, we appreciate it!" I dodged bodies between us and the road, creating an opening for the boys to come after me. Enthusiastic farewells trailed after us as we speed-walked down the street, eager to put space between us and the villagers.

When I was satisfied with the distance—and had checked behind us to be sure we weren't followed—I asked the others under my breath, "Thoughts?"

"I'd believe they were threatened or blackmailed," Vyrain offered, shaken from his near-kidnapping. "They were kind, yes, but a little pushy. That, to me, says ulterior motive."

"Could have been under the influence of something," Hohem suggested. "A city like this probably gets all their drinking water from the same place. If you had access, you could tamper as you liked. Put something in it to keep them all agreeable."

Luthri made a thoughtful sound. "Hmm. There's no plant I can think of that could induce a pleasant mood and heavy suggestibility without sluggishness and brain fog. And anything that comes close would need to be administered regularly, or you face nasty withdrawal."

"What would be your guess?" I challenged Luthri.

His pace slowed as he considered. "Brainwashing? This Rugaveld may very well be an outcast with a slick tongue who got lucky. If not that, then hypnosis of some kind?"

I nodded. All possibilities that had occurred to me as well. The only other one—and this was scraping the bottom of the barrel—was robots, but they didn't have that level of technology here. And anyway, where would the people go if they'd been replaced by robots?

We maintained polite expressions but did not linger as a group of near-identical knee-high fae waddled past, all chattering excitedly and jumping over themselves to say hello. While humanoid, their backs bore ovular plated shells like turtles. Their skin varied in thickness and came in various shades of green scales, and they had flat beaks for mouths.

Something about the scale pattern tugged at my memory, but it was there and gone.

In any case, I was inclined to believe this went beyond a cult. Sweet-talking alone didn't turn a population this large into obedient sheep, and they didn't strike me as the religious type. What else brought on that level of fanaticism? Rugaveld threatening them into submission wasn't out of the question. We should have explored the island more. Perhaps there was a hidden prison in that network of caves where family members were tortured to keep the rest in line.

"So, how are we approaching Rugaveld?" Hohem inquired. "It's got to be a trap, right?"

"It has to be," I agreed, nodding. "Let's see what we're dealing with first. If the building is secure, we'll poke around for another entrance. Maybe we can—"

Vyrain released an emphatic groan, interrupting my blossoming plan. "I get that we didn't know what the situation would be, but we've been sneaking around for no reason, Mar, and it's starting to get ridiculous. Unless they've got a dozen brainwashed *shahim* on the rooftops waiting to surprise us, I think we can handle this guy. Maybe it's time to try the front door?"

Sucking my teeth, I considered his proposition. I was loath to take the direct route; it wasn't the way I learned to do things. Being unprepared was an embarrassment at best and, at worst, death. The risk wasn't worth it. I preferred to know everything I could about a situation before going in, even if that meant it might take longer or be a little more work.

"We could split up," Luthri proposed. "Two go ahead while two hang back. That way, if it is a trap, the others will be free to mount a rescue mission. It's not an ideal…"

He trailed off, eyes glued to something past me. Warning bells went off, and I tensed.

Keeping my voice low, I demanded, "What? What is it?"

Luthri grinned and pointed. Tipping my head a degree, I used my peripheral vision to watch an impressive being, half woman and half horse—or, half *avida*, rather—disappear down a side street. No words came to mind. To think centaurs were more than a myth.

"Goddess, those are rare," Lu exclaimed. "I haven't seen a *Santouri* in revolutions. But how strange to see one in these parts, and without a herd. They're always traveling in—"

If I wasn't concentrating on getting my heart rate back to normal, I would have slapped him. "Focus, please, Lu." I forced the words past a tightened jaw. "You can sightsee later."

"Begging your pardon, love. I was saying that splitting up could work in this case."

The pet name made the twins share a look, but I pretended not to have noticed.

"It's not a bad idea," I admitted, drawing the words out as I mulled over our options. As much as the idea of splitting up soured my stomach, he had a point: without knowing what awaited us when it came to Rugaveld, a strategy wouldn't be remiss. If only we had a little more manpower. A pang of sadness hit—losing Yrra and Daethie hurt.

Making up my mind, I announced, "All right. Let's see what we're dealing with first, and then we'll figure out how we want to play this."

CHAPTER TWENTY-FIVE

IN WHICH THE PARTY IS INTRODUCED TO THE GREAT AND POWERFUL RUGAVELD

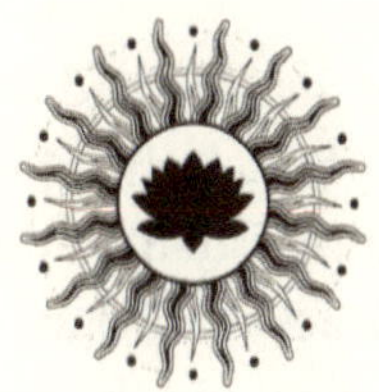

RUGAVELD'S MANOR was indeed something that could not be missed.

The house had, at one point, been a stately older building, perhaps a town hall or vacation home passed down through generations. It had since been transformed into an estate on the cliff, minimalistic modern and classic nineteenth-century elements coming together with fae architecture to create an entirely new beast. Twin towers stood proud, one on either side of the main building, while the back half was an expanse of glass and stone that hung off the edge of the earth to tempt the waves below. A smaller secondary building was attached by a skybridge lined with stained-glass windows. The effect was stunning.

We followed the road to the entrance. The streetlamps and planters on either side of the path came together to frame stone steps leading up to wide, arched double doors decorated with fine carvings of trees and wildlife and propped open to welcome visitors. Even from ground level, I had to crane my neck to look the manor over. The structure loomed above our heads, oppressive in its majesty, equal parts a dream come to life and somehow out of place next to the sea-scented air and ocean views.

"Shut your mouth. You're drooling," Hohem muttered to his

brother, prompting Vyrain to scrub a hand across his chin while shooting daggers.

Without dragging my eyes away, I asked, "Still think splitting up is the best move?"

Luthri took my query as intended. "Well, with that architecture"—he indicated the glass walls with a wave of his hand—"someone could watch you going about your life from Solfarin. So, if anything, I'd say this clinches the deal. Of course, the final decision is up to you."

Moments like these were thrilling and terrifying. Holding a leadership role meant that I had people relying on me. What if I made the wrong call? I could be sending us all to our deaths.

"We should split up," I acknowledged after a beat. It would be foolish for us all to go in at once, and the glass walls did pose an interesting opportunity.

I turned to face the others. Down the street, a small crowd of villagers converged. They kept their distance, but the eager expressions they wore were unnerving. It took me a moment to remember the topic. "Uh… okay. Shall we draw straws?"

"You should go." Vyrain ran a hand through his hair. "You're the diplomatic one, after all. Any one of us works for backup. I'm happy to accompany you for safety's sake."

"Luthri should," Hohem interjected even as Luthri opened his mouth. Lu got over his surprise quickly and gave him big puppy-dog eyes of thanks, which he shrugged off. "You're probably the best fighter of us three. Mar will be in good hands."

Men would be men, making it about me and my safety. Knowing it came from a place of affection made it hard to be bothered. Besides, I didn't mind Luthri coming with me.

"That means you two will be our contingency plan," I warned the twins.

Vyrain's face had fallen. He kept his gaze on the ground, nudging a loose cobblestone with the toe of his boot. "Whatever works, I guess," he muttered under his breath.

Hohem clapped his twin on the shoulder and pulled him close, sending him stumbling. "Think of it this way. If things go wrong, we get to come to Mar's rescue, one-up Luthri, *and* save the mission. Doesn't get much more heroic than that."

Vyrain considered his words.

"You'll be the most important part of the plan," Lu generously announced before I could come up with something to that effect. It held more value coming from him anyway.

Nodding my agreement, I gestured for them to give me their packs. "Let's split up the supplies. We'll take one bag in with us. I'm not sure how long this will take, but if it's more than a day, we'll check in every morning and evening. If we miss a check-in, assume things have gone sideways. Otherwise, if we need you, we'll signal you."

"What signal?" Vyrain inquired, shrugging off his bag.

"One you'll know when you see." I sorted through our gear, keeping an eye on the onlookers as I did so. "Keep to yourselves while we're gone, if you can. Don't accept anything from the townspeople, not even cakes from nice old ladies. Keep your wits about you."

"Mar?" Hohem put a hand on my shoulder. His mouth twitched as he fought a smile. "Calm down. We've got this—you focus on what you have to do."

I blew a strand of hair out of my face and returned my attention to dividing the supplies. "Yeah. Of course. I'm not worried, really." It wasn't the whole truth—who wouldn't be worried? But even though my nerves were stretched taut, I could trust my friends. At some point, all that was left to do was jump into the abyss and hope you land on your feet.

Luthri watched me sort through both packs. After a moment of indecision, I twisted Daethie's hair ring from my finger and tucked that into the one I would leave with the twins. Lifting the straps of the other, I began to straighten, only for him to swipe it from my grip.

"Hey!" I scowled.

He slung it over one shoulder and helped me the rest of the way to my feet in one fluid movement. "Better for you to have your hands free," he said innocently. "Shall we?"

"You can use your words," I grumbled, swiveling to face Rugaveld's mansion.

"Goddess be with you," Vyrain murmured, using a common

Ishameti phrase that doubled as both a greeting and a sendoff. He stooped to collect their bag, and he and his brother stood side by side as Luthri and I mounted the steps to the manor entrance.

It was a good thing the door was already open. The carved handles were as long and thick as my arm, and I would have looked ridiculous trying to pull on them. While no one stood inside, I didn't doubt that Rugaveld or his people were nearby. Indeed, no sooner had we crossed the threshold than one of the little green turtle people emerged from one of the side halls, tripping over himself in his eagerness to reach us.

"Welcome!" he cried in a high, breathless voice. "Welcome to Munarzed."

After confirming that the twins made themselves scarce, I met the new arrival head-on. "Take me to your leader" was too on the nose, wasn't it?

"Hello. We're here for Narille, please," I said instead, pulling myself to my full height. It was a refreshing change of pace to look down at a fae for once.

"Yes, yes, we can't wait to meet you." Quick as a snap, the turtle-man's webbed hand closed around mine—clammy and cool—and tugged me deeper into the manor. Luthri's light footsteps followed close behind. The first floor was all stone slabs, arching architectural windows, and luxurious drapes, beautiful yet devoid of personal touches but for the occasional piece of art. Floorboards creaked under our feet as we got further inside, and a faint sea-scented breeze meandered alongside us.

We passed several more turtle men. Some hovered in corners with open smiles and blank eyes, while others gracefully moved out of our way and kept on with whatever mission they were assigned. Our guide brought us through a doorway leading to a cozy, round courtyard with rows of hedges surrounded a decorative fountain several tiers high. There, he came to an abrupt halt, and I nearly tripped over his compact, part-firm-part-fleshy form.

"Welcome," a new voice called. A lithe young woman rounded the fountain. It was impossible to guess age when it came to the fae—some aged slowly, appearing half or less than their true age by human standards, while others only lived a handful of years—but she might have been an older teen. Dressed in a practical burnt-orange tunic and supple leather pants, she had deep-gray skin, pointed ears, and black hair styled in a braided crown around her head.

As she drew near, it became clear that she held a plate with an arrangement of confections similar to the ones Cantal served us before we left the shrine. She paused an arm's length from Luthri and, as the turtle servant wandered away, offered the plate with a shy smile.

"No, thank you." Lu politely pushed the plate back toward her.

She offered it to me next. "Thank you, but we just ate," I said. Considering her age and manner, I didn't think so, but I had to ask… "Are you Narille Kereti?"

The girl smiled and shook her head. "Sav," she supplied, bringing a sweet to her lips.

"Sav? Nice to meet you." I exchanged a look with Luthri, but he was as lost as I was. Turning back to her, I kept my tone soft. "Okay. Do you know where we can find Narille?"

Sav took her time, chewing and swallowing before responding. "Come with me, please." Transitioning the plate to one hand, she gestured for us to follow, twirled about, and made for the opposite side of the courtyard. Luthri and I hurried after her.

She walked with light, quick steps, her slippers barely making a sound. A short flight of stairs and expansive veranda brought us from the courtyard to another section of the manor. This side was what was left of the original house, judging by the walls of paneled wood and carpeted floors—well-maintained, but not so extravagant as the building façade and entrance hall.

The girl led us through a portion of the home and to a set of doors, which she opened into a sunny conservatory. It took my eyes a second to adjust to the light and determine what I was seeing: the most marvelous indoor garden, with a myriad of plants larger than life and colorful birds singing from golden perches that ran between branches.

On the opposite side of the room, lovingly misting the massive leaves of some vegetation that took up an entire corner of the room, stood a man that bore a resemblance to the girl. He was older, with white hair framing a more weathered—though not elderly—face. But his skin was the same shade of dusty gray, his eyes the same deep-set dark twinkles on either side of a strong nose, his movements similarly graceful. At our approach, his face broke out into a smile.

"Thank you, Savreen. Welcome, travelers." He placed the misting apparatus he'd been using on a short glass table and flicked his hand. Immediately, more turtle people appeared with cushioned chairs, rushing forward to place them behind Luthri and me.

"No doubt it's been a long journey for you," the man continued, nodding at us to sit. "We're honored to offer you our hospitality, simple though it may be."

Tassels attached to the seat swayed gently from the relocation. Did a thing as basic as a chair count as accepting something they gave us? What I wouldn't give for clearer direction. More likely, Danagil had meant it in a literal sense. But it was better to be safe than sorry.

So I stayed put. "We'll stand, thank you."

Luthri paused where he was, hand on the back of his chair and knees bending to lower himself. I caught his gaze. A pointed look was enough for him to return to my side.

Mildly nonplussed, the man wandered to the opposite side of the room to comb through the leaves of another plant. He made conversation as he worked. "My name is Rugaveld. I'm something of a head man here on the island, so if you need anything, don't hesitate to ask. Have you had something to eat yet? My daughter makes the best sweets."

So this was Rugaveld. I filed away the fact the girl was his daughter for later.

"We've heard a lot about you," I remarked. "And we're good, thank you. We've come for Lady Narille. Our sources tell us you might have been the last person to see her alive."

"Lady Narille." A fond smile broke out on Rugaveld's face. "Yes. She remains alive—and well, of course—but may I ask what business you have with her?"

I steeled my spine. "We're here to take her home."

Rugaveld gave the plant a final caress before facing us. "You are not the first to come to me with this request," he announced. "I will tell you what I told the others. You are free to speak with her; however, I request that you respect her wish to stay. You see, Narille found a home here, much like my daughter and myself. As such, I consider her to be under my protection."

Before I could counter, Luthri spoke up. "Her family would like to see her, to speak with her," he explained. "Understand where she's coming from. After that, she would be free to return. If she truly wishes to stay here in Munarzed, no one would hold her against her will."

He couldn't promise that, but I held my tongue. Better to present a unified front.

Rugaveld barely acknowledged his words, instead gesturing broadly to our surroundings. "This place… I have done everything in my power to create a refuge here. A place where people from all walks of life can come together and celebrate their differences. A place where all are welcome, and all are safe, comfortable, and honored by their neighbor. To maintain such an environment requires certain lines to be drawn."

"I understand—" I began.

"Pardon me, but I don't think you do." Rugaveld stood firm, hands clasped before him. "Too many take peace for granted. My daughter and I come from across the Great Waters, a country plagued by war. There, people must always worry over what the next day will bring. The vulnerable among us, such as women, especially. My daughter and I fled many revolutions ago. My wife, may Ni'imah cherish her immortal soul, did not survive the journey."

I opened my mouth to express my condolences, but he kept going.

"It was then we discovered this island. So much potential if one only knew what to do with it… All they needed was a guiding hand. Firm, yet kind. I provide that."

He scrutinized our expressions, a slight crease appearing in the middle of his forehead. I kept mine neutral. Where was he going with this? Did he hope that an emotional plea would convince us to drop our mission and return home empty-handed? Was this a veiled warning that he wasn't afraid to get his hands dirty if the situation called for it?

Rugaveld's stern countenance softened into a conciliatory smile. "Excuse my rambling. Narille is currently busy, but she will be available this evening and all day tomorrow. In the meantime, please make yourself at home. Stay as long as you like."

Oh, we would. If his goal was to have us tire of waiting, he would be sorely disappointed. "How kind of you," I simpered, grateful for Luthri's presence should things take a turn. "We've nothing better to do, so my companion and I will be happy to stay put until Narille's return this evening. That is, if we might be lucky enough to take advantage of your hospitality further."

Appearing pleased by this, Rugaveld nodded. "But of course. What's mine is yours. The city has much to offer, should you wish to venture beyond the walls of the manor."

He wouldn't be rid of us that easily. But since compliments never hurt anyone... "Thank you, but we had the chance to sightsee on the way here. What we've seen thus far is beautiful."

"Thank you." Rugaveld's smile broadened. "We are quite proud of our little island. There is a lovely stretch of beach to the northwest that I would recommend visiting if you have the time. And a fascinating cave system that local legend tells us is full of hidden treasures... Though I've yet to see proof of that myself. Both are popular among visitors."

Cave system? The one that nearly killed us?

"Actually, we were just there." I debated how many details to share. Perhaps this was an opportunity to coax more information from the mayor. "We didn't find any treasure, but we did encounter nightmares. It was a close call. I'd recommend avoiding that area in the future."

It might have been my imagination that his complexion turned ashy. One hand went to his mouth. "My. Nightmares? How awful. That's... Well, thank you for that information. I will need to get the word out to the residents... We will need to have that area sectioned off and have warnings put up. Ah, what a terrible thing."

His eyes roamed the room until they found Savreen standing dutifully by the doorway. He beckoned for her to approach, words pouring from his mouth, "My heart, could you show them to a room? I would like to address this immediately. Be sure they are comfortable."

The girl startled, as though suddenly remembering where she was.

"Yes!" Using the plate, she indicated the door we'd come from. "Come with me?"

I opened my mouth to protest, but Rugaveld was already delegating orders to a host of turtle people on his way deeper into his forest of a sunroom. The message was clear—a dismissal.

Well. Patience had never been my strong suit, but there was no time like the present to learn.

CHAPTER TWENTY-SIX

IN WHICH THE HEROES INVESTIGATE THE MATTER THOROUGHLY

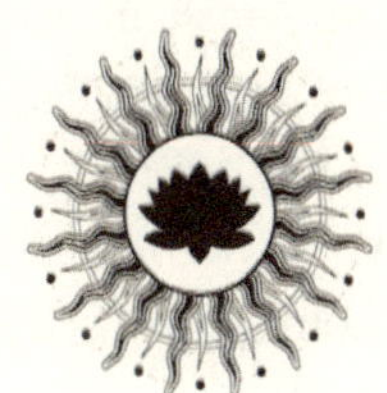

LUTHRI and I found ourselves in a cozy room with a main level and loft, each sporting a sleeping area, exposed wood beams along the ceiling, and floor-to-ceiling windows with a view of the sea. One wall was covered in tapestries and bookshelves, while another featured a doorway into the bathing space, partially hidden by a decorative privacy screen. Catching an eyeful of the freestanding bathtub and spouts had me dizzy with excitement. How long had it been since I had proper accommodations with indoor plumbing?

"Considerate of them to provide a room with two beds," Luthri grumbled in a tone that conveyed his true thoughts might lay opposite that sentiment.

I dragged my attention away from the bathtub. "What was that?"

"Nothing, love." Having removed his boots and set our bag near the door, Lu wandered to the bookshelf to sift through the titles there. His hand hovered over a nondescript volume. "Does this count as taking something they're giving us? Or no, since it was your idea to stay?"

"I couldn't tell you," I answered. "But we have some time to kill, so we might as well figure out how to make the most of it. I'm going to sweep the room."

Starting from the bathroom, I combed through each nook and cranny of the space we'd been given for anything suspicious, out of place, or concerning—strange symbols, planted chemicals, odd smells, peepholes in the walls, hiding spaces where a turtle man might fit. My search turned up nothing of consequence, but that didn't mean it wasn't there.

"Which bed do you want?" I called to Luthri from the loft.

"Doesn't matter."

Nodding, I returned to the task at hand. No wonder Rugaveld made this manor his base of operations. The view from here was marvelous, looking over the bay with its pale beaches and rich blue water. It was both a foreign and familiar sight—things on this side of The Rift just felt more vivid somehow. Perhaps that could be attributed to the presence of *mana*.

"Might as well take this time to update the twins," Luthri commented as I joined him on the main level. "I'll let them know what Rugaveld told us and where we're staying."

I'd started toward him before his choice of words registered. "You want to go alone?"

Lu paused by the door, boots in hand, with a curious expression on his face. "There's no reason for us both to go. Unless you don't trust me?"

Didn't I trust Luthri? He hadn't given me a reason not to. Sure, he could be brash, presumptuous, and conceited. He took life by the horns and didn't always know when it was time to sit down and be serious. On the other hand, his resourcefulness had come in handy more than once. He thought on his feet, fought well, and looked out for the rest of us—people he'd known a matter of weeks. That gave him several points in my book.

A burst of inspiration struck, and with a devious smile, I called *mana* for a change. Bones and skin expanded, limbs stretched, hair shortened. In an instant, I stood before him as a near-perfect copy of himself, identical but for the wings.

"Would you trust you?" I asked, nodding down at myself. I put a little swagger into the movement, cocking one hip and tossing my head in an exaggeration of his smug attitude.

"Of course I would." Luthri leaned back against the door and grinned. "Look at that honest face. Though, apparently you didn't get a good-enough feel during our rendezvous earlier, or you'd know my cock is much bigger than that. I'd be happy to give you another chance."

My blood warmed, and I barked a laugh. "Oh, I got a good feel. And no, it's not."

Chuckling to himself, Luthri opened the door. "I won't be gone long. Feel free to make yourself at home… Especially if that involves prancing around naked and/or touching yourself to thoughts of tall, dark, and handsome *Peri* men. In fact, I encourage it."

With a wink, he was gone, the sound of the closing door smothering my indignant huff.

In his absence, I did what any self-respecting young woman in my shoes would and practiced my magic. First, I spent several minutes in a meditative position on the floor. The hard surface made it easier to visualize being grounded. When my tailbone started to protest, I moved to the loft. I fiddled with one of the windows until it opened and settled in front, letting the sea breeze wash over me and soothe my frazzled nerves.

I'd missed moments like these. Not that this adventure hadn't been fulfilling, but… sometimes you craved peace and quiet, even more so in times of uncertainty. A part of me couldn't wait to get back to our campsite outside Vhalder. It had been too long since I last devoured Vee's cooking after a hard day's work, advertised our services in the town square, or broke up fights between the others when someone got a little riled up.

My thoughts drifted to Daethie and Yrra. I hoped they settled into the swamplands all right. Would the *nykse* give them trouble? Would another waterfolk come along and challenge Yrra for his new home? Not that I doubted Yrra's capabilities, but this was something I didn't know much about. If it were me, I'd want backup.

Tsk—that wasn't meditating. I refocused my energy on quieting those thoughts and grounding again, counting each breath as I drew *mana* slowly and deliberately. The power curled in my chest and dwelled there, ripe for use yet unwilling to bend to my will. I pushed down the budding frustration and kept counting breaths. It was so close, as if all I had to do was shift aside a veil, and the making technique would be revealed to me.

But the moment I was waiting for didn't come.

Opening my eyes to the view outside, I released my focus and control on my magic at the same time. Some time had passed. An hour, perhaps, judging by the golden edge to the clouds. Luthri ought to have been back by now, shouldn't he? Had the twins given him trouble? If they were gallivanting around the city, so help me, I'd kick their asses to kingdom come.

With unreleased *mana* humming through my veins, I couldn't sit still. Might as well take advantage of that bathtub while we were here. I'd have to make it quick, but the idea of cleaning up was too tantalizing to ignore. I retrieved a change of clothes—the only spare set I had—and brought it into the bathroom with me, sliding the privacy screen over the doorway.

Undressing in an unfamiliar place put me on edge. I was quick about it, getting together what I needed and turning the handle on the old brass faucet to start the water running. It wasn't hot, but it would do. You couldn't take clean water for granted here. Knowing that Luthri might return at any moment, I made it quick, scrubbing sand and sweat from my skin with a sponge from one of the shelves. When I finished, I used the bathwater to wash my clothes.

With luck, I'd have time to fit in a longer bath before we left.

A knock sounded from the other room as I pulled the clean shirt over my head. Luthri wouldn't knock, which meant that this was Rugaveld or one of his cronies.

"One moment," I called, fighting my pants in my haste to get to the door. Hair slicked back and shirt loose around my waist, I pulled it open enough to see outside. Savreen, Rugaveld's daughter, stood on the other side with a tray of food in hand.

"Good afternoon," she greeted, tilting her head to peer past me. "I'm afraid I have some disappointing news. Something has come up, and Narille won't be able to meet with you this evening. However, I took the liberty of preparing supper for you and your companion. I find there's a lot that one can overlook with a hot meal in their belly."

She held out the tray, a sweet smile on her face.

Not wanting to be rude, I accepted the offering. "Thank you. Looks delicious." The contents, a large fried fish with an assortment of side dishes, made my stomach purr with appreciation. I had to force my attention back to the matter at hand.

"I don't suppose Lady Narille happened to mention when she would be able to meet with us?" I inquired of the young host. "It's only that we have a schedule to keep to."

"I understand completely," Savreen assured me, her big, dark eyes conveying genuine sympathy. "And I've made sure to pass along the urgency. I am sorry for the inconvenience."

Suspicion aside, it wasn't right to be upset with the messenger. "Not your fault. Thanks for letting me know. And for"—I nodded down at the dinner tray—"this."

Savreen beamed, the apples of her gray cheeks flushing deep purple. "Of course. Enjoy!" She bobbed on her feet and disappeared down the hallway to tend to her next task.

Letting the door shut behind me, I retreated into the room. The tray was deposited on the desk by the bed—the temptation would be too great if I kept it close. My mouth watered imagining how satisfying the flaky, salty fish skin would be after so much dry, tasteless travel food. I should toss it, but even as I eyed the open window, I couldn't bring myself to.

I was rooting through the bag for food supplies when the door opening signaled Luthri's return. Without looking back, I called out a greeting. "Welcome back."

"Did you miss me, darling?" he crooned as he pulled off his boots.

"I've been pining away," I returned, fluttering my eyelashes for maximum effect. He grinned in reply, crossing the room. As he neared, my heart somersaulted against my ribs. *Will he greet me with a casual kiss? Grab and toss me onto the bed for a thorough ravishing?*

I put a hand to my pounding heart with a frown. That was new.

"How's everything?" I asked, pulling out the bundle I'd been searching for and settling on the floor, back against the bed frame. Luthri collapsed on the mattress beside me with a groan.

"Fine. They're set up on a ridge southeast of the manor to keep an eye on things. We'll have to risk the water supply soon, but they scrounged up some tools to try their hand at fishing in the meantime. Resourceful fellows, those two."

I made a sound of agreement. "Narille can't see us tonight."

"No?" Lu raised an eyebrow. "Can't see us, or... Can't see us?" He added an ominous emphasis on the repetition, implying what I also suspected.

"Not sure," I admitted, popping a piece of dried fruit in my mouth. "Savreen—the daughter—passed along the message. I'll raise a ruckus if the same thing happens tomorrow." Chewing, I added, "Something creeps me out about this place, but I can't put my finger on it."

Luthri nodded thoughtfully. "It doesn't feel like the townspeople are being threatened, even if that might be the most obvious answer. They didn't seem scared or nervous. I think it's more likely they're under the influence of something. Someone is pulling their strings."

"Rugaveld. Who else?" My eyes fell on the unassuming dinner tray. "They've offered us something to eat a few times... Think it could have something to do with the food?"

Lu swiveled around to follow my gaze. When his eyes fell on the plate, he abruptly stood, walked around the bed, and crouched by the plate to examine the food.

A warning climbed my throat. "Don't—"

"I know, I know." He gave the fish a dainty sniff before sitting back on his haunches. "Hm. Like I said, I can't think of an herbal compound that could achieve this result, but that doesn't mean it's not possible. Perhaps we ought to consult the *Aminkinya* again."

Savreen came to mind, the way she'd snacked on sweets from the same plate she'd offered us while we spoke with her father. The thought wrinkled my brow. "Savreen ate the food herself, remember? A drug wouldn't make sense unless he's dosing her too."

"Also not impossible," Lu countered.

He had a point. "Anyway, I don't want to stay here any longer than we have to. The mission hasn't changed—we need to find Narille and leave. First thing tomorrow, if not tonight."

An inclination of his head told me Luthri was on the same page. Continuing to mull over the possibilities in my head, I returned my attention to my "meal" when it occurred to me that I hadn't seen Lu eat anything since breakfast on the ship the day before.

"Hungry?" I offered him a handful of nuts. *Oh, could he even have nuts?*

He shook his head. "I'll be all right."

"If you say so. You can bathe if you like; I already took one."

Lu's gaze swept over me, taking in the damp tendrils of hair and the way my shirt clung to the lines of my body. My skin warmed under his scrutiny.

"I see that," he remarked.

I fiddled with the food packaging as I searched for a subject to shift the conversation. "If we can't find the stuff we lost in the swamp, you'll have to tell me where you got that bath oil you gave me. It'll be worth another adventure after this to pick some up."

"Oh, you can use mine if you like." Lu went for his waist, rifling through the personal effects attached to his belt until he produced a stoppered bottle with pale gold liquid inside.

When I opened it to examine the contents, a familiar spiced-orange scent tickled my nose. To think, he'd been carrying that all this time. I couldn't resist the opportunity to tease him. "Barely made it here with our lives, yet this survived a journey through *nykse*-ridden waters, the voyage to Munarzed, and a cave-in inside a nightmare den. Goddess forbid you go without your signature perfume."

"I take care of what's mine," was all Luthri had to say.

"Mhm. Use it the same way as the other one?" I held the little flask up to the light and tipped it back and forth so that the oil coated the interior in sunshine tones.

"That's right. You can put it in the water or apply it to your skin."

A knuckle skimmed my shoulder, the touch assessing. I pretended not to notice.

"Well, thank you for the offer." I made sure the stopper was firmly in place and passed the bottle back. "I'm all set for now, but good to know it's an option. Here's hoping we won't have to rush out of here, and I'll be able to take another bath before we leave."

"Maybe I'll join you next time."

"Maybe you will."

Lu's light tone didn't hide the inquiry underneath, but my answer gave him nothing. The bed frame creaked as he leaned forward. His next words came from right beside my ear. "If I were in there with you, you wouldn't need a bath oil. I'd gladly lick you clean."

Before I could formulate a response, he'd gotten to his feet and sauntered off toward the bathroom. I tossed another nut in my mouth and admired the sway of his backside as I chewed.

About fifteen minutes later, the sound of the privacy screen sliding across the floor made me look up from my book. I wasn't prepared for the sight that met me, but somehow I managed to maintain an impassive stare, which I was quite proud of at the moment.

"Forgot to grab a change of clothes," Luthri said by way of explanation as he strolled out of the bathroom in the nude, rippling muscle and rich brown skin on display in all their glory.

He was a shower. Or, at least, I hoped he was a shower—if he had much growing to do, I'd be shit out of luck. My eyebrows rose millimeter by millimeter as I took in the rounded shoulders and sculpted lats, the fit and flare of his obliques, the careful definition between each abdominal muscle. It was a work of art, the way his wet skin glistened in the afternoon light—like oiled mahogany. Goddess, how I wanted to taste it.

Had the temperature risen in the last thirty seconds?

Having reached the foot of the bed, Luthri bent to rummage inside the bag. I didn't realize how engaged I was until it registered that I had sat up for a better view of his backside and calves. The former flexed in a hypnotizing rhythm as he dug through our supplies.

"So sorry," he said breezily over one shoulder. "I'll be out of your hair in a moment."

I sat back against the pillows and tossed my book aside with a huff. "Oh, please. You're not sorry in the slightest. In fact, I'd be willing to bet you didn't bring a change of clothes in with you on purpose. I'll give you some credit—it's a smooth setup."

Luthri pivoted to face me—certain things taking longer to recover from the momentum than others—and put on an exaggerated pout. "You wound me, Mar. I mean, I'm flattered that you think I would be capable of such clever manipulation, but I would never resort to underhanded methods to attract the object of my affections. Unless... it's working?"

He raised his arms and angled his body, striking a pose to accentuate his ample musculature. All right, so he had my attention, but did he think he was being subtle?

I threw my hands up. "You could have, I don't know, asked?"

"Oh, so you're going to make me beg?" he drawled.

A denial sprang to my lips, but not fast enough. His knee landed on the edge of the bed. The rest of him followed, prowling forward on his hands and knees. I'd never had a man crawl to me before. The space between us shrank as my mouth opened and closed.

CHAPTER TWENTY-SEVEN

IN WHICH THE HEROES INVESTIGATE EACH OTHER THOROUGHLY

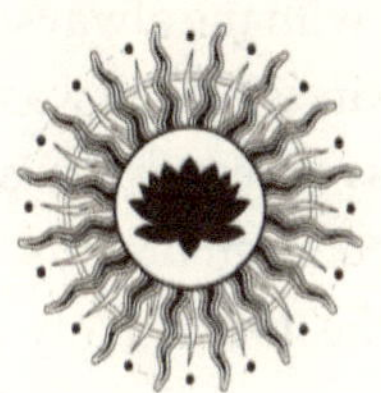

I OUGHT TO SAY SOMETHING, shouldn't I? What are words, anyway?

"May I," Luthri began, having reached my extended leg, "be granted the honor"—he dipped his head to press a kiss to my knee—"of devoting the rest of this day and night to worshiping your body in this bed? Please?"

He met my eyes with a wolfish smile.

My tongue darted out to moisten my lips. "Worshiping, huh?"

Lu's eyes were twin stars. "Your cries of pleasure will have turned the Goddesses green with envy by the time I'm done with you," he promised in a sensual purr. His fingertips dragged along the outside of my calf, making my senses sing for him.

I was having difficulty coming up with a reason to turn him down. We had the evening to ourselves, privacy, a proper bed… When would we next get an opportunity like this? And it would be easier to focus on the job if we got our attraction to each other out of our systems. Really, it would be for everyone's benefit if I let this happen. Where was the harm?

Mind made up, I let my legs fall apart and beckoned him with a finger. Luthri wasted no time. He swooped in to close the space between us, pinning me in place with his weight, and claimed my lips in a heated kiss. I closed my legs around him and met his fervor head-on.

Oh, yes. This is long overdue.

My hands dragged over his shoulders and chest, following the jagged striped markings that covered his torso and arms like a tattoo. He was firm in all the right places, hard and smooth and too beautiful for words. The scent of orange and spices was so thick in the air that I could almost taste it on his lips. I breathed in as if I could absorb it into my bloodstream and keep it with me always—keep *him* with me always.

My shirt clung to his skin where it was moist from his bath. That wouldn't do. I broke our kiss to rectify the issue.

"My clothes," I gasped between breaths. "Take them off."

Luthri's hands found the hem of my shirt. A less-than-graceful combination of pulling and wriggling bared my upper body to the air. My nipples peaked right away, eager for attention. Lu hovered in place, one hand outstretched, transfixed as though he'd never seen a woman's breasts before. If I didn't know better, I might have pinned his expression as pain.

I checked in just in case. "You all right?"

He hesitated to answer me. "I think… I'm having performance anxiety?"

A shocked giggle burst from me. Looking back, it might not have been the best response to that particular confession. "What happened to all that bravado from earlier?" I teased. "Aren't you the man whose mission it was to fuck a member of every race? Who 'forgot his clothes' so that he had an excuse for showing off his body to his latest conquest?"

He leaned back to tuck a strand of hair behind my ear. "Normally I don't care this much," he said quietly, a thread of raw emotion in the statement. My smile faltered.

Do I shrug it off? Keep things moving?

Emotional conversations weren't my forte, but actions spoke louder than words in times like this. I took a hold of his face and pulled him in for another kiss, this one tender. Keeping the pressure light, I pressed my lips to the seam of his mouth, then one corner, the bulk of his lower lip, and jaw. When I relaxed back against the pillows, he followed, returning my nibbles with more confidence.

"I'm here," I murmured into his ear, drawing slow circles across his shoulder blade. "I have you. Me and you, hmm? No pressure, just us. Nothing else matters right now."

Lu's breath warmed my neck as he sighed. "I don't deserve you."

Barely resisting the urge to shake some sense into him, I pulled back to fix him with a firm look. "Let me be the judge of that. Now, are we doing this or not?"

A hand gripped the waist of my pants, ready to pick up where we left off. "Oh, we're doing this. In a moment, you're going to be incapable of anything but screaming my name."

"That's a lot of talk," I chided even as anticipation heated my blood. Our mouths met again as Luthri worked my pants down my legs. Things ramped up a notch once there were no clothes between us. His tongue invaded my mouth, seeking out mine with the eagerness of one long denied. At the same time, Lu's arms came around and dragged me into his lap.

In the new position, I could press myself against him as we kissed, luxuriating in the feel of his solid body against mine. His length was a hot brand against my inner thigh, insistent in its need. Like an echo, mine responded, muscles deep inside my core pulsing in demand. Kissing was nice and all, but it wouldn't alleviate the ache that was coming.

"Give me your fingers," I ordered, urging him on with a suggestive roll of my hips.

"So impatient."

Despite the reprimand, Luthri indulged my request, shuffling back enough to get his arm in between us. His fingers hunted through my folds. The touch incited a fresh wave of heat, and I had to clench my muscles to keep from writhing on his hand… But before he found the right spot, he paused and withdrew. I opened my mouth to argue, reaching to pull him back.

The protest died on my lips when Luthri brought his hand to his mouth. He locked eyes with me as his tongue emerged to coat his middle and ring fingers in saliva. I could guess what he was doing. Arousal coiled in the pit of my stomach, and I wet my lips.

His hand dropped. I widened my stance to make room, using his shoulder to support myself. This time, his fingers glided into place, finding my entrance and pushing into me without delay. He tested the give with one first, and when my body was delighted to accommodate him, transitioned to two. Then began a slow and steady assessment.

Brow pinched with focus, Luthri swept his fingers in a half circle, testing several internal spots along the way. I hummed my approval. He pumped in and out a few times while scissoring his fingers, a winning combination. But when he made a beckoning motion, pressing his fingertips into the sensitive palate of my g-spot, I rewarded him with a breathy moan.

"That's the spot," I told him, canting my hips to meet his hand. He repeated the motion with more fervor and swooped in to graze his lips along the side of my neck, causing me to shudder in rapture. His fingers moved inside me in tandem with his mouth against the delicate skin of my throat, sending little shivers throughout my body.

Merda, but the boy learned quickly.

"You're good at this," I praised, letting my eyelids flutter shut to savor the sensations.

His teeth grazed my ear. When he spoke, voice roughened by desire, it sent an electrifying quiver through my core. "This is nothing, *kiannim*. We're just getting started."

My imagination took off, stomach pitching with excitement. Humans could be quite creative. What sorts of things did a sexually experienced and well-traveled *Peri* man consider standard for a romp in the sheets? Intent on finding out, I reached between us. Luthri's breath caught as my hand closed around his cock. I pumped once, twice, and he hissed in pleasure.

I found his ear with my mouth and traced the lobe with my tongue.

"Good?" I inquired, the word all but moaned. The movement of his fingers had stuttered, so I could safely assume I affected him at least half as much as he did me. I pushed my hips into his hand—a gentle reminder that had him resuming the motion and driving me toward release.

After another moment of mutual gratification, Lu's free hand fell on top of mine. He directed me to squeeze tighter and adjusted my hold around his shaft to maximize the area of contact. Inspired, I added a twist of my palm at the end of each upward stroke. He groaned his approval, a masculine sound that had my pussy clenching tighter around his fingers.

"You keep that up and this will be over too soon," he warned, breathless.

"All that talk, and for what?" I taunted him, redoubling my efforts as my own breaths came short. "It would seem that the legendary lover is but an ordinary man after all."

Luthri's fingers hit a particularly delicious spot, making me gasp. My legs grew weak. I leaned into him, using his arm for support. The added weight didn't faze him. If anything, he returned the movement, subtly indulging in the intimacy of the moment.

I'd closed my eyes to encourage the building climax when Luthri's touch disappeared, leaving an overwhelming feeling of emptiness and a deep ache that had yet to be sated. A soft whimper was all the objection I could muster, I was so far gone, but my grip on his dick tightened. A hand threaded itself into my hair and tipped my head back to expose my throat.

"You're going to sit on my face," Lu rasped, "so I can taste it when you come."

The brazen request and filthy language roused a new fire in me. I'd never sat on someone's face before, but I'd be damned if I let the opportunity pass me by—especially with such a nice one on offer. As I untangled our limbs, a dark shadow above his shoulder caught my eye, and uncertainty replaced mounting lust.

"What about your wings? Won't that crush them?"

Lu shook his head, releasing his hold on my hair so that I could move freely. He smoothed the strands he'd mussed before pulling away.

"The only benefit of their unfortunate state is that they require little consideration," he said as he threw himself down onto the bed. "Now" —he beckoned with both hands—"do as I say and smother me."

How did he manage to charm me more every day? If things

continued this way, soon enough I'd be putty in his hands. Glad I'd had the chance to bathe, I slunk across the covers to where Luthri awaited me. Getting on top took some effort; I nearly took off his nose with a knee, but as I lowered myself into position, I had to admit it was a nice view.

Lu's arms came around to grip my thighs, fingers dimpling my flesh. His words were muffled. "Don't let me discourage you, but… if I can breathe, you're doing it wrong."

That was all the warning I got before he hauled me over his nose and mouth and greeted my clit with an enthusiastic swirl of firm, wet tongue. Any thoughts I might have had stumbled to a halt. I threw my head back, not entirely in control of my body, as he drew an indiscernible pattern against sensitive flesh. Back and forth he went, tasting me as though his life depended on it and soaking us both in a combination of saliva and my own wetness.

Tension throughout my body signaled the impending orgasm would be magnificent.

Just when I thought I couldn't take any more, his tongue breached my entrance, splitting me in half with its unexpected size. My spine went rigid. The appendage writhed like it had a life of its own, reaching parts a human's could never. The foreign sensation stunned me at first—I didn't know if I should push him away or pull him closer. But his tongue woke long-neglected nerve endings, and I could no longer care about anything but finding my pleasure.

I gasped. Cried out. My thighs clamped around his head like a vise, and my hand found his hair, fisting a handful of the silky near-black locks without care.

"Oh, yes! Oh, God, do that again!" It barely registered that I was speaking English. Luckily for me, Luthri spoke fluent body language. His long tongue wriggled and thrashed against my inner walls, simultaneously meeting the instinctual need to be filled and pressing buttons I didn't even know existed. I ground against his face, a wanton creature desperate for the release that threatened.

Each twist of his magical tongue pushed me higher. Every jerk of my hips wound me tighter. Delicious tension gathered in my core to a point that bordered on pain—then, blessedly, miraculously, it culminated. The gratification was immeasurable. Infinite synapses fired at once, exploding like fireworks across my senses, and all was right with the world.

A loud crack split the air.

I didn't realize what I'd done until the tremors abated, when I rolled off Luthri and found myself on the floor. One of the legs of the bed frame had collapsed under our combined weight. Not due to ardor, but because in the throes of that breathtaking orgasm, I'd subconsciously used the *mana* gathered from my earlier practice session to accomplish what I'd been attempting and failing to do for the past weeks: expand my body beyond its natural limit.

Unfortunately for Lu, I'd been on top of him at the time.

Excess *mana* escaped in wisps, giving the appearance of white smoke leaving my body through every pore. Waving it aside, I rushed to check on him. He appeared no worse for wear physically, although all his energy was currently devoted to catching his breath.

"You take direction well," he announced between puffs. "Much longer and the Lady Hermenia would have been along to guide my soul to the underworld."

Regret obstructed my throat. "I'm sorry. I should have—"

"No!" he exclaimed, shooting up from the bed. "Don't be sorry. That was the greatest thrill I've had in a long time, and I once fucked a giantess."

Breathing a sigh, I crawled beside him. "You know, it's generally frowned upon to discuss past sexual liaisons with a new partner. Especially… Well."

I nodded down at our situation.

"A story for next time, then." Luthri let his head fall back against the pillow, eyes closed. His lips, curved in bliss, were swollen from our activities, and his chin glistened with the evidence of my arousal. Going by the proud erection jutting from his groin, the brief setback had done nothing to discourage his libido.

I doubted he would object if I picked up where we left off.

Watching for a reaction, I took his hard length in hand and moved to straddle him. Luthri's breath caught, and his head came up. Yellow eyes went scorching gold as he took in my position. I dragged my hand up and down his shaft, enjoying the heat of him under my palm, and his hands found the groove where my thighs met my torso. His fingers dug in, but I didn't mind.

"Ready?" I asked.

"Do you need me to beg again? Because I will."

I chuckled to myself. "No. No, I think you've earned it."

He held his breath as I slotted him at my entrance. I went slowly, savoring the gradual stretch and satisfying fullness. Luthri's head tipped back, eyes closing, and his lips moved as though invoking a higher being to bear witness to our lovemaking.

My arm snaked out to grab a hold of his chin and redirect his gaze where it mattered.

"I want you to watch." I punctuated my words with a forceful squeeze. His throat bobbed, and he nodded. I dropped the rest of the way without warning. He bottomed out deep inside, and my muted gasp harmonized with his unrestrained groan of pleasure. Once we'd adapted to each other, I circled my hips, testing my range of movement.

But before we could get to the good part, Lu sat up, nearly upending me. He supported me with one hand while the other came up to caress a breast.

"I've been waiting for this," he whispered into the underside of my jaw. "For you. To hold you like this, touch your naked skin… See you take me." His lips traced the column of my throat. "This is perfect. You're perfect. I had to tell you that."

I didn't think I was the kind of person who succumbed to charming words, but it had been too long since I had this. Or had I ever had it? The one relationship I'd had—one of the temporary members of our band some years ago—hadn't been quite this intense. Other casual partners could drop a dirty one-liner, but romance? That was something else.

Eyes half-lidded, I surrendered to Luthri's touch. He sensed the shift and adjusted his hold, moving under me in steady, measured thrusts that took my breath away. I could have let him do all the work—heaven knew I deserved it—but I ground onto him instead, matching his pace thrust for thrust and driving him even deeper.

It wasn't long until he was thrusting into me from below with ravenous intensity, and I could only hold on and enjoy the ride. It would be worth the soreness tomorrow. On one stroke, he hit a spot that made my toes curl, and my fingers dug into his back. "There!"

He responded instantly, tilting my body toward him at the slightest angle, and did it again with devastating accuracy. At the same time, a thumb pressed against my clitoris and massaged the spot. I saw stars. My vocalizations escalated, panting becoming loud moans and uninhibited whimpers. That seemed to do something for Lu, too, because though the pace didn't change, his grip on me tightened, and his breaths came shorter.

I wasn't thinking when my teeth closed around his earlobe in a punishing love bite. His resounding growl made muscles far under the skin clench, which made me constrict further around his cock. A second orgasm hit me out of nowhere. His thrusts grew frantic, stuttered; then he sank deep and stayed there, gripping me close with a stifled moan of release.

We held each other as we came down. Adoring hands ran over limbs and through hair while sweet words were exchanged, interspersed with delicate kisses. It was everything I hadn't realized I needed: touch, intimacy, affection, warmth. Why had I put this off for so long? If I'd been less committed to fighting myself, I could have had heaven at my fingertips the entire time.

After a cursory clean-up, which included a lackluster attempt to reattach the wooden leg that had broken, Luthri and I lay together in the (slanting) bed and cuddled.

"What's this?" Lu asked as his thumb traced a faint scar on my bare thigh.

Memories played behind my eyes: hitchhiking from D.C. to New York with nothing but determination and the clothes on my back, fleeing soldiers to climb the fence around Niagara Falls, and getting nicked by a bullet as I plummeted toward The Rift. Finally, patching myself up on the other side and figuring out what came next as a sixteen-year-old girl in an unknown world, on her own for the first time in her life.

I'd come so far.

"The cost of freedom," I responded, electing to leave it at that.

Lu contemplated my answer. "Couldn't you fix that? With your magic?"

"I could."

I didn't elaborate, and he didn't push.

Listening to the faint sounds of the ocean, we dozed until moonlight filtered through the windows. At some point, I woke to Luthri gently massaging my scalp and running his hands through my hair, as though he couldn't bear to go without touching me for an entire night. I nuzzled against his chest and breathed him in.

With my guard down, dark thoughts crept in. Things were too perfect; it was only a matter of time before they fell apart. So much was left to do, which meant there was so much that could go wrong. Fears and insecurities that usually sat on the sidelines clamored for attention. Normally, I would shake them off and keep myself busy. Now...

"I'm terrified," I confessed aloud. Luthri's hand stilled. "So many people have been here, have tried and failed. What if I make a mistake? What if we fail too, and all of us are lost?"

"Shh," he whispered into my hair. "You're not doing this alone. There's no way to predict what the future holds, yet it holds so much power over us. Don't give it more than it's earned."

Suddenly exhausted, I let my eyes shut. Luthri's lips brushed my forehead. I angled my face up for a kiss and found comfort in the gesture.

This moment, at least, was ours.

We made love twice more that night.

CHAPTER TWENTY-EIGHT

IN WHICH THE PARTY MEETS THE HEIRESS

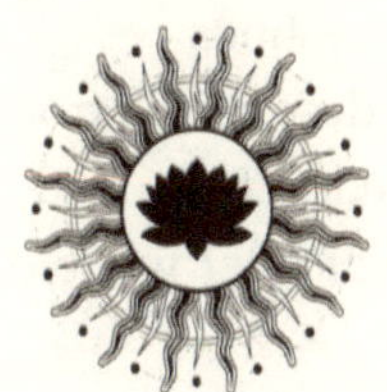

DAWN INTRUDED, as it always did, bringing a dose of reality alongside golden rays of sun. Half covered by a blanket, I lounged in bed as Luthri got dressed to go out and report to the twins. He pulled on his shirt and was stepping into his pants when I startled.

"Oh, wait!" I pushed myself up onto my elbows and patted the mattress beside me. "I forgot to look for your scar. Take 'em off and present yourself for inspection."

"It's too late now," Luthri stated, already lacing the ties with deft fingers. "You'll have to wait until next time. Don't worry—I'll even bend over so you can get a good look."

Feigning outrage, I huffed and settled back against the pillows. Lu sauntered over and, ignoring my exaggerated scowl, took my head in both hands to plant an enthusiastic kiss on my forehead. I caught a firm hold of his collar and yanked him down for a real one.

"I won't be gone long," he said, giving my chin an affectionate wiggle.

"I'll be here." So long as nothing unexpected came up, I'd stay put until he returned. It was the whole point of doing this in pairs, after all. Hopefully, we'd catch Narille today and convince her to come with us, and this would be the last check-in we do.

Luthri crossed the room. He paused at the door to pull on his boots, blew me a kiss, and was gone. As soon as he was out of sight, I tossed aside the blanket and went to fetch our washed clothing, now dry, from the bathroom. I dressed and ate a meager breakfast of more fruit and nuts. The sheets we'd sullied went in the sink to run under cold water.

It may have been an unnecessary step, but I took the time to disarrange the covers on the loft bed to make it appear slept in. Better to not have anyone asking questions.

Luthri returned as I was descending from the upper level.

"All's well," he reported. "They had to risk the town's water supply, but no ill effects. Whatever we're dealing with, it's not in the water."

"Well, that's good to know. Best avoid any they hand us directly nonetheless."

Luthri nodded his agreement. I fetched our canteens from the bag and filled them from the sink after testing a mouthful of tap water. It was a touch tinny, but potable. My canteen went on my belt for easy access while we were out during the day.

"All right, let's go." When I made for the door, Lu didn't move.

"Should we be wandering around on our own?" he questioned. "I wonder if it would be more prudent to wait for news of Narille, in case she plans on coming to us."

I angled a sidelong glance his way. "And miss our chance for unchaperoned sleuthing?"

Lu blinked, and his face brightened. "You make an excellent point."

While we discovered no secret passages, dungeons where people were being tortured, or chambers with hypnotizing apparatuses (what would that look like, anyway?), we did uncover some truly terrible art. Luthri and I barely made it through one particular hallway with straight faces after spotting an elegant bust of a turtle man with a comically confused look on its face.

"Maybe the artist was going for thought-provoking," Lu reasoned as the side of his face twitched. "One of those things where you wonder what the subject was thinking."

"Probably stupefied by the idea anyone would pay money for that."

"Now, now. That could be someone's great-grandfather."

Shaking my head, I paused to check the wall behind a tapestry, tapping the wood paneling with a knuckle to listen for hidden compartments. Nothing.

"Hm." I waved Luthri onward, and he fell into step beside me. "I still think there's got to be something we're missing. Maybe elsewhere on the island, if not here. I don't believe for a second that this is nothing more than a kindly old man who turned around a failing town."

"We could ask Hohem and Vyrain to conduct an investigation of their own." Luthri's gaze shifted around the hall, looking anywhere but me. "But… is it possible that there's no evil mastermind? That these people are happy and healthy, and nothing is wrong?"

His hesitation made me second-guess myself. Was I being too pessimistic? Jumping to conclusions? Even the Solfarin residents thought something was up, and they'd know the island better than anyone else in the region, wouldn't they?

"Is it possible? Sure," I conceded, "but not likely. Nothing is this perfect. Do you honestly think an organic civilization of this scale could exist with no complications whatsoever? People are messy. They fight and—"

I cut myself off as Savreen appeared at the far side of the hall, flanked by two turtle men. Upon noticing us, she perked up and lengthened her strides. The servants hurried to keep up. Inwardly, I pulled a face. On the outside, my mouth stretched in an approximation of a smile.

"There you are!" Savreen exclaimed, coming to an abrupt halt. She glanced at the turtle people by her side, who pivoted at her wordless order and ran off the way they'd come.

"You weren't in your room," she continued, directing her attention back to Luthri and me. Her tone, though light, held a petulant undercurrent. "I'm glad I found you. Lady Narille wanted to extend an invitation to join her for the midday meal. I figured you would be eager to accept."

"That's perfect," I agreed. It was difficult to gauge how long we had been wandering the manor—was it already that time? "Should we go there now, or...?"

Savreen nodded. "If you'd come with me."

I gestured for her to lead the way. She took us on an unfamiliar route through a seldom-used sitting room and outside to the veranda surrounding the inner garden. Patio furniture had been placed in a sunny area directly in front of the fountain, and it was there that the Kereti heiress enjoyed a spread of refreshments, a slim book in hand as she snacked.

Narille was not at all what I expected. She was a stately woman, all limb, her lanky figure covered by a shapeless, draping dress not often seen in the North. Her skin was smooth and pale gray, bordering on colorless. She had no hair except for short, ash-colored eyelashes framing large, red eyes like rubies set inside her skull. Altogether, it made for a unique alien allure.

At our approach, she set down her book and stood, smoothing out her skirt to fall flat.

"Hello," she greeted, big eyes blinking. "Welcome. Please, take a seat."

I didn't move, and Luthri remained a regal statue at my side.

"Thank you, but we're hoping this will be quick." *Manners,* I chided myself. *Got to lure with honey, or however the saying goes.* Clearing my throat, I began again. "My name is Mar, and this is Luthri. It's a pleasure to make your acquaintance, Miss Narille, and we're glad to see you're in good health. I assume you already know why we're here?"

"I'm aware." Narille returned to her chair, floating into the seat as though weightless, and crossed her long legs. "I'm open to discussing the matter, but I make no promises. Have you had the chance to try Savreen's cooking yet? She is uniquely skilled."

Again with the food. It was tempting, though, I had to admit. The traveling diet didn't compare to fresh foods, and it did look delicious. "We're all right, thank you," I forced myself to say. "Your family is worried for you. Worried enough to offer a large reward in hope of news."

One of Narille's feet bobbed impatiently. "You're not the first to speak with me, so yes, I know. It has been a frustrating experience, if I'm being honest. I could not have made my stance any clearer to my family."

"Well, they're still confused, apparently." My hands gestured as I talked, as if that could help sway her. "They didn't see it coming, and it threw them off. I think if you visited them in person and explained your side of things, they would understand."

"You don't know my family."

"No, I don't," I agreed. "But family is family, isn't it?"

Narille picked at the food on one of the plates. "I'll tell you what I told the others. It's really none of your business. But as you can see, I'm not being held against my will, and I'm not being mistreated. You can tell them as much. I'm happy here, and I have no plans to leave."

My palms grew moist as despair threatened. I pressed them against the thighs of my pants. She didn't appear to be in distress, but was that enough? Could we leave it there and go back to her family with nothing but a secondhand account of her well-being?

Would they give up the reward we'd come so far to get based on that alone?

"Look at it this way," Luthri interjected, surprising me. "Fine, you don't care whether your family is comfortable with your decision or not. But you said yourself you're frustrated—you don't want people bothering you anymore. This is the best way to settle the matter so that you can live out your life in peace. Come with us, put their minds at ease, and we'll personally escort you back to Munarzed. How's that?"

A strained smile pulled at Narille's lips. "I'm sorry, but all that traveling to prove a point that, as far as I'm concerned, is already proven? I'm sure you can see my dilemma."

What else was there to argue? "We came all this way," I tried.

"I don't mean to chase you out." Narille spread her arms, indicating the space at large. "Munarzed boasts unrivaled hospitality, and I can say it's not an exaggeration. Visit with us a while. Socialize, see the sights, and enjoy everything the city has to offer. I'm sorry that I can't give you what you came for, but the visit will not be an entire loss, hm?"

Luthri and I exchanged meaningful glances. If she wouldn't come with us, we'd done all we could, and our work here was done. Frustration and disappointment warred in my chest. We'd be leaving empty-handed, but we had no reason to stay on Munarzed any longer.

I turned back to Narille. "Thank you for your time."

Heavy under the weight of failure, we left the Kereti heiress to her lunch. Luthri and I crossed the courtyard to where Savreen waited under the shade of the veranda, watching us with an inscrutable expression on her face. Glazed eyes blinked and focused gradually as we neared, as though returning from some place far away. She must have been deep in thought.

"How did it go?" she asked, her attention narrowing on the two of us.

"Not as well as we'd hoped," I answered honestly. "I think we'll head back to our room and work on a new plan, so long as we can take advantage of your hospitality for a little longer."

"Of course." Savreen's expression lifted. "I'll show you the way."

"I think we can find our own way, but thank you." Taking a hold of Luthri's hand, I walked past her toward the door in long, even strides.

"If you're sure," Savreen called after us. "I'll be by with supper before long. Let me know if you get peckish before then—I have a recipe for suncakes that will change your lives!"

"I'll let you know!" I raised my free hand in farewell as we ducked out of view. The moment we did, I lowered my voice and looped in Luthri. "We're going to have to think on another direction to come at this. I'm not satisfied leaving things the way they are—there's no way her family will cough up the reward based on our word alone."

"I agree." Luthri matched my timbre. "I'd be down for a kidnapping. Say the word and I'll signal the twins. We could smuggle the lady out of here before nightfall."

I couldn't help cracking a smile, although my heart wasn't in it. "As fun as it would be to abduct an heiress with you, I don't know that we're at that stage in our relationship yet."

"I know what you taste like," Luthri said in all seriousness, prompting me to shush him. Heads bobbed in acknowledgment as we passed a group of turtle people.

"You can't say that kind of thing out loud," I grumbled. "Let's get our stuff and reconvene with the boys to discuss our options. This place gives me the creeps."

Not being able to convince Narille to leave with us was a failure, and on top of that, we hadn't gotten any closer to solving the mystery of the island. It was tempting to see this whole trip as a waste of time. But there had been high points, even if we almost got eaten once or twice along the way. And if we put our heads together, maybe we could come up with a solution.

Our room was as we left it that morning. Collecting our things took all of five minutes with how little we had with us. I took an extra minute to fix the bed. Unsettling atmosphere aside, Rugaveld had been an excellent host, and it was the polite thing to do.

Luthri loitered by the bookshelf. He stroked the set of spines in front of him and breathed a wistful sigh. "They wouldn't miss a book or two, would they? They have so many."

"You tempt my patience, Luthri Mendersson."

"Oh? Do I tempt anything else?"

I hauled our bag over one shoulder and pivoted, meeting his saucy wink with a warning stare. "We take nothing that's not ours. Come on, we've been so good!"

"I believe the rule was we take nothing that's *given* to us," Luthri pointed out as he followed me to the door. Having gotten to know him, I didn't bat an eye when I was relieved of the pack. The hallway outside our room was empty, ideal for an absconding.

"Semantics," I countered, stepping out. "It's the spirit of the law, not the letter."

"Is it a law, though? More like a suggestion, really," Lu mused to himself.

Sometimes, questing alongside a group of boisterous young men felt an awful lot like mothering. It was a good thing Luthri was easy on the eyes. Summoning an impressive amount of restraint, I intoned, "I am not arguing this with you. We don't need souvenirs."

I wasn't paying much attention to our surroundings. I didn't think it was important, given that we were thirty meters from an exit, and we'd been given no reason to be worried yet.

A glint in the corner of my eye had my hackles rising. Our bag dropped to the ground, drawing my attention to a wide-eyed Luthri as his mouth opened to warn me.

He was too late.

CHAPTER TWENTY-NINE
IN WHICH THE PARTY OUTSTAYS THEIR WELCOME

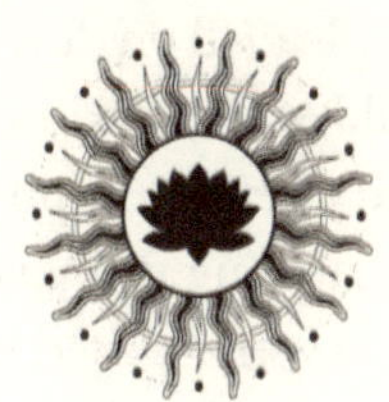

BEFORE I COULD TURN AROUND, hands seized my arms, pinning them to my sides. Magic thrummed through my veins, turning nails into claws and teeth into fangs, but the person behind me was prepared. They whipped around and slammed me against the wall with enough force to steal the breath from my lungs. A hand threaded into the hair at my nape, fingers twisting upwards, nails digging into my scalp. I hissed in pain as they made a fist and pulled. Simultaneously, a cold blade kissed my side, freezing my muscles in place.

"Don't." The word was whispered into my ear with the softness of a lover.

Rugaveld had me. Trapped—and confused—I fought back panic. No matter what, I needed to stay clear-headed. Could I summon *mana* for a large-scale change before he got to use that knife? Doubtful, with what little practice I'd had. Could I even do it under pressure?

"I'm sorry to see that you found your accommodations lacking," Munarzed's enigma of a mayor said from behind me in a frosty tone.

Lu had gone still as death, hands held up to show that he was unarmed. That didn't mean much for a mage, and Rugaveld knew it. Blood turned to ice in my veins. How would we get out of this? I needed to signal the twins. Four could give us an advantage—

With a barked order from the man at my back, Savreen scurried forward. "I'm sorry," she whispered, holding a plate out to Luthri. His eyes narrowed at the unassuming sweet that sat there, a sweet that had held charming memories between Cantal's sendoff and the similarity to a dessert from my childhood in Fortaleza. My heart fell to my stomach.

"Don't let them—" I began. My head was wrenched back without mercy, and fiery pain shot through my scalp and neck. "Ugh!"

"Please!" Lu's desperate plea fell on deaf ears. His throat bobbed.

From my position, I could watch and do nothing as he considered his options, his expression darkening in phases. He came to the same conclusion I had—between catching us by surprise and the dagger too near my heart for comfort, we were backed into a corner.

Decision made, he reached for the plate.

My vision blurred, combining with a burn in my sinuses from the effort of holding back tears. Guilt, regret, anger, and frustration swirled together in a nauseating cocktail. The doubts I managed to hold at bay most of the time came flooding in: Luthri was in danger, and it was my fault. I'd let us all down after all. I should never have been trusted with this quest.

This was the end. We were going to be permanent fixtures in a lunatic's play village.

I pulled at the hand that held me, but it was like stone, and a sharp pain by my ribs told me Rugaveld would not afford me another verbal warning. Gritting my teeth, I ignored the tightness in my chest urging me to action and went slack. Now wasn't the moment. If I was smart about it, I could get his guard down and an opening would present itself.

Luthri had finished chewing and swallowed.

"Now we wait for it to take effect. Tie yourself up," Rugaveld ordered.

A turtle guy hurried forward with a length of rope. As they trussed Luthri like a Thanksgiving turkey, another rope wound around my arms, wrenching my shoulders back. Once it was done, hands forced me to the floor and released me. I curled into myself to nurse the ache in my jaw from where it had hit the wall, afraid to look at Luthri for fear of what I might see.

Rugaveld paced the hallway, leaking anxious energy into the tight space. "I dislike doing things this way, you know. It causes so much unnecessary stress," he lamented. "All you had to do was eat the food. If you'd just done that in the beginning, we wouldn't be here."

"Sorry to be difficult," I spat.

The mayor came to an abrupt halt, considering me. "You're their leader, aren't you? Where are the other two you came here with?"

My lips pressed together. It was a good thing I hadn't gone with Luthri on his check-ins; if I had, they could have tortured the information out of me. If they caught Hohem and Vyrain unawares, there was no telling who would come out on top.

"No matter." Rugaveld resumed his pacing, jerking his head to indicate Luthri. "Give it another minute. Once he's under our control, we'll know everything he does."

Any pride left crumbled at his statement. Maybe Lu could fight it somehow? Even if he did, Savreen was right there. She sat cross-legged in front of him, staring as if ready to start asking questions the moment the drugged food kicked in or however it worked. Luthri's head was bowed in defeat, making my heart pinch.

What could I do?

"Is this what happened to all the others?" I asked, though I could guess the answer.

"Hm? The others who came for Narille? Obviously. You'd think people would stop coming after word spread that no one leaves, but money is a strong motivator. It's rather sad, if you think about it. Oh, well—that's life. Money is everything to those who have nothing."

In any other scenario, I might have been offended by the implication. If this was the end, though, I wanted to understand, and Rugaveld appeared to be the sort inclined to gloat.

"What is it?" My chin jerked to indicate the plate. "In the food."

Rugaveld followed my gaze. "You mean you didn't know? Why did you avoid it?"

Did the *Aminkinya* not speak to anyone else? Well, we did a great job of squandering that advantage. I shrugged as best I could with my arms tied. "Call it a bad feeling."

Ignoring my question, Rugaveld swiveled toward his daughter. "Is it done yet?"

"Not yet," Savreen responded after a beat.

He made an irritated sound in his throat and resumed pacing. "You've seen what we created," he continued, apparently returning to our conversation. "It's beautiful, isn't it?"

Something told me he wasn't referring to the manor. What did he want from me—validation that their creepy town was nice? While my friend and I were tied up and held against our will? Let me add a song and dance while I'm at it.

"As beautiful as a hellish prison can be," I muttered.

"Our country is at war."

"... Yes, you mentioned—"

He spoke over me. "But it goes far beyond that. In my homeland, we were forced to enslave our own, creating a cruel caste system where our people can't choose their line of work or marry for love. I've seen what that does to people. What it did to Savreen's mother, as a member of a lower caste. I thought, 'If it were possible to achieve order without cruelty... If people did what they were told willingly—happily—things would be better.'

"Now, picture a society where everyone pulls their weight. Everyone follows the law. No one is better or worse than his neighbor, and every individual works selflessly for the good of the nation. Imagine how successful that would be! That's what I wanted, and I've been given a chance to make that happen. Thanks to me, Munarzed has become the perfect nation."

Much like when witnessing a horrific accident unfold, I found myself unable to look away. This guy was certifiably crazy. Did he truly think that sob story justified this? The retort that he was no better than his countrymen climbed up my throat, but Luthri beat me to it.

"What perfect nation takes away a person's free will?" my companion growled from across the hall. Sweat beaded across his brow, an outward sign of his struggle. His criticism caught Rugaveld's attention, and the mayor stalked across the room to crouch beside Savreen.

Leaving me unattended.

Rugaveld thrust the tip of his dagger under Luthri's chin, forcing the *Peri* man to look him in the eye. His tone was chilling. "When you have a responsibility to protect that which you hold dear, you find that some concessions must be made. However, anyone would agree that our efforts have improved this island. Before we came, it was a melting pot of depravity."

This was my chance. The rope dug into my forearms when I tested it again. I'd have to be careful with the transformation—bring that part of me inside my torso instead of trying to expand within the confines of the rope. Before that, I would need *mana*, and a lot of it.

I maintained the defeated posture and observed Rugaveld and his puppets through my lashes. Praying that my actions would go unnoticed, I began amassing what I needed.

The magic in my chest roused at the first wisp, as if knowing what I planned to do. The great cat I likened the sensation to stretched and pawed the ground, eager for action. I kept my breathing even and drew slowly, steadily, gathering power for what I hoped would give us a decisive victory. A form took shape in my head—*yes, that would do nicely*.

Rugaveld looked to Savreen, who shook her head, and huffed his displeasure. "Here, have another," he said, grabbing a second sweet and forcing it between Luthri's lips. His fingers caught Lu's teeth—or perhaps it was the other way around—and he winced.

"You know it doesn't work that way," Savreen scolded, snatching her father's hand to determine the severity of the wound. She dabbed at the welling blood with the hem of her skirt.

"Magic is confusing," Rugaveld grumbled under his breath.

Their conversation drifted into one ear as I focused on collecting *mana* and preparing for a change. Of course—he controlled the residents with magic. He must have a unique ability that let him produce a mind-altering substance or otherwise turn food into a weapon.

A flurry of thoughts derailed my efforts, even though I couldn't afford the distraction. There was no cure, in that case… But *mana* returned to nature when the mage wasn't around to control it anymore. So if I killed him, that would end his influence for everyone affected, shouldn't it? It wasn't a decision to be made lightly. Murder never was. Then again, what was one man's life compared to Luthri's life and the lives of the villagers?

What other options were there? He was too far gone to convince. We held no power other than the potential to surprise them and deal a blow there was no coming back from.

And with Rugaveld and Savreen occupied, it was now or never.

I started the process again. *Mana* came when I asked, merging with the anger and fear boiling inside me and reaching a point of no return. When the quantity hit dizzying heights, I held onto the image I had in mind and let loose, pushing controlled doses of magic to every corner of my body and demanding its obedience.

The effect was electrifying and near-instantaneous.

My neck extended to make room for a line of sharp frills. My mouth, open in a silent scream of victory, morphed into a narrow snout filled with sharp teeth. Skin became a tough hide coated in shiny crimson scales. Claws sprouted from my hands, now paws the size of a man's chest. My tail, prehensile and pure muscle, curled around me as I got my bearings, sweeping a turtle guy off his feet and nearly bringing down the wall by my shoulder.

For a split second, nobody moved, taking in the dragon/sea monster beast I'd become. I might not have had the skill to craft wings, but the rest was effective without.

My eyes narrowed on the threat. No time to waste.

I lumbered forward, intent on getting Rugaveld away from Luthri. The mayor had enough time to shove his daughter out of the way and raise his dagger before I plowed into him, knocking the blade from his hands and taking him straight through the paneling at his back. Someone shrieked as a shower of debris hid him from view.

I blinked dust and sunlight from my eyes, struggling not to cough. I could show no weakness right now. A slim figure stumbled to his feet in front of me; rage turned it red. I advanced, my scaled and clawed feet sliding on the polished stone. My first thought was to bite, but leading with my teeth was unwise—killing him that way would mean having to taste him.

My jaw clicked shut, and I swung my neck instead, slamming Rugaveld against the floor with the force of a truck. He was fast for an old man, though, back on his feet before I'd prepared another blow. Fear twisted his features, his confidence shaken.

I have him right where I want him.

But rather than stand and face me, he darted for the shelter of the manor. *So, that's how we're playing this?* Loosing a rattling growl, my tail came around to block his path, sweeping rubble along the way. Despite a limp, Rugaveld vaulted over the extra appendage. I pursued him, ducking under the ceiling and into the hallway. My shoulder upset a cabinet of curios and sent a painting careening to the floor. It barely registered, no more than dull thumps in the background.

The phrase "to be drunk with power" made sense now. Once I got my unwieldy bulk moving, there was no stopping me. My vision had a blurry golden overcast, and my lungs heaved to provide the larger body with enough oxygen, but the blood pumping through my veins was hot and *mana*-fueled. My purpose was clear—the man in front of me would die.

"Mar!"

My ear twitched at the sound of my name, but it faded into white noise. Behind me, the hall filled with mist, obscuring details from view. My attention remained in front. I gained on Rugaveld, even as he rounded corners, overturned furniture, and slammed doors in an attempt to shake me off. It wasn't enough. Like a juggernaut, I plowed through every obstacle he presented.

This person threatened someone who was mine. I would make him pay.

We burst through the doors to his beautiful conservatory. Birdsong cut out at our intrusion, and a cluster of colorful star-shaped flowers that had been soaking up the sun in a planter nearby snapped shut. Rugaveld drew up short, turning this way and that. He could keep running, but he couldn't hide, and judging by the despair on his face, we both knew it.

I stalked forward. All fight left him, and he dropped to his knees, wincing as bone cracked against the marble floor. I almost felt sorry for him. Almost.

How many had this man enslaved? How many lives had he interfered with when it wasn't his place, Lady Narille's included? If anyone deserved to die, it was this monster.

"Please," he whispered, a plea for his life carried on a breeze of breath.

I hesitated. Of course I did. As determined as I'd been to chase him down, there was no coming back from this. It would be a permanent stain on my soul. But what other option did I have to put a stop to this? How else could I set the others free? How could I save Luthri?

No. This was the only way.

The shape of my mouth and throat made words difficult, and a deep rumbling bellowed from my cavernous chest in place of the intended statement. I tweaked my form and tried again. "You know I can't let you go. We show you mercy, and this never ends."

Rugaveld bowed his head. "I wanted to make things better," he tried, voice small.

I had nothing to say to that. Pity didn't serve me here, so I stopped listening. He could explain himself to whatever god or goddess received him in death.

Putting everything I had into it, I dealt the killing blow.

My feet dragged as I retraced my steps to where I'd left Luthri, praying he was all right. As I went, it became harder and harder to hold onto my form. A bone-deep fatigue took root. Scales sloughed from my arms and back, melting into the air as my hold on the excess *mana* loosened. Each footstep lightened until a normal human foot landed, bare and unburdened.

Damn it. I must have lost my boots somewhere in the change.

The peculiar mist had dissipated enough to make out twists and turns in the hall, but no details. Instinct drove me forward, but every stride was a guessing game. When the hall at last opened to fresh air and light, relief turned my legs to noodles. I barely summoned the strength to step over an unconscious turtle person in my path rather than kicking him aside.

A head of short blond hair popped out from the wreckage. Upon noticing me, an unrestrained grin broke out on Vyrain's face. "Mar! Thank the Goddess you're okay."

"That was a hell of a signal," Hohem exclaimed. Noticing my disheveled appearance and unsteady gait, he rushed to help, but I brushed off his hands. I had eyes for one thing only.

Stomping past the twins, I closed in on Luthri. The *Peri* man crouched by what remained of the outer wall, Rugaveld's dagger in hand, tending to where the rope had bitten into his wrists. At my approach, the creases of concern marking his face smoothed. He reached for me with both hands as his wings jerked above his shoulders in a happy dance. Gripping his forearms for support, I sank to the floor between his knees and let my head drop.

"Gods of old, Mar, that was incredible. But where did you disappear to?" Luthri's eyes scanned me from head to toe, taking in the various cuts, skewed clothing, and bare feet.

No doubt I was covered in dust, same as everyone else, but I would live. Fatigue was my primary enemy now. Nevertheless, I couldn't relax until I was sure it was over.

"I had to take care of Rugaveld. How do you feel?" I studied his face for signs of Rugaveld's spell. He appeared alert, but the color had washed from his skin, turning him an alarming shade of taupe. A side effect of the sweets? If killing Rugaveld didn't solve the problem for some reason, we might need to tie Lu up again until we could figure out an alternative cure.

Behind my back, my hand felt around for a stray piece of rope.

Luthri shook his head. "I'll be fine," he said. "I just need to find a bathroom soon."

His stomach concurred with an ominous gurgle. If possible, he paled even further, and his fingers dug into my arms.

I absolutely would not laugh. Some of the tightness in my chest eased, though.

"All right," I conceded, dragging my protesting limbs back into action. "Let's do that, and then let's find Narille and go home."

CHAPTER THIRTY

IN WHICH THE PARTY PREPARES TO BRING THE CAMPAIGN TO AN END

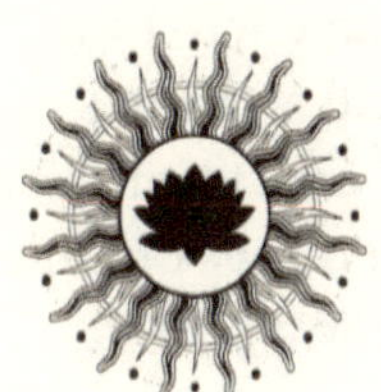

AFTER FINDING Luthri a bathroom and leaving him there at his urging (*"Trust me, Mar, you don't want to be around for this. I'll find you all afterward."*), we wandered the halls of the manor for some time before Hohem had the nerve to speak up.

"You have no idea where Narille is, do you?"

"We'll find her," I assured him. "I'm not worried."

After being released from more than a year of mind control, she was probably hiding in a room somewhere, alone and confused. To be honest, I half expected her to find us. Either we'd stumble across her, or we'd use Luthri's nose to sniff her out when he returned.

I couldn't wait for this day to be over. Hell, I was even eager to be back on the road again. My unpracticed transformation had left my body one giant bruise, and I struggled to keep my eyes open. After this, I'd need a long nap, a hot meal, and another bath. The order wasn't important. We might need to stay in Munarzed another evening or two to recover. There was the shipping schedule to worry about, too —when did Gerda return next? I couldn't remember.

Even thinking hurt. My next exhale bordered on violent.

Vyrain must have picked up on my discomfort, because he kindly offered me his canteen. Mine must have joined my shoes, lost in the kerfuffle at some point.

I helped myself to a generous swig and replaced the cap with a satisfied sigh before handing it back. "Thank you. You guys got here in the nick of time, you know."

"Well, I should hope so." Vyrain returned the water to his belt. "We were waiting on that signal, but much longer and we would have stormed in regardless. We've never been so bored."

Hohem was quick to chime in. "I can't believe we missed all the excitement. Crazy to think that all this was because of one power-hungry madman. Though, I can't blame him… If I had the opportunity to take over an island, I would have done the same. I mean, look at this manor—it's a work of art. Well, it was before Mar gave it a new skylight."

"Open floor plans are all the rage these days," I quipped.

"What would you know about real estate? We live in tents. The last time you were in a building with four walls was an *opashi*'s shack in the woods."

"It was a shrine," Vyrain chastised before I could. "A holy place."

His brother waved him off. "Yeah, yeah."

We neared a familiar door—the parlor off the courtyard, if I wasn't mistaken. The last time we'd seen Narille had been in the courtyard, and my mamãe used to say that when you lost something, you should be sure to check the last place you saw it.

I stopped Vyrain with a hand on his shoulder. "Let's go this way."

Hohem, a step ahead, had to turn back. He held the door as Vyrain and I ducked inside, and we were outside a second later. The roof and pillars cast long shadows over the paneled floor of the veranda, most of the day stolen one way or another. This better not have been the day the shippers returned; if we just missed them, that would be the icing on top.

"Mar?"

The thread of caution in my name got my attention, along with a burst of motion. Across the way, half-hidden by the vibrant greenery decorating the courtyard, ruby eyes observed us. Upon noticing she was caught, Narille emerged from behind the dense bush. It was impossible to miss the long, curved blade in her hand as it reflected the sun.

My heart thumped in warning. The twins drew themselves upright by my side. Adrenaline giving me energy I didn't have, I raised my hands. "It's okay! Lady Narille, it's okay, we're friends. I know things are confusing right now. Do you remember me?"

Something—my words, the nonthreatening gesture, an unknown influence—gave her pause. As quickly as she'd taken an aggressive stance, her pace slowed, and she came to a stop.

"Do I…?" Narille's head tilted as she considered her answer. "Yes, I remember. Mar."

"So you know who I am." I nodded at the twins, who had yet to relax. "Hohem and Vyrain—they're also with me. We're here to help. Now that Rugaveld's spell is broken, you're free to do as you wish. We hoped that you might be open to leaving the island?"

Understanding dawned. "You're leaving," she repeated.

"Yes," I confirmed. "There's a shipping vessel that will take us. You too, if you want."

"We hope you'll come with us," Vyrain added from beside me. He vibrated with the impulse to make her acquaintance but restrained himself given the fragility of the moment.

Any remaining tension leeched from Narille's body. The blade twirled in her hand and came to rest with the tip pointed at the ground. "I need to get my things. Will you wait?"

A breath whooshed out of me. "Of course! Or we can accompany you?"

We had nothing better to do, and I would be more comfortable being able to keep an eye on her. Maybe it was nerves left over from my fight with Rugaveld, or perhaps Luthri being out of sight so soon after his life was threatened unsettled me, but I hadn't relaxed yet.

"Yes, let's do that. I know a way off the island that we can take advantage of." Narille's gaze bounced from head to head. "There was one more… What happened to him?"

"Ah, the sweets didn't agree with him. He'll catch up." I cherished the thought that this would be an inside joke soon. If Narille knew a way off the island, we could be back to the mainland in no time. I could breathe easier knowing familiar territory lay within reach.

"Lead the way." Hohem stepped aside with a flourish.

Narille angled her body in the direction she'd come. "This way," she said, and waited for us to start moving before she did. Vyrain took his chance to inspect her when her back was turned, eyebrows crawling his forehead. Hohem mouthed something at me. At my questioning gesture, he shrugged it off and followed after the rest of us.

The heiress appeared to know the manor layout intimately, leading us inside to the second level. Would we be crossing the skybridge to the other section of the manor? But no, we kept to the main area, ending up toward the glass rear of the building. As she retreated into her room to gather her things, leaving the door open behind her, I considered her weapon.

It wasn't out of the ordinary to see such a thing. While many fae used magic, not all of them had the ability, and a blade, bow, or rudimentary pistol went a long way in evening the playing field. For most, it would be an additional thing to carry. Had she brought it with her to the island when she first arrived? Or borrowed it from Rugaveld's collection?

The twins stood in the doorway, observing Narille as she packed. Pushing myself to my tiptoes, I leaned into Vyrain and peered over his shoulder. The willowy woman navigated the room from one side to the other. She could have sped it up, perhaps, but maybe she needed to think about what to take with her after living here for so long. If not that, maybe there was some mental fog left over from Rugaveld's magic.

When she joined us at the door, she had a single bag slung over her shoulder, smaller than the one Hohem carried. *She's lived here how long, and that's all she owns?* I wouldn't have blamed her for cleaning out the place, but all right.

"You sure that's everything?" I checked.

"All I need," she confirmed. "We should collect your friend before proceeding, no?"

"He'll find us. At least, he said he would."

"Maybe we ought to check on him?" Vyrain's suggestion received a blank look. "I mean, I'm all for letting him find us, but that might be difficult if we're halfway back to the mainland."

"Do you remember where we left him?" Hohem asked, running his fingers through his shaggy locks. "I haven't had the chance to map out the manor yet. It's a labyrinth."

I studied the hall nearest us, opposite the way we'd come. "I think it was that way, but it's not that big. We're bound to stumble across him eventually if we stick to familiar routes."

Narille took the discussion in stride, inquiring, "Do you often lose each other?"

"This particular one, only if we're lucky," Vyrain quipped, putting on a charming smile as though that would soften the blow of his words. "Unfortunately, he has a knack for not staying lost. Hard to shake off—like a bad cough after staying out too long in the cold."

Seeing as Luthri wasn't there to defend himself, I chimed in. "Well, that's not very nice."

"I mean it in the nicest way possible, of course—"

"Better leave it there," Hohem remarked, clapping his brother on the back.

Vyrain took his advice, though not without muttering something about 'finding his stride again.' How Narille maintained a stony expression throughout the exchange was a mystery—a structured upbringing left her immune to such antics, perhaps. Poor Vyrain's usual low-reaching jokes and indiscriminate flirting wouldn't stand a chance.

After a brief discussion, we agreed to let Narille show us her route off the island, with the expectation that Luthri would catch up before we made it too far. She brought us back toward the front of the building and down the staircase to the main level. Several steps ahead, Narille disappeared around a corner moments before a resounding *OOF* carried our way. The twins and I exchanged a look and hustled to cover the remaining distance.

"Pardon me," Luthri exclaimed as he steadied the heiress with a hand on her elbow. His eyes widened at noticing the unsheathed sword. Upon seeing us, he relaxed somewhat, mirroring my own relief. "There you are. Where did everyone go? The house is a ghost town."

"No idea," I answered, giving him a once-over. "How are you feeling?"

"As well as can be expected. Things may be iffy the next day or two, but I'll live."

Hohem interrupted our cheery reunion. "Killing their leader and bringing down a few walls might have had something to do with the change in atmosphere," he commented. "Can't imagine anyone would take kindly to that sort of insurrection."

"Rugaveld is dead?" Narille's voice went strangely high-pitched.

"Yes," I confirmed. It didn't occur to me that the place would clear out immediately. "People were in a hurry to leave, I guess. They've got a lot to figure out now that they're free."

Luthri nodded thoughtfully. "As do we. What's the plan?"

"Lady Narille knows of a way off the island," Vyrain informed him.

"If it works, we won't have to wait for the shippers to return," I added. "Let's get going. The sooner we can be off this rock, the sooner we can get on with our lives."

A shadow flitted across Lu's face, but he made a sound of agreement.

The heiress, finding herself the center of attention once more, took the lead without protest. "This way," she intoned, pointing toward the building's main entrance.

We walked together down the long hallway, past the gaudy drapes and statement pieces of art, to the great double doors, which were no longer propped open. Narille applied her shoulder to the wood. Vyrain rushed forward to help, his brother hot on his heels, and together the three of them pried the panels apart enough to slip out into the waning daylight.

Narille held the door and waved us through. I crossed the threshold second to last, Luthri behind me, and nearly walked into Hohem's back as he stopped short.

"What—" The back of my neck prickled.

Framed in the space between the twins' braced shoulders, Savreen stood tall before the manor, gripping a sword that seemed too large for her slim hand. A number of townspeople stood around her, many bearing weapons of their own.

Fear rooted my legs as a rush of adrenaline flooded my body. *How could puppets still move with their strings cut?* Killing Rugaveld should have ended his control. Unless…

Unless it wasn't Rugaveld's magic at all.

Things came together, too little too late.

Scenes flashed through my mind: Savreen offering us sweets the first time. Narille asking us if we'd have the chance to try her cooking. Savreen's proud announcement: *"I have a recipe for suncakes that will change your lives."* The lady we came across right after entering the city said exactly the same thing. It couldn't be a coincidence.

Savreen was the *amafarin*, the witch. And I'd killed… Well, not an innocent man, but not the one directly responsible for this. How did I not see it? What could be done now?

In my current condition, I'd be no use in a fight. Could the boys take all of them? Unlikely. Could we hide somewhere until we had the opportunity to make a break for it, either commandeer an island boat or wait for Gerda's crew…?

My head turned at the sound of a click to see Narille shutting the front door behind us. She dropped her bag and kicked it to the side, forgotten, as she held her sword ready.

CHAPTER THIRTY-ONE

IN WHICH THINGS TAKE A TURN FOR THE WORSE

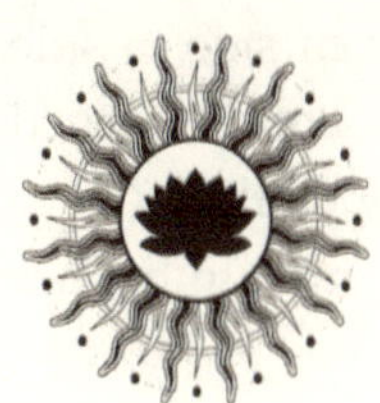

It was an impressively diverse group of people, as far as angry mobs went.

Well, how about that? I'd finally learned to look on the bright side. Shame that it was moments before we all died violent deaths on a remote island.

It also struck me how organized the group of villagers was. There were no overzealous individuals growing restless, shouting over one another, or jostling for position. I could almost see the benefit of mind control. It made for an intimidating sight, if nothing else.

"I'm done trying to do things the right way and be nice about it," Savreen declared, her voice wobbling. She brandished her rapier, and a handful of her captives copied the movement with their own equipment, as though she was too distressed to worry about who was doing what. "This was supposed to be paradise. Safety. Our future." Her face scrunched as tears rolled down her cheeks, and the next words were sobbed. "You've ruined everything."

"*We* ruined—!" Luthri barely cut off his protest in time.

He wasn't stupid; he also recognized there was a chance to deescalate the situation. Where Rugaveld was set in his ways, Savreen was young and emotional. She might be open to convincing, or at least negotiating with. Either way, we'd have to tread carefully.

I asked for space with a hand on Hohem's arm. As the twins shifted so that I could move up, I addressed the young woman. "Savreen, I'm sorry, but this isn't right. I understand where you're coming from, but these people want the same things. They have their own families who love them and their own hopes and dreams to fulfill. You should let them go."

Savreen's head jerked from side to side. "I gave them peace," she hissed. "We did that. Dad and I rescued them from the demands Narille and her family put upon them."

Using her sword, she pointed to the heiress standing frozen by the door.

"You don't know what it was like here before. People worked themselves to the bone and barely scraped by, only for her ilk to come in and demand tribute! What sort of life is that?"

Her sword lowered as she admitted, "At first, I thought Narille was a mistake. Taking someone important attracts attention. But when people kept coming for her, my dad saw an opportunity. We needed people to build all this, to keep it running, and she made the perfect bait. You would have been taken care of—clothed, fed, housed. Comfortable."

It's as if she's playing with dolls and not people. My shoulders shook from the sudden chill. Keeping my voice level, I tried again to reason with her. "Some people live hard lives, but it doesn't mean they're unhappy. Did you ask them what they thought of your plans? In my experience, people appreciate being able to make their own choices. Sure, mistakes come with the territory. It may not be perfection, but that's a good life for most of us."

Savreen's head shook faster. A section of black hair split from the woven crown and flopped against the side of her face, framing wide, crazed eyes. "It's not a good life if you're only working to further someone else's agenda, having to look over your shoulder at all times or risk losing everything you've built. It's not right. No one wants that."

"You leave if that doesn't work for you," I argued. "Take freedom with your own hands. Build the life you want for yourself, one where your wins are entirely yours to celebrate. Yes, it will be hard, but you can't take advantage of other people to make that happen."

My appeal fell on deaf ears. Savreen wasn't listening anymore, muttering her next words to herself as if too caught up in her own head. "This way, there's no pain, no anger, and no sadness. That's how it should have been, anyway. Without Dad… I don't know how I'm going to do this by myself."

Her free hand balled into a fist.

"But I'll figure it out. *You* need to be gone."

The group rushed us at once. My hands came up instinctually, though there was little flesh and blood could do against wood and metal carried with the intent to kill. The twins stepped in front of me, forcing me back, and met the villagers head-on. The world dissolved into chaos—grunts of effort, flashes of magic, cries of pain, and bodies crowding together into one suffocating mass. A blade clanged against stone as Luthri fended off Narille behind me.

"Nonlethal force!" I hollered, hoping the twins could hear me over the din. It would be helpful to be a beast right now, but trying to summon *mana* brought on sharp jolts of bone-deep pain, like a stitch in the side but throughout my entire body. I managed enough to toughen my skin and turn my nails into weapons.

Luthri disarmed Narille in the time it took me to fight through the discomfort. He'd melted and rehardened a section of ground to lock her feet in the cobblestones, making it impossible for her to do anything but swipe ineffectively at him. Evading her wild swings, he bent to snatch up her sword just in time to dodge another villager and knock him out with a well-placed strike to the head.

He came to a sliding stop at my side. "Can you do another change? Like before?"

As much as I hated to admit it… "I don't think so. That took a lot out of me."

Lu stepped forward to disrupt a turtle person's charge, neatly knocked the club from its hand, and sent it flying. The villagers' movements were not as fluid as they should have been. Whether Savreen was an inexperienced fighter or it simply became too much to coordinate a hundred people attacking at once, our opponents were sloppy. Good.

"No problem." Luthri paused to assure me. "We'll figure something else out. I'll do my best to keep them away from you. If someone makes it past, do what you need to do."

"Don't have to tell me twice," I muttered. He passed me Narille's sword. I might not know what I was doing with a weapon like that, but I wasn't about to turn it down. Being armed put me in a much better position. If we got out of this alive, I'd have to work on my stamina.

Having something to look forward to filled me with purpose.

Luthri and I faced the onslaught side by side, determined to defend ourselves while doing as little damage to the people under Savreen's control as possible. Unfortunately, they were hellbent on making that hard for us. Lu took down two more stragglers before a group of people broke off from the swarm, diverting their attention from the twins to what they saw as sitting ducks: us.

I would have loved to sit back and watch Luthri fight, but I didn't have the opportunity, as one assailant dodged his attempt to corral them right away. The young woman went for my legs. She appeared unarmed, so I dropped the sword to counter her tackle. My arms locked around her torso, and I threw my weight backward, twisting to pull her to the ground. Dazed from the takedown, she froze. It gave me the opening I needed for a rear naked choke. When she went limp, I gave it another second before letting her fall from my arms.

Running my hands over cramping muscles as I caught my breath, I checked in with Luthri. The *Peri* man was a blur of magic, fists, and talons. He would use a burst of air or light to push an aggressor aside or create an opening for himself, then deliver a stunning blow or lock them to the nearest structure to incapacitate them. He'd taken down three—make that four—in the time it took me to face one, and he'd hardly broken a sweat.

Given a brief respite, I caught his attention and exaggerated a stretch.

"Whew," I exclaimed. "You know, this isn't bad at all. To think I was worried."

Luthri's lips curved. "Oh, you think so?"

"Yeah. I'm tempted to ask for a real challenge."

"Well, you're a formidable adversary."

"I'm glad you agree."

I retrieved the sword, and we squared off against the next wave. With every opponent, we drifted closer to where Hohem and Vyrain fought their way to Savreen. She certainly wasn't going easy on us. At one point, I twisted my ankle trying not to impale a villager in the gut. Lu attracted their focus, giving me a moment to recover, and an arrow narrowly missed his neck.

I whirled around, searching for the hidden archer. There! The *Santouri*—a beast of a woman by all accounts, even before the horse parts—kept to the sidelines, waiting for a break in the action to set loose her deadly projectiles. What could I do here? Could one of the others afford to confront her if I covered for them? First, I needed to take stock of the situation.

Where did we stand?

Our efforts thinned the crowd, but we weren't untouched. Hohem was missing part of an ear and had a gash across one brow, forcing him to keep his eye closed. The combination turned his blond hair pink with blood. Vyrain limped, and the collar of his shirt gaped to reveal the beginnings of a nasty bruise along one side of his chest. He cradled one arm close to his torso.

Luthri wasn't faring much better. More than one shallow cut decorated his forearms from aggressors who'd gotten too close. His reaction time had slowed, and he no longer used bursts of magic recklessly. No doubt he also felt the ache of magical depletion.

Even with exhaustion weighing down my body, I was in the best shape out of the four of us. That being said, I couldn't tell what or how much pain to attribute to a new injury. The nick in my side from Rugaveld's dagger had long since stopped bleeding. My ears rang, my jaw throbbed, and my ankle twinged, but that was all inconsequential. I'd make do.

Lu, in between bouts again, put his hands on his knees and lowered his head. The *Santouri* on the edge of the action nocked another arrow.

"Luthri!"

His head whipped up at my shout and followed my pointing finger to the source of danger. Understanding smoothed his features, then resolve hardened them once more. Another warning sprang to my tongue.

Aaand he was already moving. I scurried after him, sword in hand. My body had never been so burdensome, but if I could hold the gang at bay long enough for him to dispatch the problem, we'd be golden. Teamwork, right?

The archer made note of our trajectory and adjusted her aim. Lu pulled up short. Momentum sent him into an oddly graceful twirl, the arrow striking centimeters from his foot. The next arrow stared me down, steady in the archer's grip, as she trotted backward in an attempt to put more space between us. Luthri was having none of it.

He darted forward, weaving left and right. Uttering a grunt of annoyance, the archer threw down her bow and reared up, pawing at the air with hooves the size of dinner plates before charging. Despite the expansive cobblestone square, the space between them disappeared in an instant. Luthri went in low. The *Santouri* cocked back an arm, hand folded into a fist, putting the entirety of her stalwart build behind it.

I didn't see them make contact. Force slammed into my back like a freight train, sending my legs crumpling. I'd gotten too caught up in Luthri's battle—how could I have forgotten that I had a fight of my own? Having the good sense to roll, I narrowly avoided another strike. Wood struck the space by my ear. My attacker raised their weapon again—a railing spoke or chair leg serving as a bat—and the hit reverberated through my crossed arms.

I clenched my jaw against the pain and swiped for their unprotected ankles, latching on when I felt fabric and calf. They toppled, falling harder than I had, and their head cracked on the stone. A strange spasm ripped through their body, and they didn't move again.

Remorse would have to wait. Gulping air as though I'd never breathe again, I crawled to where my sword lay abandoned on the ground. My hand found the hilt, and my gaze lifted, searching for Luthri. He straddled the *Santouri* woman's back, hanging onto her thick, braided hair for dear life as she bucked and spun. Laughter bubbled up; I choked it down.

The last few combatants circled like vultures. Threatening them with the sword was enough to make them think twice—apparently, Savreen wanted the townspeople dead as much as we did. Grunts and clatters abounded out of sight, but I couldn't look, not yet.

Behind the line of assailants before me, the twins had reached Savreen and her last line of defense. My grip on the sword tightened. Hohem and Vyrain exchanged blows with their opponents, dodging wood and steel to clap back with fire and fists. They were exhausted, but Savreen's eyes were wide with fear now. Satisfaction loosened some of the tension in my body.

She deserved to feel fear in the end. Bitterly, I hoped she realized how wrong she'd been.

One of Savreen's guards struck out. As Vyrain evaded his attack, Savreen darted in to follow it with a jab of her sword that caught him under the left arm. He made a small sound and stumbled to one side. Hohem was there, slipping into the opening she'd made with ruthless efficiency. For the span of a breath, the two stood nose to nose. Hohem's hands snaked around her throat. It looked gentle, but that wasn't taking into account fae strength.

He yanked. Her neck yielded. As if the universe reset, everything stopped. Villagers dropped like stones where they stood. A breeze whistled through the open space, cooling perspiring skin and filling aching lungs with the refreshing scent of sand and brine.

It was done. Over. We won.

Grin overtaking my face, I sought out Luthri. He still perched astride the *Santouri*'s unmoving body, confused. My shuffling approach had him springing to his feet. Up close, the threat the half-animal fae woman posed was undeniable. Armed or unarmed, it made no difference with a body made of muscle stacked upon muscle, all of it deadly.

Now that the flood of adrenaline faded, my limbs shook. Things I hadn't allowed myself to think or feel in the thick of it came rushing in with a vengeance: I killed at least one person. We'd been sliced up, smacked around, and shot at with arrows. Luthri, nearly trampled.

Upon reaching the man in question, I gripped his face in my hands. A mix of fae, Portuguese, and English fell from my lips as I shook him. "Valuen's sake. What in the world were you thinking? You could have fucking died. No, why do I ask? Of course, you weren't thinking. You absolute idiot. First-class nincompoop. Porra-louca!"

"I'll admit it went a little better in my head," Luthri acknowledged wryly. "But it was worth it to hear these love names. At least, I can only assume they're love names."

A half-mad laugh escaped me. Watching me closely, expression tinged with worry, Lu's hands folded around mine and moved them to rest over his heart. His touch kept the deep chill of shock at bay, and the rhythmic *thump-thump* grounded me. I closed my eyes.

"They're not dead, are they?" He eyed the fallen figures around us uncertainly.

"Probably not."

"We should… Er…"

My spine snapped straight. Of course, we had things to do. Day would soon give way to night, and we would need a plan for moving forward. I pulled out of Luthri's grip. When my knees buckled, he caught me, slinging an arm under mine for support.

"So you can hold me up," he stated with a wink. "Otherwise, I might fall."

Yeah, all right, he could have his little joke.

Together, we made our way to where Hohem and Vyrain waited by Savreen's corpse. The twins rested on the ground, one kneeling and the other sprawled in front of him. They must have been drained to not even have the energy to stand. I started to ask if they were okay, but it occurred to me that the position was unnatural.

The words caught in my throat as terror seized me.

They weren't resting at all. Hohem held his motionless brother in his arms, clutching him to his chest. Vyrain's arm trailed off Hohem's lap and onto the ground, limp and pale. Scarlet blood stained Vyrain's side, Hohem's lap, and the stones beneath them. Too much blood.

I held onto a delusional hope that it wasn't one of theirs, that perhaps they'd gotten in the path of an arterial spray by accident. But then Hohem's face tilted upward. Tears tracked two shimmering lines through the layer of grime coating his cheeks. Upon seeing us, his lips moved. No sound came out but a broken inhale. Facing forward once more, he let his hold on his brother relax, wordlessly answering the question I couldn't bring myself to voice.

For Vyrain's head drooped to one side, blue eyes open but unseeing.

CHAPTER THIRTY-TWO

IN WHICH THE PARTY MUST DECIDE WHAT COMES NEXT

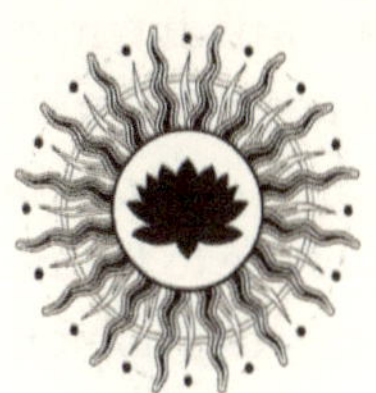

WE'D THOUGHT we were prepared for any outcome. None of us were prepared for this.

I stared for a long while, unwilling to believe what my eyes were seeing. Where did we go wrong? Could I have prevented this? How dare they, how dare she—but Savreen was a crumpled form not far away, and there was no one left to blame.

A hand on my shoulder brought me back to the present. My throat burned as if on fire. Luthri squeezed, telling me he was there, that it was okay to take things one step at a time.

Putting my hands out, I dropped to my knees and crossed to Hohem on all fours. The nightmarish scene wavered in my vision as I blinked back tears. I tried not to look, turning my attention to Hohem instead. He let me put my arms around him, buried his face in the crook of my neck, and released a quavering cry that started low and climbed to an unbridled scream.

"Not like this," he moaned between gulping breaths. "Not like this."

Heart a solid lump in my throat, I squeezed my eyes shut and held him tighter, rocking back and forth as he trembled like a mother with her babe. My hands moved in methodical circles along his back. What could anyone say to ease this kind of loss?

Dropping the tenuous hold on my emotions, I joined him in shedding tears, and we keened together to grieve our friend, brother, and companion. Lu wandered off to free the people he'd trapped during the fight, leaving us in peace.

Dusk fell before Munarzed's people began to stir. Citizens shook off the stupor as though waking from a hundred-year sleep. One by one they stood, stumbled, and sat back down to get reacquainted with their limbs. Some stayed where they were, staring into the distance. Some let their emotions spill over right away, curling into a fetal position and bawling like children. A few chose to let their anger out by kicking and pounding at the walls of Rugaveld's manor.

One of them made for Savreen's body, fire in his eyes. Luthri gently but firmly cut him off before he could get too close. The air filled with scattered wailing, restrained sniffles, and violent curses. It soothed me —the reaction, so human, reflected the turmoil in our hearts. We had something in common now: we all lost something irreplaceable on this hellish island.

A tentative shadow blocked what remained of the sunlight.

"My deepest apologies," Narille began, her red eyes swimming with sorrow.

Lu's somber gaze met mine with a question, but I shook my head. I'd have to pull myself together eventually. It took several measured breaths to find my composure and put some steel back into my spine, but I patted Hohem on the back one last time before getting to my feet.

Clearing my throat, I led with, "You've nothing to apologize for, my lady; we're aware of the situation. It's a pleasure to make your acquaintance for real this time. Are you… Well, I'm not sure how to… Do you remember everything that…?"

Narille bowed her head. "The Lady of War smiles upon you, Mar. Yes, I remember what was seen through my eyes and done with my hands. I imagine it was the same for everyone here. While a… unique experience, it is not one I would ever like to repeat."

That was putting it lightly, going by the haunted expression she wore.

"I'm sure. In that case, I suppose we should ask you again, now that you're in full possession of your faculties… Would you leave Munarzed with us and return to your family?"

A single nod, and we had her answer. "I will. I cannot wait to be home."

The hard knot in my chest unraveled, my next breath coming easier. Having the next steps sorted was something. That gave us direction, even if it would be temporary. The beginnings of a plan formed: we'd escort Narille home, collect the reward, return to Jük and Vee in our camp outside Vhalder, and take the next while off to process things.

Having that figured out momentarily quelled the rising panic. "Excellent. I'm not sure when the next ship will be here, but we'll leave as soon as we're able to secure passage."

"I will need to collect my things and find my guards. I should speak with the villagers as well… Assuage what concerns I can." Narille's eyes drifted to where Hohem knelt by the maimed body of his brother. Her features softened along with her tone. "You are heroes, all of you. I will do what I can to ensure your friend's sacrifice is not forgotten."

A muscle ticked in Hohem's jaw. "Brother. He's my brother."

"Brother," Narille quickly corrected herself. "I thank you, and my family thanks you."

A loud crash drew our attention to the manor. The front doors had been pulled off their hinges, leaving the entrance open to the elements and whoever dared set foot inside. It proved to be many. People from the main part of town rushed past us, eager to get in on the action, many toting large boxes or bags with the intent to fill them. I couldn't blame them.

I attempted to bring some levity to the situation. "Well. We'd best get out of their way."

"I will find you later," Narille stated, a grim set to her jaw. Before she left, she paused, adding, "I suspect it will be a late night. Look after yourselves, if you can."

"Same to you."

Her focus lingered on Hohem, as if she wanted to say something else but thought better of it. She nodded once more and sauntered off in the direction of the main street.

One looter rushed out of the manor with the first haul of the night. Someone else had made it their mission to tip over each and every planter along the cobbled hill leading into town. It was the beginning of the end. Poetic, all things considered.

Breathing deep, I pivoted to return to Hohem's side, only to walk straight into Luthri. "Heavens above," I exclaimed. "How long have you been there?"

"Not long." He pulled me into his side. "You all right?"

No. I'm crumbling like an old foundation. "I will be," I told him, returning the half-hug. Examining his wounds out of the corner of my eye, I asked, "You?"

He didn't appear too injured, but it was easier to worry about others than myself. The cuts on his arms ought to be cleaned. In fact, a mender should look at us all for good measure. Surely there was one somewhere on this island? Then the dead should be buried or burned—

Ah, great, I'd missed his response. "I'm sorry… I wasn't listening."

"Don't mind me," he urged. "Let me know if there's anything I can do to help."

I expressed my gratitude with a light squeeze. "Will do."

That brought me to the next order of business. Approaching Hohem, the lump returned, constricting my throat. I came to stand behind him. Misery marked every part of his body, from the slouch of his shoulders to the defeated set of his mouth. It would have been best to leave him to his grief, but some things couldn't wait. Gently, I set a hand on his shoulder.

"We should think about what to do with the body," I said quietly.

Not a muscle twitched. "I need more time. Please."

Who was I to argue? "Okay. We'll be here when you're ready."

Not wanting to stand there, I set off toward the manor stairs. It was a good place to keep an eye on things, and Luthri had already gotten comfortable. Mainly, I needed to sit. I could only push myself so far, and I'd reached that limit some hours ago.

Lu's arm came around me as I collapsed on the stoop beside him.

"It wasn't your fault, you know," was the first thing he said.

The beginnings of a protest formed on my lips, but without the energy, I settled for a grunt of agreement. The only way to avoid this would have been not coming here in the first place, and that line of thinking made my brain hurt. What a lovely mess we'd gotten ourselves into.

I rested my head on Luthri's shoulder and shut my eyes.

In the distance, a string of cottages burned, turning the airspace above orange and red. Smoke billowed into the air, a testament to the darkness being released. The acrid fumes carried all the way to where Luthri and I sat. Prompted by the harsh reality we faced, my thoughts turned bitter. Trauma, grief, pain—they had varying effects on people, and almost never kind ones. Were they taking things too far? Maybe. Maybe they weren't taking things far enough.

Another set of looters scurried past, clutching bags to their chests and lugging a small, ornate box between two of them. Any other time, I'd be tempted to join in, to pick that stolen house clean of riches that weren't deserved. Funny how priorities changed.

More and more people joined those outside, gathering in groups to confirm that their oppressor was truly dead and contribute to the celebratory destruction. Leaning on each other for support, Lu and I watched the townspeople scream their defiance into the sky, jump for joy, and embrace in the streets as the town burned around them.

Munarzed's brief reign of prosperity had ended.

As Narille predicted, no one slept. Sleep deprivation blended with tender bruises, broken spirits, and the dull throb of overworked muscles. When the sun rose, we were more zombie than Savreen's victims had ever been. As such, we had to prioritize, taking things one step at a time.

Murmuring words of support and compassion, Luthri and I were forced to pry Vyrain's stiff body from his brother's arms. We built a small funeral pyre in the courtyard to lay him to rest. Narille came to join us, saying a few words of thanks and a northern prayer for his spirit. With friends old and new present, we burned the body, scattering all but a small amount of the ash into the sea come dawn. The rest Hohem kept on his person.

"To bring him home," he said, "wherever that ends up being."

His eyes, though distant, stayed miraculously dry. I cried until the tears stopped coming. It was cathartic in a way; I couldn't remember the last time I'd let go of everything and just *felt*.

A ship arrived later that day, though it wasn't Gerda's. It didn't matter whose it was, so long as there was room, but therein lay the difficulty—we weren't the only ones who wanted off the island as soon as possible, and people fought for a spot. Narille firmly stepped in to claim enough for us all: herself, the three dour older women with similarly alien features she'd introduced as members of her household, Luthri, Hohem, and me.

We made our way to the beach south of the city, passing two bodies hung on hastily erected crosses. Birds had already begun to scavenge for their breakfast, but there was no mistaking the shadow-hued skin and slighter, feminine figure beside the man's. The barbaric display made my nose wrinkle, but if it gave people peace to desecrate their bodies, so be it.

The rest of us waited to one side with our meager belongings while Narille spoke with the ship's owner. I wasn't the only person who had never made a high-born lady's acquaintance, and Narille, in her delicate layers of fabric and embroidered overcoat, made an impression on everyone she met. She walked with authority, spoke with grace, and had a particular method of eye contact. As such, no one was surprised when she waved us forward despite having no money to offer.

"Convenient," Luthri murmured from beside me as we boarded.

I nodded absently. My focus remained on Hohem, who carried one of our packs even though I had all but begged him not to worry about it. Once we got settled, my priority would be finding him something nutritious to eat and somewhere quiet to rest.

However hard we all had it, Hohem was in his own bracket. Exhaustion, discomfort, and hunger were temporary, physical things. Sorrow cut through to the soul, stripping away all traces of humor, along with the light in his eyes. It was as though he'd aged ten years overnight. He moved like a ghost—frail, quiet, going through the motions.

I chewed on my bottom lip, unable to watch my friend suffer and equally unable to tear my eyes away. It wasn't that I was heartless—my own sadness cut deep, but it was a heartache I knew would heal given time. For Hohem… would time be enough?

Narille and Luthri, having noticed the same, had their ways of looking out for him. Narille periodically asked questions to keep him involved. Luthri pulled enough weight for the both of them so that Hohem could take it easy as we prepared to leave. He'd tried to banter once or twice, but the jokes didn't land. There was a right and wrong time to try mending things with humor. Luthri, for all his experience with the world, hadn't yet learned the subtleties.

People continued pouring onto the ship, jostling others aside in their eagerness to claim a spot. Coins glinted as they exchanged hands. The owner passed orders along to hustling crew members, who rushed customers into the bowels of the ship to make room for more.

Grateful we wouldn't have to fight, I told Narille, "Appreciate you taking care of that. And covering our fare—the journey up to now hasn't exactly been kind."

Her head jerked in an odd gesture somewhere between a nod and a shake. "It's the least I can do in return for your aid," she replied. "We would not be here without your efforts." Mischief lent a spark of life to her eyes. "And it was no trouble. I simply told him they could keep the shipment they'd brought for Rugaveld. I figured no one will miss it."

My eyebrows climbed my forehead, and my opinion of Narille shifted in a more charitable direction. Maybe it was worth trying our luck after all. "Any chance we could get private quarters? The peace and quiet would go a long way after the last couple of days."

"That, I cannot promise." The heiress's gaze searched for the ship owner, but he was deep inside a writhing crowd. "When things are calm, I can inquire with our captain."

"I'll keep expectations reasonable. Thank you again."

Hohem had dropped his bag and slid down the side of the ship, folding his legs underneath him. His head tipped forward, eyes closed.

I excused myself from the conversation to join him on the floor, scooting back until my shoulders hit wood.

I nearly asked him how he was doing, but that would have been a stupid question.

"We'll be able to get settled in soon," I said instead, hoping that having something to look forward to would provide him with some small comfort.

He didn't open his eyes. "Thank you."

If only I had something better to offer him. A hot meal, a proper bed, anything. He might have volunteered for it, but this trip turned out to be more than we bargained for. Hohem took it on without complaint. First, our mishaps with the man-eating beetles and waterfolk family. He almost lost his life in the swamps along with Luthri and Vyrain. He toughed it out with his brother while Luthri and I were cozy in Rugaveld's mansion. And finally…

He'd had a difficult time of it, indeed.

We rested in relative silence until the captain started turning people down, then chasing them off the ship when they objected. I tensed as it looked like we might need to help him achieve order, but Narille didn't move, and she was my guideline right now.

I caught her attention and indicated the aggravated rabble left behind. "Will they have someone to maintain order temporarily? Keep things organized until the next ship?"

A pained expression crossed her face. "Normally, that would be the case. That's why our local government is never designed around one or two people. With the changes Rugaveld and his progeny implemented, however, not to mention the trauma we've all suffered these past cycles… I doubt anyone will be up to the task. It is out of our hands."

Narille had a good head on her shoulders. Some things were too big for a single person. In this case, doing the "right thing" simply wasn't feasible, no matter how much we might want to help smooth things over. No use torturing ourselves over their fate. Still, a pang of regret hit, as if I had a personal responsibility to Munarzed's people.

While private spaces on the ship were few and far between, we were given a storage room. It was tight for seven of us, but we couldn't complain with the other travelers crammed in toe-to-head and elbow-to-elbow in the main areas. The captain ruefully remarked that they didn't have enough provisions to feed a hundred extra mouths, so most of them went hungry too.

We spread out as much as we could on our mats and put together a scant meal between our supplies and Narille's. Hohem declined his portion of travel fare, but the rest of us were eager to fill our bellies. As we chatted and ate, he retreated to one corner, burrowed into his bedding, and curled up facing the wall. Luthri and I exchanged a look.

Narille leaned in. "If it would help," she whispered, "I know of at least one *opashi* in Solfarin. We could take a brief detour for everyone to cleanse their spirits."

It wouldn't be worth the delay, but her suggestion did give me an idea. "That's all right, thank you. Let's focus on getting you home. We'll worry about that in our own time."

She nodded and returned to her meal.

When the meal concluded, no one dawdled. The priority turned to clearing enough space for everyone to lie down and get comfortable, passing out blankets, and stripping out of unnecessary layers. Luthri and I ended up on opposite sides of the room, so there would be no hushed pillow talk, but that suited me just fine.

Moments after setting my head down, using my arm as a pillow, I drifted away to sleep, lulled by the steady rocking of the ship and weariness like I'd never known before.

CHAPTER THIRTY-THREE

IN WHICH THE PARTY RETURNS TO THE ROAD

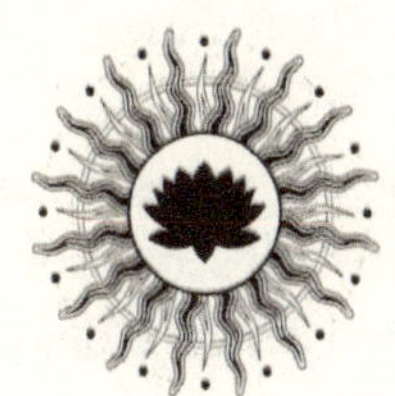

UPON LANDING IN SOLFARIN, Narille took the lead once more, guiding us to a tall brick building near the center of the city. A dwarf greeted us at the door. When he saw Narille and her guards, his eyes bugged out of his head. After partaking in light refreshments, we were brought before an official-looking middle-aged man, an *Alf* like Hohem, hunched over a desk. He spotted us, did a double take, and shot upright, tripping over his chair in his haste to stand.

"Lady Narille!" he exclaimed. "You're alive!"

"The Lady of War smile upon you, Varalt," the heiress greeted, offering a shallow bow. "I would share the details of our situation, but the tale is long-winded, and we are eager to return home. Oh, but these are my brave rescuers: Mar, Luthri, and Hohem."

The official's aquamarine gaze roamed over each of us in turn, and recognition sparked to life. "Ah, yes. Last week's arrivals. They were in and out so quickly, we didn't get the chance to meet. Glad to see you've returned in one piece and that you were successful in returning Lady Narille to us. What a victory to your credit! I can't wait to hear the whole story."

Silence followed his animated monologue. *Is this where I contribute?* "Thank you," I said, not sure what else was expected of us. In my mind, I'd already passed the torch to Narille, prepared to sit back and become a side character. My work here was done.

And a victory, huh? If that's the case, why doesn't it feel like one?

As if reading my mind, Luthri squeezed my hand. I squeezed back.

Narille forged ahead, all business. "It will get around, I've no doubt, Varalt. In the meantime, though, I must ask you for a favor. I will need to borrow some funds for our travel. My father can take it out of Solfarin's dues for the next quarter if you would be amenable."

Varalt agreed right away. "Of course, it's my pleasure. How much do you need?"

As they discussed business, the rest of us shuffled across the room to admire the art. The town hall's interior designer must have been related to whoever decorated Rugaveld's grand old house, for they had the same questionable taste. I could believe the painting of nude fauns prancing about in a meadow dotted by flowers was a curated display of fae artistry. The one of a roughly sketched snake woman choking on her own tail, I wasn't sure about.

Narille joined us before I could ponder the meaning too deeply.

"We are all set," she announced, slipping a full purse into the folds of her cloak. "Unless you have other business to conduct in the area, we may move on straightaway."

"Better sooner rather than later," Luthri advised.

I nodded my agreement and began to catalog a mental list of needs. "All right. We ought to pick up a few things before we leave. More food supplies, drinking water, clothes—"

"Oh, no need for all that," Narille interrupted with a small smile. "We'll be taking the train. It's much faster, and they will include refreshments with our ticket. When we reach Ild Lamon, my home, my family will provide you with everything you need for your return trip."

I opened my mouth—and closed it. The train *would* be faster, not to mention more comfortable. So long as it wasn't our money being thrown at luxuries, I could allow it. I could even look forward to it. "Good point," I conceded. "Sounds like a plan."

"No complaints here," Lu added.

My gaze strayed to Hohem, who hovered near the paintings, lost in his own world. He wasn't listening. Oh, well. He would support whatever decisions got us home in one piece. Hopefully, taking the train would bring him some comfort as well.

Eager to be home, Narille said a quick goodbye to Solfarin's administration and swept out with the rest of us on her heels. As we traveled the roads to the front gate, I took in the city for what might be the last time. It might not be Munarzed at its best, all neat planters and folks navigating the streets as if choreographed, but it made for a lovely picture.

Hah. Hardly through with the meat of the mission, and already I'd begun to reflect.

We briefly stopped by the entry checkpoint to report our departure. The scribe on shift, emotional over Narille's return, marked the day's record as an afterthought. Narille artfully excused herself with the justification of getting on the road, and we were on our way.

As the terrain shifted, the earth growing a richer shade and softening under our feet, Yrra and Daethie came to mind. Could we see them before heading north to the Kereti capital? We would need to come back with their share of the reward either way, but they should know about Vyrain. An updated timeline wouldn't go amiss either.

I quickened my pace. "Lady Narille—question for you. Two of our party chose to stay in the wetlands on the way here. Could we stop by and check on them? We'd planned to return that way, but if the route is too winding, we can come back later."

"There is no need for formalities between us, Mar," the heiress chided. "Call me Narille, please." She cocked her head, contemplating my proposition. "Where in the wetlands?"

"It's a straight shot." I indicated the general area.

"And how long will meeting with your friends take?"

"I can't imagine it would be that long. A quarter span, half span, perhaps."

Calculations ran behind Narille's ruby eyes. "We could afford a minor digression. If we miss the evening train, though, it will be several spans before the night train comes through."

It would be worth it. I shrugged one shoulder. "Who's in a rush?"

Narille tipped her head. "Then, please lead the way."

Admittedly, I wasn't sure where Yrra and Daethie could be found at this point. The wetlands spread several kilometers in either direction, covering what must be several hundred acres in total. Had Yrra claimed the entirety of the territory, or would they keep to the areas with deep water? Would they stick together or live separate lives as neighbors?

Despite the uncertainty, I guided the group toward the marsh our friends called home. The distance was greater than I remembered, and the journey stretched well into the afternoon. When we hit the first pool, I kept my eyes and ears peeled for signs of *nykse*. Facing them once was more than enough. At least this time, our party was largely composed of competent women. It would be easier for five of us to drag two men.

It hadn't occurred to me that Narille's type might not be keen on wading through bogs until I thought to check in. Narille showed no signs of frustration, holding her overskirt out of the way as her long legs sliced through the water, but her companions all wore identical frowns.

To hell with it. Cupping my hands over my mouth, I called, "Yrra! Daethie! It's us!"

Luthri cast a horrified look my way, and Hohem's indifference shifted to wariness, but I'd be ready if danger arose. I was a force to be reckoned with when well-rested.

The soft buzz of wings heralded a new arrival. My stance relaxed when a sharp female voice purred, "Well, well, well, if it isn't the first intruders of our new home."

Heads snapped around, but the speaker didn't reveal themselves immediately.

"Oh, shush, you," I retorted, sloshing through the muck in the direction of Daethie's voice. "I won't believe you've forgotten us. It hasn't even been a week."

A flutter of movement drew my gaze to the delicate branch of a lone, spindly tree and the tiny figure perched there. Despite her hostile greeting, joy lit the pixie's little face from within. "Honestly, we didn't think you'd come back. Chances didn't look good."

"Yeah, you know, all the missing people make sense now—it's a wild story."

A story that Narille's imposing presence at my back reminded me we didn't have time to tell. Clearing my throat, I started to address Vyrain's absence, but the words clumped together and didn't budge. Better to wait for Yrra, anyway, and tell them both at once.

Daethie rubbed her hands together, her gaze sharpening. "You have our money?"

"We're headed there next," I told her. "I haven't forgotten."

Her eyes strayed. "Oh, so this is that lady, huh?"

"Lady Narille," I confirmed, looking to the sky for patience. "Who else would it be?"

Daethie's crass manner was perhaps even more grating when combined with the haughtiness of knowing we were within her territory. *Why on Earth had I missed them—some guilt-driven desire to torture myself for a perceived failing?*

"Maybe Luthri got tired of chasing after your stuck-up, know-it-all ass and turned his focus to building a harem of baldies." Daethie shrugged. "You never know."

"It's a pleasure to make your acquaintance," Narille offered, unbothered.

I moved the conversation forward before the pixie could take advantage of the lady's kindness. "Daethie, where is Yrra? We'd like to update you both and get going."

"He'll be by soon. There's lots of work to do, you know, though we are getting comfortable. As it turns out, *nykse* taste like fish." Daethie smacked her lips to punctuate her repulsive suggestion. A shiver ran down my spine at the image that came to mind.

I'd opened my mouth, lecture prepared, but a muted splash upsetting the surface of a pool nearby distracted me from my mission. Yrra swam for us, a lithe figure cutting through the water. As his feet reached land, he emerged, slicking back his hair with a casual swipe of his hand. Warmth spread throughout my chest at the sight of my friend.

He looked to be in his element. Newfound confidence straightened his back, and he'd adjusted well to the land, having fashioned himself a seaweed belt more suited to an aquatic lifestyle than linen or leather. It covered the important bits, just barely.

Daethie, having noticed my line of sight, landed on my shoulder with a huff of displeasure. "I've told him he should let it hang free—it makes a statement—but the poor thing's spent far too much time around you 'civilized' folk and grown self-conscious."

A navy hue suffused Yrra's ears and the apples of his cheeks.

"Daethie," he chastised, more strength behind his normally subdued tone. As the churlish pixie took flight to join him, he nodded a welcome to Narille and her guard. Sharp eyes scanned our party, and when the heads didn't add up, his azure brows drew together. "Where is…?"

Hohem spoke before I could. "Didn't make it," he stated in a voice rough from disuse. Whether intended or not, his hand went to the satchel on his belt containing what remained of his brother. It was enough for Yrra to put the pieces together. His eyes closed.

"I'm sorry," he said quietly. "Vyrain was a good man. He will be mourned."

Heads hung all around in an impromptu moment of silence.

Considering the timeline, I was forced to break it. "We… wanted to update you before we continued on to the capital to collect the reward and return Lady Narille to her family. We'll come find you again when we've seen this through. If the swamp hasn't proved a sustainable resource by then, you'd be welcome to accompany us back to Vhalder."

Yrra opened his mouth, but Daethie was faster.

"You think we're trying to get water out of a rock?" she exclaimed, crossing her arms. "Have a little faith. We'll have this spot turned into paradise in no time. People will be jumping at the chance to cross through this way instead of getting robbed for some dumb bridge."

Yrra made a sound of agreement. "I appreciate your concern, but I think this will suit us fine. Although…" He ducked his head. "Maybe we could still visit every once in a while. If you can keep us informed should the camp move, that would be appreciated."

"Of course," I agreed readily, though my heart squeezed in my chest. "We will miss you, but I'm thrilled for you. I hope you can make this a wonderful home."

Yrra and Daethie exchanged bashful smiles.

Narille cleared her throat. "If that's all…"

"Yes!" My spine snapped straight. "Well, best of luck with everything. I'm not sure when we'll be able to swing by with your share of the reward, but I won't forget."

"Better not," Daethie warned, a chirp of her wings driving home the point.

"I won't," I assured her, raising a hand in farewell. "See you soon."

While I would have been satisfied traipsing through the wetlands, Narille directed us politely but firmly toward the bridge. More a pier than a traditional bridge, the sturdy wood platform wound throughout the marsh, guarded by several large orcish fae and not far from the area we crossed when we last came this way. How we missed it the first time, I had no idea.

The rest of us kept quiet as Narille took care of payment, and we crossed the bridge without issue. It was clear that the novelty of this whole thing had worn off long ago, not just for our immediate party, still grieving, but for Narille and her guards as well. Feeling the push, we picked up the pace. Home could not come soon enough.

Things took an unfortunate turn when we made it to the tracks after the last daytime train had passed. Despite everyone's frustration, no blame was cast. We settled in beside the railroad to wait for the night train, eating a quick meal and dozing in shifts.

At last, the rattling of the rails had us all jumping upright, and lights pierced the gloom. The train was an odd beast, bulky but aerodynamic, with the front engine a tarnished silver tone and quaint wooden coaches following in a neat row. No earsplitting squealing of brakes was necessary, though a hot puff of air met us as the train slowed to allow us to board.

A few words with the conductor, and we were steered toward the rear, passing rows of benches, only some of which were occupied, and shelves for luggage. The dining car, quiet at the time, still smelled of food. *Would it be too optimistic to hope for a hot meal at this hour?*

The rest of the coaches were geared toward long journeys, with plush seats covered in dark velvet that called my name. By the look of it, they could be turned down and made into sleeping quarters. Some already made use of them. However, we didn't stop there. Narille waved us onward into a carriage sectioned off into quarters to provide greater privacy.

"Restrooms." Narille tapped a panel before pointing to the opposite side. "And sleeping quarters. There will be more than enough space for us all. Please, make yourselves comfortable."

While more luxurious than the public transportation I was familiar with, it wasn't a cozy room in a villa by the ocean either. Had such comforts spoiled me already? Would it be difficult to return to tents? Maybe getting that cottage would be the right move after all.

I stood tall by Narille's side as the others found their spaces and pulled out sleeping gear, playing my part as the group's rock even as my eyelids grew heavier by the second.

Luthri's head popped out, expression hopeful. "Mar… Would you like to—"

A sharp shake of my head shut him up, and he obediently retreated into his room. I waited another moment before excusing myself to use the bathroom. My period had begun, necessitating the mutilation of a spare shirt to tide me over until I could retrieve proper supplies. Alas, the hazards of travel for a woman were plentiful and common.

As I emerged, a conductor swept through the carriage to collect fares. Narille made no move to reach for her purse. Not knowing what to expect set me on edge. What if she didn't keep an eye out for the finer details? Being unprepared could land us in all sorts of messes.

"Do we not need to pay?" I murmured, joining her once more.

Narille shook her head. "Traveling with a Kereti daughter has its perks. My family was largely responsible for the expanse of the railroad and keeps it running with significant contributions. There is not enough business to merit such a system otherwise."

Well, la-dee-dah. But government subsidization made sense in this case—the train, though useful, was mostly empty. I couldn't imagine they got that much business. And even less now that Narille was safely accounted for, though it would take time for that news to get around.

Not something I needed to worry about. "Good night, then, Narille. Sleep well."

"Good night, Mar. The same to you."

I nodded to the heiress and slipped into an empty sleeping section. The velvet benches were as comfortable as they looked, and sleep had no trouble finding me.

CHAPTER THIRTY-FOUR
IN WHICH THE PARTY COLLECTS THEIR PROMISED REWARD

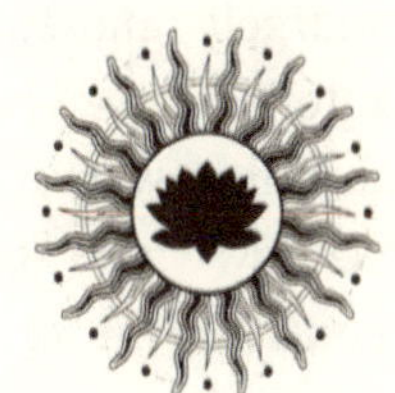

Fae trains might not be as advanced as modern human engineering, but they served their purpose. It brought us through plains and forest to the mountains over the course of two days. We collected more passengers a handful of times, each stop quick and efficient. By suppertime on the second day, our destination came into view.

The sight of Ild Lamon, the Kereti capital, could strike a wise man dumb. A multi-tiered fortress of sun-bleached stone carved into the side of a mountain, it could surely withstand anything thrown at it, whether that be an enemy siege or rampant tourism.

Disembarking the train was only the beginning. I'd never seen so many stairs and hills in my life, and certainly not so many made of solid granite. Narille paused long enough to explain that her family resided at the top, because of course they did. While the streets of Ild Lamon were a work of art—dwellings hewn into the mountain along the inside and mighty walls across the way—I did not look forward to the climb.

At least this is it.

I soothed myself with thoughts of what we could do with the reward money. I didn't have a plan beyond taking time off to process this whole thing and enjoy myself. We could hire someone to help out with menial tasks around camp so that Jük and Vee could relax and spend more time with Ked. I could even settle them into a home of their own, some place quiet, for Ked's sake, but near enough to the action that Vee could make some friends.

Getting into the city took longer than expected due to Narille's popularity. Lost in daydreams, I took a position in the back as Narille made her way through throngs of delighted people. Hohem and Luthri felt similarly out of place, judging by the way they kept to one side. We nodded and smiled but went largely ignored. Fine by me.

It was a pleasant surprise to learn they had a rudimentary elevator composed of a platform and pulley system. I filed in with the rest of the gang, and we were hauled slowly and steadily to the top tier of the castle city. A wide balcony courtyard fit for royalty met us at the top, along with a host of guards excited to see their beloved lady. The few that hung back warmed up with some reassurance from their friends.

My gaze strayed to the entrance carved into the mountain. The main doors had to be decoration. How could three-story-tall pieces of wood serve a functional purpose?

As they opened a side door for us, Narille took my hands in hers. Eyes sparkling, she implored, "Please, come in and visit for a while. My parents would love to meet you."

She cast a meaningful glance in Hohem's direction.

The offer was tempting. But we'd suffered weeks of travel, been through the emotional and physical wringer, sat around on a train, and now found ourselves faced with jubilation we didn't feel. Judging by the expressions on my companions' faces, they were no more eager for the opportunity than I was.

Squeezing her hands, I replied, "Thank you for the offer, but we're tired. Ready to be home. I'm sure you feel the same."

"You can sit the entire time, and I will make sure my parents keep it brief," Narille wheedled, a light tug on my hands inducing me to take a step toward the entrance. "Your efforts deserve to be celebrated. You'll have your reward and be equipped to set out before the day's end, I swear it."

Another cursory evaluation of my companions told me they were down for whatever would get us out of here with the least amount of effort. And I, for one, didn't have the energy to fight her further. "If it's quick," I allowed, trying to keep the misery out of my tone.

Narille squeezed my hands before letting them drop, any guilt there might have been overshadowed by her eagerness to see her family again. A drove of guards met us at the entrance, and we were ushered inside the mountain castle.

The grandeur of Rugaveld's mansion paled in comparison to the opulence of the royal family's dwelling. *Mana* sconces and chandeliers bathed the interior in light, showing off high stone walls carved from floor to ceiling, alcoves with statues cast in precious metals, and wide hallways that seemed to never end. Soldiers in layered cloth armor were spaced every few feet, standing tall even as they called out eager greetings.

As the guards started to thump their staffs against the floor in a thundering welcome, Narille returned the greeting with that odd nod/shake of her head. We progressed down the main hall to a humongous throne room. An underground river with footbridges spaced across it ran through the center of the marble floor, ending at an unoccupied platform that resembled a church altar with chairs.

While I was admiring the castle features, mouth wide open, we were accosted by a small crowd of friends and family. Our party was edged out of the throng as numerous adults and children with the same colorless skin and ruby eyes surrounded Narille, all making cooing sounds and reaching over one another to stroke her limbs and skirts.

It made for an odd sight, but there was no mistaking the love in the reunion. It only served to amplify my need to be home.

Narille broke off from the group to introduce us to her parents and siblings, and before we knew it, we were being funneled into a banquet hall and seated at long marble benches rooted to the floor. We lost sight of the heiress, but time flew. Within the hour, we were being plied with food and drink, from rich roasted meats and root vegetables to pastries and beer. Another hour or so later, Luthri and I were spinning and stomping along with dancers as drums pounded a rhythmic beat.

It was impossible to tell the time of day inside the mountain, but I had to put my foot down when the celebrations showed no signs of slowing. Narille was seated with her parents, deep in conversation. How they could talk during all this, I had no clue. I kept my approach slow so as not to intrude. She noticed me right away, perked up, and waved me over.

I tried to ask her if we could go, but I couldn't make out her response over the sounds of the festivities. Narille said something to her parents and stood, using hand gestures to suggest that I gather Lu and Hohem and our things. Eager to get going, I scrambled to comply.

Narille guided us out, flanked by several guards. I was pleased to see that it was still daylight when we emerged from the mountain—no later than midday. That gave us time to make some headway on the return journey before nightfall.

"Thank you for humoring me," Narille began as we found ourselves in the tower courtyard once more. "I am sorry that we couldn't speak more, but my family..."

"I understand completely," I assured her. "I'm sorry to cut things short, but we should be getting on the road. We have a long way back home."

"Of course. If you wait here, I'll have your money sent out to you. Oh, but... Hmm."

The heiress tapped her lips with a finger. "It would be more than you three can carry, I think. I can send some people with you to spread out the load and help deter bandits, or I can send you home with an *avida* and cart." Without waiting for an answer from us, she added, "Let me confer with my parents and get back to you. Thank you again for everything!"

With nothing else needed, the heiress hurried inside with her guards to rejoin the party.

"That was... something," Luthri murmured at my side.

It was, indeed. Unable to shake the feeling that something was off, I posed a question to the air. "Does any of this rub you the wrong way?"

"Hm? Does what?" Lu followed my gaze to the doors.

"I don't know, the ease of everything. Getting here, the beautiful city, getting our money. It's not... screaming 'Munarzed' all over again?"

His hand closed around mine. "Perhaps you're suspicious because you've been burned before?" he suggested, brushing his lips against my knuckles. "Residual warning signals that a couple of peaceful days hasn't quite been able to erase?"

"That could be it," I admitted. Munarzed left a mark on all of us, it seemed. My focus strayed to Hohem. The stark hurt in his expression had faded during the lively mood of the last two hours, but he still appeared too frail, as though a stiff breeze could send him to the ground.

Was it better to try to get him to talk or keep avoiding the topic? They said time healed all wounds, but loss was a funny thing. Maybe it would be worth looking into a mind mender—a therapist. Did Vhalder have one? A small town might not have a specialist like that. Perhaps Luthri, with his mother's connections, would know someone who could help.

It wasn't long before there was movement, but it wasn't Narille. A half-door, one of a series between two tall pillars off to one side of the main entrance, swung open to reveal a middle-aged man dressed in casual clothing. He led a narciso-yellow *avida* mare out by a set of reins. A laden cart covered in canvas followed at the animal's heels, attached by a series of straps and wooden supports on either side.

Huffing and puffing, the handler made a beeline for our group.

"Yer the ones getting the reward for the lady's return?" he asked breathlessly, as if there was anyone else who stuck out as sorely as we did. He held out the reins and continued, "We loaded it up for ye. Be kind to 'er, yeah? Devynn's a lover, not a fighter, but she'll bite if she needs to. Don't forget it."

When I didn't move, Luthri accepted the reins, casting a concerned glance my way.

"Really?" I couldn't quite believe our luck. The value of an *avida* and cart might pale in comparison to the reward money, and they *did* have a marble mountain castle, so it shouldn't have come as a surprise… Well. To think things went this easily for "heroes."

The handler misunderstood my reaction. "Oh yeah. She'll give you a nip on the arse."

"No, I..." It wasn't worth it. I let the matter drop. "Yes. Okay. Thank you."

Eyeing the beast of burden, I plotted out our next steps, starting by taking stock of what we'd been given. True to the Kereti family's word, the provided cart contained more money than I'd ever seen in my life, plus more than enough travel supplies to cover a couple of weeks for three people and an *avida*. I rested my elbows on the rear platform, considering the bounty.

We needed a map, which we could find somewhere in the city before leaving. The rest—food, clothing, cooking utensils, and sleeping accommodations—was all accounted for. We couldn't take the train again with all that, which meant a long trip home. What else was new? At least with the supplies, it would be a pleasant one.

I closed the canvas covering, hiding the money from view, and explained my plan to an attentive Luthri and indifferent Hohem. We agreed to hunt for a map and set out without delay. Lu tried to get me to sit in the cart, but I refused, telling them we could take turns when our feet got tired. Otherwise, we should conserve Devynn's energy.

Trekking down the spiraling streets of Ild Lamon, we prepared ourselves for the migration home. A kindly man gave us directions to a shop selling paper goods and sundries. There, we got our hands on a map of the Kereti territories and splurged on a sketchpad and a set of metal puzzles to serve as entertainment in the evenings. If the shop owner found it strange that we paid with such a large denomination of coin, they said nothing.

"I guess that's it, then?" Luthri questioned as we left the shop.

"I guess that's it," I agreed. "Mission accomplished. Goddess bless. Let's go home."

I took Devynn's lead from Hohem and clicked my tongue. The animal lumbered forward, launching the cart into motion. Just like that, our quest drew to an end.

CHAPTER THIRTY-FIVE
IN WHICH THIS CAMPAIGN COMES TO AN END

We had to deliver Daethie and Yrra's share of the reward, of course, and it made sense to do that first in order to lighten our load. The distance to the tidal marshlands they now called home took a full week to cover on foot, with breaks dedicated to letting our poor pack animal rest and graze. Most of the journey was accomplished in relative silence, as we focused on covering ground more than socializing amongst ourselves.

When we reached their swamp, evening had fallen. We parked the cart on solid ground and tethered Dev the *avida* to a grove with plenty of greenery to snack on. Daethie and Yrra joined us, and perfunctory salutations were shared. Their endowments disappeared somewhere safe. Yrra showed us the lost supplies he'd been able to retrieve from the muck, which weren't much, but we had no need of them with the items from Narille's family.

Returning to our roots, we spent the night camping out under the stars.

Breakfast the next morning was spent reminiscing on the past. Luthri enthusiastically told us of a time he and one of his older brothers convinced the rest of their siblings that *zanna* was meant to be swallowed for a more comprehensive, inside-out clean. It lasted months before their mother caught on and had the boys running errands for half the town to make up for it. Hohem cracked a smile at one point—perhaps it brought back fond memories of his childhood.

I shared light-hearted stories about some of the other folks who had been part of our gang, however temporarily, including a stodgy older fellow who got along famously with Jük and a bratty young woman with an equally snot-nosed son. Ked cried when the latter had to go; the rest of us were glad to see them gone.

The conversation eventually stagnated. Leftover breakfast gruel in the pot had long since gone cold, and my temples pounded from the marsh's signature stink of wet earth and rotting organic matter. It was time to be back on the road.

I studied the map while the boys got our things together, assisted by Yrra and supervised by Daethie. Minutes later, we were hugging goodbye and promising not to forget each other.

"Don't forget to write," I told Yrra as I wrapped him in a quick embrace. "Solfarin isn't far, and you've got all that money now, so there's no excuse. We'll check for news at Vhalder's birdkeeper every few weeks so as not to miss anything."

Yrra inclined his head. "Be sure to update us if you move."

"Of course. And let us know if you need anything."

"Why? Would you come rushing to our aid?" Daethie cut in.

"Sure. We're family." The words slipped out before I thought it through, but I didn't regret them. I kept going. "Which is to say, you're important to me. We might not have known each other all that long, but I'll always remember this. This journey, the memories shared."

"Aw, Mar." Daethie flashed her sharp teeth in a way that suggested an insult was coming. "You're less emotionally constipated than usual today. I'm proud of you."

"I was talking to Yrra," I huffed, making a face. "And I'd return a compliment, but you're as insufferable as usual. Hope you fly into a sentient tree and get slapped out of the sky."

She grinned, returning, "Hope you fall into a ditch and break a leg."

As good as well wishes, coming from her.

Backing up, I waved one final time, committing my friends' faces to memory before leaving them behind. Luthri and Hohem joined me for the short walk back to the cart.

"You're not going to cry, are you?" Lu teased, noting the dejected set of my mouth.

I shot him an exasperated look. "So what if I did? It's hardly any of your concern."

"No concern whatsoever. Just reminding you that I've got two perfectly good shoulders and an absorbent shirt if you need to lay your head somewhere."

"Would be hard to have a good shoulder cry while walking, don't you think?"

Lu mulled it over and settled for, "We'll have to stop every quarter span until the urge is satiated or we reach Vhalder. Whichever comes first."

I shook my head, but the bit of banter did wonders for my mood after the last couple of weeks. I'd gotten through companions leaving the nest many times before—this, too, would pass. That did raise other questions, though. Would Luthri also be leaving when we returned to Vhalder? His priorities had seemed to shift over the course of this trip, but we hadn't had that conversation yet. Truth be told, I didn't look forward to it.

As we got the cart together and set off, Luthri continued, lost in his musings. "On second thought… even if we reach Vhalder first, say the word, and we'll keep it up. Really, it's no hardship on my part. In fact, if the opportunity arises to take it somewhere private…"

"That's enough of that," I interrupted, not wanting to disturb Hohem with wherever that was headed. "Let's keep up the pace, shall we? We have a long way to go."

Luthri fell silent, and we trudged onward toward the horizon awaiting us.

Fair weather met us on the return journey, and uneventful days blended together into a week, then two. Upon reaching the familiar forest, the trees provided a welcome reprieve from the sunny plains, and the cooling nights had some of us sleeping in more than one layer.

Most of the way in, Luthri determined something was amiss.

"You know I would never dispute your leadership," he began, flashing a sheepish expression, "but we're a bit north of where we ought to be. The main road is that way."

He raised an arm to point, but I caught it and shifted closer.

"I know." Lowering my voice, I explained, "I thought it would be good to stop by Cantal's shrine. It's on the way, and the spiritual guidance could do us all well."

I said "us," but this was for Hohem's sake. The plan was formed before we got on the road, but nothing had changed since. Hohem walked with us, and… that was about it. He seldom engaged in conversation, even when Luthri was making an ass of himself. He would respond when asked but didn't make an effort to share his thoughts as they came.

If not for the fact he rose in the mornings without protest and maintained the pace we set, I might have pushed the issue. For now, I settled for the infrequent conversation and celebrated every small improvement. The balance of being supportive without being nosy was not easy to achieve. As far as whether I managed it or not, the jury was still out.

The shrine was as we remembered it—quaint but well-kept, giving the clearing a homey, sacrosanct feel. We found Cantal in his garden, harvesting persimmon-like fruits from a vine. He looked up, eyes narrowing, but the tension in his shoulders disappeared as he realized it was us. The corners of his eyes and mouth even wrinkled in almost a smile. He straightened and dusted his hands on his robe as we neared.

"Fair travels?" he asked, tucking his crate of fruits under one arm.

"Ahh… I wish we could say yes." My hands hunted for something to do as I tried to figure out how to put this. Wishing for pockets, I had to settle for looping my thumbs in my belt.

Cantal didn't miss a thing. "Hm. You're missing some folks, you know."

The nonchalant way he said it opened the wound anew, but he had no way of knowing. I breathed out slowly and acknowledged the hard truth. "Yrra and Daethie are well. They decided to stay out there. As for Vyrain... We lost him. In Munarzed."

The cleric paused to scrutinize our faces this time. Any trace of humor faded. "I'm sorry to hear that," he said quietly, sounding like he meant it. "He was a good soul."

I nodded, swallowing down the emotion that threatened. *Why did we come here in the first place? Prioritize.* The words came, eventually. "We wanted to thank you for everything. I especially wanted to express my appreciation for the training. Because of you, I was able to get a proper grasp on *mana* and changing. Without it, I think... we might have all been lost. As it was, we were overwhelmed. I underestimated the risks involved."

"*We* underestimated the risks," Luthri cut in, not letting me take the blame alone. A swell of gratitude rose, washing away a bit of the guilt that had piled around the memories.

Cantal waved off our words. "What's done is done." His gaze strayed to Hohem. "If it would not be an intrusion or too much of a delay, I would prepare a funeral for your brother. A traditional ceremony for sending loved ones into Hermenia's care. I can be ready by nightfall."

Hohem bowed his head. "Tell me how I can help, *Opashi*."

Cantal directed us to collect wood and stack it before the statue of Hermenia. We took great care in choosing dry castoffs so as not to damage any trees. After a quick supper of salted fish and stewed legumes supplemented by homegrown fruit at our host's insistence, we gathered around the modest pyre for the ceremony.

First, the *opashi* knelt on the ground and produced a tuft of tinder. He muttered a few words of prayer as he arranged it around a small pile of sticks and began to fiddle one against another between his hands. I couldn't remember the last time I'd seen someone start a fire the old-fashioned way, but none of us interrupted, sitting with closed mouths and straight backs.

The sun dipped behind the mountains before a spark caught, multiplying quickly into a raw orange flame. The cleric fed it twigs one by one until it was a roaring blaze. Then, clearing his throat, he spoke, the confident tones harmonizing with the crackle of burning wood.

"Fire, as with life, is bright but temporary," he began. "When angry, it burns hot and fast, destroying everything in its path. When calm, it can be harnessed as a tool, lending a helpful hand in times of need. Today, we seek the comfort of its warmth to soothe the wounds of loss. We seek the beauty of its color to turn the Goddess's gaze our way, that she might smile upon a weary traveler and take the soul of Vyrain Sinthaid of Wysalar into her loving embrace."

Cantal raised his hands and lifted his face skyward, eyes closed. Several seconds passed before he turned his attention back to us. He picked up where he left off, intoning, "Now, we are given an opportunity to say farewell. Let the flames burn away the resentment, guilt, anger, and other things best forgotten, leaving our spirits light and resilient once more."

The old man stood to hand us each a stick and nodded to the fire. The warm glow highlighted the age lines decorating his face. "This is the part of the ceremony where those who knew him say their goodbyes," he told us. "You may speak out loud or in your heart, whatever feels right. Take as long as you need—even if that's the rest of the night. When you're ready, add your kindling to the pyre, and let your burden burn along with it."

Glancing at the figures on either side of me, I shifted to ease the pressure on my knees. If Hohem did want to sit here all night, I'd need to get comfortable. "What do we say?"

"Whatever you do not want left unspoken," Cantal replied. "I will keep the fire burning."

I nodded and closed my eyes. The guilt came first, so near to the surface.

I'm sorry about the way things ended; you deserved better. I hope you'll forgive me.

After the guilt came regret, the things I'd never told Vyrain and should have.

I'm blessed to have known you, however short our time together. You were a light in all our lives, with your strength and your humor. Thank you for everything. I hope that wherever you are, it's comfortable, and the people are kind to you… If there are others, that is.

Silence overtook the clearing as we all participated. Did Cantal have anything to add? His expression revealed nothing. What did Luthri have to say? Head bowed, he joined the rest of us in quiet, but he'd barely known the man, and half the time, they'd been at each other's throats.

Hohem stared into the fire, his fingers digging into his thighs. I hoped he was kind to himself. However many regrets I might have, he had it worse. When I thought of Munarzed, I recalled Hohem gripping his brother's broken body as though it were yesterday. His wails of grief haunted me. Did he see it when he closed his eyes? Did he blame me?

Cantal's words shook me out of that line of thought. *'Let the flames burn away the things best forgotten. Add your kindling to the pyre, and let your burden burn along with it.'*

Well, I guess that's it. My hand squeezed around my stick. A few more silent words, and my arm swung. The weight of my regrets joined the wood to be devoured by flames.

Luthri added his a moment later. The smokiness in the air increased, as though our burdens polluted it. Some time passed before Hohem shuffled forward to lay his stick in place. A bland mask over his face, he returned to his spot without a word.

"Do you have anything of his?" Cantal directed the question at the remaining twin.

Hohem's hand went to his belt. His brows furrowed. "I have his ashes, but…"

When he made no move to continue, Cantal stoked the base of the fire, remarking, "The departed are carried with us regardless of whether we are physically burdened. It is your decision… But while the memories belong with you, held close to your heart, I believe the body belongs to the earth whence it came. Perhaps it is another thing best given to the fire."

Hohem's eyes followed the motion of Cantal's hands as he contemplated the proposition—carry his brother's ashes around for the rest of his life or let go of the last thing he had to remember his sibling by? He pulled out the little pouch, rolling it between his fingers. Closed his eyes. Sucked his teeth. Then he reached forward and added the ashes onto the pyre.

Beyond taking the occasional name in vain, I'd never been a spiritual person. Evidence pointed to religion being a hoax. Ghosts? An afterlife? Who knew. But when the fire leapt for the sky, a collective gasp rang out, and peace settled over the group like a comforting fog.

Maybe there's something to it after all.

"He is with Hermenia now," Cantal announced, getting to his feet with a grunt of effort. "His spirit will join the ranks of those who came before, becoming *mana,* and find his way back to us someday, whether in the form of raw energy or another physical form."

The *opashi* placed a kind hand on Hohem's shoulder. "Come along, boy. I've a stiff drink if you want it and a cot you can borrow if you don't. I'll watch the fire once you're settled in."

The two made their way inside to bed down for the night.

Hypnotized by the dancing colors before my eyes and the swirling thoughts behind them, I stared into the flames long after they were gone.

"This is for you."

I dumped a bag in front of Cantal, the rattle of coin against coin piercing through the hubbub of Hohem and Luthri wrangling our cantankerous *avida* into place.

The cleric, mending a blanket on the stoop as he watched us pack up, paused his work. "That's not nec—" he started.

"It is," I insisted, shoving the money closer to him. "Consider it compensation for the food and showers from last time, or use it for the shrine. Either way, it's yours. Thank you."

One weathered hand pushed the bag back toward me. "I've done nothing outside the realm of my calling. It's been my pleasure to serve."

"Be that as it may"—I nudged it in his direction once more—"we're in your debt and will hear no protests." Backing up so as not to give him the chance to return the money, I went on to say, "We'll be on our way now. Thank you again, and the Goddess be with you."

The *opashi* clicked his tongue in reproach, but bowed his head. "And with you."

I returned the farewell gesture and pivoted to join the boys. Navigating the path, I passed the small pile of smoldering ash—a stark reminder of the perils we'd faced—and said my last goodbyes, hoping that it would somehow reach the person it needed to.

CHAPTER THIRTY-SIX

IN WHICH THE PARTY RETURNS HOME

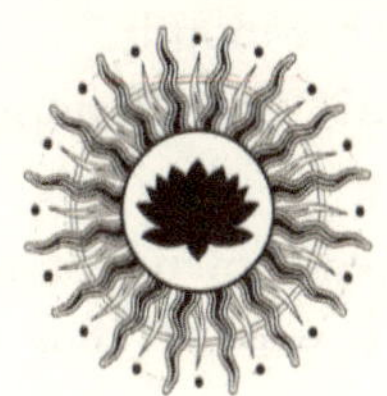

With weight lifted from our hearts, the final stretch went smoothly. Lu's sense of direction worked like a compass to guide us home, and we avoided the section of road overrun by insects. Autumn came on schedule, adding a faint chill to the breeze and coloring the trees a richer shade of their usual pastel hues.

Before we knew it, we were climbing the hill to the clearing we called home.

There were more tents than there had been when we set out, and a fresh-faced girl with red hair and expressive almond-shaped eyes prepared a brace of rabbits fireside. It appeared our company had grown again. I hadn't the chance to ask for our family by name, as Vee hurried out from her tent, squealing in excitement, to gather me in a tight embrace.

"So glad to see you safe!" she cried, holding me at arm's length so she could look me up and down. "We got your letter, but news of the island nation all the way out here has been so limited. And with Yrra and Daethie staying, we thought that perhaps you would also decide to give us up for the city life. Not that we would have blamed you!"

"I could never," I assured her as she clasped my forearms in an *Epitgig* greeting.

"This is home," Hohem agreed, gaze softening as he took in the familiar space. Across the way, our male *avida* snorted a welcome to Devynn, who lifted her head to regard him. Vee noticed Vyrain's absence, and her face fell.

"Vyrain is missing. Did something…?"

I spared Hohem the discomfort of having to explain. "The situation on Munarzed was more of a mess than we realized. Vyrain was brave and fought well, but…"

"Oh!" Vee's hand flew to her mouth.

"Are Ked and Jük around?" I asked, hoping to tell the story with all present.

"Picking up some things in town." Shaking her head, Vee shot a sympathetic look Hohem's way. "Come, settle in. You must be exhausted. We've had some new additions and other news, but there's time for all that. Oh, poor dears. Here, let's set up your tents."

The doting mother would hear no objections. She followed us to the back of the cart, and her eyes went wide when the cover was lifted to reveal stacks upon stacks of leftover supplies and numerous bags of coin. Hohem and Luthri wasted no time unloading.

"What a bounty!" Vee exclaimed, reverent.

Pulling one of the bags from its place, I explained, "On top of the promised reward, the Kereti family outfitted us well for the return journey. The cart and *avida* were also their contribution. We'll have to figure out what to do with all of this."

Vee nodded. "It would be a good idea to bury the money. Perhaps in several locations. And open a line of credit in Vhalder so as not to attract attention with so much coin."

A warm blend of relief and gratitude swept through me. I'd almost forgotten what it was like to have her around. "Sounds good. I'll leave that planning to you."

"Morak can help with this as well; let me find him."

Vee disappeared before I had the chance to ask about the new arrivals. She returned before long with a redheaded boy, who collected the bags I'd set down without complaint. Working together, Luthri, Vee, the boy, and I unburdened the cart while Hohem set up our tents.

Jük and Ked arrived as we were introducing Devynn to our male *avida*. The ornery old *Epitgig* almost smiled—must have been a trick of the light. In celebration of our return, he went out again to buy ingredients for supper. Ked, still wearing Lu's gifted earring, tugged me along to introduce me to the new friends. They were siblings: two girls and a boy, adolescents, all with the same mild manners and foxlike features.

Dinner was remarkably quiet without Yrra, Daethie, or Vyrain around. We told our story in pieces between mouthfuls, leaving out the gory details for the children's sake. Ked and Vee hung on every word. Jük made an effort to seem indifferent, but his spoon missed his bowl twice.

When I got to the part about Vyrain's funeral, we shared a moment of silence. Vee grasped Hohem's hand and, deciding that wasn't enough, gathered him in a fervent hug instead. Him being twice her size, she had to put significant effort into her grip. Ked enthusiastically joined the two of them. Inspired, Luthri and I followed suit. Jük even reached over to pat his wife on the shoulder. The group hug lasted until the siblings excused themselves to bed.

Things returned to normal, for the most part.

As it turned out, being rich didn't make much of a difference. It was all relative—the reward money may have been life-changing for one or two people, but divided amongst eight, less so.

That was how Luthri and I found ourselves at The Bitter Brother rather than a more luxurious establishment, sharing one of the benches where I'd met him for the first time some months ago. Strange how things had a tendency to go full circle.

"Used to being on your own, you must be glad for the peace and quiet now," I remarked, sipping from my third cup of flower wine. I'd forgotten how nice it was to relax with a drink at the end of a long day. The pleasant buzz of alcohol loosened my muscles and cast everything in a rosy glow, allowing me to temporarily forget responsibilities and enjoy myself.

Luthri considered my statement for a beat before shaking his head.

"I had siblings, remember. I think I miss it. Being part of something, having friends like this… It's like being part of a big family again. I was starting to take things for granted."

What an optimistic way of looking at it. I shrugged, swirling the liquid in my mug. "It's normal for people to come and go in this lifestyle, so you're not necessarily going to be part of the same thing all the time. Not like a true family."

In that infuriatingly observant way of his, he understood what I wasn't saying. His gaze turned sympathetic. "That must be hard."

"It's not easy," I admitted, thinking of all the people I'd gotten to know and lose over the years. "But that's life." To my utter stupefaction, my eyes began to water. Hurrying to address the evidence with my sleeve, I exclaimed, "Ugh, what's with the waterworks? Don't look."

Lu's head twisted dramatically to face the dining room. "I don't see anything."

"It's the alcohol," I grumbled, taking another gulp nonetheless. The burn going down brought my thoughts to another uncomfortable place —namely, our relationship, or lack thereof.

I was the one who had said to keep things casual, but what happened now? Did we go our separate ways? Did Luthri stay and resume his personal "quest," sleeping with me during the week and coming to the bar to pick up sidepieces on the weekends?

Was there a chance of cementing this? "Us" becoming a permanent fixture?

Whatever the case, better to know sooner than later. I was already more invested than I'd like to admit, and the unknown was beginning to chafe.

"So," I started, keeping the question casual, "what's the next chapter for you? Thinking of sticking around, picking up work around here? Visit your mom? Maybe find another group of poor souls setting out on an adventure and see if you can tag along again?"

His reaction to each suggestion didn't reveal anything useful. "Well, this last one emptied my purse, so… it might be some time before I can get back on the road."

So, he'd be leaving too. I kept my tone light. "Ha. Well, at least you've got another notch in your belt to show for it." Staring into my mug, it occurred to me that I'd need another drink soon. Maybe something stronger—the cheery sweetness didn't feel right.

"Another notch?" Lu contemplated my words. "Oh, sleeping with you, you mean?"

My shoulder jerked in acknowledgment. "That was your goal, right?"

"In the beginning." Talons rapped against the table in a progressive rhythm. "But I won't lie—I've enjoyed our time together very much. We mesh well, you and I. Don't you think so? It's hard to believe we've only known each other a few weeks."

"Well, a lot happened in those weeks," I reasoned. "A lot of experiences that bring people together. Sharing a campsite, traveling the same roads. Almost dying a handful of times."

"Don't forget the fucking."

"That too. The highlight of the trip, really."

"I might even go so far as to say I like you," Lu continued, watching my face.

I gave him nothing. "You know, I have that effect on people."

He barked a laugh. "All right, we both deserve more credit than this. Let's not be stubborn about it. Are you hoping I'll leave, Mar? Or are you asking if I want to stay with you?"

I want you to stay. I could say it. But people deserved to make that choice for themselves, without outside influence. So I waved off his question. "That's up to you. You're an adult."

Luthri's lips pursed. Amusement danced in his eyes. "Goddess, you're difficult. I love it. Let me try that again, and don't think so hard this time. Would you be happy if I stayed?"

That was easy enough to answer. "I would."

"Then it's settled."

Behind a mask of nonchalance, my heart soared. Did he mean—?

Luthri leaned back—forgetting that there was nothing but open air behind him—and would have upended himself onto the floor if I hadn't leapt to catch his arm.

"Eita! I would ask how many you've had, but you're not even drinking," I scolded, yanking him back into place beside me. He recovered quickly, scooting closer so that he could sling an arm around my shoulder. His lips brushed against the shell of my ear.

"I'm drunk on love, *kiannim*," he whispered.

"You're ridiculous," I sputtered, but the word choice hit home, sending butterflies swarming in the pit of my stomach. I couldn't let myself melt—who knew what 'love' meant to a man like Luthri? It could be something he threw around without regard for feelings. I needed clarification; even if we weren't on the same page, we should at least be in the same book.

"When you say 'love'..."

He expected my hesitation. With a twinkle in his eye, Lu responded, "The day they invent alcohol derived from meat, I'll be almost as happy as the day you agreed to be friends with the possibility of something more. Mar, you enchant me. I'm absolutely charmed. Entirely besotted. And, most importantly, I'm the happiest I've ever been. If you let me, I would get on the roof right now and sing your praises to the people of Vhalder so that everyone knows—"

His voice had steadily risen, attracting the attention of several nearby patrons now reflecting his dumb grin. Hiding my face, I hissed, "Okay, okay, I get it! That's enough!"

Planting an elbow on the table, Luthri leaned forward and caught a hold of my chin, directing my gaze back to him. "You don't have to say it back," he told me, "but I wanted you to know. No questions about it, no doubts: I'm in this as long as you want me."

My face grew hot. "I hear you."

"Good." Lu released my chin. "And if you need, I'll say it again."

"That won't be necessary. You've been plenty clear," I muttered under my breath, busying myself with counting the *mana* lamps on our side of the dining room.

Motion caught my eye. On the opposite side, a stool had been set in front of the stairs that lead to the second floor. An *Alf* bard with a stringed instrument strapped to his back was excusing himself from a conversation with one of the faun bartenders.

I blinked. "Live music, huh? Didn't think this was that kind of venue."

Luthri followed my gaze. "A serenade. Isn't that lovely?"

Once comfortably perched, the musician pulled his instrument around to his front with a flourish and greeted the room at large. "Hello, everyone. I'm thrilled to share a brand-new ballad with you today, straight from the capital. Chances are it's your first time hearing it, but if not, well, lucky you—you get to enjoy it again. Tips are much appreciated."

A smattering of laughter rippled through the room. Clearing his throat, the musician strummed a simple tune and began to sing:

Let me tell you the tale of an island nation,
Beauty unsurpassed, under subjugation.
A hero came along—
The subject of this song—
To liberate its people from a terrible evil

'Twas foretold long ago that a fair-haired youth
Would one day be a lauded hero—a half-truth
Little did they know
He'd give his life to overthrow
A tyrant with a city built on mind control…

"Well. Now we know which was the chosen one," Luthri whispered, breaking the spell.

Horrified, I swiveled to face him. "Did you just—? That is not appropriate."

Lu sobered instantly, regret chasing all humor off his face. "Ah, I'm sorry… I felt that it—I mean, you know I—sometimes a joke is all that comes to mind."

"You should work on that."

"Sure." After a beat, Luthri took the opportunity to add, "And maybe you could work on that prickly exterior of yours? It's not the most effective way to make friends, you know."

"That's my best feature," I countered in a frosty tone. "Weeds out the weaklings so that only quality is left." Cackling at my own joke, I drained my cup.

Luthri's shoulders relaxed. "So. What do we do now?"

"For now… get another drink." I tapped the side of my empty flagon.

He laughed and signaled the waitress, who acknowledged us with a brief nod. When a fresh drink was placed in front of me, I answered his question. "What do we do? Anything we want. We have each other; we have money. The world is our oyster."

Lu dropped a hand to my thigh and squeezed. I responded by resting my head against his shoulder. We enjoyed the music like that for a while, engaging one another with low conversation whenever a detail in the song wasn't quite accurate. Overall, it was a beautiful tribute to our friend. What better way to immortalize the tragedy of Munarzed?

After some time, Lu ventured, "What's an oysturr?"

Oh, brother. Where do I begin? Thank the Goddess I was having this conversation drunk. I wrapped my hands around my mug and breathed a deep, cleansing breath. "All right. I can't believe I'm doing this, but… I think it's time I told you where I'm from…"

THANK YOU FOR READING THE STEADFAST ONE

We hope you enjoyed it as much as we enjoyed bringing it to you. We just wanted to take a moment to encourage you to review the book. Please visit The Steadfast One on Amazon to leave your review.

Every review helps further the author's reach and, ultimately, helps them continue writing fantastic books for us all to enjoy.

The Treasured One
The Steadfast One

Gladiator meets Heartless Hunter meets Bloodguard in this new adult fantasy romance. ***Four deadly trials will reunite them. One secret will tear them apart.*** *When a mission goes wrong and ends with her best friend dead, Drusilla Valerius is rescued by someone she never expected to see again: Marcus Scaevola. The only man she's ever cared for—the man who spurned her feelings six years ago. Marcus should've known Dru wouldn't be the same woman he left all those years ago, and is he's unprepared for her distrust of him – and her uncanny ability to kill. But he has a purpose for seeking her out. Bound by loyalty, he convinces her to train King Cato of Anziano, one of the last countries yet to fall to the tyrannical Imperium, in the Valorem Blood Trials. Unlike years' past, the Imperium has a heavy hand in it, hiding beneath the guise*

of peace and unity between their two countries. When both Dru and Marcus find themselves joining the competition – Dru to take the place of an innocent and Marcus to protect the king – they're forced to trust one another with their lives. Now inescapably entrenched in the gory, duplicitous world of the blood trials, feelings long-buried surface, blurring the lines between duty and honor, love and loyalty. But Marcus carries a devastating secret–one that could destroy the foundations of Dru's world... ***Don't miss this adult romantasy debut combining the second-chance romance of*** **Heartless Hunter** ***by Kristen Ciccarelli with the deadly trials of*** **Gladiator.** ***With their lives and their hearts on the line, will love be enough to thwart the might of the Imperium?***

GET TRIAL OF BRONZE AND BLOOD NOW!

A fairy hunter desperate to save herself. A blighted knight hunting for his freedom. A looming war. *Unexpectedly resurrected, Gwendolyn finds herself kidnapped by her mortal enemy: the fae. A distressing prospect considering her monster-hunting mother trained her to eradicate them. Worse, a bargain has been struck with the fairy lord on her behalf, and Gwendolyn knows too well that such deals always come with a terrible price. Trapped in the fairy lord's glittering court each night and banished back to her own world upon waking, Gwendolyn must find the terms of her bargain quickly if she hopes to survive and outsmart him. Yet, despite her inherited hatred of fae, the fairy lord is not without his charms. Gwendolyn struggles to resist his allure when every time they meet, he offers her anything she could ever wish—a bargain that would no doubt cost her entire soul in trade. She soon discovers the only creature in this twisted realm she can truly trust is a man as trapped as herself; a blighted knight made from the pieces of a hundred failed heroes. Cursed down to his literal bones, he cannot help but hunt her on his master's orders. Despite this, Gwendolyn's*

heart aches for him, his situation so very like her own. She knows, despite his insistence that she cannot trust him, that if she were to break his curse, they might actually stand a chance of fighting their way out together... ***Don't miss this Romantasy debut where the monster hunting vibes of*** **VAN HELSING** ***meet the glamorous ballrooms of*** **BRIDGERTON,** ***in the Victorian style of Emily Wilde's*** **ENCYCLOPAEDIA OF FAIRIES.** ***Perfect for fans of*** **The Labyrinth, A Court of Mist and Fury,** ***and*** **Queen of Roses.**

GET A FAIRY HUNTER'S GUIDE FOR THE RECENTLY [UN]DEAD NOW!

For all our Romantasy books, visit our website.

GLOSSARY OF FAE WORDS & PHRASES

Amafarin (AM-ah-FA-r/lin): Someone who uses magic for evil. Loosely translates to "witch."

Aminkinya (AH-min-KIN-ee-yah): A warlike matriarchal fae race resembling pixies from English folklore. They live in large nests in the ground and have a queen much like bees.

Alf/Alfen (AHL-fen): A humanoid fae race that tends to be conventionally beautiful, light-skinned and modelesque with blond hair and blue eyes. Some know them as the "fair folk."

Avida (AH-vee-dah): Large riding beasts that resemble colorful elk-horses. Males have antlers.

Bavga (BAHV-gah): An Epitgig curse meaning a useless, low-value person; freeloader.

Epitgig (eh-PIT-gig): A rowdy goblin-like race known for their "music."

Galyak (GAL-yak): A type of fae with the appearance of a hag that can control the weather. Inspired the Cailleach in Gaelic mythology.

Gian du tiannar (GYAN doo tee-AN-nar): An *Aminkinya* phrase meaning "fate knows best." The phrase implies accepting strong feelings more than anything to do with fate as we know it and is often used to justify fighting and to soothe the pain of a loss.

Ishameti (ee-SHA-meh-tee): A group of fae united under House Wysalar. Translates directly to "People the Goddess is with," or more colloquially, "Goddess-blessed people".

Kainna (KAI-ngah): Pollinating insects similar to bees.

Kapitiya (CAP-i-TEE-yah): A word association game played like Japanese Shiritori.

Kiannim (ki-AH-nim): A *Peri* word meaning "precious one," often used in a family context between parent and child or between lovers.

Lya (lee-YAH): Large livestock beasts somewhere between a rhino and a cow. Used primarily for milk and, in some places, for their meat.

Mana (MAH-na): A powerful elemental force that exists all around the fae realm. Mages draw it from their surroundings to fuel their abilities.

Massiya (MA-see-yah): A semicircle pastry with savory filling.

Mensa (MEN-sah): An herb that provides a relaxing effect. Can be smoked or consumed.

Nykse (NICK-see): A water-dwelling creature that lures males with a hypnotic song to breed them against their will, then kill and eat them. Inspired tales of nixie, nøkken, and mermaids.

Opashi (oh-PAH-shee): An honorific form of address for holy men.

Paya (PAI-ah): A cereal grain resembling rice that's eaten in several regions of the fae realm.

Rinsom (R/LIN-sum): A large, fluffy, red flower like a big chrysanthemum.

Santouri (san-TU-r/lee): An indigenous race in the North that resembles centaurs.

Shahim (SHA-him): Colloquially "Hand of the Goddess." Magic user that can competently wield all four categories of magic: mending, breaking, changing, and making.

Skair (scare): *Aminkinya* insult meaning pea-brain or idiot.

Thracks (thracks): A tabletop game involving trying to roll marbles into certain patterns.

Vali (VAH-lee): A type of nut-bearing tree common in the fae world.

Vodt (vohte): Large coins worth about an hour's wage. 1 *vodt* is worth 3 *tarn* or 18 *jinni*.

Zanna (za-ngah): A root tasting faintly of licorice that can be chewed to clean one's teeth.

ACKNOWLEDGMENTS

A huge thank you to Rhett and Steve at Aethon Books for taking a chance on a new author with the publication of my debut novel, The Treasured One, and now its sequel. It is such a precious thing to see my ideas come to life and this series start to flourish. I hope to someday return the favor by providing you with a hundred bestsellers!

I would also like to thank the incredible Bookstagram community and wonderful fellow authors who raise others up instead of tearing them down. It feels like having my own found family, and you have all been such a blessing on this journey. I especially want to thank my fellow Aethon authors. Additional appreciation is owed to Brit, Alex, Jaz, Rae, and the rest of the MoP and ASS group chats… if you know, you know. And an even bigger thank you to my wonderful assistant, Jazmine, for taking some stress of content creation and organizational things off my brain so that I can focus on writing. I hope the books are worth it!

Thank you to Lara and Dayane for helping me with Marcia's backstory elements and making sure her Portuguese was up to par. Representation is important, but it needs to be done right—even if it's only small pieces, and even if it's difficult. With their expert guidance, I've not only written a book and character I can be proud of, but hopefully also given the Ceará culture the respect it's owed.

Finally, the biggest thanks of all to you, wonderful reader, for giving my book a try out of all the hundreds that are almost certainly on your TBR and the thousands of incredible Romantasy books out there. If you enjoyed The Steadfast One, I would be honored by a review—it helps us authors out more than you know.

Don't hesitate to connect with me on Instagram—I'd love to hear from you!

www.ingramcontent.com/pod-product-compliance
Lightning Source LLC
Chambersburg PA
CBHW020248030826
48979CB00030B/2659/J

* 9 7 8 1 9 6 4 5 0 5 1 7 6 *